The Struggle Within

By Rebecca Jayne Heipel

I couldn't have done this without the help of my best friend,
Nicolas Vleeshouwers, who spent endless hours reading,
questioning and pushing me every step of the way.
Ik ben een slechte konijn :)

And of course, my deepest gratitude to Su Scarfe
for doing all of the editing and proof reading.

PROLOGUE

Have you ever wondered how things might have been?

Like if you had turned left and took the shortcut instead of the long way to school one day. Or you hit the snooze button one extra time and miss your bus. Perhaps you call in sick to work one day, just to enjoy the sunshine, and then get assigned as team leader on a project that nobody wanted. Or perhaps your mother doesn't try to kill herself on your eighth birthday. Maybe, just maybe, things might have been easier? Perhaps I might not have ended up in this situation.

These thoughts were filling my head as I tried to draw a breath into my lead-lined lungs. A dull, throbbing ache pulsed through my ribcage as I leaned over to cough, a dry rattle emerging from my lips and blood drivelling down my chin. My head lulled forward onto my chest, supported by the coarse ropes that held me up. Slowly I tried to raise my head up, fighting against the alarm bells that were ringing inside. A heavy haze fell over me as I struggled to remain conscious. A sudden chill overcame me and I cried out in pain as the ropes dug farther and deeper into my ribcage.

A lone light bulb flickered above me, slowly swaying in the breeze I now felt pass through the room. Shadows danced on the walls and in my imagination. Cries echoed around me and I was unable to discern if they were real or not. Were they actually happening or were they a vague recollection of how I got here? Uncertainty and confusion welled up inside me as tears gushed down my face and I fought back the sobs. How did I end up here? Where is here? Why is this happening to me?

I looked at the wall in front of me and tried to focus, but the shadows were playing tricks with my eyes. The dimly lit wall kept revealing a dark stain that kept growing bigger with each swaying pass of the light bulb above my head. A dark, rusty stain on a dirty brown wall. The stench of vomit suddenly filled my nose as the breeze quickened around me, and a low groan from behind me gave the impression that I was no longer alone. As I fought against the ropes to turn towards the noise, a sudden blackness embraced me.

CHAPTER ONE

It was a typical Sunday afternoon of last minute shoppers mingling about the aisles of the local grocery store. Frazzled mothers with their small children whining for candies and sweet cereals, or their crying babies and toddlers long past due on their afternoon naps. Adolescents sulking along the aisles, trying to remain inconspicuous as their parents fruitlessly attempted to make the weekly grocery shopping a hip and social event. Elderly men and women using their shopping carts as walkers while the store served as their weekly social gathering hole, exchanging gossip about their grown adult children and pictures of their grandchildren. Young twenty-something women in their fuzzy velour pajamas, talking on their bedazzled cell phones and toting around small puppies in their oversized purses, pretending that they were the local versions of Paris Hilton and Lindsay Lohan. Acne filled, bored teenagers dressed in hideously orange smocks, mindlessly filling paper bags with groceries or stocking the shelves with store brand canned products, all while carefully pushing the cheaper products farther back behind the more expensive name brands.

Myself, I was leisurely strolling along the aisles with a mostly empty cart. My cupboards were barely ever stocked as I mostly ate out and my only real needs were that of the liquid nourishment kind. The contents of my cart were mostly props as I enjoyed my source of afternoon entertainment by absorbing the energy of the people around me—ears peeled for a new 'character' I could incorporate into my latest tale. I stopped mid-aisle and grabbed a can of kidney beans in each hand, pretending to compare calorie and nutritional content as I eavesdropped on a nearby conversation of a new mother on her cell phone.

She was arguing with her partner about their individual responsibilities and how she was apparently slacking off on her end. Only a few seconds of eavesdropping provided me with the obvious knowledge that her partner was your stereotypically sexist male that expected to be waited on hand and foot, even after giving birth to their child.

I chuckled and put both cans back on the shelf. She was nothing new in my day-to-day observations; however, new mothers never ceased to make me laugh. They simply reaffirmed my choice in remaining childless. I left her fuming in the aisle and turned down the baking aisle just in time to see two elderly ladies arguing over which type of prune juice worked better. I quickly turned on my heels, unable to maintain my composure and slammed right into a young woman.

Her hair was a rich, chocolate brown that flowed softly onto her shoulders and down the middle of her back. Two dragonfly barrettes clipped her hair back just enough so her ears barely poked out, teasing you. Her skin glowed a pale rosy ivory, not enough to be a natural redhead, but more than enough to make you think that she might have family who are. Her lips sparkled with a shiny pink lip gloss and smelled of cherries. Her blue eyes jumped out at you with a cold steeliness that cut you straight to the heart. I breathed in sharply, a lump instantly forming in my throat as my stomach lurched and my heart began to beat wildly. The whole world around me stopped suddenly and all I could see was her.

She lost her balance as she stumbled backwards away from me and I grabbed her arm gently, steadying her.

"I… I'm sorry," I stammered, my usual cool composure shaken.

She smiled radiantly back at me. "It's okay, probably my fault anyways, I'm a bit of a klutz."

Her smile permeated into my soul as she bit her lower lip and giggled, casually looking at her arm and my hand still holding it. I quickly dropped her arm and looked back at her sheepishly. I mumbled a vague apology and she patted my shoulder, her eyes flickering with mischievousness.

"Thank you for the rescue, kind sir," she said, then continued down the aisle away from me.

Then as quickly as the moment started, it was over and she was gone. The world around me reappeared, only this time it was ugly, grey and bleak. I knew that I had to find her again. Her presence was so strong that I knew I needed to capture her in words before I forgot. I closed my eyes, impressing her image into my mind, etching every last detail into my memory.

Nicola bounced up the stairs with a hum in her step. She was going to surprise Karim with his favourite dinner:

meatloaf and garlic mashed potatoes. He knew that Patsy was joining them for dinner, but she knew that he would presume they would be doing their usual take-out. She seldom cooked anymore, and felt guilty that her new business had taken that away from her. She had to hurry though, both of them would be arriving within the hour. Bumping into that strange man at the grocery store had startled her more than she had initially realized, and she ended up leaving the store empty handed. She had gotten halfway home before she realized her error and had to run back.

Balancing the bags in both of her arms and her purse draped over her wrist, she pulled out her apartment keys and they fumbled through her fingers and fell onto the ground beneath her. She rolled her eyes in mock frustration as she slowly squatted down to pick them up. As her fingers grasped the edge of the keychain, the bag in her left arm tipped over just enough so that the tomatoes began to tumble out. She quickly dropped the keys and reached with her other hand to grab them, only to completely lose the bag in the crook of that same arm. She started to moan when the door to her apartment opened abruptly and Karim appeared, grabbing the escaping tomatoes with one hand and the falling bag with his other, while Nicola stumbled the rest of the way to the ground.

"Oh. You're home," she said with a pout as she reached a hand out to his.

Karim took her arm and pulled her to her feet. "Nice to see you too, honey."

She blushed furiously. "I didn't mean that. I just…" she said, trailing off.

He laughed, causing her to blush even more. She let herself be guided into the apartment, kicking off her shoes at the front door and slipping on her slippers. Still sulking, she followed him into the kitchen and leaned against the counter, watching him unpack the now mostly empty bags.

"I was hoping to surprise you with a homemade meal. I'm going to make your favourite."

"Kraft dinner?" he asked.

She put her hands on her hips and glared at him. "No, spam sandwiches."

"Oh goody! My second favourite," he said, laughing as he embraced her from behind. He kissed her lower earlobe and began to slowly nibble his way down her neck.

She sighed softly. He slid his hands down her waist, stopping at her hips and holding her body close to his. She put her hands onto his arms and followed them up and down, scratching his skin softly with her nails.

"I need to start dinner," she purred as he started to unbutton her shirt.

"You want me to stop?"

"No. Yes. I don't know."

He chuckled as he slid his hand under her bra and pushed her forward onto the island that sat in the centre of their kitchen. Her hips bumped it roughly and she gave a small giggle.

Suddenly, she pushed herself back to an upright position and pointed. "Oh no! The tomatoes are escaping!"

He stopped what he was doing and looked at where she was pointing. The tomatoes had rolled off the island onto the floor and were making their way back towards the front door. Looking at the seriousness on her face, he suddenly burst into raucous laughter. She followed suit, falling into a fit of giggles that soon became so strong that she wrapped her arms around her stomach and fell to the floor laughing. Tears rolled down her cheeks and she tried helplessly to wipe them away.

"Run, tomatoes, run! You can be free!" she said, still laughing and rolling around on the floor. She crawled to her knees and scrambled after them.

Behind her, Karim's laughter got even louder and she could hear a loud thump as he fell to the floor ass first.

"Stop it, oh please, please stop it," he pleaded to her, clutching his stomach.

"I've captured the hostages!" she proclaimed, holding the wayward tomatoes in the air like a victor's trophy as she turned to face him.

"Mercy, I beg you. Please. My abs can't take anymore," he pleaded.

A deliciously, evil grin grew across her lips as she pulled herself in front of him. Slowly she waved the tomatoes in front of his face.

"Please, don't turn us into meatloaf. We'll talk! We'll talk!" she said, and he fell to his side with his arms wrapped around his stomach. He started gasping for breaths between his fits of laughter as he proceeded to roll around on the floor.

Still giggling, she stood up and plunked the tomatoes into the sink and ran cold water over them. Carefully, she stepped over the still laughing Karim and finished unpacking the rest of the groceries. She gathered all of the ingredients she needed to make dinner and separated them into two piles. One was for the meatloaf and the other for the mashed potatoes. She had gotten halfway through preparing the meatloaf when Karim finally gained enough composure to stand up again. He grabbed her in a hug and kissed her.

"Busy now," she said, focusing on her task.

"I'm not hungry anymore. Well, except for you," he said.

"I'm dessert. Peel the potatoes please," she said, pushing his hand towards the pile of unpeeled potatoes.

He sighed and rolled his eyes knowing that once focused on a task, it was impossible to deter her from it until it was done. He opened the bag of potatoes and pulled a few out. Slowly, he took one in his hand and nudged it towards her pile of ingredients for the meatloaf. She suddenly stopped what she was doing and glared at him. He stifled a laugh but took the potato back to his side of the counter and started peeling it. She resumed making the meatloaf.

After a moment he again slowly nudged the potato back towards her. Again, she simply stopped and just glared at him. A sly smile crossed his lips as he knew that he was successfully torturing her OCD side. He took the potato back to his side and finished peeling it. Midway through peeling a second potato, he pushed it back towards her. Suddenly and without looking his way, she took the knife that she was cutting the celery with and stabbed his potato. Startled, he jumped backwards before realizing that the blade had landed mere inches away from his fingers. She lifted the potato into the air in front of her and inspected it intently before putting it back on the counter. She rolled it back towards him.

"You're not done with this, I can't cut it yet," she said and resumed cutting her celery.

Karim stared at her with shock and disbelief.

She looked over her shoulder at him with innocent, questioning eyes. "What?"

"You're nuts."

"I know."

"And I love you for it," he said, gushing.

"There are doctors who can help you with that," she said.

He laughed and leaned over the island towards her. He grabbed her by the back of the neck, pulled her face towards his and kissed her fiercely on her lips.

"Don't ever change, okay?"

Her eyes glittered and she smiled slyly. "Never."

I opened my eyes and peeked out from beneath the blankets. I could see the moon through the window that I lay next to. The moon was bright and the sky sparkled with stars. I looked at my plastic wristwatch and it read 12:01. Sitting up, I smiled. It was now my fifth birthday and officially the biggest and best day of my life. In a few hours I would start kindergarten and I could finally have real friends.

I looked down and saw my school from the secret room in the attic that supposedly didn't exist. All of my dolls and stuffed animals that father had saved for me after mother threw them out were up here with me. My only friends. We were quietly celebrating my birthday so we didn't wake mother. She yells at me a lot. I never know when she will or why.

Once I tried to tell her about the secret room, before I even found it. I kept hearing all sorts of noises above me in the ceiling. At first it had scared me, and when I tried to tell her she screamed while waving a knife at me. So I ran away and hid in her closet. Afraid that she might come after me, I crawled deeper and deeper into the depths of the closet until I bumped my head against the back wall and a panel in the wall moved. I crawled through the opening and found a small staircase just behind it. Enough light from the closet shone through that I could make out a few steps, so I decided to investigate. However, the farther I crawled up the stairs, the darker it got until I felt like the walls were going to eat me up. I wasn't sure how long I had crawled, but it felt like the staircase was going on for forever when I suddenly popped through a floor and into a small room. The entire room was barely bigger than my bed but looked so large and spacious, even with blankets and pillows strewn about everywhere. There was a small round window with a white bench jutting out from beneath it. When I sat on it I could see the kindergarten playground. My playground.

I came up to my secret play room almost every day. At first, I would only come up for a few minutes at a time. Just long enough to stare out at the playground and wonder what it would be like to play with other kids. But each day I would spend a little longer up there. Mother was too busy looking after my baby sister. I don't think she ever noticed whether I was even there or not, only if I was in the way.

One day I met a new friend. His name was George. I was passing my books through the tunnel, one by one, when a hand from above reached down to grab a book. I was so surprised that I almost yelped out as I tried to turn away and run. But the tunnel was too tight to easily move around in. The mysterious hand took my hand and gently shook it. My eyes grew as wide as saucers as my hand was engulfed in his, and noticed it was furry like a dog's paw. He didn't speak to me, but grunted. He let go of my hand and pointed to the pile of books at my feet then grunted again. I wasn't sure how he saw the books as only his arm extended through the hole from above. Still bewildered, I slowly took a book in my hand and passed it to him.

His arm disappeared and then re-appeared empty. I passed him another book then another until the whole pile was upstairs. He then disappeared and I crawled up after him.

I looked all over the room and saw only the books next to the window. He was nowhere to be seen. I searched everywhere for him. Under the blankets, the pillows and even in the shadows, but he had completely vanished. Unsure of what had just happened, I sat down on the ledge and grabbed the first book on the pile. It was one of my favourites, Little Red Riding Hood. I turned the first page and slowly started reading out loud.

I heard a shuffling of footsteps from behind me and snuck a quick glance over my shoulder. Shadows danced about then stilled. I heard the sound of someone's breathing slowly receding so I flipped the page and continued reading aloud. Again I heard the sound of footsteps coming up from behind me. Only this time I did not turn to look, but continued reading. I could now feel his breath on my legs and out of the corner of my eye I could see a blue furry head and bright purple eyes staring down at me fondly.

I continued to read aloud until I had finished the book, and then pretending that I hadn't noticed him beside me, I held the book out towards him and said "Next". He took the book from my hands, set it next to the pile and handed me a new book. But instead of just taking the book I grabbed his wrist and tackled him. I shrieked and giggled as I proclaimed my victory and started tickling him. He grunted in surprise and for a moment I thought he was going to toss me aside and then run away. Instead, he looked at me with mild annoyance and my breath caught in my throat. But then just as quickly, he broke out in a grin and tickled me back. We rolled around on the floor tickling each other until there were tears in our eyes, and then we collapsed on the blankets, out of breath.

Staring down at the floor I suddenly grew quiet. He looked at me with alarm so I put my finger to my lips and pointed to the floor.

"She might have heard us," I whispered, referring to my mother. We put our ears to the floor and listened carefully. Silence. We looked at each other with unease, and I looked over at the hole to the tunnel and then back at him. I bit my lip, scared that my secret was about to be discovered. But then the sounds of my sister giggling and water splashing could be heard. We both let out a sigh of relief.

I asked him if he had a name but he only looked at me with question. I told him that my father called me Shorty and pointed to my chest while saying it but he just grunted and shook his head. So I asked him if he wanted a name and he nodded eagerly. I tapped my finger against my chin and concentrated hard. I hadn't named anything before. I went over to my pile of books and started going through them. I finally stopped and held up a yellow book with a monkey on it. He looked at it and touched it gently. I smiled at him.

"Lets call you George," I said and he smiled and hugged me tightly. "I love you too, George."

We both sat back down and he passed me another book. A fairy tale. I agreed to read one more story before I had to go back downstairs for lunch. He pouted so I promised him that I'd be back everyday. George smiled at me with so much love I could barely hold back the joy inside my heart. I had a new friend.

The rest of my summer I spent upstairs in my secret playroom with George. I never saw him anywhere else in the house. With each passing day I would spend more and more time in that room. Mother seldom noticed my absence and father worked each day. I'd often go up after breakfast and not return until just before my father got home. Every few days George would introduce me to a new friend and I would read stories aloud for everyone each day. By the end of summer I was talking about starting school. Sometimes, I would just stare for hours at that playground, thinking about how one day it would be mine.

Little slivers of sunlight darted through the semi-closed curtains. Nicola rolled over, groaning as she pulled her head deeper under the covers.

"Wake up sleepyhead, time to run," Karim said, gently nudging her.

"I don't want to go to school, daddy," she mumbled from beneath her pillow. He grabbed the bottom edge of the comforter and started to slowly slide it down off the bed. She clumsily grabbed at it, pulling it back over her head.

"Five more minutes?" she pleaded.

"No!" he said with a flourish as he pulled the comforter off the bed completely in one neat yank.

She grumbled and rolled off the bed gracefully, landing on her knees with a thud. He tossed her running clothes onto her head. She sat up, her sports bra framing her face, and sulked at him. He laughed at her daily antics to avoid running with him.

"Remember," he said as he left the room, "it's you that wants to run the marathon, not me."

"Coffee?" she pleaded and sighed deeply as she reluctantly began to get dressed.

Downstairs he already was brewing a mug of single serve drip coffee. He had added a drop of vanilla extract to the beans, knowing how much it would perk her up. Next to the mug he had put a banana. Nicola finally strolled into the kitchen, still yawning. She took in a deep breath, inhaling the sweet aroma of the coffee and literally floated over to it. She swallowed half of the mug in a single gulp, smiled briefly, then quickly set the mug down and clasped her hands over her mouth. Muffled gasps of pain escaped as her eyes grew wide. Karim rolled his eyes at her and stifled a laugh into his own cup of coffee. This woman could remember intimate details about the oddest things she had seen and what shop and what date, yet she could never remember that coffee was hot and burned her mouth on it daily.

She fanned a hand in front of her open mouth and then glared at her mug of coffee. She snatched up the banana, peeled it and offered half to Karim who accepted it quickly before she could change her mind.

"Hurry up already. I want to get in a good hour this morning before work, slowpoke," he said between bites of banana.

She made muffled noises at him through her banana-filled mouth, mocking him.

Ignoring her he asked, "Hills, speed intervals or boring?"

"Hills. I hate hills," she said as she laced up her shoes. In the few seconds of conversation she had woken up completely and was practically out the door.

He laughed. "You never did like the boring runs, did you?"

She shook her head at him and held the door open with a foot, "No pain, no gain."

He tossed her a pink water belt and she clipped it around her waist. She pulled it snug onto her hips and shook her waist. He tossed her iPod and keys to her, laughing as she successfully caught the keys but almost dropped the iPod. She tucked them both into her belt and looked up to see Karim ready as well. She smiled a sly smile as she stood up on her toes and kissed his nose.

As she broke off the kiss, she tossed the keys towards him, "Race you!"

She laughed as she raced out the door, suddenly wide awake and full of energy. He instinctively caught the keys with one hand before he realized that she was out the door. He dashed after her, letting the door lock itself behind him.

It took almost fifteen minutes of solid running, dodging and traffic lights before even getting to the trails that were worth running. Nicola and Karim were extremely lucky to have found an apartment not only so close to a park, but literally a giant forest. The trails inside it were not city made, but completely created by runners like Nicola and Karim who ran daily. The sun broke through the trees and glittered amongst the fallen leaves and the freshly blooming branches.

Nicola had just entered the forest when she turned the corner, a block away from the entrance to the forest. There were three main paths you could follow. One that lead to a long but fairly flat route around the whole forest; a.k.a. 'the boring route'. Another cut straight through the trees and consequently up some fairly decent sized hills— a continuous run of ups and downs that was great for the legs. Lastly, the more entertaining yet dangerous route zig-zagged through the forest and over everything that stood in it. For more danger you ran it with timed speed intervals. The game of dodging roots and fallen logs put you in such a state of exhilaration that you could survive off the high for days. Nicola often thrived off the high and almost always ran that route. But today she knew she needed to push herself on the hills. Her upcoming marathon had a few steep hills in the course and she needed to be better prepared for them.

As she glanced over her shoulder she could see Karim coming around the corner. She knew she could keep ahead of him if she ran the easy route or the obstacles, but he'd catch up with her quickly on the hills. His endurance was much better than hers. Her goal today would be to make it to the third hill before he caught up with her. She pushed herself and gritted her teeth as she turned towards the first hill. She bore down hard and ran full force up the hill. Keeping her eyes downcast, she tried the old trick of convincing her brain that she wasn't really running up a hill but a flat surface by letting her eyes think they saw 'flat' ground beneath her. Her calves called her a liar halfway up the hill and she chuckled through her already panting breaths. One of her favourite parts of her morning run was how alone she felt despite running with Karim. Lost in herself, surrounded by nature and the sun warming her skin. The world was hers to conquer.

She cleared the first big hill fairly easily and let herself slow down as she descended it. The next set of hills was a series of smaller ones. Up down, up down, up down. Literally a few steps up and then back down. Like really big speed bumps that she wasn't tall enough to take in a single step. She glanced over her shoulder but Karim was nowhere in sight. She smiled and pushed herself to speed up even more. When she cleared the series of speed bump hills, she glanced behind again and this time she could see a small figure bouncing behind her. She frowned at it. She hadn't even hit the second big hill. She was hoping he wouldn't be in sight until she had cleared at least that one. She pushed her head towards the ground and dug her feet in deep and pushed herself harder than normal. As she rushed forward she kept glancing back, watching Karim get closer and closer. She ignored the burning in her parched throat and pushed herself even harder. But with each glance back the figure in the distance kept gaining. The next hill would be over the next ridge, just past the large maple tree. She made a mad dash for it, and as she cleared the maple tree she looked back again and discovered that she had lost him. She smiled brightly as she ran towards the next hill.

At the bottom of the hill she looked back again, saw no one and stopped abruptly. The maple tree was as small as an ant in the distance. If she had seen him gaining on her only a few minutes ago, he should have cleared the tree by now. She waited, running in spot, for him to come around the tree but saw no sign of him. She started to run back towards the tree but then realized how silly that would be. He would catch up with her on the next hill. He might even be watching her now, waiting for her to go up the hill, pretending she was faster than he. Resolved, she turned back to run up the second hill.

Halfway up the hill she again looked back and was surprised to see a figure at the bottom of the hill. Impossible. How could he have gotten there so quickly? She squinted, trying to ascertain if it really was Karim but the sun was too bright to discern if it was real or just an mirage. So she continued up the hill still trying to outrun him. At the top she looked back only to discover that not only was the figure even closer, but it still remained a blur. She rubbed her eyes to clear them but the figure remained a blur against a fairly clear background. She called out to him, but he neither answered nor acknowledged her. She picked up her pace and ran quickly instead of cautiously down the hill. She knew this was risky as she was prone to klutziness, but the mysterious runner behind her both encouraged her to keep ahead and frightened her slightly. She constantly kept looking back only to see that despite her increasing speed, her mysterious runner was catching up. Yet with each step closer, she gained no more visual clarity of him.

Suddenly she felt overwhelmed and frightened. It wasn't Karim behind her. He would have answered her by now. She would be able to tell if it was him. She could feel the presence behind her getting closer and closer and her heart began to race wildly. She risked a look back to see that the runner was almost within touching distance and yet his face remained a blur. She turned away from him and pushed herself to run even faster down the hill. Almost immediately she felt her foot snag a tree root. As she started to fall over she pulled her body into a ball as tightly and quickly as possible. Her hip jarred against the ground and took the brunt of her crash. But she didn't stop there. Unfortunately she was still in the middle of the hill and she continued to roll, head over feet, down the hill. When she risked a peek she could see the mysterious runner blurring into the background. She came to an abrupt stop at the bottom of the hill and lay sprawled out. She could hear Karim calling out to her from far away then felt his strong arms scoop her up in his.

She called out to him in a daze, unsure of if she was really in Karim's arms or if he was just a figment of her imagination. Where had he come from? How had he gotten in front of her? Asking if she was okay, he gave her a quick look over for any obvious wounds. Ignoring him, she kept asking about a man who was behind her. Karim looked around unable to see whom she was talking about.

He scolded her for endangering herself by foolishly running down the hill at such a fast speed.

Nicola tried to look up the hill but Karim was holding her to face the other way. Still confused, she insisted that she look up the hill, fighting to get herself out of his arms so she could face the hill she just fell down. He struggled to keep her in his arms and tried to calm her down. She just kept frantically pointing behind him and Karim turned to look over his shoulder and back up the hill. He shook his head and swore to her that no one was there now and no one else had been on the hill when she fell. She shook her head violently, intent on what she had seen and felt. Finally he turned so she could look up the still empty hill behind them.

"There's no one there, honey," he said. "And it couldn't have been me, I passed you at the beginning of the first hill."

Nicola looked at him with surprise. Had he really passed her that early on? She pushed herself out of his arms, stumbling as she tried to keep her balance. Bewildered, she looked between Karim and the hill. He took her hand and gently tugged at it, leading her down the path.

"Let's call it a day. You were probably just lost in thought and you imagined that you saw someone," he said.

She shook her head in disagreement but let him lead her out of the forest.

CHAPTER TWO

Nicola rushed out of her house, debating on whether to wave down a taxi or just power walk to work. Her run had shaken her so much that she had taken much longer to get ready for work and was now quite late. Patsy had already texted her, worried, but Nicola assured her that she was fine. Much easier to lie by text. Her stomach grumbled loudly, making the decision easy for her.

She walked down the block to the deli and grabbed herself a sandwich before hailing a taxi. Once inside the taxi she quickly dug into her sandwich while checking her emails on her phone. She figured she should at least start working a little, especially since Patsy had just set up her mailbox on her phone for her. She had several new emails, but one in particular caught her attention. The subject was written in caps and simply read, "CANCER SURVIVOR NEEDS HELP".

Curious, but also skeptical, she wondered if it was one of those 'give me all your information' email scams. Patsy kept telling her to set her email settings more strictly, but she dreaded the idea of going through all of her spam mail to find emails from potential clients. Tentatively, she clicked it open.

Dear Ms VanBurgen

I doubt that you remember me but my name is Gregory Sanchez. We went to elementary school together. I was the quiet and awkward boy that was always picked last for sports. I hope that the years have found you well. I recently relocated to this beautiful city once the doctors gave me the all-clear after being in remission for a full year now.

The reason I'm emailing you is partially to reach out and say hello and hopefully make new friends in this new city, but also because I require your services. I have read that you acquire unique items for a living? I am in need of a couple of wigs for myself since my chemotherapy has not only caused me to lose all of my hair, but I've had the unfortunate experience of having a rare side effect of permanent baldness. Sadly for myself, most businesses that provide wigs for cancer patients are mostly for children and I've been unable to find suitable wigs for myself. I'm hoping to obtain wigs made out of human hair. I've sent you a couple of pictures of myself when I had hair and am hoping you can find something suitable for me. Cost is no concern, but speed is.

Sincerely, Gregory Sanchez

Nicola wiped the tears from her eyes. He looked so young and vibrant. She hoped that he still retained some of that vitality now. She forwarded the email to Patsy and added at the top "Emergency, do this ASAP" before replying to him.

◇◇◇

"As you can see, despite the newer rules, this space used to be a modified living and work space," the real estate agent said.

She waved a hand towards the ceiling, where several fluorescent ballasts were hanging empty.

"The previous tenant used special fluorescent tubes to create natural lighting. But there are also several hanging lamps to accommodate the space more easily."

The agent looked at her client. He was quite unresponsive and frankly, quite creepy. He wore a trench coat and fedora on this hot, muggy spring day. Even though they were inside and it was quite dark in this unit, he wore sunglasses. But she was eager to rent out this unit as the warehouses usually stood empty for the most part, due to recent rules that were quite strict for the tenants. They forbade anyone from being able to actually live in their units. Ones like this were to be monitored since the original design layout was ideal for artists and entrepreneurs, making them ideal for living conditions and were now hard to re-rent.

The client walked aimlessly around the room, gingerly touching the walls. He disappeared through the open doorway into the kitchen and bathroom area. The agent stood patiently in the middle of the studio space and waited for him to return. She knew that she should follow him and give more details, but the idea of being in that confined space with him gave her the chills.

When he hadn't returned after ten minutes she begrudgingly walked into the kitchen. It was quite dark so she tried the switch on the wall, but nothing turned on.

She called out into the darkness to him, "We will put fresh new bulbs in all of the lamps and overhead fixtures before you move in, otherwise you can see that the space is quite clean."

She heard the floor behind her creak as a hand touched her shoulder. She jumped back and screamed before she realized it was her client. She leaned over, clutching her heart, panting.

"You scared me," she said as he walked past her and back into the main room.

"I'll take it," he said, his voice soft but gruff.

The agent smiled and guided him towards her briefcase, still on the floor in the main room. She pulled out a contract, already pre-filled out, and put it on her briefcase. She held it up to him and passed him a pen from her hair.

"Just sign here... here... and initial here, then this place is yours in 24 hours," she said as he signed the forms and smiled.

Nicola sat at her desk, scores of papers strewn about from one end of it to the other. She sat with one knee pulled up to her chest, her boots on the floor beneath the desk. Her left hand, holding a now cold chai tea latte, was draped around her left leg, sliding up and down her knee-high bright rainbow socks, while her right hand bounced a pencil upon the many documents that lay before her. She had thought that spreading them out might have made them easier to sort, but she was wrong. It only made it worse. Too many documents depended on another and the chains were countless.

Setting her drink down onto the floor beside her, she ceremoniously swept the papers into a single pile. Then she opened the lone drawer in her desk, which was actually more of a glorified kitchen table from Ikea, and pulled out a pad of post-its. She took the first one and set it to the leftmost corner of the desk. Grabbing a sharpie, she neatly wrote upon it BILLS. She took a second post-it and put it a few inches adjacent to the first, and wrote CLIENT NEEDS. On a third post-it, POTENTIAL SUPPLIERS FOR CLIENTS, and on the fourth she wrote SHIT PILE. She then grabbed the still-daunting pile of papers, took a deep breath, and grabbed the first one off the pile.

She stared at the piece of paper in her hand and proceeded to give herself a long internal pep talk that was more procrastination than motivation. She told herself that it would be a piece of cake once she actually got started, and at the thought of cake her stomach grumbled loudly. She looked eagerly at her door, knowing she had just eaten but still debating on whether or not she should try to sneak out. She was already reaching under the desk for her boots when there was a knock at her office door. She yelled for Patsy to come in as she fumbled under the desk for her boots.

Patsy, her assistant-slash-secretary-slash-godsend from another holy planet that existed in the nether regions, came into her office. Patsy was 5'2", slight, fair-skinned, and had a neat asymmetrical bob that cut from her chin to just below her shoulders. She had appeared to Nicola shortly after Nicola bought the office and was mid-renovations, with a full messenger bag slung over her shoulder, a paint brush in one hand and a chai tea latte in the other.

"The first day is free," was all she had said to Nicola. From there on was history. The two had meshed together perfectly. It was like they were twins from the same pod.

Today, she held a small grocery bag in her hand. She walked over to Nicola's desk in silence and set the bag down. She took two of Nicola's post-its, found an empty space on the desk, stuck the post-it down and wrote LUNCH on it. Beside it she put the other post-it and wrote MAIL. She proceeded to empty the contents of the paper bag. She set hummus, a package containing a variety of chopped up vegetables in stick form, an apple, and a container of greek yogurt with granola, on top of the post-it marked LUNCH. She produced a bottle of water and set it behind the pile of food. She folded the bag up neatly and tucked it into her front pocket. Then she took a small pile of mail out of her back pocket and put it next to the post-it marked MAIL, and walked out the office.

"I'll be heading out later this afternoon to get the wigs. I've already found a dealer, so don't even think of avoiding that pile you have on your desk. You're not allowed out until your meeting at three. If that pile isn't at least half done, I'll go to the meeting in your place," she said defiantly as she closed the door behind her.

Nicolas sighed and muttered to herself about how Patsy could be quite spooky and wondered who really was the boss here. She cracked the bottle of water, dipped a carrot into the hummus and took a bite. After a long drink she straightened herself up in her chair and grabbed the first piece of paper from the pile. Easy pickings, new client. She scanned the sheet, highlighted the client's request and put a pink post-it on the top righthand corner and wrote out a short list of needs in her illegible shorthand. She then tapped on her iPad and composed a new email to Patsy.

The iPad had been yet another one of Patsy's brilliant ideas. She swore that iPads would change the world. They were lighter, easier to commute with, simple to hook up with wifi and had millions of practical apps. And she was right. Just months after she had started using it, Nicola started seeing businesses everywhere else using them. Restaurants, sales clerks, even hotels. While it did take a few weeks before she warmed up to the idea, Nicola was glad she had trusted Patsy. With a few simple add-ons, Nicola could meet up with clients anywhere, pass on the goods and complete the transactions with secure credit card payments even in the middle of a field. As long as she could find wifi she could do it.

The subject of the email was 'Client Needs'. She always emailed Patsy a list she would compile from her paperwork. Patsy kept their computer records up-to-date and Nicola felt it fair to give Patsy first dibs on what she wanted to find. She looked at the first sheet she had just highlighted and typed in the requests and then added it to the new pile of CLIENT NEEDS. She grabbed the next piece of paper from the pile and scanned it. Again, another easy grab: office hydro bill. She closed the email and tapped a bright orange square with a white lightening bolt in it. Gone were the days of standing in line at the bank to pay a bill or mailing in a cheque and waiting ages for it to clear. A simple tap of the icon opened up the app. Login, password and then boom. Enter amount owing, click okay, connect to bank via the app and poof. Paid. She shook her head with a small chuckle. If only all of life were that easy. She highlighted the amount paid on the bill, drew a line through it with her sharpie and wrote PAID on it, and put it in the bills pile. She opened a second email, this time to herself, and wrote in the amount she just paid and that it was for hydro. She'd have to remember to update the company cheque book, a chore Patsy often volunteered for but Nicola couldn't give up. Not that she didn't trust Patsy, but more that she felt the need to be responsible herself.

She grabbed another sheet from the pile, closed her eyes and crossed her arms over her chest, hugging the paper close. "Three times lucky?" she asked herself out loud. Yes, indeed, another bill, but this one just a receipt confirming payment. She simply added it to the bills pile.

She reached for a carrot and out of the corner of her eye she saw the pile of mail. It was a small pile, only 4 envelopes. Probably more bills. Except that one envelope stood out. It was a pale pink and had several hearts drawn on it. She smiled and slid it out from the bottom of the pile. It was April, well past Valentines day, but Karim had probably thought she needed a romantic gesture to pull her out of their blues. The two of them had been trying for the past year to conceive. After a rough year without success, she had finally decided to go to a fertility clinic and seek the help she apparently needed. Her first appointment was later this week. She smiled fondly as she opened the envelope, wondering what words of encouragement he had written her. She reached inside, pulling out a card, and a plethora of glitter rained onto her desk. She looked inside the envelope. No letter, no paper, just more glitter. She looked at the card. It was the size of a baseball card, but on the front was a picture of her smiling, holding the key to her office. On the back was simply the words 'Be Mine'. She laughed. She gave the card a kiss and took a selfie on Snapchat. She added 'Of course, always' to it, and sent it off to Karim.

She carefully placed the card against her iPad and continued into the slowly dwindling pile of paperwork.

With a bigger smile on her face than earlier, she resumed her battle and grabbed the next sheet. She quickly fell into a routine: scan sheet, highlight the specifics and then either pay it right away via her iPad or add to the ever growing email to Patsy. It was starting to look like a busy month. Several regular clients as usual, but an even larger number of new clients. She knew Patsy would be excited. She loved the challenge of finding lost and obscure items and procuring new suppliers.

The time flew by quickly and before she knew it, it was well past lunch. Her earlier snack was long gone and her tepid chai tea latte suddenly looked very inviting as her stomach grumbled again. The pile of paper was finally sorted and all that remained were the three pieces of untouched mail. She hit 'send' on the email to Patsy and tidied up the piles of paper. The bills pile went into a folder for later filing and the client needs into another folder for Patsy to weed through and pick her favourites. Nicola would deal with the half she didn't want.

Her door opened and Patsy came in smiling. Nicola tried her best to give her colleague a look of authority, but knew that she was failing at it miserably. Nicola could feel the invisible hand patting her on the head, mocking her leadership, but in a friendly way. Nicola held out the folders and Patsy took them eagerly.

"Want to go out for a quick bite before your meeting and my errands?"

Nicola's stomach rumbled eagerly, answering for her. Patsy laughed.

"I'll meet you in the hall in ten minutes, don't forget your wallet, it's on you today." She stopped suddenly, noticing the valentine card on the desk. "Cute picture. From when you first bought the office?"

Nicola smiled. "Yeah, Karim sent it to me."

"In a pink envelope? Really? Such a sweet man you have!"

Nicola nodded with agreement as she reached down to grab her boots. As she slid the first boot on, her phone beeped with a new message from Karim.

"Speak of the dev—" Nicola let her words trail off.

Patsy stopped and turned back to face Nicola. "What's wrong?"

Nicola held her phone out and Patsy stepped back into the office to see what was on the screen. A single sentence stumped them both: *'Nice picture, where did you get it?'*

CHAPTER THREE

Patsy loved this part of the job. She loved shopping in general, she loved the hunt of finding bargains, and even more she loved the challenge of finding rare and unique items. A personal challenge of hers was to find the oddest thing in the shortest amount of time. Often she and Nicola would both go hunting for the same thing and see who could find it first. Of course she had the biggest advantage: the internet. Nicola, bless her heart, was ridiculously old-fashioned for someone so young, although Patsy was slowly but surely converting her to the world of technology. Nicola still preferred to hunt through the shops and through her clientele. Patsy, on the other hand, used the internet to hunt things down and often could find the same thing in the same place that Nicola would. However, Patsy had to admit that Nicola had an uncanny ability to know exactly where to go to find something, even if it was a store she had never been to before. It was like Nicola was some sort of magical divining rod.

Shortly after receiving Nicola's email, Patsy sent out calls to some old classmates from university. Within minutes she had two stores that specialized in quality human hair wigs for adults, both of which were inside city central and one of which that had two wigs of the similar colour and almost the exact same hair style. She supposed it was unfair to consider this as a time record since she knew the odds were in her favour. Regardless, she had her stopwatch running. She pulled it out of her pocket and smiled as she went into the store to get the wigs.

Inside the store the clerk greeted her. "You must be Miss Klein. I have the wigs right here."

He disappeared briefly behind a curtain and re-emerged with a large box in his hands. He set the box on his counter and opened it. He pulled out two wigs and set them out for Patsy to examine. She put one of the wigs on a styrofoam head then pulled out her phone to cross examine it with the picture she had. She shook her head.

"Sorry, they're too dark," she said. "Do you have any lighter ones?"

He shook his head.

"How long would it take to get lighter ones?" she asked.

The clerk shrugged his shoulders. "Could be weeks. Our supply is limited to rejects. These wigs are perfectly fine, but for whatever reason they are rejected from the hair for cancer children society. So we don't acquire them quickly, but rather quite randomly."

She called Nicola and after a quick conversation she turned back to face the clerk.

"So our client must be psychic. He just emailed us saying that he understands if we can't get the exact length and he wonders if we could find him a wig with the same colour in a longer length. He's willing to cut it himself," she said.

The clerk pondered a moment then disappeared behind the curtain again. After a few minutes he came out with another box. He pulled out a wig with hair that ran almost five feet long.

"This was a custom request for a client a few years ago. She took immaculate care of it, and in her will gave it back to us so we could re-sell it."

Patsy let the hair fall between her fingers. It was exquisitely soft. She couldn't believe how luxurious it felt. She compared her picture to it and smiled.

"It's perfect, I'll take it."

The clerk put it on the styrofoam head.

"If I may, could I cut the excess off so there's enough for your client to style the hairstyle they want and we can use the excess to make another wig?"

She nodded. "I don't see why not."

The clerk pulled out a pair of scissors and hair elastics from his belt. He pulled the hair into a ponytail just below the nape of the neck and then quickly braided it. He cut the wig just above the first elastic then put it into a small express postal box. Patsy filled out the paperwork and he assured her it would be delivered by that evening. She smiled, emailed Nicola and the client, stopped her stopwatch and left with a skip in her step.

Nicola stood outside the restaurant and inhaled deeply. She slowly let it out as she gave herself a quick look over. She was wearing one of her nicest dresses, one that Karim had bought for her and not only had she put on makeup, but she had gotten Patsy to help her do her hair in a fancy 'do. She even wore jewellery. Karim often criticized her for not being able to go to a 'nice' restaurant, so she promised him that tonight they could go wherever he wanted to. So here she stood outside one of the most expensive restaurants in town, a fancy seafood restaurant. It was one that he and his fellow casting directors often took their more famous clients in order to impress them. And Nicola could see why. She had barely even made it inside and she was as impressed as she was intimidated. She looked at the doorman past the awning-covered red carpet. She could do this, she told herself and she took a deep breath as she stepped towards the carpet only to stop abruptly. She looked down at her feet and realized she was still in her folding slip-ons. She laughed nervously and opened her bag-sized purse. She pulled out a pair of black sling back heels and slipped them on. After readjusting her dress she walked towards doorman and let him usher her in.

She stood, shell-shocked, inside the doorway. It was even more impressive inside than she could have ever imagined. The walls were a crimson maroon red with intricate white flowers etched along the top edge of the wall. The ceiling was cream coloured with mini crystal chandeliers dropping down from them, and rich dark purple drapery pulled in tight bunches going from chandelier to chandelier. Like the piping around a fancy cake. The tables were mahogany, a medium chocolate brown, and the tables were set with pristine white china. Unknowingly, she took a step backwards and the doorman gently nudged her towards the hostess stand before closing the door behind her. The hostess smiled at her.

"Reservation ma'am?" she asked, and Nicola slowly nodded, her eyes as wide as saucers.

"Name?" the hostess asked.

"Karim—" she started.

"Ah yes," the hostess interrupted. "Right this way," she said as she quickly disappeared around the corner.

Nicola rushed after her and tripped over her shoes. An arm reached out to grab hers and steadied her just in time to prevent her from falling over completely. She looked up into Karim's eyes and he shook his head at her with a half-cockeyed smile and guided her to their table.

He slid her chair out and she sat down into it, reminiscent of how he would do this at fast food restaurants, and smiled back at him. He let the waiter seat him and then poured them both a glass of wine. As they toasted she noticed that he took more of a large drink than a sip, finishing almost half of his glass. She set her glass down and gingerly picked up the menu. It was stiff like cardboard but velvet to the touch. The pages inside appeared to be inscribed with gold lettering. She let her fingers glide along the smooth and cool paper.

"I already ordered for us," he said, and she set her menu down with a small pout.

She saw he had a hand on the table and reached out to grab it, but just as she was about to touch his fingers he reached his hand into his pocket and pulled out his cell. She quickly retracted her hand back to her side and took another sip of her wine.

She looked up at him, shyly at first, then shook her head. They had been going out for over five years, so why was she acting like it was their first date? When she finally looked back at him he was reading something on his cell. She sighed and leaned back in her chair. She watched him send someone a message and then put his phone away into his pocket. He took another drink of his wine, finishing his glass. He filled it up again and gestured to the waiter for another bottle. Finally he looked her way and she perked up immediately before realizing he had seen their food as the server came from behind her and put two dishes in front of them. Both were soup. His a hearty clam chowder while hers was a very thin minestrone. He dug into his soup eagerly.

"Karim," she said and he mumbled a response between sips.

"How was your day?" she asked.

"Fine," he said rather quickly then dipped some of the restaurant's famous focaccia bread into his soup.

She took a sip of her soup. Despite its lacking of vegetables the broth was quite flavourful.

"How is work?"

"Fine," he answered.

She put her spoon down with such force the table rattled slightly. Karim finally looked up at her.

"Your soup is going to get cold," he said then resumed eating his.

She pushed her soup towards the centre of the table.

"I've lost my appetite," she muttered.

He shrugged his shoulders and kept eating.

The waiter magically appeared just as Karim finished his soup. He scooped up Karim's bowl and looked at Nicola's still full bowl.

"I'll take it to go," she said, garnering a strange look from the waiter before he left their table.

Moments later two more dishes appeared. They both got a combined greek and salmon salad with blue cheese and nuts sprinkled on top. Again Karim dove into his salad and Nicola ate a little but mostly played with hers.

He carried on more of a conversation with his phone than he apparently was willing to with her.

After the salads came the main course. For him a steak with all of the fixings and her a vegetarian ravioli. She sighed and smiled inside. At least he could order food well enough. She looked up at him, his nose buried in his phone. She took a bite of her ravioli and it melted in her mouth. The pasta was fresh, probably made that afternoon in the restaurant itself. The tomato sauce was perfectly spiced and the cheese slid and oozed around the spinach with such delicacy. Suddenly she had an idea. She reached into her jacket pocket and took out her phone. She sent a text to Karim that read 'Are you on a date with me or your phone? Should I be jealous?' She added a winking smiley face and hit 'send', then put the phone away. She continued eating, glancing up at him between bites. He finally got the message and instead of looking amused he looked upset. He went to reply then set his phone down.

"I've been dealing with work," he said.

"You promised me no work for three hours. Just us," she said softly. "Would it kill you to ask how my day was?"

He glared at her. She simply stared back at him and shrugged her shoulders.

"You asked me to go to dinner here," she said.

"And you asked me to go to the bar with you and Patsy," he retorted.

She set her fork down gently.

"I asked you to go for drinks as a double date. Because Patsy has a blind date. You said yes. Then you asked if we could go for dinner somewhere nice first and I said yes. But what does that matter? We're on a date, together. We should talk, laugh, have fun. Not just stuff our faces. We can do that at home for much cheaper. This isn't fun. This is painful," she said.

He opened his mouth to respond then snapped it shut. He sighed heavily as he lowered his head into his hand his eyes looking downward and away from her.

"You're right. I'm sorry," he said.

She looked down at her pasta awkwardly. She picked up a piece of her ravioli and put it on his steak. He looked at her like she was crazy.

"You need more vegetables with your meal," she said seriously. He burst out laughing.

"You are such a nut," he said, shaking his head.

The room was filled with smoke and laser lights spinning around the room like small darts. A broken disco ball chugged around in a slow circle, spattering the room with jagged spots of low light. A low crooning voice poured out of the speakers, filling every square inch of the room. Bodies thumped against each other on the dance floor, grinding to the music. The floor stuck noisily to her feet as they walked over to the table. Karim had set their drinks on the table and was holding out a chair for Nicola. She smiled and took her seat as he first tucked her chair in then Patsy's. Patsy only half noticed Karim tucking her seat in under her as she glanced around the bar, looking for her date, and sighed.

"Always the gentleman," she said absently.

"Always a pleasure, mi'ladies," he said as he sat down beside Nicola, took his drink and clinked glasses with her.

Nicola took a long drink, finishing the majority of it in one go.

"Mi'lady must be awfully thirsty. Should I order another already?" he said mockingly. Patsy pushed her glass over towards him.

"Please," she mumbled.

Nicola shot him a knowing look while taking Patsy's hand and squeezing it. Then she giggled.

"Maybe this is just what the doctored ordered," she said, sneaking a glance at Patsy who was still scanning the crowd, then back at Karim and mouthed the words 'two for her' while subtly indicating Patsy.

His free hand reached over and grabbed her thigh with a squeeze. She took his hand in hers and squeezed it back with a smile. Subconsciously, Nicola scanned the crowd. Looking for him. Not knowing who he was, but still looking.

"Nicola," Karim said.

She mumbled a vague response back to him and he snapped his fingers in front of her face.

"Stop it," he said.

"Sorry, what?"

Startled, she snapped backed to reality and realized what she had been doing. Her face flushed red with embarrassment and she mumbled another apology to Karim. He reached over and dragged her chair closer to his, pulled her into a tight embrace and stroked her hair softly. He whispered into her ear, telling her to stop over-analyzing everything so much and to just relax. But their dinner earlier had left her feeling uneasy. She just couldn't shake the feeling of being followed out of her mind and it chilled her to the bone.

She turned her head and nuzzled it into his chest.

"Okay, you're right. No more thinking tonight. But I could still use another drink," she said coyly as she finished the last of her drink.

He hugged her tight against his chest one last time before standing up.

"I think I'll grab us some food for us too. Patsy? Wings?" he asked, tapping her on the shoulder.

She looked up from the crowd and managed a small nod before resuming her visual search. Karim disappeared into the crowd, a carefree saunter in his hips. Nicola smiled as he disappeared into the crowd and then started to ponder over how quickly she could get him back to their place when a sudden presence in his chair broke her naughty reverie.

"Nicola! Darling, how are you? It's been forever!" a shrill voice said, and she looked up through her daydream to see a mid-thirties woman sitting in front of her. She had jet black hair that probably would've reached the floor if it hadn't been done braid upon braid with most of it tucked up neatly upon her head and several smaller braids flowing down the back. Her eyes were a sparkling green and her skin an alabaster white. She wore a sharp black jacket and a red blouse peeking out from beneath it, with a matching white pinstriped skirt. Nicola smiled at her, desperately trying to recall where she had met this woman before.

"Linda. Linda Torrance?" the woman said, a hopeful look in her eyes.

Nicola bit her lower lip and tried to fake recognition but she had always been a terrible liar.

"I'm sorry, I can't remember. I mean, I remember you... " she said, flustered, "but I don't recall how."

Linda laughed, a low throaty guttural laugh that surprised Nicola considering her petite stature. "It's okay. You haven't seen me since you were a teenager. My mother and your mother were friends and business acquaintances," she said smiling, a mouth full of perfect pearly whites shining brightly in this darkened room.

"Oh, right. Macklee?" Nicola said, sighing as she did her best to feign happiness at their reunion. Just what she needed in her already horrible day. A reminder of her mother. She wondered if Karim could work abroad and if changing countries was difficult.

Linda calling her name out to her broke Nicola out of her daydreams yet again. Was she still here? Nicola feigned her best smile as Linda proceeded to tell her that she had moved back to help her ailing mother, but that she would hopefully pull through. Also, that despite her best efforts, her mother was being quite stubborn about handing over her duties and had barely handed over the legwork. Linda had convinced her mother to do only the paperwork for now until the doctor gave her a clear from bed rest. Nicola rested her chin on her hand and nodded frequently while pondering how to get Linda to leave. Suddenly Karim showed up setting drinks and wings on the table along with a plate of veggie sticks and blue cheese dip. Linda abruptly stopped talking and gave him a good look over.

"Why, hello handsome," she said.

Karim poked Patsy in the shoulder and she grabbed her drink and a wing while Karim leaned over to give Nicola a kiss on the cheek. He turned to face Linda.

"Who's your friend, honey?" he asked.

"Karim, Patsy, Linda. Linda, Karim, Patsy. Linda's mother and my mother used to work together when I was a teenager," Nicola said with enough sugary sweetness to kill a diabetic. "Karim is my boyfriend and Patsy here is a good friend who also works with me," she finished with a big fake painful smile plastered onto her face.

Karim took Linda's hand and shook it firmly. "Pleased to meet you, Linda. If I had known you were here I would have brought you a drink."

Patsy nodded and offered Linda her hand as well.

"Oh no, that's ok. I don't drink. Against my religion. In fact, I'm meeting some new clients here in a few minutes. I just saw Nicola and had to stop to say hello."

Linda reached into her purse and pulled out a small, blue jewelled card holder. She popped it open and withdrew a card. She handed it to Nicola as she got out of the chair and offered it back to Karim.

"Call me if you want to catch up, darling."

She kissed Nicola on both cheeks and then strode off to the back of the club. Patsy rolled her eyes and sighed, chugging her first drink quickly. Karim watched Linda walk off, jiggling her butt, and Nicola swatted his leg with her clutch. She shot him a dirty look as he laughed at her and took her hands in his.

"Must be nice to be able to meet with clients at a loud club like this," he said.

"Strange is more like it. You know that company, Macklee?" she asked as he shook his head no. "Lucky you. It's a frightening and menacing company," Nicola said.

Karim suddenly jumped out of his seat and pulled Nicola to the dance floor. She yelped in protest but let him take her anyway. He pulled her deep within the throng of the crowd. A loud thumping could be felt through the floor and up into their bodies. They laughed and started grooving to the music. Karim smiled at her, with his eyes full of mischievousness and his famous lopsided grin that made her heart race each time she saw it. He slipped his hand down her back and settled it just below her waist. Slowly he pulled her closer until their hips bumped each other softly as they grinded to the music. He ran his other hand through her hair softly, then suddenly grabbed it tightly and tugged her head ever so slightly. Her heart began to race and her breath quickened as a soft gasp escaped from her lips. As quickly as he had yanked her hair he let it go again. His other hand pulled her slightly trembling body into his. She looked up into his eyes, bewildered and excited at the same time. His grin was huge.

"I love you," he whispered into her ear.

She leaned up and kissed him. A rough hand suddenly pushed into her ass and she fell into Karim, breaking off the kiss. Startled, she looked around to see who had pushed her but only saw a crowd of fellow tipsy dancers. Karim looked at Nicola as she proclaimed that someone had grabbed her ass. He laughed and patted her butt fondly.

"It is a nice ass," he said, but stopped abruptly and looked over her shoulder with concern in his eyes.

"What's wrong?" she asked, her happy blissful state quickly being overrun with panic.

He mumbled a response that sounded like he said it was nothing but she didn't believe him. She craned her head over her shoulder, trying to see what had upset Karim. He put his hands on her shoulders and pushed down on them lightly. He told her to stay put before he went over towards the door and the bouncer.

Frantically, Nicola began to scan the crowd, looking for anyone that might stand out. But she was enveloped deep within the smoke and crowd. She couldn't see much more than the band in front of her and Patsy weaving her way through the crowd towards Karim and the bouncers. She was surrounded by dancers, all grinding away in their own private world, unaware of her or anyone else, yet she had the distinct feeling that all of their attention was on her. Everything started to swirl about her, getting closer and closer, faster and faster. The smoke grew thicker, making it difficult to breath and she tried to swallow her breaths more deeply but her lungs refused to cooperate. The disco ball got faster and the smoke started to cling to her clothes. Suddenly everyone was looking at her, like she was some sort of freak. She could see them start to point at her, to laugh at her. She put her hands over her head and tried to force them out. But it was crushing her down. She tried to push her way out of the crowd, but she was trapped. She fell down to her knees, clinging tightly to herself.

"Nicola?" a voice said breaking through the crowd as a hand appeared out of nowhere. She took it and let it herself be pulled out.

"I'm sorry, I shouldn't have left you there. C'mon, over here." Karim said as he pulled her close to him and led her out of the crowd.

She followed him to the bar and then out through to the back. He led through a series of doors until they found themselves in a small office filled with computer screens, all sporting different angles of the bar they were just in.

Patsy was huddled over the screens with a scrawny looking security guard, scanning the screens.

"They're going to see if they spot the guy who grabbed you and find out why he put the letter in your pocket," Karim said.

"Letter??" she exclaimed.

Karim held a bar coaster in his hand and slowly she took it from him. On one side was the bar's name and logo. The other side was usually blank, but scrawled on it were the words 'I'm watching you'. Tears filled her face and Karim hugged her tight. He kissed her on the forehead and reassured her that everything would be alright.

The bar manager pointed to the screens now showing the dance floor. There were six different angles. He asked when the incident had occurred and Karim told him less than a half hour ago. The security guard said that he could roll back the videos but that it would take him a few minutes to do so. And that he would load the last half hour directly onto the computer as they needed to continue recording the rest of the evening and it would be easier to view on a separate source. He also told them that the police were on their way. Nicola nodded numbly and sat down, taking the coffee offered to her and sipped absently while Karim and Patsy scoured the live stream video looking for anyone suspicious.

A hour later two police officers had joined them and Karim had identified the moment when Nicola had been pushed against him and presumably when the culprit put the note in her pocket. The bar manager was able to pull up a grainy but fairly good picture of the man who appeared to be the one who had accosted Nicola. He printed it up and gave it to the police officers. They went off to search the club for him. Karim knelt in front of Nicola, took her hands in his and held them on her lap and smiled, reassuring her again that they would find the man and this ordeal would be over soon.

She nodded and smiled weakly. She leaned her head against his chest, too exhausted and overwhelmed to be happy yet. He kissed her on the forehead. They both looked over as one of the police officers came back in with a frown on his face. He was shaking his head as he shared the bouncers' consensus that they saw the suspect leave more than an hour ago, most likely right after the incident. He affirmed that they would continue their sweep of the club; however, he told Karim that the three of them should go home and try to rest; that they could come down to the station tomorrow morning and file a report then. But to not expect to hear anything for a couple of days since it would take some time to find the man's identity with only a picture. The officer put a hand on Nicola's shoulder.

"Don't worry ma'am, we'll find him," he said, nodding to them before disappearing back into the club.

Patsy was shaking her head back and forth, obviously more disgruntled at not finding the assailant than her date standing her up. She was biting her lip, trying to hold back her words. Karim held out Nicola's jacket and slipped it onto her shoulders. Patsy huffed but left the office as Karim took Nicola's hand in his and led her out of the bar.

Dad had left early in the morning to head into the city. The car needed some repairs and dad had made an appointment to get it

looked at that day. My Uncle Phillip was going in with him, taking his own car, in the likelihood that the car couldn't be repaired right away. Our day had passed as normal with the only difference being that dad had called in saying he would be late, as the shop was able to fix the car but he couldn't pick it up until closing time. My sister and I were sad because it meant dad wouldn't be home in time to tuck us in and read us our regular bedtime story.

Long after we had gone to bed I found myself unable to sleep. Finally I decided to go downstairs and heat up some milk with anijsbokjes. I knew mother wouldn't make any for me, so I crept downstairs as quietly as possible. A soft red glow pulsed from the fireplace as I walked past it through the living room and into the kitchen. The moonlight that fell through the window was bright enough that I could make my way to the stove to turn on one of the gas burners without having to turn on any lights. The tick, tick, tick of the stove lighting itself startled me as it echoed loudly around me. I hesitantly looked up above my head, as if I could see my mother potentially waking up through the ceiling. After being sure that I heard no movement from above, I took a pot and put it on the burner. I found fresh milk, dated from that morning and probably from the cow I had milked myself. I carefully measured one cup into the pot and turned the heat down to a small, low blue flame. I easily crawled onto the kitchen counter to open the cupboards and found the anijsbokjes with the other Dutch treats, hidden on the top shelf. I found it, broke off a single block and put it back. I slid off the counter, grabbed a mug and a whisk and looked back at my pot. The milk was just starting to boil. I dropped the block in, started whisking it and turned off the stove.

I had just finished cleaning up and was sipping my milk at the kitchen table when the silence was abruptly broken by the ringing of the telephone. It echoed loudly throughout the house, like a fire siren blaring down the street. I paused with the mug halfway to my mouth with uncertain guilt as the telephone rang a second time. I looked through the living room, towards the staircase, then to the ceiling above me and then back to my mug. I put my mug down and hesitantly answered the phone as it shrilled for a third time. As I picked up the phone I could hear the sound of my mother's feet hitting the floor above me.

"Hello?" I asked, my voice timid and quiet.

A very loud and gruff voice answered me. He spoke a large blur of words that I couldn't understand. I wasn't sure if he was speaking too quickly or his voice was just muffled. Then I heard my father's name amongst the words.

"Is daddy with you?" I asked.

I saw my mother coming through the living room out of the corner of my eye as the man continued to ramble on. She looked tired, worried and very stressed. I held out the phone to her.

"He says he's a police officer. He said daddy's name... mommy?"

Tears started to fill her eyes as she took the phone from me and roughly pushed me away from her.

"Mommy, what's wrong?" I asked her but she turned away from me, as if I wasn't even there. I sat back down at the table and resumed my drinking. I didn't know what was happening, but I knew it couldn't be good.

Even with her back to me, I could see my mother's body language quickly changed dramatically. She started to hunch over, curling her body to the wall and over the phone. I could hear her tears falling down her face as she choked back sobs. I put my drink down, walked over to her, and wrapped myself tightly around her in the biggest hug I could give. With her spare hand she clutched my shoulder with a frighteningly strong grip then roughly thrusted me away from her and I went sprawling to the ground.

She set the phone gingerly onto the receiver.

"Mommy?" I asked maintaining my distance.

"Go upstairs and pack a suitcase for you and your sisters. You're going on a trip," she said, her voice hollow.

"Mommy?" I asked again.

"Get out of my sight!" she suddenly screamed as she pushed me away from her.

Startled, I got to my feet and ran upstairs. I grabbed a suitcase out of my parents' closet, stopping briefly to look at their empty bed. Sobs filled my throat but I choked them down and quickly made my way to my bedroom. I found my sister asleep in my bed. She must have snuck in after I went downstairs. I turned on my light and she moaned, turning her head beneath the pillows. I opened my dresser drawers and randomly just threw clothes into the suitcase. Shorts, dresses, t-shirts, undies and socks. I added the book I was currently reading and my journal. I closed the suitcase and went to my sisters' bedroom.

Taking the flashlight my parents kept on the edge of our door frames, I turned it on, waited a moment listening for my baby sister's soft breathing to remain steady and then rolled the suitcase to the dresser my two sisters shared. I added the same number of clothes for my sister and for the baby I did double. I also took the clean diaper pail and filled it full of cloth diapers, baby powder, bath toys, diaper cream, wipes and as many toys for both of my sisters as I could squeeze in. With what little space remaining in the suitcase I put in colouring books, crayons and some writing paper. I dragged both the suitcase and the diaper pail out of the bedroom before quietly closing the door.

The suitcase was too heavy for me to carry down the stairs so I took the diaper pail first. I set it at the front door and then went to get the suitcase. As I started up the stairs my mother emerged from the kitchen. Her face was flushed red and soaked with tears that had *barely stopped flowing. She looked distraught and distant. As if she wasn't even here anymore.*

Without looking at me she asked, "Are you all packed?"

I nodded, afraid to talk. Afraid that she might start crying again.

"Go wake up your sisters and get them dressed. Your uncle will be here soon."

I looked at her with surprise, she never let me near the baby.

"Even the baby?" I asked quietly, afraid both to lose the privilege and to face her wrath.

She turned and hissed at me to leave her alone and hurry up so I ran back up the stairs and quickly dragged the suitcase down, literally riding it like a sled down the stairs. Mother didn't even notice.

I ran back upstairs and turned my bedroom light on again. I shook my sister until she finally started to show signs of life.

"Wake up!" I hissed at her.

She looked at me, her eyes full of sleep and confusion.

"Wake up," I said again, but this time more gently. "Get dressed. We're going on a trip."

She again looked at me with confusion but slowly sat up.

"A trip?" she asked.

"Yes, a trip. Get dressed. I have to get the baby ready."

I left her, hoping she was awake enough to get herself ready. I stopped at the doorway as she asked me, "Where's daddy?"

I looked down at the floor and answered meekly. "I don't know."

My baby sister was just starting to wake up from all of the noise we were making. She cooed at me as I turned on the bedroom lights. I reached in and carefully lifted her out of the crib. It was the first time I had been allowed to pick her up. I hadn't even been allowed to hold my other sister when she was born. She cooed and giggled and babbled in baby talk as I held her close to me, afraid I might drop her if I wasn't careful. I changed her diaper even though it had looked dry and then I changed her pajamas for a warmer winter set. A bit warm right now, but if we were going out to our uncle's it was bound to be cold to get from the house to the car.

My other sister finally stumbled into the room and I ordered her to get dressed, pointing to the clothes I had laid out on her bed but she promptly fell onto her clothes attempting to fall back asleep. With an eye on my baby sister I ran from the changing table to smack my sister on the butt. I hissed at her to hurry up and she sat up abruptly, a look of fear crossing her face as she realized the seriousness of the situation. She knew I wasn't joking. I took the baby, put her on my hip, took the diaper bag in the other arm and looked over at my sister, now half dressed.

"Don't forget your teddy," I said as I left the room.

Downstairs mother was still sitting in the living room but my grandparents had arrived and were arguing with her over us kids and where we were going. I dropped the diaper bag off with the the suitcase and went into the kitchen. The grownups ignored me as I set the baby into her highchair. I grabbed a spoon out of the drawer and gave it to her to play with. I peeked through the window that separated the kitchen from the living room and could make out that all of the grownups were quite angry with each other and I hoped that they would continue to ignore me.

As the grownups continued to argue I began preparing a bottle for the baby. As soon as the milk felt warm I turned off the stove and took the bottle out. I screwed on the nipple top and put my hand in the underside of the bottle forcing all of the air out until a stream of milk popped out. I smiled softly as the baby cooed and clapped her hands in excitement, the spoon I had given her to play with now long gone onto the floor.

I squirted some of the milk on the inside of my wrist. Happy with its temperature I walked over to her, flying the bottle like it was an airplane. Zipping from side to side of the kitchen, performing loop de loops as she continued to squeal louder and louder. Out of the corner of my eye I could see that the grownups were too engrossed in their argument to have noticed us yet. I sighed inside, but kept my smile on the outside. My other sister rounded the corner of the stairs into the living room. Her shirt was on inside out and backwards, but otherwise she was successfully dressed. She had her teddy in her hands and her thumb in her mouth, a habit she had broken a couple of years ago, but given the current tension in the house I couldn't blame her. I wished I was five years old again although I was only eight years old myself. I waved her over to the kitchen and she ran past the grownups quickly. She took a seat at the kitchen table as I gave the bottle to the baby.

I asked her if she was hungry but she shook her head no, her eyes now wide as saucers as she sat facing into the living room, watching the grownups argue. I took her chair and slid it to the other side of the table so she could watch the baby. She neither argued or complained but merely looked at me with scared eyes and a tremble in her lower lip.

"It'll be okay," I mumbled, trying to believe those words myself.

I grabbed two bowls from the cupboard and placed both of them in front of her. In a lower cupboard I got out the Fruit Loops. Normally sugary cereal was only for special occasions, but I assumed that being woken up at three in the morning was just that. I poured us both a small bowl, overfilled them with milk and put a spoon into my sisters hand. She slowly scooped out some cereal and put it in her mouth. She chewed, as if in deep thought and contemplation. Then she suddenly realized how hungry she was. She gobbled up the remainder of the cereal in a flash and then started on mine. I had only managed one bite myself but could barely swallow it, so I just pushed it towards her.

I heard the front door slam abruptly and looked up from the table. My grandparents were gone and my mother was alone in the living *room. I didn't know what to do. So I poured another bowl of Fruit Loops and hesitantly took it to her.*

"Mommy?" I said softly as I pushed the bowl towards her. "It's Fruit Loops."

She looked up me, her face still soaked with her tears and looking like she was a hundred years old. Her face was full of crinkles and had dirty spots on it. She looked so sad. I continued to hold out the cereal towards her. Hesitantly she took it from me and took a bite. I shifted from foot to foot while she ate the cereal until she finally looked up at me, clarity and a new steeliness in her eyes.

"This doesn't mean anything," she said softly.

I looked at her with confusion, unsure of what she meant. But fear filled me and I took a step back. Suddenly she threw the half-eaten bowl at me. I whimpered and ran back to the kitchen as mother started sobbing again.

◇◇◇

Karim had already hopped into the shower and Nicola lay on their bed, still dressed. Due to Patsy's insistence they had gone directly to the police station and filed a report right away instead of waiting for the morning. They had spent hours at the police station filling out paperwork, and halfway through Nicola had been ready to just leave and forget all about it, but Patsy had insisted that she saw someone. By the end of the evening, now early morning, everyone was tired and Nicola felt that police thought they were crazy. She was embarrassed that she had let herself get so wound up over something so trivial.

Her phone chirped. Probably Patsy. She pulled it out of her pocket and saw a new text from a unknown number. It read *'Nice ass'*. She sat up abruptly and looked around her room. She called out to Karim, knowing he couldn't hear her over the shower. She sent a message back, demanding to know who this was. Shortly after, she received a text complimenting her features and saying how beautiful she was. She messaged back, again asking who it was and she received yet another message complimenting her. Frustrated, she pounded out another text threatening to contact the police if he didn't identify himself, and just as she went to hit send another text came through saying goodnight. She hit send anyway and stared at her phone, willing him to text her back. But he never did.

She heard the shower stop and looked up from her phone. She quickly shut off her phone and put it on the charger, then set it to silent. She stripped out of her clothes and crawled into bed naked. She pulled up the covers just as Karim came out of the bathroom and crawled into bed, snuggling up close beside her. He smiled as he ran a hand along her naked body under the sheets.

He leaned over, with a smile on his lips and whispered into her ear, "Forget something?"

CHAPTER FOUR

Nicola walked into the office, dragging her feet behind her. She attempted to kick the door shut but only succeeded in moving it a few inches. She sighed heavily, turned around and pushed the door shut gently. Turning back she saw Patsy staring at her with surprise and concern. Nicola held out two paper bags towards her with a weak smile then lowered them as she stumbled into her office. Patsy quickly followed her in, sliding her chair with her.

Sitting at her desk, Nicola set down the papers bags, pulling out two chai tea lattes and cheese danishes. Patsy took one of the drinks, sipped it and made a face. She passed it back to Nicola and took the other one. Nicola chuckled.

"Sorry, didn't sleep well, I need extra caffeine."

Patsy just stared at her and shook her head. "Adding a shot to a chai is sacrilegious," she scoffed at Nicola.

Nicola bit into her danish and chewed a few bites before taking a long drink from her chai, and proceeded to tell Patsy about the texts she received the night before, after they left the police station. Patsy covered her mouth with her hands as she voiced her surprise and asked if she had told anyone else yet, or even the police. Nicola shook her head no, arguing that the police probably already thought that they were a bit over-zealous. Patsy looked at the ground awkwardly and mumbled an apology, but Nicola laughed and reassured her that she'd rather have a nut on her side than no one.

Patsy reached her hand out over the desk and smacked Nicola in the arm before grabbing Nicola's phone. She browsed through the texts quickly, then handed the phone back, shaking her head slowly from side to side as she bit her lower lip. The number was untraceable—to the point that Patsy thought it could have been sent via an app or online.

Nicola shrugged her shoulders. "It was probably just a crank text."

But Patsy shook her head violently and grabbed Nicola's hand. "Don't let the stupid police tell you that bullshit. This might just be some crazy secret admirer but it is someone."

Nicola looked at Patsy, her face so serious and intent, and sighed. She didn't know what to do and just wanted it to go away before it got any worse.

Patsy shook her head again and tightened her grip on Nicola's hands. "No maybes—" she started, and Nicola went to protest but Patsy cut her off. "You need to take this seriously. Be aware of your surroundings. Keep an eye out for people acting suspiciously."

Nicola reluctantly agreed and nodded.

Patsy let go of her hands. "Hopefully, it's nothing more than a secret admirer, but you never know," she said as she got up out of her chair. "I have to go pick up some orders, so I'll be back later. Message me if anything else weird happens."

Nicola nodded in agreement as Patsy left her office. After she had gone, Nicole slowly opened the desk drawer above her lap and pulled out the valentine she had received. She looked at it and then glanced back at her cell phone.

As usual it was noisy in the café, so Patsy decided to walk down to the next neighbourhood; a more artsy type of neighbourhood with a more natural and organic vibe compared to the movie-rush of this café. The neighbourhood that she lived in. There was a café just outside her apartment that she frequented daily. The only reason she went to the other café was for Nicola. She preferred their chai tea latte. However, every now and then Patsy bought her a chai from her favourite café, El Naturo, and poured it in her mug. Nicola had yet to notice and Patsy was debating whether or not to confess to her boss about the occasional switch.

The walk was unusually calm and quiet. No taxis honking their horns, no cursing as people cut each other off on the road, and the sidewalk was relatively bare. She decided to pop in her headphones and listen to some tunes while she attended to her emails. She walked with a little hop in her step as she powered her way through a dozen or more emails. She wove her way expertly through the sparse crowd and stopped diligently at the traffic lights without evening looking up. The beeping signal for the visually-impaired indicated when it was safe for her to cross, and she knew the way by heart.

She turned down a small side street unknown to many that led to the back entrance of her apartment. It was quite narrow and only a few of the people who knew about it could even fit through; it was very much a one-way pedestrian access only path. She exited the pathway and turned left to go to the café and her phone suddenly flew out of her hand as she bumped into someone. An arm wrapped around her waist to catch her and the other deftly caught her cell. She looked up to see whom she had bumped into and her jaw dropped slightly.

He was only a couple of inches taller than her with a clean-shaven face, and was young with delicate, feminine features. He had short, sandy-blonde hair and wore a pair of loose fitting khakis and a bowling shirt. She couldn't help but gaze into his dark blue-green eyes. He smiled and handed her phone back to her. With her free hand she plucked her headphones out of her ears and smiled back an even goofier grin than the one she already had on her face.

"Thank you," she stammered.

Still holding her close, she could smell the scent of freshly laundered clothes and Ivory soap on his skin. He grabbed her hand as she took the phone and squeezed it briefly before letting it go.

"Can I buy you a coffee as an apology for bumping into you?" Patsy asked.

"I should be buying you a coffee for the honour of your company," he said, his voice only slightly low but a bit gravely. He finally let go of her hand and the two of them walked into the cafe.

The barista saw them and smiled a greeting. "The usual?" she asked, and they both nodded.

He waved to Patsy, ushering her to get them a table as he paid for the drinks.

When he brought them over he had three drinks and Patsy blushed a deep red.

"Oh my god, I'm so sorry. I forgot that on Tuesdays I get my boss a drink too. They must have assumed I was picking up for her," she stammered.

He just smiled at her and Patsy could feel her heart start to patter.

"No worries. Do you have to take it to her right now?" he asked, and Patsy shook her head no, smiling a lopsided, giddy grin.

He set her drinks next to her and then sat down across from her. "My name is Gregory, what's yours?"

"Patsy."

"That's a beautiful name, just like you," he said as she blushed feverishly, and he laughed softly. "Do my compliments bother you?"

She shook her head no.

"Good, because there's plenty more where that came from," he said as his fingers lightly grazed hers.

She could feel goosebumps growing all over her arms and was grateful for the long sleeves she was wearing. She studied his face intensely, partially shaken by the amount of unease he was causing her, but also wildly intrigued.

"Do I know you Gregory? You look very familiar," she asked, but he shook his head no.

"Maybe in a past life. But no, I just moved here last week."

She shrugged her shoulders and started to get up from the table. "As much as I'd like to stay and chat more, I do have to get back to the office and preferably before these drinks get too cold," she said reluctantly.

He nodded his head and waved a farewell as she strolled off. Barely a block away she glanced over her shoulder to see if he happened to still be looking at her, but he was already gone.

Nicola slid her car into her usual parking spot on the outskirts of the forest. Despite being one of the few entrances to the hiking trails, this area was seldom used. Most likely because it was due to the lack of signage, or simply because the main entrance was only a few hundred yards away. In either case she was always happy she didn't have to fight for one of the three spots available, and was grateful for the lack of other runners in her vicinity.

One of her biggest pet peeves was the city yuppie joggers. The forest served as a sanctuary for both the inner city and suburban dwellers. It was a large forest— spanning over thirty acres. The majority of it was riddled with trails, many of these undiscovered by but a few people who could discern the subtle entrances to them. It was within these trails that Nicole usually found herself. However, it did require a good twenty minute run from the outer edge of the forest, at any entrance, to find a way in. The yuppies usually stuck to the outskirts of the forest and spent as much time yakking out loud about useless nonsense as they did jogging—not quite a fast enough pace to disrupt their never-ending banter amongst each other, and of course included anyone they crossed paths with into their conversation.

This drove her slightly mad as her running was a time to get in touch with mind and nature. She embraced the solo aspect of running and preferred to let her natural surroundings be her soundtrack. Mostly, she enjoyed starting her run with absolute silence and letting herself get lost into her own thoughts.

After quickly checking the laces on her shoes and tapping her toes onto the ground to settle her feet into them better, she stretched out a single leg in front of her. She pointed her toes, then flexed them upward and pointed one more time. She repeated this with her other leg. She rolled her head in circular motion, cracking it slightly as she did. Satisfied, she reached back into her car and grabbed her water bottle. She slid her hand into the cozy that fit around the bottle, which served as a glove she could easily put on while also maintaining enough grip that she didn't have to worry about it falling off as she ran. She tossed her cell phone back into the car and nudged the car door closed with her knee, took a sip of water and locked the car door with a loud beep. She never really stretched much before she started as her light jog from the outer trails to the inner trails served as her warm up.

The sky was still blue from the warm afternoon, but storm clouds were lingering at the city's edge, making their way towards the forest. The dark menacing clouds threatened to turn her run into a shower, so she took off with a dash and quickly disappeared into the depths of the forest.

As usual, this part of the trails remained empty. A few signs were scattered along the trail, some urging owners to pick up after their pets with a roll of little plastic baggies under the signs, while others had Smoky the Bear on them and warned of forest fires. Her favourite was the collection of signs advertising a litter-free forest. On most of these signs people had attached pictures of a litter of kittens and drew a big X through them. The pictures were faded with age, showing just how little the city really maintained this forest.

She took in the silence around her. The wind caressed her hair as she ran, her ponytail bobbing from side to side with each step she took. The sunlight trickled through the leaves of the trees like small slivers of light. Old, dead branches crackled and leaves crunched under the pounding of her sneakers. The only other sound was that of her steady breath. She rounded the first bend and then took off. She looked ahead to the next bend and pushed herself hard to reach it as fast as possible. As soon as she was about to round it she abruptly slowed herself back down to her slower pace. She took a big swig of water, gargled it and then swallowed it quickly.

A lone bird chirped ahead of her, warbling a love song to its wayward mate perhaps. Or merely expressing its sadness as autumn approached. Soon the birds would migrate south and the forest would feel even more empty. She bounded down the path like she had every other day since she found this area over a year ago. It was so easy to run here, her body on autopilot and her mind flowing freely. She did her best thinking while running here— venting her frustrations out into the trees, logically processing out solutions—and often left her run satisfied with the decisions she had made during it. The clarity she achieved while running sometimes scared her. But she knew a run on a treadmill could never give her the same sanctuary as this.

The sunlight flickered through the leaves, like a dance encouraging her to amp up her pace. Deeper and deeper into the trees she ran, her heart racing and her mind soaring with a million thoughts. Her upcoming appointment with the doctor at the fertility clinic weighed heavily on her mind. While she and Karim had only been trying to conceive for the last two years, she had stopped using her birth control right after Karim had moved into her apartment four years ago. While back then neither of them had wanted children, their use of condoms quickly became casual and she honestly couldn't remember the last time either of them bought new ones. Either she was incredibly lucky at having never gotten pregnant or just horribly unlucky now.

In either case, Karim had already received a clean bill of health from his doctor, so now it was her turn. Her own gynecologist couldn't find anything physically wrong with her, so he had recommended she try a fertility clinic where his wife was a doctor. 'A little help isn't a bad thing, even if the plumbing isn't broken,' he had insisted. She supposed he was right. The two things that kept her hesitant were the enormous cost for something that was not guaranteed to work, and the overwhelming fear that even with help she wouldn't be able to conceive a child.

Maybe she wasn't meant to be a mother. Maybe she really didn't want to be a mother. Maybe the universe was trying to stop her from becoming like her mother. So many maybes and no definite answers. Nicola did not like the vagueness of the situation as it was the thing that was putting her on edge so much these days. She knew Karim felt the backlash of her crankiness, even though she tried very hard to keep her doubts inside her and hated showing her emotions in the face of uncertainty. She preferred to bottle everything up until she knew whether she had the right to be happy or sad. No point in being upset if five minutes later the whole situation could change for the better. So she buried everything deep inside herself and waited for the answers to reveal themselves so she could consciously choose how to feel. But no matter how hard she tried to keep it from him, she knew she overflowed like an unattended kettle on the stove as it boiled.

He had been distancing himself from her the last few months, ever since she got the news from her doctor that nothing was wrong with her. Sometimes she felt like he was disappointed with her. That somehow, it was her fault. When they first got together, years ago, she had happily agreed with him that children were a menace to society and completely unnecessary in life. It was one of the biggest things that drew her to him. She had grown up the eldest of three. However, she grew up isolated from them and was treated as an outcast. Although during her teenage years she had spent the majority of her free time looking after her siblings, she never grew close to them until recently, when they all had moved out of the house. Her mother's lack of motherly affection towards her only fuelled her desire to remain childless.

So, after several years of dating and discovering that while men were happy that you didn't have children at that particular moment, the desire to never have children tugged at their hearts in such a way that she found herself single over and over again. It had reached the point where the only relationships she found herself in were meaningless sex ones. No one talked about children in the bedroom, especially if it there were only a one night stand. It left her hollow inside sometimes, but it was less painful than being dumped for her lacking desire of motherhood. When Karim came around, she thought she had been dreaming and she couldn't believe her luck. To not only to find an attractive, desirable man her age that was also attracted to her, but to find one who wanted cats instead of children! The two of them had hit it off instantly and the rest was history.

Until a few years ago. Her sister, Cassandra, had just gotten married while she had a very large bun in the oven—twins in fact. They had barely finished the ceremony when the bun decided to pop out. Nicola and Karim dragged the frazzled couple into their SUV and rushed off to the hospital. Nicola was coaching her sister in the back seat of the car, while her brother-in-law Philip, a very large man, sat in the front, his bear paw of an arm stretched out to reach his new wife's hand. Despite the hospital being a short drive away from the chapel, her sister's contractions kept getting closer much more quickly than anyone could have anticipated. Nicola barely had time to grab her emergency kit from the back seat when her sister grabbed her shirt and wrenched her back onto the floor beside her and through gritted teeth growled, "GET THEM OUT OF ME NOW!"

Nicola quickly pushed the wedding dress out of the way as her sister propped herself up onto her elbows. As she quickly threw a towel on the car seat under her sister, she could see the baby's head crowning already. Philip, already a few steps ahead of her, had pulled out a bottle of sterilizing liquid and gloves. She doused her hands quickly and he helped her put the gloves on. When she turned to look back, the baby's head was already halfway out. She muttered a few curses under her breath before ordering Philip to look under the driver's seat for the baby blanket she and Karim had gotten them along with some sterile wipes.

She gently cradled the baby's head, then its shoulders, as her sister pushed amidst her screams. The first baby popped out quite easily and Nicola took the blanket, placing the baby boy into it. She pulled on the cord, trying to get to the placenta so a clear path could be made for the next baby. As the placenta fell out of her sister, Nicola furled her brow in confusion. Her sister gasped softly and the car was suddenly eerily silent.

"What's wrong?" Cassandra asked, and Nicola could only look quizzically at the placenta. A second cord, stemming from beside the first, grew out of it and continued back inside her sister. Nicola slowly and gently pulled on it, afraid of possibly hurting, what she hoped, was the other baby attached to the other end.

"What is it!" Cassandra shrieked through gritted teeth.

"I don't know. It has two cords?... Is that normal?" Nicola stammered.

"I don't ca—" her sister started and was abruptly cut off by her own screaming.

Suddenly, alongside the placenta cord, another head appeared. Nicola yelled a hurrah! as she let go of the cord in her hand. She suddenly realized that the first baby would be in the way of the second baby but she didn't really have anywhere to put him. So she set him gingerly on her lap and took the other blanket from Philip, dropping it just in time on the car seat for the other baby to pop out. Again, she helped ease the baby out and onto the blanket. Gratefully, the second cord was indeed attached to this baby. A baby girl.

Her sister collapsed onto her back and sighed. "I better get better anniversary presents than these two monkeys get for their birthdays," she muttered. As if on cue, the twins, silent until now, suddenly broke out crying. The entire car erupted into laughter.

"Here, try to sit up," Nicola said to Cassandra as she slid the remainder of the emergency kit under her sister's back while carefully balancing one baby in her lap and the other in the crook of her arms. She got Cassandra to slide back enough so she could prop her jacket under her head. Then Nicola took the baby girl and placed her onto her Cassandra's belly.

"Just hold her here... I need to grab the other one. They're still attached to each other," she said as she grabbed the baby boy and put him into her sister's left arm before repositioning the girl into Cassandra's right arm. She smiled brightly at the sight of her new niece and nephew.

"Ahem," Philip said as he cleared his throat loudly.

Nicola and Cassandra turned to face the new father. In his right hand he had his cellphone, held up high and close to the rearview mirror. He angled it slightly so you could see his head, the top of the car seat, his wife holding their babies, and Nicola.

"New baby selfie?" he asked, as demurely as possible. Nicole and Cassandra had to bite their tongues to stop from bursting into giggles. He snapped a picture almost as quickly as he had asked, and the sisters burst into laughter, tears rolling down their faces.

"Can you see that they're attached still? Pretty cool huh?" asked Nicola.

"Didn't know that was even possible," said Karim.

"Maybe we can keep them that way. Easier to keep an eye on both of them?" said Cassandra, her voice filled with motherly love. Nicola laughed softly.

"We're here," Karim announced.

Nicola looked out the window. She hadn't even noticed when he had slowed down the car to pull into the hospital. The passenger door abruptly opened and she let herself get pulled out. She watched as her sister and the twins got taken out of the car quickly and efficiently. They disappeared through the emergency doors. Nicola stood next to the car, her clothes soaked in blood and other bodily fluids.

Karim, glove on his hand, took hers and squeezed it. "Sorry, precaution. You're kind of all gross now. Might have cooties."

Nicola just stared at the hospital emergency doors fondly. "I want one," she said softly.

Karim, pretending he hadn't heard her, let her hand fall out of his. "Sure babe. Whatever you want."

CHAPTER FIVE

Nicola rushed into the diner. It had been ages since she had last been there. She looked around for Herb, the owner, but couldn't see him anywhere. It wasn't their normal day for their weekly lunch date at the diner, so she wasn't surprised, but still a little disappointed. A hug from Herb always cheered her up. The hostess let her pick her own table after she scanned the room for Karim, surprised that for once she was the first one there, especially since she was almost a half-hour late. The server had just brought her a milkshake when Karim finally strolled in, cellphone glued to his ear. He waved the hostess off when he saw Nicola and walked over to the booth. He sat down across from her, still avidly talking on his phone. He appeared to be disgruntled and kept lowering his voice as he got more and more agitated. The server brought him a coffee, his usual, and set it before him. Karim poured in sugar and cream, stirred the mug once then took a drink. Finally he ended his call. He set his phone down in front of him and began playing on the screen.

Nicola tilted her head sideways and made a face at him but he didn't see her. She waved a hand near his coffee, but he was too engaged with his phone to take notice. Finally she nudged his phone gently with her finger and he jumped in his seat slightly, snapping his head up at her.

"What?" he said aggressively, and she quickly pulled her hand back to her side of the table, shrinking back in her seat.

"Hello to you, too," she muttered under her breath as he continued playing on his phone.

The server finally interrupted the awkward silence at their table with their lunch. A BLT with fries for him and chicken strips with a caesar salad for her. Karim looked up long enough from his phone to give the server a grunt before digging into his food. The server gave Nicola a look of sympathy before bustling off to the other end of the diner. They ate in relative silence for a few minutes before Karim finally looked up from his phone.

"I can't come with you tomorrow. Something's come up," he said.

Nicola set her fork down. "But it's for both of us. I can't go alone," she said.

"Why not? This part doesn't really concern me does it?" he said.

She looked at him with surprise and hurt. She opened her mouth to respond then just closed it. She bit her lip and swallowed her pride.

"No. I guess it doesn't. I had just thought you would want to be aware of the procedures," she said slowly.

"You can fill me in after," he said before going back to his phone.

Nicola shrugged and gingerly picked up her fork. She pushed her salad from one side of the plate to the other, her appetite suddenly gone.

Karim pulled out his wallet and set a couple of bills on the table. He slid out of the booth and kissed her on top of her head.

"Gotta run. See you later," he said as he dashed out of the restaurant before she could protest.

She turned to see him run out, the phone glued to his head.

Nicola sat down with her usual glass of wine and a plate of grapes with cheese. It was unusually quiet in the condo that evening. Ordinarily there was a party on the weekend somewhere in their building. The building was owned mostly by rich parents whose late-teen, early-twenties children attended the nearby university. When she and Karim had bought their condo a couple of years back, the building was in the process of being renovated. They got a great deal since they offered to do the majority of the internal renovations themselves. Just as they had finished, the neighbourhood became popular and the building skyrocketed in value. Then the partiers came. The condos got snatched up by wealthy families following the latest trend in neighbourhood house buying and let their children trash the units.

Not that she nor Karim really minded. When the students started moving in, they themselves were both in their early twenties and enjoyed crashing the occasional party. And while Nicola did believe that most of them were immature delinquents, they did leave their partying to the weekend. Which made for a good relationship between them all.

She pulled out her iPad and propped it on the table against her half-empty wine bottle. She made herself comfortable on the couch and logged in. She scrolled through the many, many apps on her iPad until she found Skype. She swore that Patsy just added apps when she wasn't looking. She found her sister online and called her. The iPad chirped as it connected the call then rang as it called Cassandra. After a few rings her sister answered. Well, actually her niece answered the call. Three years old, tall for her age and with long brown ringlets that framed her face. She resembled Shirley Temple both in hair and facial features.

"Auntie Nicky, Auntie Nicky!" she cried out in delight when she saw Nicola's face. She then ran off, presumably to find her twin brother.

Nicola smiled and clutched the wine glass to her heart with a big sigh. Suddenly Cassandra's face popped into view, in the far back. She waved, her hands covered in flour.

"I'll be there as soon as I get the bread in the oven!" she called out, then disappeared back into what was most likely the kitchen. At the same moment her niece returned with her brother in tow. He was lagging behind, letting his sister drag him by the hand to the monitor and putting up great resistance. He had a frown on his face and a disgruntled sneer on his lips. His was mouthing something that Nicola couldn't quite make out but could guess had to do with his cars. His most recent obsession was with toy cars, especially old classic ones.

They both popped onto the screen and her niece mashed her face into the monitor camera to give Nicola a kiss. When her nephew saw it was Nicola, a half smile came upon his face. They sat down in front of the monitor, both fidgeting, very hyper and spitting images of each other. Heart-shaped faces with smooth skin and those luxurious curls.

"Hi, Auntie Nicky!" they said in unison.

"Hi guys, how are you?"

"Good!" they chimed. Nicola smiled.

Despite their obvious differences—one being a boy and the other a girl—the two mostly spoke in unison when spoken to, or finished each other's sentences. She wondered how teachers would cope with these two once they were in school.

"Do you still play with the toys I got you guys for Christmas?" she asked, Christmas having been only a few months ago.

"I love my cars, they're my favourite!! I want more," he answered excitedly while his sister answered with "What did you get me?" They both looked at each other and he burst into giggles while she looked downward at her toes and bit her lower lip.

Nicola chuckled. "I got you the doll whose hair changes colour with water, sweetie."

Her niece's eyes lit up with recognition. "I love her! We play in the bathtub!"

"Are you guys ready for pre-school?" Nicola asked.

"Yes, Auntie Nicky," they said.

Just then her sister emerged from the kitchen, fresh faced and hands free of flour. She was pulling her apron off as she approached the kids. She leaned down to them, whispered in their ears and they tore off. They mostly took after their mother with their smooth pale skin and their long, curly, brown hair. Cassandra wore it down to her waist and most often, like today, in a loose braid. The three of them also had heart-shaped faces and thin lips.

Before Nicola could ask, Cassandra said, "I told them I put on Sesame Street in the living room and made Nutella sandwiches. I'm not sure what they love more, Nutella or Sesame Street," she said smiled fondly.

"It's a shame that soon they'll be exposed to the more horrendous kiddie television shows," said Nicola.

"I know, huh? Can't keep them inside forever. Well I could, but I'll be damned if I homeschool them. This fall is the beginning of my break."

"Do you have anything planned for yourself?" Nicola asked.

"I was thinking I'd spend the first couple of months relaxing and cleaning house. Then I'm planning on tackling some of the small home renovation projects we've put off since getting married. Next summer I go back to school to finish off the few courses I dropped out of last minute in university," she said.

"That sounds amazing Cassandra!" Nicola exclaimed.

"Pffft, it's less exciting than it sounds. Ask me again in a year when I can get a proper job," Cassandra said, chuckling. "But how about you? How's Karim? How's the business? Any luck with, you know…?" Cassandra asked as she rubbed her tummy.

"I'm good. The usual. Work is great. Patsy was the most amazing thing to happen to me. She's a great employee and an even better friend. I've no idea how I would have survived these first two years without her. I can't wait for you to meet her. I'm sure you'll like her as much as I do. Smart, witty, funny, and does her job amazingly well," Nicola gushed.

"That's good. I know father thought you were a bit nuts, hell, we all thought you were a bit nuts, but truthfully, you've always been good at finding things. I guess no one thought you could make a living out of it," Cassandra said.

"Oh geez, thank you ever so much for your never-ending support and confidence," Nicola said rolling her eyes mockingly.

"Awww come on sis, you know what I mean. I've always supported you. You know that. No matter how insane you ever sounded, I've always been there for you," Cassandra said.

"I know, I know. I was kidding." Nicola said.

"So? What else?" Cassandra asked.

"Hmmm, nothing really. Karim and I are working too much. We see less of each other since we moved in."

"Yeah, I know that feeling. It was the same with us. You start to take for granted that your significant other will just be there once you move in. You end up working less on your relationship. But don't let it continue like that, you'll end up growing apart without even realizing it. We have a date night each week, just a few hours set aside for the two of us. No kids, no work, just us," said Cassandra.

"That sounds great. What do you guys do on your dates?"

"Everything we used to do. Cuddle with a movie, go bowling, dinner, be lazy and lie in bed together. Anything and everything really," she said.

"I think we could definitely use that," said Nicola.

"Speaking of cuddling, how's it going? How many times are you going to make me ask you?" Cassandra asked, crossing her arms across her chest and sporting a comical frown.

"It's going. No news yet. Fingers still crossed."

"Go for twins. Get it done in one shot. Best thing to unintentionally happen," Cassandra laughed.

"I think I'm going to focus on getting pregnant first. One or two doesn't matter. Just want it to actually happen," Nicola said.

"Yeah, yeah, I get ya," Cassandra said as she looked back over her shoulder. "Sounds like the little terrors are done their sandwiches. Time to get back to them. Talk to you soon. Hugs," she said as she blew a kiss to the camera.

"Bye Cass, talk soon," she said and waved a hand as she ended the call. Nicola finished her wine and set the glass down on the table. She stretched and laid out on the couch with a yawn.

A mischievous grin grew across Nicola's lips as she picked up her cell and sent a naughty text to Karim, asking him if he wanted to have a 'play' date night. She then stripped off her pajamas, took a picture of herself lying semi-naked on the couch and sent it to him before he had a chance to read the first text. Giggling, she contemplated what other pictures she could take when he replied back quickly with a 'YES'.

She put her clothes back on and quickly sat up. Her head was woozy and the room spun a little as she realized she had gotten up too quickly. She set a hand on the coffee table to settle herself when her phone chirped indicating a new voicemail. She looked at it curiously. She didn't recall hearing it ring. She picked it up and touched the home button. One new voicemail but no missed calls. She picked up the landline from her desk and dialled her phone. After a moment it rang loud and clear. She hung the landline up and stared at her phone. Curious, she dialled her voicemail. The message started out blank, as if the person calling had not known when to speak. After almost a whole minute, she went to hang up the phone when the sound of heavy breathing could be heard. A low guttural panting followed by a low moan continued. She clutched her phone tightly and shivered, wishing she had the strength to just delete the call but frozen with disgust and fear. Finally the breathing stopped, just as abruptly as it had started. She heard the sound of a kiss being blown into the phone followed by a chilling, stark monotone voice calling out to her, "Love you sweetie, can't wait to see you." The sound of the automated voice asking her if she wanted to replay the call broke her from her terror and she quickly hit the button to delete the message.

CHAPTER SIX

The click of the front door shutting stirred her out of her slumber. Nicola lifted her head up from under the pillow and looked over at the blue glowing lights of the digital alarm clock. It read 04:00. She rolled over and saw that Karim's side of the bed was empty. She rolled back towards the door and saw the kitchen light turn on. She could hear Karim tip-toeing around. She put her head back under the pillow and curled the corner up just enough to be able to see. The kitchen light went out and she could hear the soft pat of socked feet making their way down the hallway.

He stopped outside their bedroom and slowly slid the door open, then he quietly closed it as he made his way towards the closet. He opened the closet door and started undressing. Silently, Nicola crawled out of bed and snuck up behind him. She wrapped her arms around him and he jumped.

"Christ, Nic, you scared the shit out of me!" Karim exclaimed.

She murmured softly and kissed his back. She reached around his waist, unbuttoned his pants and pushed them to to the ground. He turned around and kissed her. She reached a hand up, stroking his hair tenderly before abruptly pulling her hand out of his hair and stepping away from him.

"Why is your hair wet?" she asked.

"I had a shower at work," he said shrugging. "What's the big deal?"

"It's four in the morning. Why are you showering this late? Why not just come home and shower?" she asked.

"I showered hours ago babe," he said, pulling her closer towards him. She held herself away from him.

"My hair takes hours to dry, yours takes minutes," she said trying to push herself free. "Let me go."

He pushed his mouth onto hers and she tried to fight against him. But he wrapped one arm around her waist and pulled her in tightly. He finally broke off the kiss and she pressed her hands against his chest, gaining a few inches of space.

"What is wrong with you, Karim?"

"Me?" he said grabbing her arm and shaking her as he pulled her back against him. "What's wrong with you?" He kissed her again and pushed her onto the bed. She looked up at him defiantly.

"Why are you so late?" she asked.

He leaned over her menacingly before reaching a hand up her nightie. "I was busy with work," he said, attempting to pull her nightie over her head but she fought against him, pulling it down.

Finally he stopped trying. "Christ, Nic," he said, standing up and grabbing a pillow from their bed. "I thought you wanted me. Or was that just another ruse to try and get my attention," he said taking a blanket from the closet.

"Karim, what the hell is going on? Why won't you just answer me?" she pleaded as she moved to the edge of the bed.

He turned to glare at her. "Why can't you make up your mind about what you want. An interrogation or 'play' time? 'Cuz I'm not willing to do both simultaneously," he grumbled as he started to leave the room.

"He called me," she said suddenly.

Karim stopped and looked over his shoulder. "Who, your secret admirer?" he asked as he left the room.

Sitting defeatedly on the bed, Nicola stared after him for a moment before hanging her head down between her legs.

The waiting room was filled with women, mostly in their late thirties or older. Several of them looked cheerful while a few looked tired and frazzled. There were magazines strewn on the waiting room table that were mostly planned-parenting orientated and a few medical magazines about birthing, fertility and family health. The walls were painted an off-white cream colour, and with a cheerful banner of storks carrying babies trimming the upper edge of the wall where it met the ceiling.

Nicola walked into the room and quickly felt self-conscious. She was much younger than the majority of the women here, and she very much felt out of place. At least most of the women appeared to be here without their partners, she thought. She walked up the to receptionist, checked herself in and sat down with a clipboard full of several forms to fill out. The first few forms asked for personal information, medical history and other data-related forms. The last few were more detail-orientated regarding the specific wants, needs, desires and expectations of the patient. She was starting to feel a little overwhelmed by it all and wished that Karim had joined her for this visit, especially considering it was her—well, their—first attempt at seeking help outside of their own bedroom about getting pregnant. She had just finished the last form when the receptionist called her to an examining room.

She sat down in the chair and started tapping her fingers on her lap; a nervous tic of hers that seldom appeared unless she was under high stress, which she guessed she was. Her biggest anxiety was that the doctor would tell her that she couldn't be helped at all. She looked around the room and tried to calm herself. On one wall she saw the doctor's certificates of achievements and doctorate degrees. Another wall had various pictures of the womb and a variety of detailed descriptions of the various forms of conception. She started to stand up to examine the posters better when the door opened and the doctor walked in, holding Nicola's forms and chart. She closed the door behind her and took a seat across from Nicola behind her desk. She smiled as she set the folder down and looked cheerfully at Nicola.

"So, Miss VanBurgen, my name is Dr. Bluin. I'm one of the three fertility specialist here at this clinic. I see that you are looking to have a child, yes?" the doctor asked.

Nicola nodded eagerly.

"I also see that you're young, healthy, in great shape, eat well and generally don't participate in bad habits like smoking, excessive drinking or drugs," she continued.

Nicola nodded in agreement.

"I have to ask, since I see that you are alone. Are you in a committed relationship? Or is this a solo pursuit to parenthood?" the doctor asked.

"I have a boyfriend of five years. Unfortunately, he was busy with work and unable to make this consultation appointment. But he's eager to hear what information you have to give me and whatever opportunities we may have," Nicola said.

Dr. Bluin nodded. "Alright then. So let's go over the facts I've gathered from the paperwork and see if I'm missing anything before I give you your potential options," she said.

"Okay," Nicola said, suddenly finding herself perspiring.

"You've been having unprotected sex for the last two years. In the last year you've start taking vitamins aimed at helping promote your fertilization. You've changed your normal exercise routine to again help promote fertilization, and pretty much tried the majority of the old wives' tales from the internet?" she asked as Nicola nodded in agreement.

For the next hour the doctor proceeded to explain to Nicola how there were in fact hundreds of possibilities as to why she wasn't able to conceive. That some were easy to detect and solve, while others still remained mysteries to them all. That once they had ruled out the obvious they could work on determining what course of action they wanted to take. Even within that capacity there were several variations and options. Anything from the lab artificially inseminating her eggs to a surrogate mother to a simple drug therapy schedule.

The options were never-ending and the amount of information the doctor was producing was quite overwhelming at first, until the doctor realized that Nicola was attempting to write down everything she said. She chuckled and put a hand on top of Nicola's and reassured her that everything she was saying would be available both in hard copy and email, so that Nicola and her partner could go over all of the details at their leisure. But after ruling out any corrective therapy or surgery, the clinic usually encouraged the mothers-to-be to try their drug therapy regime for at least a year before jumping into in vitro fertilization, as it was not only more costly but more invasive. The doctor handed her a folder thick with information.

"Whoa," Nicola said softly as she took the folder from the Dr. Bluin.

"If you open it to the pink-coloured tab you will see pages about the fertility drugs. Now we can wait until the test results are done in a week, but I like to explain all the potential options even if the test results turn some of them down, simply because I feel it's better to give you the control," the doctor said smiling.

Nicola nodded eagerly and the doctor continued explaining the different types of drugs and how they affected her body and whether or not one could see positive changes right away or not. Dr. Bluin also explained that the main downside for most of the drugs was the inability to know if they were working unless she actually got pregnant. Nicola nodded, her excitement growing, knowing that there were several options she could try and that she wouldn't be getting the boot quite yet.

The doctor ended her spiel, explaining that despite all of these options and while they prefer to do in vitro fertilization as a final option, the clinic felt that it was a step in the right direction for the men to come in at some point and do a sperm donation, so that the clinic could do all the tests for all parties involved. The doctor also asked Nicola if she could ask Karim to get his doctor to send in his test results regarding his fertility as soon as possible, or if he could come down to the clinic himself for testing.

Nicola stood up, a big grin across her face as she shook the doctor's hand. She was much more encouraged now than she had been an hour ago. The doctor smiled back as Nicola left her office.

Tears poured down my eyes as I woke up remembering where we were. Why had they taken us away? Where were mother and father? Why wouldn't anyone tell us anything? I peered inside the crib next to my bed, expecting to see my baby sister, but instead there was a different baby in there. She was breathing softly but with a slow hissing. Like she wasn't able to get all of her breath inside her. Her skin was a frightening yellow colour, almost like someone had painted her as a joke. Her lips were quite pale and even though she was a baby, she appeared to be quite small and thin. Like she was missing all of her baby fat. I left her sleeping and made my way out to explore what I had hoped to be my Aunt Sally and Uncle Tom's house.

The remainder of the house was eerily quiet. Sunlight poured in everywhere, revealing a very clean, tidy and sterile house. No toys, no books, no mess to be seen anywhere. I knew my aunt and uncle had two children. Presumably the baby I saw was my cousin Tammy; they also had a boy who was my other sister's age, named Daniel. But no one was in sight. I guess living in the suburbs meant sleeping in, unlike the farm where each day started when the sun rose.

I found the living room, which was just like ours. There was a small bookshelf filled with children's books and adorned with pictures of Daniel, but none of Tammy. The kitchen was quite small, but also newer and shinier than ours. I was about to try and figure out how to get some water to drink when I heard my aunt's voice. She was baby-talking to someone, probably my baby sister.

I followed the sound of her voice until I found a door slightly ajar. I knocked lightly on it, but no one answered. I knocked on it again this time pushing it open and poked my head inside.

"Good morning, Aunt Sally," I said, and she looked up, finally hearing me. Uncle Tom was still asleep on his side of the bed, while Aunt Sally was playing with my baby sister. From the extra pillows and baby blankets in the bed it was obvious that she had slept with her in their bed. I thought it strange since their own baby slept in a crib and it was large enough to hold them both. I slid onto the bed beside her. She gave me a side hug and then resumed playing with the baby.

"Is anyone else awake?" she asked. I shook my head no. "Cereal is in the cupboard below the sink and to the left. Make sure you feed your little sister when she gets up," she said.

"Thank you, Aunt Sally." I slid off the bed and ran off to the kitchen.

After opening several cupboards, mostly just for fun, I found the cereal. Fruit Loops, Frosted Flakes, Cap'n Crunch. I was in cereal heaven! I pulled all of them out looking for the boring ones we usually ate at home but couldn't find anything else. So I poured myself a large bowl of Cap'n Crunch and dug in. I was on my second bowl of cereal when my sister wandered in, rubbing the sleep out of her eyes. I poured her a bowl of frosted flakes and the two of us ate in silence. The only noise was the crunch of cereal between our teeth and the slurping of milk. After we finished, I instructed her to find our toothbrushes and brush her teeth while I cleaned up. My aunt had a dishwasher, but as I wasn't used to such extravagances I washed and dried the dishes by hand. As I finished, my aunt came into the kitchen with my baby sister. She put her into the highchair and began to prepare breakfast.

Back in the bedroom my little sister had pulled apart our entire suitcase. Tammy was still asleep in her crib but my sister and the toothbrushes were nowhere to be found. I wandered until I found the bathroom and my sister in it. She was diligently brushing her teeth. She handed me my toothbrush and I joined her. We brushed in silence, an unspoken truce between us. If neither of us said anything, then no one would ask the questions that neither of us really wanted the answers to. We walked to the living room and I left her on the couch while I quickly went back to the bedroom to get her colouring book. I brought it to her and left her to play on her own.

Sounds of sizzling and crackling mixed with the smell of bacon and coffee wafted from the kitchen. I could hear the sound of the alarm ringing in my aunt and uncle's bedroom, followed by the smacking sound of my uncle's hand as he slammed the alarm off. He grumbled but got up and I heard the bathroom door shut moments later. I decided to explore the house a bit more. We hadn't been here since my aunt and uncle got married a couple of years ago, and I only remember the flower girl dress I wore. I couldn't remember much else. Down the hall and past our bedroom was both the bathroom and my aunt and uncle's room. Around the corner was another door, this one fully open. I poked my head inside the room and was surprised to see a huge mess. Toys and clothes were everywhere. Beside one wall was a toy box, opened and most likely empty. Next to the toy box was the closet, its doors open but hardly any clothes hanging up in it as they were mostly scattered on the floor. On another wall was a bookshelf filled with even more toys and books, and on the third wall a large spaceship bed. My cousin Daniel was obviously awake and elsewhere. I was surprised not only at the mess, but at the vast difference between Daniel's room—this toy-filled room—and Tammy's room, the latter of which I had awoken in that morning. Daniel's room was decorated with posters, had brightly coloured walls and race car curtains. Tammy's room was so very plain.

Something felt wrong, but I couldn't put my finger on it. I guess things were different in the city. I wandered back into the kitchen and saw that my aunt had prepared breakfast: sausage, eggs, bacon and pancakes for herself, my uncle and Daniel. I stood in the doorway staring, watching the three of them eat. Why hadn't she told me she would make breakfast? I was shocked and hurt. She was even feeding my baby sister. My baby! Where was Tammy? As if she heard my thoughts, Tammy started wailing. I was still staring at the scene in front of me when my aunt's shrill voice finally cut through.

"What are you waiting for? Go get her," she ordered.

In a muted daze I wandered off to the bedroom to find Tammy rolling around from side to side, wailing loudly, her face soaked with tears. I softened quickly and reached into the crib to get her. She was heavy with a wet, night-filled diaper. I tried to hold her away, not wanting to get myself wet, but she was surprisingly heavy. I looked around for diapers, a changing table, anything, but nothing was obvious as to where to change her. I put her back into the crib only to be rewarded with her bursting back into tears. My aunt shrieked at me to quiet her down so I rushed over to the dresser and tore through the drawers. I found disposable diapers and a fresh change of clothes. I ran back to the crib and pulled Tammy out. She instantly quieted down. I put her on the dresser and stripped her down to nothing. I saw no garbage can or laundry hamper, so I dropped the diaper and dirty clothes onto the floor for the moment. I found wipes in another drawer and cleaned her head-to-toe. I put the clean diaper on her and dressed her in pink and white striped leggings, a bright red skirt, and a white shirt with yellow daisies. I took her into my arms and she clung to me tightly. It almost felt like she was afraid I might put her down again. I kicked the dirty pajamas towards the closet and carefully bent down to pick up the diaper.

After dropping the diaper in the bathroom garbage I carried Tammy into the kitchen. My uncle was cleaning up the dishes, Daniel was playing with his food, and my aunt had just finished cleaning up the high chair. She noticed me as we walked in and smiled. She took my baby sister out of the high chair and wandered off to the living room. I looked from my uncle, to where my aunt was, to the now empty high chair, and then back to my uncle. It was apparent that I was being ignored by my uncle and that I was supposedly to look after Tammy. I put her into the highchair, found some pablum and heated it up. Tammy cooed and bounced in her highchair. She was such an easy baby. So happy when you gave her just a little attention. She ate her breakfast eagerly and relatively neatly for a baby. While I was feeding Tammy, my uncle cleared the table of Daniel's dishes and urged the boy out of the kitchen, and I felt remarkably alone.

After feeding Tammy, I brought her into the living room where everyone else had gathered. My uncle was sitting in his arm chair reading a newspaper; my little sister was still colouring; Daniel was playing with race cars on a mat that resembled streets and buildings; my baby sister was watching Daniel eagerly; and my aunt sat on the couch watching the children play. I set Tammy down next to my baby sister so she could watch. As soon as I set her down my aunt shrieked at me.

"Keep her away from him!" She jumped off the couch, picked Tammy up and rushed her off to the far corner of the room to a playpen that I hadn't noticed before. It was old, dingy and well-used, probably Daniel's from when he was a baby. After depositing Tammy into it she sat back down onto the couch and resumed watching her son. Again I looked from my aunt to Tammy and to my uncle, and again, it felt like I was being ignored. I looked over at my *sister who had abruptly stopped her colouring, her crayon in her hand poised mid-air, and a look of complete shock on her face. I put my finger under her chin and pushed her mouth closed. I moved myself closer to her and away from my aunt and feigned interest in her colouring.*

The atmosphere in the room was bizarre. Everyone was ignoring me, unless I was doing something wrong and they were mad at me. Tammy was being treated like she was overly contagious and Daniel was oblivious to it all.

"Where's mommy and daddy?" my sister asked suddenly. I felt my heart quicken and my chest tighten. I wanted to know too, but I was afraid to ask.

Without missing a beat my aunt answered quickly, "Your father is dead."

Nicola stepped out of the doctor's office feeling better and much more confident than she had when she had first walked in. Her eyes sparkled and she had a little skip in her step. She walked over to the receptionist with large, strong strides and a big smile on her face. She set her purse down on the counter in front of her and the folder of paperwork from the doctor to the side.

The receptionist looked up at her and smiled warmly.

"Do you need to schedule your next appointment?" she asked.

Nicola shook her head no as she unzipped her purse and pulled out her wallet.

"I will be back, but I need to discuss my options with my man first," she replied as she set her wallet aside so she could dig through the giant mess inside her purse.

Finally she produced her insurance card with an 'aha!' and handed it to the receptionist. The receptionist took it in hand, flipped it over and dialled the number on the back. She held a single finger up to her, indicating for her to wait a moment while she processed the card.

Nicola took this opportunity to re-arrange the contents of her oversized purse so she could put the folder inside. She moved everything to one side and tried sliding the folder in, but to no avail. She removed half of the larger items and tried again, but still no luck. The receptionist stifled a small giggle that Nicola didn't notice. Finally she just grabbed the outside of her purse and shook it to lay flat on its side and forced the folder in. Then she squished the remainder of her items back inside. She had just zipped it up when the receptionist handed her her card back. Nicola smiled and thanked her before realizing she had put her wallet back inside the purse. She bit her lower lip and giggled. The receptionist did her best to keep a serious face as she handed Nicola paperwork to sign. Thankfully she had put the wallet in relatively last so she was easily able to put the card away. She signed her papers, smiled again and went to leave.

She had just reached the door to leave the waiting room when she realized that she had forgotten her jacket. She looked around the waiting room and saw it draped over a chair. She let go a sigh of relief as she went to retrieve it. As she picked it up off of the chair she discovered a small basket underneath it. It was wrapped in cellophane and tied off with a large yellow bow. Peering inside she could see it contained a variety of baby items such as bottles, diapers, wipes, creams, et cetera. Attached to it on the front, below the bow, was a large white envelope with her name written on it. Slowly she looked around the waiting room, looking for someone she knew but saw only a few older women reading their magazines, awaiting their turn to see the specialist.

Cautiously, she plucked the envelope from the basket and opened it. Inside was a card with a large stork carrying a baby in a makeshift hammock and the word 'congratulations' written across it. Opening the card she found a handwritten note that read: 'Congratulations on your upcoming bundle of joy. I hope it can bring you as much happiness as I want to bring you myself. Sincerely, your secret admirer.' The card slipped from her hands and fell to the ground as she gasped. She wrapped her arms around her chest and scanned the room again. Tears sprung into her eyes and she felt a chill rush through her body.

Nicola walked back to the receptionist, stumbling slightly, and interrupted the conversation she was now having with a nurse. The receptionist looked up at her as Nicola pointed to the gift basket still sitting under the chair that her jacket was on. She asked the receptionist if she knew where the basket had come from. The receptionist cheerfully told her that it had been delivered while she was inside having her appointment with the doctor, and that she had signed for it herself—although she did admit that it seemed a bit strange as it was the first time that they had ever had anything delivered for a patient here. Nicola nodded numbly and asked her if she knew who had delivered it. The receptionist again nodded eagerly and looked through her things on the desk in front of her before producing a business card which she handed over to Nicola. She explained that she had made the delivery man wait while she Googled the business to confirm that it was legitimate company, and even called them before accepting the delivery. Nicola took the card gingerly with trembling hands. The receptionist asked if she was okay and Nicola quickly nodded and ran off before her tears could spill over.

CHAPTER SEVEN

The café, as always, was filled to the brim with people. The old brick walls were adorned with pictures of celebrities posing with the owners, and aside from that, they remained bare, the old school-brick layout a wonderful compliment to the exposed wood beams in the ceiling. Multi-coloured LED Christmas lights were wrapped around the beams, and low-level mini pars added the appropriate ambience to the room. The tables and chairs, although mis-matched, had a flowing symmetry to them as they all resembled old saloon bar furniture from the days of the wild west. They were in fact a collection of old set pieces from the local film studio. The café was actually co-owned by two local production companies and not only used for filming, but was a common place to hold interviews.

Karim made his way through the crowd, waving a hand to the barista as he navigated his way to the back of the café to his private table. Karim, like many other casting directors, not only owned a share of the café, but also had a regular time slot that he came to the café daily, thus enabling him a guaranteed spot at the casting directors' table. As he cleared the crowd he saw Patsy already sitting at the table, drinking a frozen coffee drink and polishing off one of the café's famous croissants. She stood up and they kissed each other's cheeks lightly before he sat down to join her.

Karim sat across from her awkwardly, his fingers tapping his knees absently. He opened his mouth to speak, then stopped. He took a deep breath and went to speak again when the barista suddenly appeared with his coffee. He clamped his mouth shut abruptly as she set his coffee down in front of him. She set a tub of sugar cubes next to Karim's coffee and disappeared into the crowd.

Patsy smirked slyly as he slowly put the sugar cubes into his coffee and stirred the spoon inside the mug with great determination. She couldn't help herself and chuckled at his awkwardness. He looked up at her with surprise and she bit her lip, stifling out a meagre apology. He let out a long sigh.

"Whatever it is you need to talk about, just spit it out, Karim."

He looked into her eyes, afraid of what he had to say. Worried that he would appear to be either ungrateful or just a jerk. He started cracking his knuckles, one by one.

"Jesus Christ, Karim! Just spit it out!" Patsy blurted as she slapped his hands apart. He jumped slightly but settled back into his chair.

"I think there's something wrong with Nicola," he finally blurted out.

Patsy stared at him with utter disbelief. "What on earth are you talking about, Karim?"

He took a deep breath and looked directly into her eyes.

"I think she's imagining this stalker," he finally said.

Patsy gasped. "How can you even think that? We have proof!"

"You have a card that was mailed to her, that's it. It could have come from anyone and it could have been with good intent. Doesn't mean it's from a stalker."

"What about the incident at the bar? The times she's seen him when running? The note in her pocket?" Patsy asked incredulously, appalled at the horse blinders on Karim's eyes.

"She thinks she's seen someone, but she hasn't actually seen anyone, nor have I. There was no one on the trails with us that day, and even the bouncer couldn't describe who he thought he saw touch her, and he admitted he could have just seen someone dancing close to her. None of the video footage actually shows anyone pushing her," he said.

Patsy sighed. There was some merit to his statement, but she also knew that Nicola wasn't the type to make things up. She processed everything with a logical, albeit sometimes odd mind, preferring sound facts to back her up.

"I'm sorry but that's not possible. There's no way Nicola would be imagining this."

"A few months ago I would have easily agreed with you. But recently, things have been rough between the two of us. I think the stress is just getting to her..." he said, letting his sentence trail off.

Patsy's eyebrows furrowed together and her lower lip curled as she tried to look concerned, but inside she really was thinking, debating whether or not Karim was being one hundred percent truthful. She knew the dynamic between those two had changed in the past couple of years, ever since Nicola had decided that she wanted a child. But he had never refused her desire to have a child, never once suggested he was against it, and even though he originally—like Nicola—hadn't wanted children, he seemed more on board with the idea than she had. Nicola had not once brought up anything of any concern regarding the two of them other than the inability to conceive. In fact, Nicola couldn't stop talking about how wonderfully supportive he was through the whole ordeal. It suddenly made Patsy wonder how supportive he really was. Of course Patsy was mistrustful of most men, even Karim, despite all that Nicola had told her about him. However, in the couple of years that Patsy had known Karim, he never once came to her about anything. So, why now?

"It must be difficult focusing all of your energies on trying to have a child," she said carefully.

"Yes. Of course. That takes up most of my thoughts," he agreed.

"So, what part of it has been rough? I can't imagine wanting to have even more sex really being a problem." Patsy winked as she smiled at him coyly.

"Uhhh, no, that's not the problem. It's more of... there's a growing distance between us recently. She's become obsessed with the idea of a baby and it's all she ever talks about."

Patsy studied him carefully. His head was in his hands and he rubbed his face roughly with them. As he took a deep breath, his eyes flickered ever so slightly from side to side. It was true, Nicola had baby fever and it had grown greatly over the last year. But, in Nicola's defence, they had been trying for two years now with no success. They were both young and healthy, which meant most likely one of the two of them had something physically wrong, and the potential of not being able to have a baby was a possibility that loomed heavily in Nicola's mind. Patsy knew as much as Nicola had confided in her many times, and the two of them had endlessly researched the countless reasons and possible diagnoses either Nicola or Karim could have to prevent conception. But Patsy was unsure how baby obsession could lead to fake stalker.

"I suppose that's true. But having a baby is now top priority on her list. You know how she is. She likes to get things done in a timely manner."

"It's just… I don't know anymore," he muttered.

"Do you not want to have a baby?" Patsy quietly asked.

"Of course I do!" he answered defensively and almost a little too quickly.

"Then why the issue about baby talk?" she asked, trying to figure out how to probe the conversation into his theories on Nicola's fake stalker. Patsy wasn't quite sure how they went from Nicola faking her stalker for attention to the real issue—Karim and the baby—but she was happy that he was finally opening up to her.

"I just want to have a conversation about something else other than what colour to paint the room or what toys we should get. She's not even pregnant yet. Can't we enjoy our adult lives right now? While we still can?" he said, frustrated, and Patsy's heart broke. The poor man just wanted more TLC. She pulled him into an awkward chair hug. He let his chair slide closer to hers and embraced her tighter. She patted him lightly on the head.

"It'll be okay. Just talk to her about it. She probably doesn't realize it's bothering you. Ask her to have a date night, no baby talk. Just you and her. I'm sure she'll understand," said Patsy, rubbing his arm.

"What if she doesn't?" he said, sniffling.

"Then you tell me and I'll talk to her."

Patsy gave him a big hug and quickly broke off the embrace. As he broke apart from her, his face glided close to hers, so close that she could feel his breath on her skin and the graze of his lips along her cheek, and then as he touched her lips ever so slightly with his. He paused at her lips briefly, and for a moment she thought he was actually going to kiss her. But then the moment passed and he was sitting upright in his chair. Patsy smiled brightly at him but hid her bewilderment at his erratic behaviour.

"Thank you, Patsy. You have no idea how helpful you've been," he said as he squeezed her leg, and only then did she realize how high up her thigh his hand suddenly was.

Standing at the cashier, Nicola stood frozen, staring at the two of them. Had he just kissed her? In this café, in front of everyone? She watched Karim glide his hand up Patsy's thigh and the giant smile on her face. Nicola could feel her face growing red with anger and tears starting spilling out of her eyes.

"Your change?" the barista's voice chirped, breaking Nicola out of her trance. Nicola rubbed the tears from her eyes with one hand and took her change with the other. She pushed her hand into her pocket and thrusted herself into the crowd and made her way to the door, forgetting about her chai tea and trying to forget about what she had just seen.

I closed the door quickly, eager to resume my earlier activities. Scanning the room, I noted that it looked much cleaner and functional than when I had first signed the papers. The only additions I had made aside from food, was a bevy of electronic equipment. Smiling smugly, I recalled putting 'electronics geek services' under my business description for the lease. I was definitely getting my geek on, but only for myself.

Thanks to modern technology what I needed to do was much more easily done than it would have been only a few years earlier. I had searched online until I found a messaging site that allowed you to send text messages at scheduled times. It was a site professing love and marriage and other 'timely' events, with a premise that it offered the ability to send a loved one a text message while sitting there with them just before you proposed or gave other news to help set the mood. Minus the proposal, for now, it was exactly what I wanted to do.

I had spent the last hour setting up messages to send her to profess my undying love for her. It even gave the option to send voicemails. Altered, of course; you typed in text and their computer slapped together a voice recording from their bank of actors' voices. Sounded almost real. You could even send voice messages, at an additional cost of course, to sound like some of your favourite celebrities. The only problem was trying to find a way to receive messages back from her. Right now I didn't want that, although I knew eventually, when she was ready, she would want to contact me too.

I was in the process of literally copying the messaging site's entire programming code and seeing if I could reprogram bits of it to allow me to receive messages. I sent a text to one of my two phones, received it, and then replied back. Nothing. I tweaked the program a bit more and tried again but got the same results. I tweaked more, then resent the same message. I got it and replied. *Eureka!* I thought and I jumped up, fist pumping the air. Quickly I typed in a message to her and was about to hit send when I realized that I could see the number I had sent the original text from on the second phone. Frustrated, I slammed my fists into the table. That wouldn't do. She needed to be able to contact me but I had to be untraceable. An alarm went off on my phone. I looked at it quickly and with a grimace on my face closed my laptop. I got up, unbuttoning my shirt as I went to my closet.

Suddenly I reached my hands out to the ceiling and breathed in deeply. I could feel her all around me. In the linoleum beneath my feet, in the small breeze that flowed through the warehouse, and in the very walls behind me. From the moment I had touched her shoulder I had wanted more. Needed more. Her smiled touched my soul, reached down and clutched my heart so tightly it hurt as much to think about as it did to not. I was a willing victim to her innocence and charm. She brought out parts of me I had never felt before and wanted to feel even more. But her rejection was crumbling the dream I was so desperately trying to lay out for us... for us! I felt that our meeting was so fleeting, and I yearned to recapture the essence I had felt then.

Tears started rolling down my cheeks. It couldn't be over already, I didn't want to lose this feeling, this raw strength of energy she had brought to me. I opened my eyes and a new determination came over me. There was a bleakness that threatened to overrun me and tear away what little joy I had in my heart. It had to be destroyed. I couldn't fall prey to it again. I ripped open the closet door and began to tear out what little contents were inside. Underwear, socks, shirts, pants. A shoebox of sex toys and condoms. Nothing was what I wanted or needed.

Then I spotted a box of crayons and a notepad. Feverishly I penned out a love note to her, not entirely sure if I would give it to her or not, but merely satisfied to express what was burning inside my heart. When I finished, I was sitting on the ground, covered in sweat and dirt but my racing heart was finally calm. I stood up, leaving the note on the floor, stripped naked and stepped into the shower.

CHAPTER EIGHT

Nicola slammed the door to her office so hard that the flower vases lining the entrance hallway trembled and shook, threatening to tip over. She flung her heels, already in her hands, across the hall. One bounced harmlessly off the wall while the other one hit it square-on with the stiletto and left a neat and tidy dent in the wall. Slowly she fell back against the door, her chest heaving. She had run aimlessly about after she had seen Karim with Patsy and had lost track of time. Her legs ached and her heart was heavy with pain as she could finally no longer hold it inside. She slid down the wall to her knees and burst into tears as she started screaming.

She cried and cried, pounding her fists into the floor and moaning with frustration. Slowly the sobs subsided and her eyes finally shed the last of her tears. She lay on the floor, her hair pulled sporadically out of her braid, looking like a prom date night gone wrong. Her face was soaked and what little makeup she wore probably resembled that of a clown. Her clothes were covered in dirt and dust from lying on the floor. The sound of the elevator moving forced her to slowly get up onto her feet and look towards the office door. Patsy was returning from errands.

How could Patsy do this to her, she thought, her chin trembling and tears threatening to erupt again. She shook her head firmly, no time to dwell on it she told herself, she had to get to the bathroom and clean herself up. She couldn't let Patsy know she knew. She had to confront the source first. She had to confront Karim. She pulled herself to her feet and made a mad dash for the bathroom as she heard the elevator doors slide open. She was just locking the bathroom door when she heard the office door open.

"Hello, I'm back!" Patsy's cheerful voice rang out, and Nicola flushed the toilet and turned on the water at the sink. Hopefully Patsy would hear this and not continue the conversation long enough for her to clean herself up.

A quick look in the mirror revealed that her makeup was thankfully relatively waterproof. She took a baby wipe from the cabinet beside the toilet and wiped her face clean. Aside from redness she looked okay. She ran cold water over the baby wipe and gently dabbed it over her face, trying to get rid of the puffiness from crying. She undid her braid and tousled her hair a bit and then tied it up into a ponytail. Taking a deep breath, she stepped out of the washroom.

Patsy was sitting at the front desk sorting through the mail. She looked up at Nicola and smiled.

"Went for a midday run?" she asked.

Nicola paused looking up at the clock and realized that several hours had passed since she had seen Karim and Patsy together that morning. She nodded, happy that Patsy completely misinterpreted the redness of her face.

"Yeah. Needed to let off some steam," she replied. "I'll be in my office if you need me."

She quickly walked past Patsy and into her office, closing the door behind her.

Sitting down at her desk she let a big breath of air out, surprised to realize that she had been holding her breath. She dug her cellphone out of her pocket and opened it to iMessages. Without thinking, she typed out 'Need to talk ASAP. When are you free?' to Karim and hit send.

She stared at the delivered message, willing him to read it now. Then realizing the silliness of this, she shut off her phone and placed it face down on the top of her desk. She shook her head, as if trying to clear it of the impending doom that ran in circles inside it. Her phone chirped, followed by her iPad. It was Karim. His response: 'I know. Me too. After work? The café?'

Her heart sank. Were he and Patsy that serious? Was he going to break up with her? Her hands trembled as she slowly typed a reply 'Want more privacy. Home?' and hit send. She swallowed deeply and stared at the delivered message, watching as her phone indicated he was typing back a reply. A simple 'Sure' was all he said. She put her phone down, her eyes threatening to spill over with tears again. She quickly wiped them away as Patsy knocked on her door.

She called out for Patsy to enter as the door opened a small crack. Nicola's high heels popped inside and began dancing.

"Forgot to put these on after your run?" Patsy said with laughter in her voice, and Nicola smiled.

"You know me and heels. Figure I'd try leaving them behind… maybe sneakers will work with this dress, no?" she said halfheartedly.

Patsy set the heels down next to the door. "Sneakers no, but nice sandals would," Patsy replied and closed the door behind her.

Even knowing that Patsy would have to be a willing participant, Nicola couldn't find herself being upset with her. All of her anger and frustration was aimed at Karim. She put her phone in her pocket, slid her sandals that were sitting under her desk onto her feet and wiped the tears from her eyes. She wanted to be home before Karim got there, otherwise she'd lose her nerve.

Patsy watched as Nicola dashed out of the office. Nicola had mumbled something about running out to the store briefly and being back in a couple of hours. Patsy started filing the paperwork into the computer since Nicola hated data entry. Actually Nicola hated anything to do with computers. It was Patsy's ongoing battle to slowly win Nicola over to the 'dark side' of technology. A battle she was slowly but surely winning.

She told herself that if she finished the data entry by three o'clock, she would reward herself by going to the pita place that she loved, even though it was farther away than her usual dinner trek and she would have to borrow Nicola's delivery bicycle to do so. She had skipped lunch; her conversation with Karim had left her stomach on edge. It was also a good half-hour ride away and she would have to run the rest of her errands on the bike if she did that. But those amazing pita wraps were worth the effort.

She heard the groan of the elevator and looked up from the computer with surprise. Clients never came to the office, so Nicola must have left something behind. Nicola didn't think that their office had the right look for their business since it was almost always either full of junk or completely spotless. They kept minimal stock on site and tried to make the majority of their regular clients' supplies come directly from the supplier. Saved money on both ends.

She had just resumed her work when someone knocked on the door. She slowly got up from her desk and walked over to the door. Carefully and quietly, she put the chain lock on the door. The warehouses were mostly abandoned but she didn't want to take any chances. She also dialled 9-1-1 on her phone and hovered her finger over the send button. Slowly she turned the door knob and slid the door open a couple of inches.

She was standing behind the door so wasn't able to see who was on the other side. She asked who was there and a medium-high gruff voice answered her saying he was Gregory Sanchez. She sighed with relief, turned her phone off and closed the door. She undid the chain, opened the door and started to welcome him, but stopped abruptly as he took a step inside the door.

"Have we met before?" she asked, positive that she recognized him from the cafe earlier that week.

He chuckled. "Patsy, right?" he asked as he reached his hand out to shake hers.

Reluctantly she took his hand and shook it firmly. She started to reach up to touch his wig, asking if it was one of the wigs she had found for him, when he quickly extended his hand up to catch hers before she could touch his wig. He lowered her hand and released it gently.

"Sorry, I'm still a little sensitive," he said and she blushed furiously, appalled at the line she had almost crossed, and muttered an apology.

Patsy ushered him inside and rolled her chair out for him to sit in. He sat down as she briefly disappeared into Nicola's office, returning with her office chair. She rolled it behind her desk and sat down.

"What brings you here today, Mr. Sanchez?"

"Call me Gregory," he said with a smile. "I came to see Nicola. We had coffee the other day and she gave me her number but I've yet to get a cellphone. So I thought I'd drop by and thank her again for finding me the wigs so quickly."

"It was our pleasure. We aim to please," she said smiling back. She found herself leaning towards him and blushed, straightening herself up, hoping he hadn't noticed.

He ran his hand lightly through his hair. "You did a great job. I can hardly tell it's not my own hair."

"Thank you. It was just luck that some friends of mine knew the right place to go to. Unfortunately, Nicola isn't here right now. I'm not expecting her back until the late afternoon. Can I just tell her that you stopped by?" she asked.

He nodded then leaned forward onto her desk. "I can always see her another time, I think I'm going to stay in this city for a little while. I like what I see," he said grinning.

Patsy cocked her head slightly, a puzzled look appearing on her face briefly before she realized what he was indicating. A wave of red washed over her face and he laughed lightly.

"If I may be so bold," he started, "Would you be interested in dinner tonight, with me?"

Patsy's jaw dropped slightly. She was pleasantly surprised. He was good looking, even with his feminine features. His voice was soft spoken but filled with authority. She found herself unable to resist him for reasons she couldn't fathom. Probably because she was used to having to do all of the chasing and most of the work. She managed to nod her head up and down slightly but couldn't find the words to answer. He took her hand and kissed it, causing her to blush even more and stared deeply into her eyes. After what seemed like hours but was probably only seconds, he let her hand go, and grabbed a pen and a notepad off of her desk. He scribbled down a few words then turned the notepad to face her.

"Meet me here tonight at eight. Tell Nicola I said hello and that I look forward to our next coffee outing," Gregory said as he stood up from the chair. He gestured a small wave as he left the office.

She smiled fondly as he left and put her chin in her hands and sighed. There was something a little off about him but she couldn't place it, and chalked it up to the fact that he was simply shorter and leaner than most men she had dated. Regardless, she had a date with a hottie and that's all that really mattered right now.

Already deep into her second glass of wine, Nicola sat tensely on the couch staring down the clock. The second hand seemed to slow down, and every time it ticked, it was so loud it echoed throughout the whole room. She shook her head, trying to clear the nonsense out of it. The trip home hadn't take that much time as she made each connection quickly, like fate was either mocking her or urging her in what it was proclaiming was the right direction. However, once home she kept finding excuses to have to leave. She set each one aside and finally cracked a bottle of wine. Wine made her lazy enough to lounge on the couch and hopefully give her the excuse not to leave, but a bit more strength and courage to confront Karim.

Nicola heard the jingle of keys and the soft whoosh of the door gliding open. She reached over to the table and poured a new glass of wine. As she set down the bottle, a bouquet of flowers popped into her face. She set her wine glass down and took the flowers eagerly. She breathed their soft fragrance in deeply, closing her eyes as she inhaled. Karim kissed the top of her head and she sighed softly. Nicola fought the urge to shake her head but mentally steeled herself. She was worried that he was lulling her into a false sense of security before dropping the bomb. She opened her eyes and set the flowers on the table. She offered him a glass of wine which he eagerly took. She took a small sip of her wine as Karim sat down on the couch beside her.

He played with the glass in his hands for a few minutes before taking a sip himself. She resisted putting a hand on his thigh; instead she just visually took him in. She loved him so much. More than anything in the world. But that couldn't stop her. She had to know the truth. She had to confront him regardless of the consequences. He took her hand in his and gently squeezed it.

"How are you baby?" he asked softly.

Nicola gave a half-assed smile. "I've been better. You?"—sarcasm already starting to seep into her voice.

He didn't seem to notice. "I'm alright. The usual I guess," he answered. He tapped his fingers nervously on his knee.

They both looked at each other, half staring the other down, half avoiding. The silence started to grow awkward but neither of them appeared to have any idea where or how to start.

Nicola finally broke the silence and simply blurted out, "I know." Karim looked at her with a questioning look on his face. "I know about Patsy," she said quickly.

"You know what about Patsy?" he asked, appearing to be genuinely confused.

"I know about you two," she said accusingly, her voice warbling slightly.

"Us two what?" he asked.

"Don't play stupid Karim, I saw you two together," she said, her voice starting to raise slightly and a shrill tone growing in it.

"Together? What are you talking about honey?" he asked as he moved closer to her on the couch, close enough that his leg leaned up against hers.

She slammed her glass down on the table with such force that the wine sloshed, threatening to spill over. "I saw you with her today at the café. How long have you two been sneaking behind my back?" she asked.

His confused expression faltered slightly before a slight tremble grew in his eyes. Nicola was suddenly seething. His expression gave it away so easily. Despite begin a smooth talker at work, he had never been a very good liar.

"Well?" she asked

"Today was the first time—" he started but she quickly cut him off.

"Oh, that makes it all better doesn't it? You've just started. Thank god I caught it right away," she said her voice dripping with sarcasm.

Karim set his wine glass down on the table and put a hand on hers. "Started what? I don't understand what you're talking about."

She slapped his hand off of hers and pushed herself off of the couch and to her feet. She threw her hands up in the air, exasperated, and shook her head.

"Nicola?" he asked softly, reaching out for her arm. "We just had coffee and talked," he said as he tried to pull her back down to the couch. She yanked her arm away from him and took another step backwards.

"Suuuure," she said. "Just how stupid do I look?"

"I don't know what you think is going on between us, but I can assure you that it was the first time I've been alone with Patsy. I swear there's—"

"So you admit that you and Patsy are getting together?" she said, cutting him off. "That you're fucking my assistant!" she cried out as tears started spilling out of her eyes.

She ran out of the living room and down the hall. Karim quickly jumped up from the couch and chased after her. He caught her by the arm in the hallway and turned her to face him. Nicola tried to pull herself free but he held her tight.

"How could you do this to me?" she wept.

"You actually think I'm sleeping with Patsy?" he asked her incredulously.

"I saw you kiss her. In the cafe," she cried, still struggling to pull herself free from his grip, but he held her firmly against the wall.

"I never kissed her," he declared, hurt written all over his face. She hesitated and stopped struggling.

"Sure looked like you did from where I was standing," she said softly. He loosened his grip on her and sighed.

Nicola pulled herself out of his grasp, violently yanking her arms free. She stepped away from him and held her other arm out, trying to hold him back. "Stay away from me," she said.

He looked at her, heartbroken, and took a step towards her. She stepped back and found herself up against the wall again. She slid to her right and he put a hand on the wall, stopping her. She slid to the left and again he stopped her.

"I'm not sleeping with Patsy. I needed advice from her. That is all," he said, holding his voice stern yet wavering. She could see a mixture of hurt and anger on his face as he breathed heavily, his body leaning in against hers.

"I don't believe you," she said defiantly.

He took her chin in his hand and held her face up to look directly into his eyes. "Look into my eyes and listen: I. Am. Not. Sleeping. With. Her. Not now, not ever," he pushed his mouth onto hers and, at first she resisted, then finally gave in to his kiss. Tears spilled down her cheeks as she abruptly broke the kiss off and began to pound him on the chest.

"Don't do this. This isn't fair," she whimpered as he forced her to kiss him again. She pounded on his chest again but he wrapped his arms around her and pulled her in close. She caved in and returned his kiss. He unbuttoned her shirt and slid it off her shoulders.

"I hate you Karim," she whispered as she pulled his shirt over his head and tossed it onto the floor behind them. He yanked her skirt down to her ankles and then hoisted her up off the ground and she wrapped her legs around his waist as he pushed her roughly into the wall. "You love me and you know it," he growled.

The room was dark, warm and cozy. The double layer blackout curtains she had invested in were a great asset on these bright summer mornings. Karim had already left for an early breakfast meeting, his usual Saturday morning gossip catch-up with his fellow industry friends. Nicola like to refer to it as the I-fucked-this-girl-how-about-you breakfast group. Karim laughed the first few times she called it that, but later asked her to stop referring to it as that since it appeared to actually be mostly just that.

However, it did mean that Nicola had at least two more hours until he would return and hopefully crawl back into bed with her. So she had at least a couple more hours to do whatever she wanted, although she would probably get out of bed now, eat some breakfast, have her chai and then crawl back into bed with enough time to warm it back up for the two of them. Karim had mentioned something to her when he left, but she was too groggy from sleep to remember. Thankfully he left a note behind that read: 'let's have a lazy day and not leave bed. I'll bring doughnuts.'

The prospect of cuddling all day brought her great joy. It had been ages since they had been this close. The strain of having a baby seemed to be pushing them apart, and

Nicola was embarrassed at the fact that she had actually thought that Karim was having an affair with Patsy. They were both under a lot of stress from their jobs, and like most couples their age, they had just started to drift apart. Relationships needed to be worked on twenty-four hours a day and couldn't be taken for granted. She had no one to blame but herself for her irrational behaviour, and she promised herself that she wouldn't let herself jump to conclusions like that again.

She pushed the covers aside and tossed her feet onto the cold hardwood floor, shivering as she reached down under the bed for her slippers and slid them on. Naked, she wandered towards the bathroom, thinking she might take a shower. But at the door she changed her mind and decided to put on the kettle and have a cup of tea before her shower. She went to the kitchen, turned the kettle on and prepped her cup of tea before she realized she was still naked. Laughing, she decided she would drink her tea en route to the shower.

As the kettle was boiling, she pulled out her cellphone and saw that she had three missed calls—all from a blocked number—and also had three new voice mails. Turning on her phone, she dialled her voicemail and set it to speaker so she could prepare her tea. The first voicemail was only ten seconds long and was blank. She erased this message. The second message was only a few seconds longer but she could hear heavy breathing in the background the entire time. Like someone was almost panting. Picking up the phone she quickly deleted the message, shivering as her skin was suddenly covered with goosebumps. Hesitantly, she hit play for the third voicemail and a low, grumbly voice was heard, almost rasping.

"Do you remember me, Nicola? It's George. I've missed you. I've been watching you."

The phone slid from her hand and landed on the countertop with a thud, the kettle now shrilling behind her. Her heart was pounding as she stared absently at the wall across from her. She knew it! Someone had been watching her and now she had proof!

Her whole body started shaking and trembling. She hugged herself tightly as her legs suddenly felt like they were full of jello and she had to grab the countertop to keep herself from falling over. She shook her head and her body, trying to regain control. Almost as quickly as it had started, the trembling passed and she pushed herself upright, finally noticing the shrieking kettle. She turned the stove off and took the kettle off the burner, her hands still shaking badly enough that she didn't risk pouring the kettle, especially since she was still naked.

She knew she had to tell Karim. She had to tell him now. She couldn't wait for him to return from his breakfast. Nicola knew where they met each week. She ran to her room and threw on the first outfit she touched, grabbed her keys and her phone, and dashed out the door.

CHAPTER NINE

Nicola sat in the taxi, wrenching her hands together, biting her lower lip and fidgeting about in her seat. She knew she should've just run to help release her growing pent up tension, but the restaurant was on the other side of town. She looked back down at her phone, wondering if she should call Karim first. But he'd probably think she was just being paranoid. If she made him listen the to message first, he'd understand. Finally the taxi pulled up outside the diner. She quickly paid the driver and dashed out of the car.

What had started out as light rain when she left was now a torrential downpour. In the ten-foot run from the cab to the door, she managed to get completely soaked.

She wrenched open the door, fighting against the gust of wind that threatened to slam the door shut into her face, and pulled herself inside. The diner, as it usually was during the lunch hour, was quite full. Nicola scanned the room, looking for Karim and the other guys from his agency, but didn't see anyone. She took another step in, still looking around, when she bumped into Herb, the diner's owner. He put his hands onto her shoulders as he took a step back, his face breaking out into a huge grin. Pulling her back in, he hugged her tightly.

"Nicola!" he gushed, "How are you? Long time no see."

She smiled back fondly. "Hello, Herb, how are you? You look well."

He chuckled, his laugh like a bear's growl of excitement, and slapped his well-endowed stomach. "If you mean I still look like a happy fat man, then I suppose I do look well," he said, laughing even harder.

He started to usher her to a booth but she shook her head and apologized. Nicola explained she was looking for Karim and the boys.

Herb looked at her with confusion and scratched his head. "You're a day early, love," he said, and she looked at him, perplexed.

"It is Saturday, isn't it?" she asked, and he nodded in agreement.

"They changed their brunch day to Sunday. I'm less busy then and the others have family errands to tend to on Saturdays," he said.

She slowly looked over the whole diner before returning her gaze to Herb. "When did they change the day?" she asked slowly.

Herb scratched his chin as he thought. "Hmm, hard to say. I think maybe four or five months ago?"

She kissed him on the cheek, gave him another hug and ran out of the diner, shouting over her shoulder, "Thanks Herb, I'll be back again soon."

More than two months had passed since we first got to our aunt and uncle's house. Three weeks since the crazy man almost abducted us.

One week since my sister and I had spent the weekend with our aunt's parents; a wicked, evil couple that thrived on scaring us by recanting how the father had died more than once by accidental electrocution, and punishing us by forcing us to kneel on a bed of sharpened pencils for fifteen minutes at a time. They even shaved my sister's head where gum had settled when she fell asleep chewing it. The cruel ignorance of being ignored daily by my aunt and uncle was welcome over her parents' wickedness.

We still went to the pool daily, and usually for the whole day, but Daniel was banned from ever asking us if he could join us. The lifeguard was happy to see us, and started taking her break just before we left to go home for dinner, to walk us home. It felt weird that she was so kind to us and didn't even really know who we were, and that our own aunt didn't even care about us. We barely saw our baby sister. Our aunt had fallen head over heels in love with her and doted on her day in and day out. Even bought her all sorts of new things. I had once made the mistake of putting Tammy in one of the new outfits my aunt had bought for my baby sister, and my aunt had screamed and hollered at me until I tore it off of poor, confused Tammy.

Today was Sunday and the pool was closed for maintenance. It was one of those rare occasions where everyone was together and playing together. I had found a selection of board games in the back of the linen closet and discovered a barely used version of The Game of Life. I pulled it out and blew the thick layer of dust off of it.

I brought it to the living room, set it on the coffee table and loudly asked "Who wants to play?" My sister jumped up at the prospect of a board game. Sunday family game night was a big part of my family. Daniel perked up as well. My aunt hesitated, and my uncle jabbed her lightly in the rib cage. She caved in and I opened the box quickly before anyone could change their minds.

The game was a hit. My uncle showed his sense of humour by having only boys in his game car, even marrying two boys together and having only boys as children. In contrast, Daniel chose to only have girls, while my sister decided her children were actually dogs. It was the first time since we had gotten there that not only were we all having fun, but we were having fun together. The doorbell rang but no one even noticed. Then someone started knocking, lightly at first, then harder and harder until they were practically pounding on the door.

My uncle finally stopped his laughing long enough to say, "Oh my dear, I think we have guests," he said as he got out of his chair. We all stopped playing to look in the direction of the door, and the ringing doorbell and the knocking continued. We all looked at each other and burst into giggles. My uncle sauntered over to the door to open it, his arms raised high as if to greet the queen, laughter still bellowing out of him.

As he opened the door, his laughing stopped abruptly. We, too, stopped laughing and looked back at the door, a sense of unease filling the air. Our uncle had stepped backwards to let our guest in, and to all of our surprise, in came our mother. My sister and I were in shock. We had no idea she was coming. Based on the look of surprise on our aunt's face, neither did she. Our mother let herself in, looking a bit tired, but otherwise all right. She gave my aunt a look and the three adults disappeared into the kitchen. My sister and I were still frozen in our seats. We looked at each other, excitement growing between our eyes. Were we finally going home? We could hear the adults mumble something about a hospital and someone almost being well enough to come home. Then something about the kids.

Our mother emerged from the kitchen and I stood up quickly.

"Mother?" I asked softly as she whisked past me and into my aunt and uncle's bedroom.

My aunt followed her and my uncle stayed behind at the entrance to the kitchen. I looked at him and he cast his eyes downwards. My sister tugged at my pants and I looked at her with confusion. Did mother not see us?

A few minutes later mother came out of the bedroom, the diaper pail in her hand and the suitcase in our aunt's. I clutched my sister's hand and tried to contain my excitement. My aunt passed the suitcase to my uncle and he disappeared outside. Mother set the diaper pail by the door as our aunt picked up our baby sister. Mother brought the baby's coat over and dressed her on the couch. The couch that we sat on only a couple of feet away from her. My sister crawled over to our mother and tugged at her pants.

"Mommy?" she whispered.

Mother gave her head a kiss and whispered something into her ear. My sister suddenly perked up and ran for the hall closet. My uncle came back in and took the diaper pail outside. Mother stood up, taking our baby sister into her arms as our aunt plunked a hat onto the baby's head. As our uncle came back inside, the grownups gathered once again, this time at the door. Mother hugged them both, said thank you, took my sister's hand and left. I ran for the door but my uncle caught me and held me back.

"MOMMY!" I screamed at the top of my lungs. I struggled against my uncle, watching through the still open door as mother put my sisters into the car, got into the driver's seat and left without a single word to me.

◇◇◇

Nicola looked up at the building in front of her, then back down at the card in front of her. She wasn't entirely sure when she had decided to come here or how she even got there. But since she was here, she might as well investigate. Perhaps it would soothe her nerves a little. The logo from the card was the same as the one on the sign. She smiled: first good sign, she thought, and it was also open, so she went inside.

The flower shop was filled to the brim with a large assortment of flowers, not only local ones, but most likely imports as well. The entire wall surface of the shop, minus the door leading customers in and the door to the back, was entirely comprised of clear glass coolers. The rest of the shop had a variety of displays featuring toys, golf accessories, chocolates, and many other gift-like items. Nicola was impressed with its large variety. This place made gift giving easy. She wondered if it was a new business. A clerk popped out from a cooler holding a bouquet of daisies and tulips, both coloured shades of green and blue. She noticed Nicola and waved a greeting before going behind the desk.

"How may I help you today?" the clerk asked her, smiling brightly.

"I'm hoping you might be Miranda," Nicola said. The clerk nodded eagerly and Nicola let out a sigh of relief as the clerk finished wrapping the flowers and set them below the counter. "I called you a couple of days ago, about a delivery to a doctor's office…" Nicola started.

The clerk looked at her with confusion in her eyes for a moment then broke out in a huge smile. "Yes! I remember your call." She looked at Nicola's trim figure. "And I can see why a baby basket delivery might distress you. You're not pregnant are you?" she asked.

Nicola shook her head no. "Did you know that the doctor's office you were delivering to was a fertility clinic?" Nicola asked and the shocked look on Miranda's face was a clear enough answer.

"No, I didn't. Only that it was a doctor's office. The man placing the order said it was a surprise."

"About this man. I know you described him to me over the phone, but I was wondering if you had any records of the order with his name on it," Nicola asked, and again, Miranda shook her head no.

"I am so sorry. I remember that he paid with cash and he didn't need a signature on delivery, so there was no need for contact information," Miranda said with a frown on her face. She had opened the delivery book and was already looking for additional information.

Nicola looked around the store. "What about security cameras?"

Miranda slapped her hand on the counter. "We have those! There's a television in the back that shows the two cameras. One's out back and the other is in the store."

"That's great!" Nicola exclaimed. "Do they record?"

Miranda opened her mouth as if to answer, then furrowed her brow and her lips into a pinch. She tapped the side of her face with the pencil in her hand. "I dunno. That's a really good question. You would think that they would, wouldn't you? Do you wanna take a look?"

Nicola smiled from ear to ear. "Are you sure that's okay?"

"Probably not, but the boss it out of town this week checking out a flower show in the next city. He'll never know. C'mon." She gestured Nicola to follow her behind the desk.

The back room was merely a long and wide hallway that they had fashioned into a makeshift office. A desk was inset into the wall, along with a computer and several books on flowers. On the other side were several awards and certificates, including a cork board that looked like it was primarily used for communication. It had the shop's schedules, contact info for suppliers and a section full of post-its under a large question mark.

Miranda saw her eyeing it. "Anyone who works here can post a question, about anything, personal- or work-related. Then whomever wants can answer it if they know the answer."

Nicola nodded and looked at the computer. Miranda shook her head and guided her farther down the hallway.

Halfway down she stopped at a picture hanging in an old frame. Miranda pushed the picture in, and it slid into the wall to the left, leaving only the picture frame in place. Behind it was a flat-screen television. It displayed both the back and the interior of the shop—the main counter in fact. Nicola scanned the screen and looked around it. There was a remote control on one side and on the other a small VCR-type device. She saw that it had a cable running from it to the television. Closer investigation revealed a few buttons on it: play, record, stop, pause.

Nicola looked to Miranda. "Do you mind if I check it out?"

Miranda waved a hand as if to say 'go ahead' and she watched Nicola with great curiosity.

Nicola looked at the screen for a moment, then walked out front to the counter. She waved her hands in big exaggerated movements for a few moments then went back to the hallway. She hit stop on the machine. The screen kept showing the front and the back. Then she hit rewind for a few seconds, then play. The television screen flickered a moment then popped back to the view of the front and the back. She watched the screen intently. After a few minutes she appeared and waved her hands about. Sighing, she hit stop and ejected the tape. On top it read 'extended play 72 hours'. She put the tape back in and hit record.

"Well?" Miranda asked. "Will it help?"

Nicola shook her head no. "It appears to loop back and re-record over itself every 72 hours."

The two of them went back to the front of the store to discover that another customer had come into the store. Miranda put a hand on Nicola's shoulder as she started towards the new customer.

"I'm so sorry I couldn't be of more help. But you know what? This might sound strange, but you remind me of him. He had similar features, like he could have been your brother or a cousin. I hope you figure it out. If I see him again, I'll call you." She smiled and darted off to her customer.

CHAPTER TEN

'Why does she always get into my head? I need to focus,' I told myself as I slammed my fists onto the coffee table. I poured myself another shot of whiskey from the now half-empty bottle and chugged it down. I set the empty glass on the table next to my laptop. I wiped my mouth dry with the end of my shirt sleeve and poured myself another drink, but sipped this one more slowly. I knew I had to concentrate and not lose my focus. I had to figure out how to give her what she desired most. I knew she didn't like the gift basket because it wasn't really for her. I need to give her something special, something that really showed how much I loved her.

I logged onto my computer through multiple encryptions and fire walls before beginning my search for romantic gifts. But all I could find were the usual sappy sentimental gifts that most pathetic men give their loved ones: flowers, chocolates, wine, teddy bears. She was special. She was unique. She deserved something above and beyond. I tried revising my search to 'unique gifts' before finally starting to find a bit better selection. I chuckled, thinking that I should just email her and ask her to find it herself since that was her business. She'd probably find something better than what I could dig up on the internet, I thought to myself. Except that would leave a trail that would lead directly back to me.

I found a variety of sites that made custom candies, trinkets from scrap metal, and then finally, jackpot—a jewellery site that refurbished antique jewellery. I looked at the pictures of her on the table before me and smiled. I knew exactly what to get her.

Nicola and Karim walked into the Denny's together. She had tried holding his hand but he had quickly stuffed his hand into his pockets, obviously pretending he hadn't noticed her reaching for him. She tried to smile it off but it had hurt. They had barely made it through the door when the terror twins jumped onto her. She scooped them up and they adorned her face with slobbery kisses before she put them back down onto the ground. They both took Nicola's hands and pulled her over to their table where Cassandra, Philip, Patsy and Sarah, Nicola's youngest sister, were already seated. Sarah and Patsy were looking at some kind of brochure together and quickly hid it when they heard the twins coming back with Nicola, and smiled guiltily at Nicola. She gave them the evil eye but Patsy shrugged her off with a 'none of your business' look.

Nicola sat down next to Cassandra, the twins sandwiching themselves around her while Karim sat at the other end of the booth. He had already pulled his cell out and was playing on it. The twins pulled out the menu and placed it in front of her, pointing at all of the dishes they wanted and persuading her to choose one of them. She laughed and played along.

Patsy and Sarah continued their secret conversation over the mystery brochure while Cassandra kept trying to calm down the twins. Philip cleared his throat and looked over to Karim.

"So how's the family-making going? She keeping you busy?" he asked, a sly, knowing smile on his lips.

Everyone, except the twins, suddenly stopped what they were doing and slowly but carefully looked over at Karim while trying to look like they weren't actually looking. The twins, blissfully ignorant, kept playing with the menu.

Karim looked up from his phone. "Sorry, are you talking to me?"

Nicola glared at Cassandra, who in turn poked a finger into Philip's side. He gave Cassandra a weird look before looking back at Karim.

"Yes, any kiddies in the near future yet? My little ones need some family to play with soon," he said, tousling his son's hair.

Karim shifted uncomfortably in his seat. "Well, you—" Philip started, but Cassandra quickly interrupted him.

"You don't want to rush into having kids, it's a big decision," she said quickly cutting her husband off, but he only looked at her, bemused, and shrugged his shoulders.

"Nicky here said you've already decided and you've been trying for what, two years now?" he asked. Nicola nodded slowly, keeping her head lowered and avoiding eye contact with Karim. She turned her face away from him, afraid to catch his eye.

"It's an ongoing decision until you are actually pregnant with them, isn't it honey?" Cassandra said through gritted teeth as she attempted to stare Philip down, but he either took no notice or was naively oblivious.

"C'mon Karim, what are your soldiers waiting for? I want a niece or nephew and Sarah keeps scaring away the good men with her crime scene club infatuation," he said. Sarah shot him a dirty look and he raised his hands up to his sides, mocking a white flag of mercy. She rolled her eyes at him and glanced back at Patsy. Patsy's eyes were furtively darting back and forth between Karim and Nicola.

Karim was sitting very still with a weird look on his face. His phone was now facedown on the table and his hands were curled into fists that sat on his lap. He exhaled slowly and deeply out through his nose.

"Speaking of kids, don't yours start school soon?" Patsy blurted out.

"Yes, yes they do," Cassandra said, shooting Philip one last dirty look before giving a sigh of relief to Patsy. "We're so happy, aren't we honey?" she said moving closer to kiss him on the cheek. When she was near enough, she hissed in his ear to shut up already and drop the kid thing already. He nodded his head quickly and furiously and one of the twins looked up from the menu and asked why their daddy was a bobble head. The whole table grew silent for a moment before bursting into laughter. Even Karim joined in the laughter.

When the laughter finally subsided they realized that their server was patiently waiting for them to order. They all placed their orders and the server left, rolling her eyes at them.

"So sis, how is work these days?" Sarah asked Nicola.

"It's good," Nicola said smiling. "It's great in fact," and proceeded to tell them all about it.

Throughout her conversation she snuck glances at Karim, who continued to isolate himself with his phone, and inside she felt her heart sink.

Patsy looked up at the clock. Almost eleven in the evening. During dinner, Patsy had remembered that she had left a package at work that she had wanted to deliver early the next day, so Nicola and Karim had dropped her off at the office afterwards. But instead of just grabbing it and going straight home, she had decided to get a jump on a few projects for Nicola. She figured it was the least she could do considering all of the stress Nicola was going through. She wasn't sure if Karim had talked to Nicola yet, but even if he had, things didn't look like they were going well quite yet. Things looked like they were starting to get complicated. Patsy did a final sweep around the office and turned out the lights for the night, her heels clacking loudly as she made her way out of the office and to their private elevator—one of the perks of working in a ridiculously designed old warehouse.

Outside, Patsy decided, like she often did, to walk home instead of taking the bus. It wasn't that long of a walk and she enjoyed walking through the dark and gloomy abandoned warehouses. It got her heart racing to get home quickly and snuggle up with a glass of wine and a horror movie. The moon was hidden behind clouds, and as usual the street lamps were mostly broken. The few that did work flickered with what little life that had barely clung to them. Her heels echoed loudly amongst the buildings as she strolled down the alley-like street. She popped her headphones into her ears and cranked up her tunes and death metal filled her ears instantly. She smiled and gave a little twirl.

Suddenly a pair of hands appeared out of the darkness and grabbed at her, yanking her into the shadows and slamming her head hard against a concrete wall. Stars danced before her eyes and her head spun wildly out of control. She tried to get a sense of her surroundings and what had just happened when an earth-shattering crack filled the air around her. As the light slipped away from her, she realized that the cracking noise was the sound of a bat connecting with her skull. As she fell into unconsciousness, she heard but didn't really feel the bat connect with her stomach as she fell over onto the ground.

CHAPTER ELEVEN

The shrill ringing of her cellphone shattered her dreams and brought Nicola back to reality. Still sleepy, she rubbed her eyes, unsure of what exactly had woken her up when her cell rang again. She fumbled with her left hand, feeling around for the phone and accidentally knocked it off the nightstand and sent it flying to the floor. It rang again and Karim rolled over to her side of the bed and slapped his pillow onto her head. He mumbled about how it was too early to be calling anyone at this hour and for her to answer it already, then fell back asleep as it rang again. Nicola groaned as she partially climbed out of the bed, her body half sliding out as she fumbled on the floor for her phone. She finally found it, and as she answered it she fell completely out of the bed, landing on her back. Facing the ceiling, her legs still tangled in the sheets, she looked up at her phone and said her best 'hello?' followed by a giant yawn.

A gruff male voice asked for a Nicola VanBurgen and she mumbled a reply of agreement. The voice on the other end introduced himself as a police officer and proceeded to apologize for the late intrusion and explained that they had her friend, Patsy Klein, in the hospital.

Nicola quickly bolted upright at the news, saw it read just past midnight on her alarm clock, and in a growing panic, gushed out her concerns and worries to the police officer. Karim, still fast asleep, took no notice at her sudden change. The officer attempted to calm her down, reassuring her that Patsy was indeed all right, just a little banged up. Still in a panic, Nicola went on a tangent about leaving Patsy alone at the office so late and how it must have been her fault. Her words started rushing out of her mouth as she pulled herself to her feet. Again, the officer tried to calm her down and when Nicola finally stopped talking long enough to listen, she found herself able to calm down and to hear the officer tell her that Patsy had been attacked on her walk home, most likely a mugging as both her purse and wallet were found dumped and empty nearby.

Nicola nodded numbly as the officer explained all of this to her. He ended by urging her to come to the hospital so she could see for herself that Patsy was all right, and so he could answer any other questions she had in person.

She readily agreed, already partially dressed. Once her mid-slumber panic has started to recede, she pulled herself together easily. She tossed her cellphone onto the bed and quickly finished getting dressed. As she went to leave the room, Karim mumbled out to her. She kissed him on the forehead and told him that she'd be back soon. Without any argument he rolled over onto his back and fell back to sleep as she left.

Nicola stood outside the glass window, looking in at Patsy. The doctor was jotting down notes in her file while the nurse was administering drugs into the IV. Patsy's face was bruised and Nicola could see dried blood on her neck. Patsy was staring off at the ceiling while the doctor finished treating her, so Nicola tapped her finger lightly on the glass. Patsy blinked then looked away from the ceiling and slowly over to her right. She saw Nicola, smiled and waved her hand, indicating that Nicola should come in.

Nicola slowly opened the door and crept inside, but the nurse immediately caught sight of her and turned to face her.

"Family only," she said sternly.

"She's my sister," Patsy said weakly, and the nurse looked at them skeptically before turning towards the doctor for reinforcement, but he was obviously turning a blind eye to the women.

Nicola rushed over to her side and took Patsy's hands, squeezing them. The nurse looked between the two women, shook her head with disapproval and muttered something under her breath as the doctor left the room. The nurse quickly finished cleaning Patsy up then left the two alone.

She stopped at the door and looked back at them. "Ten minutes. Max. She needs her rest," she said as she spun on her heels and left the room, closing the door behind her.

Nicola leaned in and gently hugged Patsy. "Are you okay?" she asked and Patsy managed a weak smile.

"I think I'll survive, but can I take a beating-by-stranger-day instead of a sick-day?" she asked, and tears poured from Nicola's eyes as she choked back a gasp mixed with a laugh.

Patsy laughed at her as she reached up to clean the tears from Nicola's face. "I'm okay, Nicola. Honest. If it wasn't the middle of the night they'd probably have let me go home already..." she said trailing off.

Nicola, still holding one of Patsy's hands, squeezed it tightly. "Aren't I supposed to be cheering you up? Not the other way around?" she protested, trying to smile through her tears.

"Well, I've always been the tougher one, haven't I?" Patsy said and they both laughed. Nicola wiped the remaining tears off of her face before hugging Patsy.

"Take as much time off as you need," Nicola said.

Patsy pushed her hands against the bed, hoisting herself to a better sitting position. She grimaced slightly and Nicola quickly helped her. Nicola looked her over and noticed, thankfully, few bandages.

"Oh, I plan to. Going to milk things as long as I possibly can," she said with a giant grin on her face.

Nicola sighed but smiled. If Patsy was joking this much then she truly must be okay. "What happened, Patsy?"

"I got jumped by some guy, I think," she said. "It was hard to tell, it was dark and he was kinda small. But it sounded like a guy and he was wearing a ball cap."

"Any idea who it might have been?" Nicola asked but Patsy just shook her head. "Do you think it might have been my stalker? Do you think he might have thought you were me?" Again, Patsy shook her head.

"I'm much shorter than you, even in my heels. He took my purse so I guess he was just robbing me," she said.

Nicola nodded in agreement and the two fell silent as they pondered that thought, when there was a knock on the door and the grumpy nurse popped her head in.

"Time to go. She needs to sleep," she said sternly.

Nicola leaned over Patsy, gave her a kiss on the cheek and hugged her. "Call me in the morning, tell me how you're feeling," she said. Patsy hugged her back and whispered in Nicola's ear, telling her not to worry, that she'd be okay. Nicola hugged her again and left.

Nicola stood outside the warehouse, her arms overflowing with packages. She was juggling the last package on top and trying to pull her wallet out of her purse to pay the taxi driver. She gritted her teeth at his rudeness as he was just sitting inside his cab without even bothering to help her with her packages. Not that she had wanted help inside the warehouse, but it would have been nice if he had passed the packages to her so she could have arranged them in her arms better. Then her credit card hadn't worked so now she was trying to get cash out of her purse. She finally managed to get her wallet out and gripped the outer edge of it with her teeth. She managed to pull out a handful of singles and tossed them through the open window and onto the passenger seat and she walked away, ignoring his cursed mutterings of her lousy tip.

Outside the elevator she reached up with her foot and tapped the up button with her toe. She was grateful for her ongoing yoga classes, for her balance didn't even waver, and she leaned her back against the wall as she waited for the elevator. She could hear it groan with age as it slowly clacked its way down the elevator shaft and she closed her eyes briefly. The elevator hit the bottom floor with a loud thud and she moved away from the wall, turning directly into the elevator, forgetting that she had to open the gate. She hit the gate, almost losing all of her packages before kicking it partially open and stepping inside.

She tapped the fifth floor button and reshuffled the tower of packages to her right side. The top package was starting to slowly slide off so she quickly moved to the right side of the elevator and used the wall to reset her packages. The elevator reached her floor and shuddered to a stop. She waited a moment to let herself settle before stepping away from the wall. Again she opened the gate with her foot and the packages started to slowly spill forwards. She ran from side to side, like a cartoon character, trying to level out the tower. She rushed into the closed office door and caught the pile before it could tip over completely. Carefully, she pressed her chest into the packages, binding them between her and the door so she could reach down to open the door. Surprisingly, she found the door locked. She knelt down slightly to enter in the key code for the door, and forgetting that she was still leaning against the door, it abruptly popped open with her falling forward through the door, tripping over her feet and stumbling. Just as she thought she was about to fall over she managed to steady herself and stopped, coming to a fully upright position with all of the packages still in their neat little tower. With a sigh of relief she took two more steps forward and deposited the packages onto Patsy's desk and smiled. A week had passed since the attack, and Patsy had already come back to work at full force. Nicola had tried to put her on light duty, a.k.a.

computer work, but she knew Patsy would have finished those duties quickly.

Still smiling, she took her hands away from the pile of packages and it collapsed completely all over Patsy's desk. She laughed and shook her head, wondering where Patsy was. She checked her phone for any new messages but didn't see any, and was about to text her when she realized that Patsy probably left a note somewhere in the office for her. Most likely it was below the pile she just deposited on the desk. She looked at the scattered pile of packages with a guilty smirk and walked over to her office and started to open the door when she saw that the mailbox in front of it was chock full of invoices and a variety of other forms that had to be sorted and dealt with.

Deciding against office work, she went back to the pile of packages on Patsy's desk to sort through them. She took the first box and opened it. Inside was a set of rare china plates from the Ming Dynasty. Biting her tongue, a quick hiss escaped from her lips as she carefully emptied the box, checking that the contents hadn't been damaged, and made a mental note to remind that particular supplier the need to mark items as fragile. Luckily, nothing was broken so she took a sharpie from the desk and wrote on the outside 'China Plates – Mrs. Willows' and then put the box on the shelf marked 'fragiles' that was next to the door so it could be prepped for delivery. One by one she opened each box, identified its contents and labeled each box accordingly before putting it on the shelf.

After a too short period of time the pile of packages was gone. Having cleaned the pile clear, she could now see the note Patsy had left her on the desk. It was flourished with little hearts, flowers and stick birds along with a simple note: '*Dentist had last minute cancellation, gone to get work done, see you tomorrow. ~ Patsy*'. Nicola took the note and set it in the recycling bin. Ready to admit defeat she went into her office, taking the pile of papers out of the mailbox and opening her office door.

She took a step inside and stopped mid stride. The pile of papers fell out of her hands and scattered all over the floor. Her jaw dropped and her eyes grew wide. The door handle fell out of her hand and hit the wall softly. Slowly she looked from one side of her office to the other. Plastered over all of the walls were pictures of her: getting into taxis, going into restaurants, at parties, eating dinner, going for a run. Most of them had hearts drawn over her own face and there were X's and O's drawn on them and the words 'love you' and 'watching you' over and over again. She took another step into the office and slowly turned a complete 360 degrees. Every inch of all four walls was plastered with pictures of her. She put her hands to her face, tears already pouring down her cheeks, collapsed to the floor and wailed.

CHAPTER TWELVE

A knock on the office door jostled Nicola out of her repeating nightmare of thoughts. She sat up in Patsy's desk chair as the door opened and two police officers came in.

"Nicola VanBurgen?" one of them asked and she nodded, her face drenched with tears that wouldn't stop, and smeared in dirt and snot from constantly rubbing her face on her shirt sleeve. She went to stand up but the female officer put a reassuring hand on her shoulder and told her it was okay for her to remain seated, that they could talk to her as she was. Nicola sniffled and wiped her nose with her sleeve, thanking them.

The male officer scanned the room and then looked at Nicola, observing out loud that he didn't see anything out of the ordinary inside the office, that the 9-1-1 operator had told them an office had been vandalized. Nicola stretched her arm out and pointed to her office door. He pulled a latex glove out and gingerly opened the door lightly with his fingertips. He took a step inside and briefly scanned the room. He looked back at the female officer and waved her over. She put a hand on Nicola's shoulder and squeezed it before following the other officer inside

Nicola's office. She disappeared into the office, following the other officer, and carrying a small briefcase. Nicola could hear them walking around her office, the snapping of a camera, the click of the briefcase opening, and the rustling of papers beneath their feet. She stared absently at the empty space in front of her, and after what seemed like hours the police officers finally emerged from the office, their faces a mixture of concern and thought. The male officer had a camera in his hands and several photos in the other. He set the camera down in his satchel and bagged the photographs. The female officer came over to Nicola, notepad and pen in hand.

She knelt down beside Nicola and asked her how she was feeling and if it was okay to proceed with some simple questions. Nicola nodded absently and her eyes blinked rapidly as she tried to focus on the female officer. Out of the corner of her eye she could see the other officer dusting the door knobs for fingerprints. The officer proceeded to ask her a battery of questions. Did she call the police as soon as she discovered the pictures, did she touch anything in the office before or after calling the police, who else had been in the office that day, who has access to the office and did they always lock up at night?

Slowly, like she was on autopilot, Nicola either nodded or shook her head numbly to the majority of the questions. She confirmed that the only people who had access were herself, Patsy and the cleaning lady, and that they always locked up at the end of the day, and also pointed out that the office was locked when she had arrived. But no, Patsy did not regularly go into her office when she was out. She also mentioned that Patsy had been out most of the day at the dentist.

The officers looked at each other briefly as the male officer finished dusting the room for prints. He tilted his head a little to the left, and she asked Nicola for Patsy's contact info, assuring Nicola that they only needed to determine a timeline of accounts for both of them to better determine when the vandalism had occurred. After Nicola had calmed down, the officer asked her if anything else out of the ordinary had occurred recently.

Nicola took a deep breath. The officers both looked at her expectantly. Slowly, she proceeded to tell them about the valentine she had received in the mail with no return address and over a month late for Valentine's Day, and the gift basket that was sent her to doctor's office.

The officers exchanged another look, this one of curious surprise, and asked her if she still had either of these items. She nodded, revealing that the card was in a secret drawer of her desk and the gift basket in the closet behind Patsy's desk. The male officer went to retrieve both and the other officer squeezed Nicola's hand tightly, telling her that she was doing a great job and that they were almost done.

The male officer returned with both items, the valentine now in a plastic baggie, the gift basket currently too big for what he had presently. He excused himself briefly to go to their car to get a larger evidence bag.

While he was gone, Nicola and the officer talked about the gift basket and how Nicola thought it was strange to get as no one knew she was even at that clinic since it was not only her first visit, but a fertility clinic as opposed to a treatment centre. She assured the officer that only Karim and Patsy knew about the appointment as they were still very hush-hush about their current situation, outside of family. The officer inquired as to who Karim was and asked if she had contacted him yet, but she shook her head no, staring down at the floor.

The male officer returned and bagged the gift basket. He looked over at Nicola and asked how she kept track of her appointments and if she used a PDA of some kind. She nodded and said that she used both an iPad and an iPhone, and that her assistant had linked the two together for her. He asked Nicola if he could take a quick look at them and when she looked at him with question, he explained that they might be able to trace a hacker from them. She handed them over and almost instantly he shook his head. Nicola sat up and looked at him with worry. Still shaking his head he told her that she really needed to put passwords on both of them, making sure to make both of them different and nothing easy to guess. Nicola asked why and he showed her that not only could anyone easily look at her schedule on them without her ever noticing, but that she had several apps with their passwords saved. Anyone could easily get into her banking app or steal a lot of sensitive information. He fiddled with both of them for a minute then handed her the iPhone and instructed her to create a password and to enter it twice. Once she complied, he handed her the iPad and she did the same thing, assuring him that she was choosing two different passwords. He also urged her to not tell anyone the password, not even her assistant or boyfriend.

Nicola grew tense and asked them if they thought her friends had actually done this to her. They shook their heads and explained that it was their job to find suspects and rule them out with the evidence that they found, and that no one could be ruled out unless the evidence said otherwise. They weren't allowed to be biased. Nicola shook her head and lowered it slightly. The female officer explained that they weren't looking at her friends as guilty, but that it was easy to accidentally reveal information to the wrong people without even knowing it. The female officer got to her feet as the other officer grabbed the gift basket, his camera and the briefcase. She handed Nicola a business card with the police station number on it, explaining which numbers were direct lines to their desks, and her case number on the back. She told her to call if she remembered anything else and they both headed for the door to leave.

Nicola looked up at them. "I've felt him. Once, when I was running in the trails in the forest. I felt like someone was following me," she said softly.

The two officers looked at each other quickly and the female officer came back to Nicola's side. She put a hand on Nicola's shoulder. "I know this isn't going to be the most reassuring thing for you to be hearing right now, but you have to understand that then, in the forest, now, and in the upcoming future, you will become hyper-sensitive to your surroundings and the people in them. There is a good chance you may imagine a presence near you. This is not your fault. This is the unfortunate side effect of being stalked. You have to fight the urge to become paranoid. Do not let this creep take ahold of your life. Be aware of your surroundings but don't let them consume you. For right now, don't travel alone unless necessary, but keep your regular routine, take mental note of anything that seems off, wrong or different, and write it down. Keep track of these notes with dates and times and in a few days come to the station and give those notes to us. It'll help us try to track the perp down, otherwise, we will contact you if we have any more questions or a lead. And don't hesitate to call us if anything happens, okay?"

Nicola nodded. The officer got up and joined her partner on the other side of the desk. They both nodded at Nicola then left her alone.

Nicola stared at her office from behind Patsy's desk. She didn't want to go in there. She turned to the calendars on the wall behind the desk. There were two; one for client deadlines and the other the cleaning, trash and recycling schedule. She put her finger on today's date and noted that the cleaners would be by later that evening. She grabbed a post-it and wrote 'Please clean the pictures off the wall in this office and trash them', and put it on her office door. She wrote a second note that said 'additional cleaning request on inner office door' and put it on the outside of the main office door. She sent a text to Patsy telling her to call her as soon as she was done with the dentist and to not come in that day. With one last look at the office, she closed the door and left.

Patsy was shaking her head from side to side. Her lower left cheek looked like she had swallowed a chipmunk. The server set down a bowl of soup in front of her and a salad in front of Nicola. The girls thanked her before Nicola continued to fill Patsy in on the office situation and why she had left the cryptic text messages the previous day. After the police left, she had texted Patsy telling her to stay out of the office as it was 'contaminated', and then immediately had gone for a long run trying to work the stress out of her system. Feeling much better after running for nearly two hours, she returned to find her apartment empty.

After a long process of calling person after person and leaving half of them cryptic messages, she had given up and treated herself to a bubble bath, music and wine. Because she went directly from the office to a run, she had accidentally left her iPad at work and like usual, she had left her phone out and unplugged so it died during the night. As a result, she didn't get any of her messages until the following morning when she discovered that Karim had returned late in the night and must have plugged the phone in for her.

Patsy's eyes grew wide as Nicola described to her the horror she felt being surrounded by pictures of herself. When Nicola told her how she had left a note for the cleaning lady, Patsy asked her about the paperwork she had dropped on the floor and if Nicola had remembered to tell the cleaning lady to not throw it out. Nicola shrugged her shoulders as she took a large bite of her salad. Patsy rolled her eyes and took a careful sip of soup. Suddenly Patsy dropped her spoon into her soup with a clatter and her eyes grew wide. Nicola stopped mid-bite and looked up at her.

"What if… what if it's the guy who mugged me?" she asked.

Nicola shook her head. "It couldn't be. If he mugged you then why put up pictures of me?"

Patsy slowly nodded her head in agreement. She asked if it was safe to go to the office and Nicola shrugged her shoulders again.

"Do you think we should get one of those fancy alarm systems?" asked Nicola.

Patsy shook her head, concluding that Nicola would only forget the password within a day. Nicola swatted her shoulder. Patsy winced at the jarring in her jaw and Nicola flushed immediately and put a caring hand on Patsy's shoulder, apologizing profusely.

Patsy grinned and stuck out her tongue. "Gotcha," she said with a smirk.

Nicola growled at her and her phone chirped. She pulled it out, read the message and smiled.

"What? Good news?" Patsy asked.

Nicola nodded. "The office is clear and good to go. The cleaning lady put all of the papers on my desk. So, hurry up and eat. I've got a ton of paperwork to avoid doing," she said with a smile.

Karim rolled over, pulling the sheets with him as he did, rolling himself up like a pig-in-a-blanket. When he felt no resistance he rolled back and saw that Nicola was already gone. He rolled back to his side and looked at his cellphone. Already ten am. He groaned, still drunk from the night before. He hadn't returned until almost five in the morning. He had drank so much he hadn't even noticed Nicola leave earlier that morning. Still looking at his phone he noticed that he had missed two calls from Nicola and that she had left him two texts. Neither said anything important, just that she wanted to talk to him. He deleted them all and pulled himself out of bed.

Naked, he hopped into the shower and quickly rinsed off. He didn't have any meetings until noon, but he still wanted to get in early enough to prepare and revamp his speech. His first appointment was with a regular client who was quite upset at not getting a role she believed was rightfully hers. He sighed, hating the coddling-the-big-egos part of his job. But she did bring him good money, so he couldn't afford to lose her.

Donning a towel, he made his way to the kitchen, hoping that Nicola had made him a pot of coffee before she left as she sometimes did. He sniffed the air deeply, unable to detect the bitter aroma of coffee. As he made his way down the hall he saw the light flickering on Nicola's old answering machine. He chuckled, amused that it even worked, and hit play. The first message was from the doctor at the clinic saying she had Nicola's test results and wanted to schedule a follow up appointment. He quickly skipped over that message to the next one. Sarah's voice popped up and she sounded frantic. She didn't say much other than to call her. He saved this one and then played the final message. It was her other sister Cassandra, expressing her concern about the vandalism at the office and offering her a place to crash if she needed some TLC, and asking her what the police had said. He stared at the machine and replayed the last message.

Police? Vandalism? What was Cassandra talking about? What exactly had happened at Nicola's office and why hadn't she told him? He discerned from both messages that Nicola's sisters had left, that she had obviously called both of them and had left messages briefly describing whatever had happened. He played the messages for a third time and midway through he punched the wall above the machine and stormed off to the bedroom, looking for his phone.

Nicola sat down at the table, a chai tea latte already in her hand, nibbling on a cheese croissant. She scanned the crowd looking for Gregory. She had seen his email earlier while having lunch with Patsy, and accepted his offer of an afternoon get together even though she knew she was drastically behind in paperwork. Surprisingly though, Patsy hadn't reprimanded her for bailing on her work and even offered to sort the paperwork while she was out so it would be easier to tackle when she returned.

She smiled as she thought about the email. She couldn't wait to see how he looked in his wig. The last time she had met up with him he wore a ball cap pulled down over a handkerchief that he had wrapped around his head. Other than that he looked fine. Any traces of chemotherapy treatment had thankfully not remained with him for long. She caught sight of movement out of the corner of her eye and she turned to see Gregory as he was about to put his hands over her eyes. He grinned as she gasped in surprise. He sat down next to her empty handed.

"Did you want something to drink? To eat?" Nicola asked, but he just shook his head no, explaining that he had just eaten and didn't have much of an appetite these days. She took his hand in hers and squeezed it. He smiled back at her and reassured her that he was doing just fine. In fact, more than fine.

She looked at him quizzically and asked him what good news he had to share with her. He explained how he had gotten a temp job writing articles for an online newspaper about his cancer endeavours and his perspective on positivity playing a key role in his health improvement. She grinned from ear-to-ear and proclaimed how proud she was of him turning a negative situation not only into something positive, but doing something beneficial for others. He smiled back at her coyly, a small curl to his lips. She looked at him suspiciously and asked if she was wrong. He shook his head no, but told her that wasn't the real reason that things were more than fine.

Puzzled, she proceeded to interrogate him, guessing at the various things that could have improved his life recently and he enjoyed the game immensely. Finally, after much persuasion he admitted to her that he had met someone. She squealed like a school girl and asked him a million questions about his mystery woman. He carefully and cautiously answered most of her questions. She knew that he was holding something back from her, but she didn't care. She was happy that her friend was happy. After an hour of catching up, she looked at her cell and sadly admitted to him that she had to return to the office to finish her paperwork or Patsy might actually ban her from ever leaving the office again.

They hugged and he promised that he would introduce her to his mystery girl soon. Only after they parted ways had she realized that Karim had sent her several texts. He appeared to be getting more and more irate with the messages to the point that he even left a few angry voice texts. The last one simply stated that he was at the office waiting for her. She then noticed a single text from Patsy that read, 'didn't tell him who you were meeting; hurry back, he's pissed!'. Nicola looked up from her phone, bit her lower lip and ran off to catch the nearest cab.

Nicola rushed into the office to see a very nervous Patsy tapping away at the computer. She looked up from her desk when she heard Nicola come in and sighed a breath of relief. She indicated with her head that Karim was in her office. Nicola stopped, inhaled deeply and slowly walked in, closing the door behind her as Patsy grabbed her jacket and dashed out the office door.

Inside her office Karim was sitting in her chair. The look of anger on his face was unmistakable and Nicola wondered what she had done. She waved her hand slightly and smiled meekly as she greeted him but he simply stared her down. After a long moment of silence she asked him what was wrong.

He put his feet on her desk and tapped his fingers together lightly.

"Isn't that more of what I should be asking you?" he said slowly, his words dripping with sarcasm.

She swallowed deeply, unsure of what was happening. She slowly shrugged her shoulders and feigned an 'I dunno' look. Swinging his feet off the desk he slammed his fists down and she jumped, her heart lurching upwards as she bumped into the door behind her.

"Christ, Nic! How am I supposed to protect you if you don't let me?" he asked, exasperated.

She blinked her eyes, watching as he hunched over the desk, his whole body shaking slightly. She could hear the tremble in his voice, the desperation. Her heart slowly settled and clarity started to settle in. She took a step towards the desk, reaching her hand out towards him. He abruptly sat up, his hands still curled into fists and she stopped. Her breath quickened until she realized he was just regaining his composure. He uncurled his fists and settled back heavily into the chair. She took another step forward as he looked up at her.

"I'm sorry," she mumbled apologetically.

"Don't you trust me?" he asked, his voice full of hurt.

She nodded quickly, her heart breaking at the sight of him in so much pain. Her eyes glistened. "I tried to call you. But you didn't answer. No one answered. I didn't know what to do. I'm sorry."

He got up from behind the desk and came around to her side. He pulled her close and embraced her tightly. She wrapped her arms around him and let him squeeze her so tight that she almost lost her breath. She could hear him try to hide the tears in his voice as he started muttering, "I don't want to lose you." Over and over again.

CHAPTER THIRTEEN

Nicola sat alone at the detective's desk. It had only been a month since she was first here, but it felt like yesterday. A week had already passed since the office incident and she hadn't heard a peep from the officers, so she imagined she would get a similar berating about wasting police time. The police didn't seem to really care much about what had happened to her. She looked down at her purse, wondering how much longer she was going to have to wait here. She pulled out her cellphone to see if Patsy had texted her yet, but there was no service. The office she was currently in was in the basement of the precinct and there wasn't even a window to look outside. A loud voice caught her attention, a woman practically screaming outside the detective's office. Nicola got to her feet and cracked the door open to see what was happening. As she peeked through she recognized Patsy's voice and opened the door all the way. She stepped through the door and could see Patsy arguing with an officer at the other end of the room.

She reached a hand into the air and called out to her. Patsy looked over, saw her and waved back. She gave the officer a dirty look, stuck out her tongue and rushed over to Nicola. They grabbed each other in a hug. Patsy was apologizing for taking so long to get there and Nicola was reassuring her that it was fine as she hadn't been waiting long, when the detective appeared and ushered them back into his office. The women went in first and he followed, closing the door behind him.

The detective sat down as he pulled a file folder out from his desk and the girls sat down across from him. Nicola looked resigned while Patsy looked like she was ready to bite. The detective cleared his throat.

"Miss Klein, I hope you are doing well despite your incident. I'm sorry that we have had no progress on your case as of yet."

Patsy nodded her head as he turned to face Nicola.

"Miss VanBurgen, I must apologize for our lack of due diligence with your case. Despite our initial belief, it appears that your stalker is turning out to be more serious than we had originally presumed—especially considering what has happened to you and now your employee."

Nicola looked at him, stunned, and hope filled her eyes as Patsy squeezed her hand.

"However, I have to say that unfortunately our hands are legally tied at the moment. Not only are we bogged with more cases than we have detectives, but in cases such as yours, there are no crimes actually committed as of yet," he said grimly.

Patsy leaned forward in her chair. "What do you mean 'as of yet'," she asked.

"There are no signs of forced entry into the office so we're unable to prove trespassing, and the vandalism would be the only crime currently committed. There is no law against leaving messages, calling or sending gifts.

Unfortunately, in most cases like this we are unable to do anything until the stalker crosses the line."

Nicola looked between Patsy's upset face and the detective.

"Yes, I agree," he continued. "While it would appear that Miss Klein's assault may have been by your stalker, we have no evidence that link the two incidents together. If we did then it would be for all of our benefits. However, at the moment we have what appears to be multiple separate incidents that have nothing to tie them together. And aside from Miss Klein's assault, which we are investigating with full force, until your stalker leaves more evidence behind or actually commits a crime that we can prosecute him with, we are unable to do much more than take record of your incidents. We simply don't have the manpower to investigate this," he said.

"This is outrageous!" Patsy said, jumping to her feet. "We pay taxes for police protection." Nicola reached out to take her hand and tried to pull her down to the chair but Patsy yanked her hand away.

"I understand how you feel, but we are trying to protect you," the detective said

"By doing what? Sitting on your ass while this jerk continues to harass her? What if this," Patsy said pointing to her own face, "Is only the beginning? What if next time he hurts me or Nicola even worse?"

"Patsy, please," Nicola said. "Let's just go."

Patsy looked at her angrily. "Nicola, they need to do something."

The detective looked between the two women uncomfortably.

"No matter how angry you get, he isn't going to change his mind. We'll figure something out. C'mon. Lets go," Nicola said, standing up and taking her purse. She grabbed Patsy's hand and pulled her towards the door.

Nicola pulled an angry Patsy through the police station. She looked down at the ground as the officers stared at the two of them, some with pity and some with disdain. Patsy managed to keep her mouth shut until they got outside the station, and then she started to argue with Nicola about how they had rights and the police were just pigs, but she stopped when she saw the tired look on Nicola's face. She hugged Nicola and whispered an apology in her ear.

Taking each other's hands, they started down the stairs out of the precinct and, surprisingly, Karim met them halfway. Nicola jumped into his arms and he hugged her back fiercely. After reassuring him that she was okay, he offered to drive Patsy home.

After dropping Patsy off, Karim drove out of the city and to the park closest to their old place. He parked the car, opened her door and offered her his hand. They walked along the trails, watching the other people in silence. They wandered off the main path and deeper into the forest.

Finally Nicola broke the silence. "We used to come here all the time didn't we?" she said quietly and Karim nodded.

"I kept hoping that you'd finally stop being such a prude and let me do you in the bushes," he said was a small chuckle.

She looked up at him, shocked and surprised. "Are you serious?" she asked.

He shook his head up and down so strongly that she punched him in the shoulder. He feigned pain, let go of her hand and clutched his shoulder. She stormed off ahead of him, muttering obscenities under her breath. He dashed after her and pulled her close. He held her tight against him, her back against his stomach, and leaned his head over her shoulder.

"Why did we stop coming out here, Karim?" she asked, already knowing the answer.

"Because life got complicated. We got busy," he said, and she sighed.

"Things used to be so much easier, didn't they?" asked Nicola.

He nodded in agreement, his chin rubbing into her shoulder. "Things used to be simple, babe. Then life happened."

She turned her head to look up at him. "Are we going to be okay?"

He paused for a long moment before he finally said, "I hope so."

They stayed this way for several minutes, her hands holding his arms that were wrapped around her chest. He occasionally nuzzled his face into her hair. Finally, when a jogger ran around them and they broke apart and continued down the path. As they walked back to the car she told him how Patsy had insisted they visit the police station. His grip on her hand continued to get tighter and tighter as she told him that the police basically told her that she had to fend for herself unless the stalker actually did something drastic like hurt her. Abruptly he yanked his hand out of hers and punched a tree. She pulled him back, grabbing his hands and kissing the knuckles softly, urging him to calm down, telling him how being angry wouldn't change anything nor help. He took a step away from her and kicked the dirt like a child sulking. Mumbling an apology under his breath, he let her lead him back to the car.

As she went to unlock the car he suddenly grabbed her and kissed her. A long and hard kiss. She melted into his arms and kissed him back eagerly. She hadn't felt this kind of passion from him in weeks. He whispered something so softly into her ear that she could barely make it out, and before she could ask him what he had said he broke apart from her and got into the car. Looking at him with mild confusion she shook her head to clear it. She knew that whatever he had said, it was too long just to be 'I love you', and she felt that she had missed something very important. The car suddenly started and reluctantly she got in.

They were quiet again on the ride home, the silence both soothing and uncomfortable. She knew something was wrong, but she wasn't entirely sure what. Karim was all over the place emotionally. He pulled up to their condo, parked the car and shut off the engine. He stared out the windshield, his hands in his lap and a slightly lost look on his face. She looked over at him as she undid her seatbelt.

"I can let myself in, silly," she said as he reached a hand over and touched her leg. Still staring straight ahead, he told her that he could stay home if she wanted him to. She leaned over and kissed his cheek.

"And watch you spend the whole day on your phone instead of entertaining and wooing young girls with promises of being the next Charlize Theron?" she said mockingly. "Go. Work. I'll be fine. I just need to unwind and I'll be okay."

He finally turned to look at her and she couldn't tell if he was overly concerned or looking for an excuse not to go to work. Something seemed wrong but she couldn't put her finger on what exactly it was. He asked her if she was sure and she reassured him that she was okay and that he should go to work. Finally, with a promise of staying inside until he got home, she got out of the car and he drove off. She looked after the car and then up at their condo.

"I promise to stay inside, after I go for a run," she said out loud.

The wind whipped around her face like a breath of fresh air. That morning, the police station, Karim, everything, was evaporating away from her mind as she ran down the trail. Karim's voice telling her to stay inside chimed in and she pushed it away to the back of her mind. She pushed everything away and just let her mind go blank.

She hadn't ventured far, she only went around the corner from their condo to the high school down the road to run through the trails in the small patch of forest behind it. The path was well beaten and easy to follow. Worst case scenario was she ran into a teacher and had to explain herself trespassing on school property.

She could hear the shouts and cries of teenagers on the field playing some sport just outside the forest. She caught patches of colour between the trunks of the trees, and the sounds of car horns and trolley buses clanging could be heard in the near distance. Despite the solitude, she felt protected here. She'd never run here before, but it was close to home and the school was within shouting distance.

She came upon an intersection in the trails and chose to go in the direction she thought would take her farther into the forest. The pictures of herself from her office floated up in her head. The week after the incident had been quiet. No messages or texts from her stalker. She had tried to put it out of her head, but the randomness of how he would contact her put her at unease. She worried that if she relaxed he would see it and react. She knew that she had to do something herself if she wanted control of her life. Sarah and her crime scene buddies had offered their services, and she was seriously considering taking them up on the offer. The detective had said they didn't have the time to help her so what would be wrong with letting those who did have the time investigate? She knew that while the police thought little about the pictures left behind, she knew better.

Her getting into a taxi with friends, with Karim at a bar, in her favourite red dress—something about these pictures nagged at her mind. She tried to push the thoughts away but they refused to hide. She saw herself going into the bakery. No, she was already there and she was eating a cupcake. She knew there was significance to this picture but she couldn't put her finger on it. There was a picture of her and Karim standing next to a BMW. A picture of her and Patsy at a club. Was there something about just one of the pictures that nagged at her, or was it all of them?

Then it hit her. The cupcake picture was a selfie. Patsy had introduced her to selfies a few weeks ago and she couldn't stop taking them. She even went as far as to buy herself a selfie polaroid camera and started taking pictures with clients. If that picture was a selfie that she took herself, then the stalker couldn't have taken it. But if the stalker didn't take it, how did he get it? She suddenly stopped running: Facebook. The stalker was someone from Facebook. All of the pictures were on her Facebook account and Patsy had set her privacy to über_high. So unless the guys who ran Facebook were stalking her, her stalker had to be a friend of hers. She felt around for her phone, wanting to message Patsy right away. This was something they could figure out. She hardly had any friends on Facebook. She cursed under her breath as she unzipped half of her running jacket before she finally found the actual pocket her phone was in and yanked it out triumphantly, only to have it go flying out of her hands and bounce onto the dirt path in front of her. She rolled her eyes at the sky before bending down to pick it.

A rustle from the bushes behind her startled her. She paused and slowly looked over her shoulder as she called out to the bushes. Silence. She waited and scanned the bushes around her thinking that if it was an animal it would probably move again. But after a moment, still nothing. Turning back to her phone, she picked it up and the bushes behind her rustled again. She whipped around to look at them directly this time, still in a half crouch. Again, silence. She turned on her phone and the bushes rustled again, this time only a few feet away from her. Startled, she fell down to the ground. She called out again and still no answer. Hesitantly, she got to her feet and took a step closer towards the bushes, picking up a small rock off the path. She tossed it in the bush expecting to provoke the animal to move again but all she heard was the thud of the rock landing in the bush. A second later a rabbit jumped out of the bush and onto the path in front of her. It looked at Nicola, cocked its head sideways then bounced into the bushes on the other side of the path.

She let out a sigh of relief and turned on her phone again and started to text Patsy when the sound of a large crack, like a branch being stepped on, came from the same bush. Nicola looked up from her phone and saw the bush rustle again. This time she immediately turned and took off down the path. She looked over her shoulder and thought she could make out the the form of a person behind her, but she couldn't be positive. Regardless, she ran down the trail as fast as she could, her heart racing so loudly she could barely make out the sound of footsteps pounding behind her. Farther and farther she ran down the path until it came to an abrupt end. She stopped and looked behind her. She couldn't see anyone but she could feel that he was close by. She looked around for another trail out but couldn't see one. The bushes rustled again, and she could hear small cracks of branches from down the path and then a low, gruff voice. She thought she heard her name. She tore off into the trees, off of the trail.

She tried to focus on the sounds of the school children, wanting to find the school grounds where she would be safe, but they were a million miles away. The branches of the trees scratched at her face and mud sucked up at her shoes. The ground began to get soft and sloppy. She looked over her shoulder but couldn't make out much beyond the trees. Pushing herself harder she continued to run wildly through the muck, stealing glances over her shoulder. Suddenly she tripped over a large tree root and fell face first into the mud, hitting her head on a large tree root. Dazed, she rolled over onto her back and scrambled backwards. She looked around frantically, afraid that he was already there. She could hear voices in the near distance and the sound of feet slopping through mud. She tried to push herself into a sitting position up against the very tree she just tripped over but stars spun in her vision and she stumbled back onto her bottom, landing in the mud. She put a hand to her head and tried to steady it. Still a bit groggy but afraid to dawdle, she used the nearest tree trunk for support and pulled herself first to her knees and then, despite the screams ricocheting in her head, to her feet and stumbled forward.

Finally she broke free of the forest, and looking around she realized that she was at the far edge of the school grounds. The kids playing were but specks in the far off distance. She looked behind herself at the forest and then back at the kids playing. Determined, she stumbled her way towards them. Suddenly she heard voices from behind her and stopped to look over her shoulder. Emerging from the forest, not far from where she just was, a small group of high school boys ran out, covered in mud and cheering. Most of the boys faces sported mud and gigantic grins. She stared at them dumbfounded. They ran towards her, noticed her and high-fived her as they ran past. She watched as they joined their group of classmates on the field. She stumbled backwards, towards the forest. Her knees grew weak and wobbled as she crumbled down to the ground and everything went black.

CHAPTER FOURTEEN

The shrill ringing of her cellphone brought her out of her slumber as she tried to remember where she was. Groggy, she rubbed her eyes and slowly sat herself up before realizing she was in her bed. A sudden panic filled her and she looked down before she noticed that she was no longer in her mud-filled running clothes, but in a simple tank top and her undies. She blinked her eyes a few times, trying to remember how she had gotten home and obviously cleaned herself up without any recollection at all. She was still deep in thought when her phone rang again and she looked around her room with a bit more clarity and alertness. She went to slide out of bed but her legs were all tangled up and she went halfway onto her knees before sliding off the bed and landing on the floor with a thump. The room spun and tilted so she shook her head to clear it and her phone rang once again. She looked around the room as it continued to ring until she finally spotted it on the floor below her nightstand. She crawled over, grabbed it, and seeing that it was Karim, smiled as she answered.

"Hi baby," she said softy into the phone as she pulled herself back onto the bed and into a sitting position.

Their conversation continued with Karim offering to come home early, but she protested, knowing it was his night out with the boys. After much banter back and forth she finally managed to convince him that she'd be okay for the night and that she'd order in food instead of going to get take out. After hanging up she looked around the room with clear and more awake eyes. She realized how lucky she was to have convinced him to stay out. She winced as she stood up too quickly and touched her head lightly. It throbbed slightly at her touch. She looked around the room for any signs of the mud she might have tracked in but both the bedroom and bathroom were clear. She looked in her laundry hamper and found it was empty. A quick look in the hallway revealed a finished load of wet laundry waiting to be put in the dryer, but she couldn't find her running shoes anywhere. She shrugged her shoulders and figured they'd turn up eventually.

She made her way to the kitchen and without even consulting the fridge, she decided to make a quick call to their favourite Chinese food restaurant and made the rare order for delivery instead of take out. Satisfied, she suddenly started stripping. Even though she was obviously clean, she still felt dirty.

She started to walk down towards the shower when she noticed that there were new messages on the home answering machine. She hit the play button and went back to the kitchen to grab a beer for her shower. There was a long stretch of emptiness in the first message and then she almost dropped the beer as she recognized the voice in the message say, 'Let me guess. Chinese again? Betcha you got beef because he's not there. Always out with the boys on Tuesday nights, isn't he? Too bad I'm not there to join you', followed by a click. She stared out at the hallway, her heart racing. She was pretty sure that their home number was unlisted, mainly because of Karim's job, to stop the wannabes from harassing them at all hours. The second message was the sound of a man grunting and groaning. Like he was trying to get himself off but not succeeding. Just before the call disconnected she could swear she heard him whisper, 'I need you', then a loud click.

She ran over to the answering machine, hit save and tore the cassette tape out, replacing it with a new one. Her heart was pounding loudly. Karim had always mocked her for having such an archaic device but she loved old things. She was sure her sister could find a way to play the tape back so she could analyze the voice. She wouldn't give the tape to the police, not yet. Let Sarah make a copy and then give them that. They wouldn't know the difference anyways. She grabbed an envelope from their office desk and put the tape in it. She went back to the kitchen, put the envelope in her purse and sent a text to her sister saying they had to meet up tomorrow. Anytime was fine.

Patsy looked at the wall clock anxiously, then back at her cellphone. If she could leave in the next ten minutes she would have enough time to get home, shower, change and meet up with Gregory for dinner. She had immediately typed in the answer 'yes', but was hesitating on hitting send. She didn't want to commit before she got the okay to leave work early, but Nicola was nowhere to be seen. She knew that Nicola had met up with her sister Sarah earlier that afternoon for follow-up information regarding the taped messages, but she had thought she would at least return to work. It had already been a half hour since Nicola had received the text and with iMessage it was obvious that she had already read it. Patsy debated with herself; Nicola was super easy-going and normally wouldn't be upset with her, but with the recent stress Nicola appeared to be in a state of unpredictability. She was late more often and sometimes just wouldn't show up at all. She also confided less and less with Patsy and more with her sisters, especially Sarah. She didn't mean to be insensitive, but she felt less wanted recently and it hurt since it felt like Nicola was casting her aside. More importantly, she had just found a super rare item; pink techno racing yayoi wheels, also known as sakura, for a new client, and wanted to share in her success with Nicola and be patted on the head for a job well done. However, she decided to just leave. If Nicola got upset she'd tell her too bad. She started to compose a text to Nicola, telling her that she was leaving early, when Nicola strolled into the office.

She had two bags in her hands, a large paper bag filled with what looked like clothes and a small clear bag with little birds and flowers decorating it. Nicola dropped the clear bag onto Patsy's desk and she realized it was homemade sugar cookies.

"From Mrs. Winters. She was extremely grateful for the birdcages we found. I like the red heart ones, they taste like sugar strawberries," Nicola said as she wandered off into her office. She paused mid-stride and looked back to Patsy. "I got your email. Great job on the racing contract. Why don't you take off early today? Have an early weekend, on me."

Patsy's phone fell into her lap and her jaw dropped. It was her lucky day! She was glad she hadn't hit send on her message, she thought, as she jumped out of her chair, grabbing her jacket that was slung over the back of her chair and caught her phone as it nearly fell down to the ground. She quickly deleted the message she had almost sent Nicola and literally ran for the door when Nicola cleared her throat. Patsy stopped suddenly and looked back at her boss who was looking at her desk. She ran back for the cookies as Nicola laughed at her and then dashed out the door.

Patsy literally clicked her heels together in the air as she raced out of the office and saw a taxi was dropping someone off as she emerged out of the warehouse. Smiling broadly, she hopped into the cab and put the cookies into her purse as she flopped into the car seat. She couldn't believe her luck. Her phone chirped. It was Gregory. He texted back a smiley face with 'can't wait'. She hugged the phone to her chest and sighed.

Little more than an hour later, Patsy walked up to a well-hidden Italian restaurant that looked vaguely familiar. She thought that maybe Karim and Nicola might have taken her there once when she had first started working for Nicola, although she could be mistaken. Regardless, it had a quaint charm to its personality and the low lights emitting from it added a very romantic atmosphere. She went inside and was greeted by the host who took her to a table in the very back of the tiny restaurant. The table had a red and white checkerboard tablecloth on it, two candles, both white and partially melted, a bouquet of red, pink and orange daisies arranged nicely in the middle of the table and a bottle of champagne to the side. Her jaw dropped for the second time that day when she realized that this was their table. She looked around for Gregory but saw no one else other than the host who said nothing. Instead he poured her a glass of champagne and disappeared into the smoky haze.

Patsy closed her eyes and inhaled everything in. She couldn't believe her luck. Good looking and romantic. She's had men bring her flowers on a date before, but not like this. And to start the date with an expensive bottle of champagne? Be still her beating heart! She took the champagne to her lips and took a small sip. As she set down her glass she opened her eyes and Gregory was there, sitting quite close beside her, one of his hands on her knee and the other just about to stroke her hair. She set her glass down with a clatter and almost knocked it over. Her heart jumped as he leaned in and kissed her cheek. As he pulled away she could feel his breath on her cheek.

"Hello, my sweet," he said, his eyes twinkling.

She barely managed to stammer out a greeting in reply, blushing like a school girl. She tried to pull herself together, unsure of how he could be having such a strong and profound effect on her so quickly. It was only their third date and yet she felt like she had known him forever, while at the same time each moment they passed together brought her such new experiences and surprises. He smiled and traced a finger down her jawline to just under her chin. Pausing, ever so slightly, he pulled her gently towards him and when her breath caught in her throat he released her and slid his fingers down her neck, between her breasts and then off to the side. She was surprisingly mesmerized. She had never met a man like this before. She knew he had invited her for dinner and she normally took things quite slowly, but all she wanted was his lips on hers.

"Does it still hurt?" he asked, touching the faint bruises that still remained on her face.

She blushed and turned away, shaking her head.

He looked at her lovingly. "Are you sure?"

She nodded a yes and smiled brightly.

"Well then, now that that's settled, I've taken the liberty of ordering for us both. I frequent here enough that they have specials just for me. That is, if you don't mind," he said as she shook her head no, and he smiled that irresistible smile again. "You are so beautiful, do you know how beautiful you really are? Inside and out?" he asked, and again she shook her head no, this time a red colour slowly creeping into her cheeks as his hand was slowly making its way up her leg.

"I've never met a woman quite as lovely as you before," he said, his voice low as he leaned in closer and slid his hand under the bottom of her dress ever so slightly. He inhaled deeply and exhaled softly, tickling her neck and sending goosebumps all over her body. She didn't know why she was letting this happen or why she was feeling this way, but she couldn't help herself. Something about him made her trust him instinctively, even though he was technically still a stranger. His forwardness, which she would normally be turned off by, was completely enticing.

"You skin is so soft, it is begging to be tasted," he whispered, pecking her gently on the cheek, his hand now at the bottom of her panties. "But do you know what wants to be tasted even more?"

She slowly shook her head from side to side as her heart began to race even more and she could feel her breath growing heavy.

"Wh—a—at?" she gasped in a small moan as he slid his fingers beneath her panties and into her. He smiled seductively as she panted and then blushed furiously. They were in a restaurant, in public, and here they were behaving like high school students. She put her hands over his wrist and started to push his hand away from her but he leaned in closer and breathed heavily into her ear, licking it softly and pushed inside her even more. She moaned with pleasure and then gasped suddenly as he teased her.

"No one can see us right now," he whispered into her ear and he suddenly dropped under the table. She opened her eyes briefly and noticed that their table was now surrounded by a curtain, hiding them from the rest of the restaurant. She barely had time to register this fact when her body involuntarily jerked beneath her as he ripped her panties to the side, slid her to the edge of the bench, thrusting his tongue inside her, and quickly bringing her to climax.

Her face was flushed, her hands still clenching the edge of the bench and her body was slowly easing into a more relaxed position as he sat back up beside her, took a sip of his champagne and then kissed her earlobe. She was still panting softly, so he took her glass and offered it to her lips and she greedily drank the whole glass in one shot. He poured her another and she gulped it half down. She took a deep breath and did her best to regain her composure.

Her face was still flushed but now from the champagne. She looked at him like the cat that just ate the canary and could barely mouth the word 'wow'. He nodded nonchalantly and took another sip of his champagne.

She put her hand on his upper thigh and slid it upwards. Casually but quickly he put his hand on hers and stopped it as the curtain opened and the server came in with two plates.

"All in due time," he murmured as the server set the dishes down in front of them. For him a colourful rainbow tortellini with a white wine cream sauce and shredded chicken; for her, mini ravioli stuffed with ground beef and mushrooms in a thick and hearty tomato sauce. She inhaled the rich and aromatic scent of tomatoes and basil.

"This looks amazing," she said.

"It tastes even better. Almost as good as my appetizer," he winked as she again blushed hotly.

She quickly stuffed a piece of ravioli into her mouth in an attempt to distract from her embarrassment, and he chuckled. They both ate their meals in an easy silence, too enthralled with the delight on their taste buds to really engage in conversation. As their meal ended, the server magically appeared with two dishes of tiramisu and two lattes, hers a chai, and the server quickly whisked away their dinner plates. Patsy took a bite of the dessert and moaned with delight. It melted onto her tongue like butter, so soft and so rich.

He put a hand on her thigh again and she looked up at him, her heart beginning to race.

"Would you be offended if I told you that I need help and the only one that could help me was you?" he asked.

She blinked, confused at the sudden request. "Me? How could I help you? What could I possibly do for you?"

"You know that Nicola is my friend and I owe my world to her. Her friendship gave me life in a time when I needed it most," he started, and Patsy suddenly straightened up in her seat. She shifted awkwardly, curious at where he was going with this line of conversation, but also vaguely suspicious.

"I think someone close to her is doing something wrong to her, and as much as I want to tell her, we've only just re-kindled our friendship and I feel it would be wrong to burst in with accusations and no proof," he said.

She felt her cheeks flush with jealousy. She bit her lower lip and held her voice steady. "Is this meant to be a romantic gesture?" she asked softly.

He laughed. "I've eyes for only one person right now," he said intently as he stared deeply into her eyes. "I just can't sit around and watch a childhood friend get hurt."

She looked at him curiously, eyeing him closely while she mentally scrutinized his proposal. But before she could give it much thought, he grabbed her by the hips and slid her onto his lap. Reaching up her shirt he squeezed her nipple firmly and she squeaked, twitching in his lap. She could feel something hard beneath her. With his other hand he grabbed her hand and grazed it over his lap.

"Want this?" he asked, softly breathing into her ear, and she nodded eagerly. "Want it now?"

Her eyes flickered and she moaned softly. He put his hand up her skirt again.

"Hmmm, good girl. Already ready. Take them off," he murmured and she slid her panties down to her knees. As she leaned over to push them the rest of the way off, she heard the sound of him undoing his zipper. She turned to face him but he stopped her with his lips. They kissed long and deep, him pushing his tongue deep into her mouth. He suddenly broke off the kiss and pushed her face away from his. He grabbed her hips, pushing her skirt out of the way as he pulled her buttocks towards him, spread her legs open over his and slowly slid inside her. Once all the way in, he put his hands up her shirt and onto her breasts, holding her down. He pinched, flicked and pulled with both of his hands, taking delight in her moaning. She rode him faster and faster, almost reaching her second climax of the night when he suddenly grabbed her hips and held her down onto him. She squirmed but he held her firmly. He waited until her breathing grew more steady, then abruptly resumed his thrusting and quickly brought her to climax. She screamed as she orgasmed then quickly covered her mouth, remembering where she was. He pulled her back against his chest, her head on his shoulder, stroking her breasts softly as she slowly regained her composure.

"Will you help me, princess?" he asked her softy.

She nodded, "Anything you want."

The dim lights trembled as the train roared by overhead. The building creaked with age and groaned as it settled with the passing train. The walls were adorned with random scatterings of wallpaper left over from a bad makeover probably done in the seventies. The paper had peeled back to reveal old, faded brick. The overhead lamps resembled tacky tiffany lamps that looked like they came from someone's grandmother's house, complete with cracked and missing glass panels. The floor was stained a dark brown or black; sadly, probably real wood beneath the cheap paint. At least the tables and chairs matched. The bar was the one highlight in this whole establishment. It was a rich red mahogany that looked like it was polished and cleaned daily. The bartender, however, matched more of the room's décor than the bar itself. Old, sad, grumpy and disheveled. A little time and money and this place could easily be jazzed up. But then, where else would we go when we were desperate to have a drink to clear our thoughts in privacy? Even the empty ones.

I looked around the bar from my seat at the counter. A man who sat in the far back by the jukebox looked liked he'd been wearing the same clothes for days. A look of lost hope flickered from his eyes as he took another sip out of his glass. A faded and worn out prostitute sat across from him, feigning hope for herself that another trick might soon walk into the bar. A businessman sat down the bar from me, drowning whatever sorrows he had in an already half-empty bottle of Jack Daniels.

I set my shot glass onto the bar counter with gentle ease. Everything was falling into place. Slowly but surely. The voices in my head had left me behind for the day. Like a shadow in the background, I liked to think I could easily walk away from the voices, but knew I had to pay them great respect lest I feel the consequences. But I knew with each passing moment I was growing stronger and closer to my goal. I tossed a handful of cash onto the counter and slid off the bar stool. Slowly I glided towards the door. With a hand on the door handle, I turned to look back one last time, taunting the voices to come back.

To give them one last chance. With a sly smile on my face I realized I was free. Free to take the next step.

CHAPTER FIFTEEN

Her phone beeped from deep within her purse. Nicola was balancing a tray of hot drinks and croissants in one hand and three bags full of antiques in the other. She stopped briefly, contemplating the possibility of actually being able to retrieve her phone safely, then decided to ignore it. It chirped again and again. She cursed under her breath as she waved down a taxi with a leg shake. The driver, like most in this city, didn't get out to help her. She set the drinks on top of the cab and opened the door. She gently set her bags inside the cab as her pocket chirped yet again.

"Christ," she muttered under her breath. "Who died this time?" she grumbled as she grabbed her drinks and sat down inside the cab. She recited the office address as her phone continued to chirp.

The cabbie chuckled. "You're a popular lady," he said as he turned the car back into traffic.

Nicola rolled her eyes and pulled out her phone. It beeped in her hand as she turned it over. Fifteen new text messages. All from a private number. All had the same context: 'Missing you', 'Thinking of you', and 'Be mine'. She jumped as her phone beeped yet again in her hands.

She quickly shut the phone off and shoved it back into her pocket.

Patsy sat outside the 'Lovestruck Motel' awaiting the arrival of Karim and this week's mystery woman. In the past three weeks, Patsy had observed that Karim frequented two regular motels. This one was for his one-time girls and his visits were irregular. However, he was remarkably easy to follow, completely oblivious of his surroundings, like he wasn't even attempting to hide what he was doing. She hadn't wanted to believe Gregory at first, but when he told her at which motel he had seen Karim, and she checked it out herself, she was floored. Following Karim had become an obsession for her. She couldn't believe that he was doing this to Nicola.

The other hotel was classier and located inside the city centre instead of the outskirts, like the one she was outside right now. To the nicer hotel he brought only one woman. Her name was Miranda Holkstein. She was young, twenty-one-years-old, but not as young as some of the floozies he brought here. Miranda was an up-and-coming actress and singer. She had already starred in several movies as a child, but made the move here to take a stab at live theatrical productions, primarily musicals. Karim had taken her on as a new client to help broaden his horizons. She was his first and only non-film client. And broaden his horizons she had.

The two of them had started hooking up shortly after he signed her—or so his gossiping secretary had let on. Unlike his one time floozies, Miranda didn't have to sleep with him to get his interest. Patsy had found out from the hotel that he had been checking into room 2715 for the last four months every Tuesday and Friday evenings, checking out the following day. He paid with a credit card, from a separate bank than his and Nicola's. Patsy, with help from Gregory, had checked into that same room the other day and installed two cameras. One was hidden in the headboard and the other at the entrance to the room. Tomorrow she should have sufficient footage to help Gregory prove to Nicola that Karim was indeed a very bad man.

Today, by chance, she had seen Karim outside a café in her neighbourhood when she was out running errands. She saw him go in with a woman to get a coffee, and then the two of them sat down outside chatting and flirting. Impulsively, Patsy drove straight to the motel and awaited Karim's potential arrival. She figured she would wait a half hour, then if he didn't show she'd leave and just wait until tomorrow. Here, despite being a regular, he didn't have an exclusive room for himself.

Patsy pulled out a Tupperware container and set it on the passenger seat. She opened it to reveal carrot and celery sticks in one half and homemade hummus in the other, loaded with tons of garlic. She wasn't expecting to see Gregory until tomorrow night, so today was her day to indulge. She was halfway through her snack when a taxi pulled up in front of the motel, so she whipped her camera up from her lap and aimed it at the taxi. She peered through the lens, zoomed in and focused, but it was a false alarm. An elderly man with an obvious prostitute were getting out of the car and she chuckled, wishing the man a heart-attack-free encounter with the woman young enough to be his granddaughter. She put the camera back onto her lap and resumed eating. She had to get back to the office soon or Nicola might become suspicious. She figured she'd leave after she finished eating her snack.

She had just put the Tupperware back into her bag when another taxi pulled up. Again, she whipped out the camera and focused on the passengers. Karim stepped out of the car, then reached in and helped out the young woman Patsy had seen him with earlier. The woman was very giggly and all over him. He feigned interest with a smile so fake that Patsy was surprised that the girl had bought it. Patsy zoomed in on the girl. She still had braces. Couldn't be more then eighteen, tops. She looked over at Karim who had that big phoney smile on his face. Patsy shook her head with disgust. She didn't know what was worse—an ongoing affair or random hookups with barely legal teenagers. She snapped enough pictures to satisfy herself and watched them go inside.

She took her laptop out of her bag, turned it sideways and set it on her lap. Taking the SD card from the camera, she put it in the laptop and uploaded the pictures she just took. Quickly she put them into an encrypted folder—courtesy of Gregory—and then emailed it to him. She looked through the various folders which she had separated into two categories, FLOOZIES and MIRANDA. She opened 'Floozies' and put the new folder, with today's date as its name, into the folder. She gasped as she realized how many there were: ten. Already? Which truthfully didn't sound like much until you realized that she had only been taking pictures of him for just under a month, and he was also hooking up with Miranda twice a week. She wondered if he took Viagra.

She shook her head with disgust again, packed her bag and drove off to work.

Nicola tapped a business card absently on the desk. She didn't have anything new that she could investigate. She had given everything to her sister Sarah. She wasn't sure if reviewing old facts would help her get a jump on her stalker or not, or just provide her with more frustration.

She picked up her phone and dialled the florist shop number, but quickly hung up before the call could connect. Nicola had called both of her sisters as soon as she had left the clinic that day, and they both swore that they neither told anyone else, nor sent the basket. Cassandra even went as far to assure her that she hadn't even told her husband about Nicola's appointment. Cassandra knew he could be a bit overbearing with his enthusiasm, and knew that Nicola wouldn't be comfortable with that. Karim obviously hadn't sent it, nor had Patsy. Nicola felt useless just sitting in her office, waiting for her stalker to strike next. She wanted to get a jump on him. Figure out his next move.

She pulled a notepad out of her desk and started scribbling down facts. Time, date, location and various other notes she could recall. She had filled out two pages when a thought dawned on her. Her lips slowly curled into a smile, grinning like the cheshire cat. She got out of her chair, threw on her jacket and dashed out the door.

The shrill tone of Skype echoed throughout the house as Cassandra unlocked her front door and kicked it open with her knee since her hands were full of groceries. She nudged the door shut with her hip and sauntered into the kitchen. The Skype ring ended and she looked in the direction of the computer. After a moment of silence she started to unpack the groceries. She had emptied half of the first bag when she heard the Skype call again. Setting down the peanut butter she went over to her laptop. Sarah was calling her. Above the calling icon were several messages from Sarah. She sat down and answered the call.

Sarah's face filled the screen. Her hair was a jumbled mess and random chunks of hair stuck out erratically like she had just crawled out of bed. Her clothes looked like she hadn't changed them in days and there were orange Cheetos stains on her cheek. Cassandra laughed at the sight of her sister.

"You look amazing, Sarah."

"Are you sitting down?" Sarah asked her urgently.

Cassandra looked at her cautiously, but sat down at the desk. "Yeah. What's wrong?"

"I found something. Something impossible. I've spent the last three days researching it. At the library here, online, even at the library back home."

"Slow down, take a deep breath, Sarah. And I can kinda tell. You look like it. When did you last have a shower?"

"This isn't the time, Cass. This is serious."

"You're scaring me now. What did you find out? Did you find something about Nicola's stalker?" she asked.

"No. This is worse. Much, much worse." Sarah took a newspaper article and held it up to the screen. "Can you see it?" she asked.

Cassandra squinted her eyes. "Hold it back a little, it's super fuzzy." Sarah moved the article back a few inches.

"Yeah, okay, hold it there." She cocked her head from side to side. "Is that mom and dad? They look young."

"But who else do you see?" Sarah asked.

"I think that's Nicola. But the baby, is that me?" Cassandra asked.

Sarah put down the article. "No. It's our brother."

Cassandra's jaw dropped and her eyes literally flew wide open. Like Wile E. Coyote as he realized he had just run off the cliff. She made gurgling noises as she tried to ask Sarah what the hell she was talking about. They didn't have a brother. Suddenly Cassandra found her voice and the questions just flew out. What happened to him? Where is he now? Why didn't they know about him?

Sarah looked at her sister, her eyes slightly watery and her face grim. "He died. When mom was pregnant with you," she said.

Cassandra blinked, her hands involuntarily flexing into fists. "How?" she whispered.

"The article says he drowned. Nicola apparently was with him in the bathtub playing. Mom left them alone to go answer the phone. When she returned he was dead. They don't go into much detail on the 'how'. The only other reference beyond that to Nicola is a quote someone overheard. Apparently she told the police officer, 'We were making bubbles, but then he stopped. Why did he stop?' "

Cassandra's hands flew to her mouth and she felt tears fall down her cheeks.

"It gets worse, Cass. The newspapers all blamed mom. They chastised dad for staying with her. Mom and dad even moved out-of-state because the harassment was terrible, especially with mom being pregnant."

"That's why. That's why she treats her so badly… why we weren't allowed to play with her…" Cassandra muttered under her breath.

"What did you say, Cass? Who? I don't understand what you said."

"Sarah, mother blames her. Mother blames Nicola," Cassandra said.

The look of confusion on Sarah's face was quickly replaced with a look of clarity, followed by shock. "No. That's impossible. It was an accident. Nicola was only four-years-old. It's mother's fault for leaving her alone."

"I know," Cassandra said softly.

"We have to tell her, Cass. We have to tell her that we know."

"I don't know if that's a good idea right now, Sarah. She's already under a ton of stress."

"Cass, c'mon, she needs our support. She's reaching out to us now with the stalker stuff, but only because we can be helpful. She's afraid to depend on us too much. We have to tell her we know and that we don't blame her," Sarah argued.

"Maybe. Are you positive that this story is real? That it's really our mother and father?" she asked.

"Yes. I'm very, very positive. I even got a copy of the article from the local newspaper of the town that they lived in then. Did you know that you were almost born in a different state?"

Cassandra leaned back in her chair, trying to absorb the information Sarah had just revealed to her, still reeling from the shock of it all. But, despite the insanity of it all, it made so many things finally make sense. It explained mother's behaviour and father's reluctance to really stop it. It explained the many unanswered questions, the small lies they kept telling them.

"Sarah?" she asked her quietly.

"What?"

"How do we face mother now?" she asked. The two girls just stared at each other, neither one able to answer.

The front door opened and Cassandra's husband and children came bursting in.

"Sarah, the family's home. I have to go. Email me the articles and I'll talk to you tomorrow, okay?"

"Sure. Talk to you soon. Love you."

"Love you, too. Bye."

Cassandra closed the laptop slowly and looked up to see her husband towering over her. She jumped up and hugged him tightly. Then she rushed over to her children and squeezed them so firmly that they started to whine and complain that she was squishing them. She let them go reluctantly, a tear in her eye. Her husband reached down, put a hand on her shoulder and looked at her with curiosity.

CHAPTER SIXTEEN

Nicola stumbled into the office, defeat written all over her face. Patsy held out a chai latte for her as she walked past the desk. She stopped and looked at Patsy. She looked down at her chai, took a sip and then gave Patsy a suspicious look. "How is it that the chai you give me is always hot? We don't have a microwave," she asked.

"I'm working with your stalker?" Patsy said innocently as she batted her eyelashes dramatically.

Nicola blinked her eyes in disbelief as she shook her head and dropped her jaw slightly.

"You are seriously way too gullible," Patsy said, laughing as she got up from her chair.

She waved a hand indicating to Nicola that she should follow her, and they walked into the closet which, as far as Nicola knew, was where they kept all of the cleaning supplies for the janitor and their basic office supplies. It was quite tiny and couldn't hold much more than that. Under much duress, Nicola had, in the end, allowed Patsy to install a bar fridge in the closet so they could keep snacks and drinks on hand. Nicola herself could never remember to feed herself, let alone remember to buy anything to put in it, so it was pretty much Patsy's fridge.

Directly above the fridge was a shelf that held a mini espresso machine.

Nicola gave her the evil eye. "You drink coffee now?" she asked suspiciously.

Patsy shook her head. "Custom made, all it does is steam milk," she said, opening the fridge. Inside it were several cartons of milk and chai tea mix.

"Do we really drink that much?" Nicola asked her, surprised, as they exited the closet.

Patsy closed the door behind them. "In only one month we've paid off half the cost of the machine with what we've saved by not buying at the café. So yes, you drink that much," she said with a laugh.

Nicola shot her a dirty look as Patsy smirked back at her before nodding, impressed. "Okay. I approve," she said and Patsy laughed.

Nicola went back towards her office as Patsy sat down at her desk. "Any progress?" Patsy asked.

Nicola shook her head. "It's been a quiet couple of weeks. Maybe he's stopped." she said wistfully.

"Then I might have some bad news," Patsy said, reaching into her desk drawer and pulling out a small package. Nicola stopped and turned around. Patsy gingerly held the package out towards Nicola. "This came for you while you were out earlier."

Nicola came back to the desk and looked at the package. She went to take it but Patsy pulled it away before she could touch it. Instead she offered a pair of latex gloves to Nicola. It was then that Nicola realized that Patsy herself was not only wearing gloves as she held the package, but noticed how carefully she was holding it, with a handkerchief, to obviously not smear any fingerprints that could be on it.

As Nicola took the gloves and put them on, Patsy handed her the package. It was quite small and appeared to be an envelope for CDs to be mailed in, but it was also protruding in the centre. She looked the package over. It had her name and the business address but no return address. The postal stamp was their city. She turned it over carefully.

"Why am I wearing gloves?" Nicola asked absently.

" 'Cuz your sister Sarah is a CSI wannabe. Maybe one of her groupies can look for fingerprints and other clues on it?"

Nicola nodded and agreed that it was a good idea. Patsy handed her a letter opener and Nicola shook the package lightly, but whatever was inside was tightly wrapped and she could hear nothing. She took the letter opener and sliced the end of the package open.

She set the letter opener down and looked inside the envelope. She couldn't make out what it was so she carefully put her fingers inside, felt a small box, grabbed it and pulled it out. She set it on the desk and shook the envelope again. It appeared to be empty. Patsy already had a large ziplock baggie out and Nicola put the envelope in it.

Nicola laughed lightly. "Sure you're not a CSI groupie yourself?"

Patsy rolled her eyes. Nicola looked down at the box. It was a plain brown jewellery box. Nothing special, no store name on it anywhere. Probably bought at a dollar store. She picked it up and opened it. Inside was an old silver locket. She pulled it out of the box and handed the box to Patsy.

Still using the hankie, Patsy held the box with one hand while prying the remainder of its contents out with the tip of the letter opener. Under the padding she found a folded up piece of paper.

"Nic," she said, holding the paper out towards Nicola with the blade tip.

Still holding onto the locket Nicola took the paper, unfolding it several times to find a note that read 'Remembering old times'. She put it and the box into another ziplock baggie and then held the locket directly in front of her face.

"I remember a locket like this," she said.

"Really? When?" Patsy asked.

"A long, long time ago. I think my mother used to wear one similar to this one," she said absently. Patsy had never heard Nicola mention her mother before and wanted to ask her more but the look in Nicola's eyes warned her not to. Nicola took a deep breath, opened the locket and gasped. Patsy jumped to her feet, demanding to know what was wrong, what was inside. Nicola's face wrenched in pain and she turned the locket towards Patsy. Patsy reached for the locket gingerly and looked inside it. She saw two pictures; both, presumably, of Nicola. The first was Nicola when she was either three- or maybe four-years-old, sitting in a bathtub wearing a plastic bowl as a hat. The other one was a family portrait of Nicola, Cassandra, Sarah, and their parents. Everyone was cuddling together closely except for Nicola, who was sitting on the floor beneath them, looking quite unhappy as she stared at the vast gulf between her and the rest of the family.

Patsy looked up at Nicola, who was doing her best to maintain her composure.

"We tell no one. Not the police. Not Karim. Just Sarah. We'll give her all of this and see if she and her groupies can find any clues we can use," said Nicola, and Patsy slowly nodded in agreement.

Nicola dropped the locket into the baggie as Patsy pulled out an express post envelope.

Nicola dropped her purse on the kitchen island. She tossed her keys into the ceramic cat tray, overshooting it, and the keys went sailing onto the floor. She groaned and rubbed her temples. Kneeling down she picked the keys up off the floor and gingerly set them into the cat tray. She opened the fridge and grabbed herself a beer. She cracked it open and took a long drink.

It had been a long week for her. Patsy had called in sick more than once, but not consecutively. Which normally wouldn't be a problem, except today she had lined up several back-to-back appointments with new clients and she had hoped that Patsy would cover one or two of them, allowing her to take a break. On top of that she wasn't able to search for anything today. While she was happy to secure new clients, three of which would be ongoing clients, she always felt more productive when she spent the day hunting down rare items and securing them for her clients.

Sarah and her crime-fighting groupies had also come up empty handed. The only positive thing was that she hadn't heard anything from her stalker since the locket had arrived more than a week ago. She ignored the quiet voice in her head urging her that she was being lulled into a false sense of security again.

Nicola opened the fridge again and poked around it. Leftovers, stale bread, expired yogurt and more leftovers. Their cupboard was even more bare. Neither she nor Karim had remembered to go grocery shopping in the past month as both had eaten either at work or out too much recently, since they were both working long hours these days. They were literally passing out at home with barely enough energy to shower, let alone eat. She had hardly seen him in almost two weeks now, his face a fleeting image as she either fell into slumber or stumbled out the door to work. She looked at the clock. Karim would have left work already. Too late for take-out, so she called for delivery. She picked up their landline and hit speed dial number 6: Lucky Panda Chinese food.

She quickly placed their usual order and hung up the phone smiling. The guilty pleasure of having ordered from the same place often, they recognized her voice and knew her order by heart. She heard the door as she took a sip of her beer. She went to set it down when Karim took it out of her hands and finished it. He belched to the side, pecked her on the cheek and tossed the empty into the sink. She sighed and rolled her eyes as he grabbed two more beers out of the fridge and tossed her one. She caught it easily and set it down to settle before opening it. He dragged a stool over to the other side of the island and sat across from her.

"Hi, babe," he said smoothly, giving her his best Blue Steel impersonation.

She rolled her eyes again and opened her beer in his face. It fizzed slightly, spitting in his face. He pouted with great exaggeration but quickly turned it into a sly, shy smile. She smiled back as he reached across and brushed the hair out of her face. She closed her eyes and sighed deeply, settling her face into his hand. She cupped his hand with hers as he stood up, him leaning over the island and kissing her softly on the lips. As he sat back down she slowly opened her eyes and smiled.

They sat like that for quite awhile, enjoying the peaceful silence between them. It had been ages since they had a moment like this, and even longer since they'd been able to take the time to enjoy it. He leaned in again for a kiss, pulling her face towards him, forcing her to lean across the island. The doorbell chimed, breaking their silence, and Karim looked at her hopefully, "Chinese?"

"No, a new vegan restaurant I wanted to try out," she answered him as seriously as possible. His face fell and he looked crestfallen as she bounced out of her chair and rushed to the door, hiding the smirk on her face. When she returned she held out her hands with two unmarked brown paper bags. Karim started to look more hopeful and stole one of the two bags out of her hands before she could set them down onto the island, ripping into the bag eagerly and reaching in.

He pulled out a typical white and red Chinese food carton and held it high in the air, like he had just won the Stanley Cup.

"Yes!" he cried triumphantly. He emptied both bags quickly as she produced two more beers out of the fridge. He scavenged all of the rice for himself and the gong bao chicken. She took the ma po tofu and slowly started to nibble at it. She scored a quick bite of his rice when he wasn't looking, which prompted a chopstick war that she easily won. He handed the rice over reluctantly as she grinned, taking a large bite of the rice in victory, then pushed it back to his side.

"So..." she started.

"So?" he said as he looked up from his carton, mouth full and rice dribbling down his chin. She muffled a laugh knowing he would easily deter her from this conversation if she let him.

"I saw the doctor again the other day," she said as he grunted a reply with a mouthful of food. "The fertility specialist," she paused and looked at him carefully over the edge of her carton of food.

He continued eating. She wasn't sure if he had heard her or not.

"She ran a bunch more tests on me and said if they return negative as well, that I have a few more fertility drug options to try to increase, well, me, I guess."

He nodded absently, his interest obviously feigned.

She ignored this and continued on. "Is there anything you want to know? About what I'm going to do?"

"Is there anything I really need to know? Doesn't it mostly affect you?" he asked.

"I guess not. I mean, it's pretty much all for me..." she said letting her sentence trail off.

"Then no, not really. I'm not really needed until something happens right?"

"Yeah. Right," she said reluctantly. She twiddled her chopsticks in her fingers and then tapped them on the edge of her beer before sticking them upright in her food. She stood up from her seat.

He sighed and reached over, quickly putting his hand on hers.

"Babe, I'm sorry," he said. "Please."

She looked at him, eyes full of tears.

"I know this is important to you. It's just that, well, with all that is going on, I thought you might want to take it easy for a bit," he said.

Nicola sat back down. "I guess so," she said softly.

He took her hands in his. "What can I do to make it better?"

"I don't know. Karim, I still want a baby. And creepy stalker or not, I don't want to put my life on hold for him. They'll find him eventually, won't they?" she asked.

"Of course they will," he said reassuringly, stroking her hands.

"So I just want to keep living life like I do everyday. He's just a hiccup in my day. A temporary hiccup," she said defiantly. "We can do this, right?"

"You can do anything you set your heart to, babe." He leaned over and kissed her on the forehead. "So tell me, what does the doctor want me to do? Other than have sex with you everywhere in every position possible. Maybe we should stop going to work and just have sex all day, everyday," he said, staring off into the sky with a happy smile on his face. She grabbed his chin and shook his head.

"She said you have to wait on me hand and foot every day until the end of time. With strawberries, champagne and chocolate."

"Oh really? Why don't I believe you?" he said laughing.

"Okay, maybe just strawberries," she pinched his nose and he swatted her hand away playfully.

"Actually, she said that while I'm taking the fertility drugs to increase my girlness, you could go donate sperm to have on standby," she said, and noticed out of the corner of her eye that he suddenly grew rigid and sat up stiffly in his chair.

"On standby? For what?" he asked, a slight strain creeping into his voice.

"Well, if after the drugs don't work they can try a process called in vitro fertilization. They take my eggs and your sperm and make a baby in the lab then put it in me," she said slowly, watching him carefully as she gauged his reaction.

He frowned. "I don't think I like the idea of a lab baby. Won't the drugs work? How long will it take before we know?"

She bit her lip. She knew that he was goading her into an argument to distract her from something else, but she didn't know what.

"It's not a lab baby. It'll grow in me silly," she said as she grabbed at his hands and he pulled away.

"I'm not sure I like that option," he said, his voice even more agitated, and she stared at him with surprise.

"We don't have to do it. It's just one of the options to try if the drugs don't work. I haven't gone over all the details yet, but it can take months before we know if the drugs are being effective or not."

He suddenly started eating again, paused, went to speak , then filled his mouth with food. When his mouth was finally empty he set down the carton.

"I think I'd rather wait and try the drugs first. We'll cross the next bridge when it comes."

She grabbed his hand and squeezed it tightly. "Of course, honey. There's no rush."

She leaned over to kiss him and he reluctantly kissed her back. She sat back down, a small pout on her face, pretending to be hurt when inside she was actually crushed. She knew something was wrong. Really wrong. His mood had changed so quickly. She wondered if having a baby was what had made them less intimate. Maybe they needed a little spice and spontaneity, she thought suddenly.

She stood up from her seat and took her clothes off, leaving only her panties on. He paused mid-bite and she leaned back over the island and kissed him again. She broke the kiss and grinned at him.

"Isn't that a bit better?" she asked playfully.

He looked at her with a serious look on his face and said, "Your boob is in my gong bao chicken."

Standing up, she put her hands on her hips and glared at him. He grinned ear-to-ear, stood up and reached across the island and pulled her onto it, knocking his food all over the counter and floor.

"Yeah, babe, much better."

Sarah took the recording of the most recent voice message that Nicola sent her and examined it. One of her hobbies was solving crimes. She was the president of her branch of CSI intern members. Once every two or three months, the club would get together and re-enact an old crime scene. Half the members were responsible for setting the scene while the other half would solve it. Sarah preferred setting the scenes; she felt it increased her skills at perception better and that it was a personal challenge to set the perfect, impossible-to-solve crime scene.

She had recently acquired a voice recognition software program, and while she had been experimenting with it, she hadn't had the opportunity to try it out with an actual unknown voice. She copied the voice file from the USB stick directly into the software. She had to wait a minute while it loaded itself into the program, then once ready, she began to run basic filters through it. Her first task was to try and identify age and gender since the voice was most likely filtered through some voice adapting program. It sounded almost mechanical to her. After several filters she had determined it was either an early twenties female or late twenties male. Truthfully she thought, it probably could be any age. The filters were easy to manipulate if you didn't know the basic program that altered the original voice.

Then she tried to filter out the background noise. After an hour of pulling various sounds she was able to isolate four different sounds. There was the sound of a train running in the background, along with the sound of a train station announcement. She couldn't isolate it well enough to be able to distinguish specific words in the announcement, but she could recognize the male automated voice. She also heard the sound of a door with a bell above it that clanged each time the door was opened. She speculated that the door was closer to the person making the call than the train station. Lastly she could hear a bird chirping. She had no idea what kind of bird it was, but she was running it through the program. She had also downloaded a variety of sounds along with the program that would allow her to search the database and help isolate myriad sounds.

She wasn't sure how long the program would take to figure out what bird it was, if the program could even identify it. So she left the program running and shot an email to Cassandra and Nicola, informing them of what she had found out. There was a knock on her door and she called her roommate in. He handed her a Fedex package and quickly left. She chuckled, knowing that her nerdiness made him nervous. The amount of high-tech gear she kept in her bedroom she imagined rivalled the local police stations, and her roommate was very conservative, technology wise.

She ripped open the package to find a couple of cassette tapes and a note from Nicola. She smiled and pulled out her cassette player, eager to start the new task at hand. She looked at her clock, realizing how late it had gotten. She turned towards her computer and placed an order from her favourite pizzeria. It was going to be a long night.

Nicola waltzed into the office, a woman on a mission. She had had this brilliant idea a couple of weeks ago but had kept putting it off. She smiled at Patsy who looked back at her with wonder as she strolled into her office, arms full of bags from the local office supply store. Patsy got out of her chair and followed her, lingering at the doorway. She watched as Nicola dumped the contents of her shopping bag onto the table: glue sticks, stars and circle stickers, post-its, push pins, scotch tape, a variety of coloured string, sharpies of all colours, and several large pieces of poster board. Nicola scanned the room and settled her direction on the sliding chalk board. She went over to it, slide it to the left and revealed behind it an unused cork board. She smiled and grabbed a piece of the poster board. She tacked it in the middle of the cork board.

Then she opened up the package of sharpies and grabbed a pile of post-its. She put one in the middle of the cork board and drew a large question mark on it. Above it she wrote 'STALKER'. Then she went to her filing cabinet and pulled out a shoebox. She opened it and looked back and forth between the box's contents and the board. She bit her lower lip and tapped her thigh subconsciously. She continued to look between the two, her face a mixture of concentration and puzzlement.

Patsy cleared her throat and Nicola looked up at her. "Can I help?" Patsy asked her.

Nicola bit her lower lip. "It's not really work related—" she started and Patsy chuckled.

"Are you sure? I thought he was a new client?" Nicola stared at her for a moment, stunned, before bursting out in laughter.

She laughed so heartily that she had to grab her stomach to stop, and crouched down low when the tears leaked out of the corners of her eyes.

"Oh... my... god," she said between fits of laughter. "I haven't laughed that hard in quite awhile. Thank you. Oh god, thank you. I needed that," she said as Patsy helped her to her feet.

"So, boss. What troubles you?"

"That no one knows who this—" she said pointing at the word 'stalker' on her board—"is. I know Sarah is doing her best, but I feel that I can do more. That I need to do more. That I need to take control of this situation and deal with it myself since it's obvious the police aren't going to be much help. It's just all so unorganized right now," she said triumphantly. She then pointed to the board and her meagre supply of clues in the shoe box. "I'm not sure how to organize this… stuff."

Patsy combed through the clues and then looked back at the board, then to the pile of supplies. She grabbed another poster board and placed it to overlap the top left corner of the centre one. She took a sharpie and wrote 'CLUES' on the top centre of it. Then below it and to the far left, she wrote in smaller letters 'DATE'. Beside it she wrote 'CLUE', then 'ORIGIN', 'NOTES' and 'SUSPECTS'. Then she took the first item out of the box—the valentine sent in the mail—and tacked it under 'clue'. Beside it she wrote the date. Under 'origin' she wrote down the post office's address that Nicola had traced it to from the postal stamp on the valentine. Finally, under 'notes' she wrote 'unable to trace item farther; fingerprints?'

"Alright?" she asked, looking at Nicola.

Nicola smiled brightly. "That's brilliant! Simple and easy, yet informative!"

Patsy smiled back. "What's next?"

Nicola reached into the box and pulled out a piece of paper. On it were the time and dates of the voice messages left and whether their location was her cellphone or home machine. Patsy pulled out the locket and the two women began to fill out the board, making small notations everywhere.

"Soooo…" Nicola started slowly. "How's your new beau?" she asked suddenly, chuckling lightly as Patsy turned bright red.

"How did you know?" she stammered.

Nicola laughed and explained to her the little differences she had noticed: Patsy's makeup had changed slightly, she was smiling more. But most importantly, that she was constantly rushing out of the office at the end of the day. Patsy continued to turn more, and deeper, shades of red as Nicola continued on, asking her when she was going to get to meet this man.

Patsy racked her mind for an excuse. She knew that now was not the right time to introduce Gregory as her beau to Nicola. She knew that Gregory and Nicola still met for coffee on a weekly basis, but he had obviously not mentioned his relationship with Patsy, and she knew that it could ruin everything that both of them were working on.

Nicola's calling out her name while waving a hand in front of her face broke Patsy out of her thoughts, and she muttered an explanation of them not being serious yet, so she wanted to wait before introducing him to Nicola. Nicola scoffed at her and rolled her eyes before admitting she was just enjoying teasing her. Patsy sighed with relief and resumed working on the chart, not noticing the careful way Nicola was watching her.

CHAPTER SEVENTEEN

Gregory sat in a café, the afternoon sun slowly setting. The usual coffee crowd was dwindling as everyone was heading home for dinner and time with their families. Only the die-hards and artistic-types filled the sparse area around him. He liked this time of the evening best. He found it much easier to focus on his tasks at hand with minimal distraction, and frequented the café often around this time.

He set his laptop out onto the table and sipped his coffee, his eyes flickering back and forth as he scanned picture after picture. Patsy had not only sent him a new batch of photos but had uploaded him a whole weekend's worth of video footage from Karim's hotel room. He was quickly skimming through the videos and deleting anything that didn't have Karim in it, lest he get caught with anything inappropriate—considering how illegal it was for him to have filmed in the hotel room in the first place. He made a mental note to book a night there soon so he and Patsy could remove the video cameras before they were accidentally discovered.

He was shaking his head with disgust at what he saw. He couldn't believe how far Karim had gone to betray

Nicola. Gregory knew he was skating on thin ice, by wanting to expose Karim, but he felt obligated to Nicola. She had saved him when they were children. Brought him out of his shell and given him meaning. Without her he wouldn't have been able to exist and would have remained a hollowed-out boy, lost inside himself. He had just hoped that when he had finally found her again, he would have been able to show his appreciation and thanks in a much better way.

He looked up from his laptop and discovered the sun had almost set completely. A quick look at his watch made him realize he had to hurry, he had prior engagements to attend to shortly. He closed his laptop and rushed out of the cafe.

"I'm tired of coming home to this," Karim shouted, slamming their front door open. It banged against the wall, causing the shelves to vibrate and rattle. He rushed inside, throwing his keys at the ceramic cat tray with such force that the it slid off the island and smashed to the floor, shattering into hundreds of pieces.

"Fuck!" he cursed. He grabbed a beer from the fridge and stormed out of the kitchen.

"Christ, Karim! Maybe if you actually tried talking with me once in awhile about it I wouldn't feel the need to nag you daily. It's not my fault my body rejected the drugs so quickly and badly."

Nicola let the door slowly close behind her and inhaled a long, deep breath. She stayed at the door, listening to him storm about the apartment.

"Maybe you should just let it happen if it happens. Why do we have to try so hard?" he shouted from the living room as he turned on the television and turned the volume up.

She put her keys on the island and looked down at the broken cat on the floor, and sighed heavily. She picked up his keys and clenched them in her fist. She bit back her tears and dropped the keys on the island.

Stepping carefully over the broken pieces, she made her way to the living room. She snatched the remote from his hands and muted the television. He jumped to his feet and reached for the remote. She stepped back, took the batteries out of the remote and slid them into her pocket and tossed the remote onto the couch.

"We weren't finished 'talking', Karim," she said slowly, each word leeching out of her mouth like sharpened knives, carefully controlled.

"I'm done talking about it. It hasn't happened, I'm tired of always talking about it, I'm tired of you telling me to go to the doctor, I'm tired of having to try too hard at something that's supposed to be a thing of 'nature'." He crossed his arms across his chest in defiance, striking a typical alpha-male pose.

She dropped her arms in half-defeat. "I'm sorry that my plumbing is broken and I require assistance. Nothing's perfect Karim—"

"Things used to be perfect, before you suddenly started wanting a baby," he spit out, interrupting her.

She gasped and took a step back away from him, her arms instinctively drawing to her chest. A look of surprise and hurt fell on her face. "What are you saying?"

He sighed heavily and lowered his stance. "I'm saying I miss how things used to be. Before you wanted a baby, we never fought. We never argued over anything big. We could talk," he said softly.

She felt her anger rising inside. His words sounded right and made sense, but they upset her all the same. He made it sound like it was her fault.

"I want a baby? It takes two to make a baby Karim."

"Apparently it takes a team for us," he muttered under his breath.

"Why is the baby thing such a big deal for you? I thought you wanted one too?" she asked.

"Why is the baby thing such a big deal for you, Nicola? You never wanted a baby before, and now suddenly you not only want a baby, but it's become an obsession for you. I'm tired of this obsession. Why can't we just wait and see if it happens? If it doesn't, then maybe we're not meant to be parents. Have you ever thought of that?" he spewed.

"I'm not obsessed!" she retorted.

"Yes, you are. If I hadn't convinced you to wait until you were actually pregnant we would've already have a completely furnished baby room a year ago. You've probably already picked out its name without even knowing the gender. Every day it's doctor this, pills this, what should we do Karim, how about this Karim, baby this, baby that. I'm tired of it. I already told you what I wanted. What more can I do or say?" He sat down on the couch, putting his head in his hands as he hunched over, frustrated and tired.

Nicola stood her ground but could feel her anger simmering down as she looked at how broken Karim was. Maybe he was right. She might have become a tiny bit obsessed. Especially since she first had the thought that something might be wrong with her. Like most things, she just charged into it head first without taking into consideration how he felt. She remembered his reaction to her suddenly announcing that she wanted to try having a baby. He looked at her with a giant grin and frankly said, 'That means more sex right? All the time? You won't say no, ever?', and she had laughed. In the following months, he kept proposing new places and positions, insisting that he had been told or read that it would increase their odds. But now look at them. Barely sleeping together.

She sat down next to him and kissed the side of his head. She put a hand on his thigh. "What do you want Karim?"

"I don't want to fight anymore. I'm tired of arguing," he said softly.

She squeezed his thigh. "I can't promise that we'll never argue again. But, I'll try to be more sensitive with my nagging."

"Can we drop the doctor and the baby thing? Just for a little while?" he asked hopefully.

Nicola bit her lower lip and looked away from him. Out of the corner of her eye she could see the stress written across his face. His forehead was crinkled and he had worry lines at the sides of his mouth. When had he aged so much? When did the stress start showing?

She took a deep breath. "Okay. No more baby talk for a few months. Mum's the word. But we will talk about it again, when we're both more ready. Deal?"

He nodded, pulling her into a big hug.

Nicola walked out into the hallway and looked over her shoulder. Karim was finally going back to his office. She had to beg off of him joining her on her run. After their argument earlier, he had settled down in front of the television and she had gone for a walk to clear her head. He hadn't noticed her leave, but he noticed her return, and was upset that she had left without telling him. When she had changed into her running clothes he had followed suit and they almost got into another argument when she insisted she go alone. Finally, she had assured him that she would go to the gym in their building complex and not run outside alone. She got into the elevator and instead of going to the lower floor where the gym was, she hit the button for the top floor. She felt bad lying to him, and guilty because he was obviously trying to make amends, but she knew he would be upset if she told him that she wanted to Skype Cassandra alone. Not that he usually joined in their Skype dates, but he wouldn't understand why she didn't want him overhearing their conversation.

Once she was at the top floor, she walked to the end of the hallway and into the escape stairwell. She pulled her house keys out of her pocket and fumbled through them until she found the one she wanted. At the top of the stairwell was a small ladder that went up about ten feet before ending at the ceiling. To the left of the top of the ladder was a door that led to the roof. When she and Karim first bought the place they had convinced the building owner to give them access to the roof so they could have a vegetable garden. It lasted a couple of years before her business took off and they both got too busy to look after it. However, in that time they had managed to haul up lawn furniture, and even though they never went up there anymore, the furniture remained and the owner never asked for the key back. Nicola had the only key since she was the one who had wanted the garden in the first place. She carefully unlocked the door while dangling from the ladder and deftly swung herself through the open door. She closed the door behind her before making her way up the stairs that led to their makeshift terrace.

Looking around she was pleasantly surprised to see nothing had changed. There were some vegetables growing, reseeded from previous crops. She chuckled at the box of zucchini that had begun to slowly take over the roof. Plant one seed and get a million in return. She remembered the second year of the garden. She tried to convince Karim to buy a mini freezer because she went on a baking spree and was making dozens of loaves of zucchini bread a week. She and Patsy had started giving them away to their clients. She shook her head laughing, knowing that the clients had thought the loaves sweet when truthfully she was just desperate to not eat another piece of them. The furniture was still securely covered despite two years of mother nature.

She pulled a cover off a chair next to the patio table, and then blew the dirt and dust off of the table. Carefully she unzipped her running jacket and took it off, setting it down on the chair. Underneath she wore a tank top over a sports bra and one of those compression belts for support around the tank top. She reached her hands behind her back and under the belt. She felt around until she got a secure grip on her iPad with one hand. Then with the other she unzipped the belt, letting it fall to the ground. She set her iPad on the table and quickly put the jacket back on.

She turned on her iPad and then impatiently tapped the screen as Skype tried calling Cassandra. She wiped the tears from her eye with the cuff of her hoodie. The call disconnected and she dialled again. She knew Cassandra was home. It was only a couple of hours after preschool had let out and it was the middle of the week. They only took the kids out on the weekends, making them earn that privilege with good behaviour during the week. It disconnected again. She pulled out her phone and looked at the text message she had sent Cassandra. She still hadn't read it. She sent another '9-1-1' message to Cassandra and dialled her again on Skype. She begged her iPad to connect her and looked eagerly at her phone, shaking it frantically. Finally Cassandra picked up.

"Hey sis, what's up?" Cassandra asked before noticing the distraught look on her sister's face. "Hey. What happened? Are you okay?"

Nicola shook her head. Cassandra glanced over her shoulder quickly then back at the screen. Nicola could hear the kids squealing in the background.

"I'm sorry, I know it's almost dinner time. I just had to talk to someone," Nicola mumbled.

"What did you say sweetie? Speak up." Cassandra turned back away from the camera. "I'll be there in a minute," she shouted out then looked back at Nicola.

"I'm sorry, this is a bad time," Nicola said.

"No, no, honey. No such thing. They can eat without me. What happened? Did you get something else?" she asked but Nicola shook her head. "Is it Karim?"

Nicola nodded.

Cassandra put her hand on the screen and stroked it. "Oh baby, I'm sorry. What did he do?"

"I think... he... don't know—I think... doesn't..." Nicola blurted between sobs.

Cassandra looked over her shoulder again and shouted, "It's just Sarah, start without me," before looking back at Nicola. "What did that big jerk say this time?"

"Who's there?" Nicola asked.

"No one, just hubby and the kids." Cassandra said with a weird reassuring smile on her face.

"Then why'd you say I was Sarah?" she asked.

Cassandra looked down at her hands. She started to mumble, obviously avoiding an answer, when a shrill voice that Nicola hadn't heard in years interrupted Cassandra.

"Cassandra Jillian Brinks! You and Sarah are being incredibly rude. Tell her it's time for dinner with your family and you'll call her back."

Nicola pushed herself away from the iPad, fear filling her face as her eyes glistened, a single tear running down her cheek. She slowly shook her head from side to side and Cassandra looked at her pleadingly.

"I'm sorry, I got your text when she was right beside me. I turned the computer onto silent so she wouldn't notice it," she said.

Still looking shocked, Nicola softened her posture. "It's okay. You should go."

"Nicky...I'm sorry. I'll call you right after dinner okay?" she said.

Nicola nodded and went to reply but stopped abruptly, staring at the screen. Behind Cassandra their mother had suddenly appeared. She started to ask Cassandra what was so important with Sarah when she looked at the screen and saw Nicola. She gave Nicola the dirtiest look ever, and accused Cassandra of wasting her time before Cassandra could end the call. Nicola curled herself up into the lawn chair, her knees to her chest and her head in her lap, and cried.

◇◇◇

A taxi drove through the warehouses, its headlights a shining beacon in the late evening mist. Most of the warehouses were empty; the few that were in use operated only during regular business hours. Living in them was strictly prohibited, but nevertheless she needed to be careful not to be seen. The taxi came to a stop, its lights shining brightly on the bleak grey wall. Patsy looked out the window, making sure that there were no lights on in any of the warehouses around her. Once satisfied, she paid the cabbie and got out of the car. She leaned in the window and gave the cabbie an okay sign. He nodded back and turned his car off. She let herself into the warehouse easily, since she had a spare key.

Once inside the office she turned her flashlight on. She had speculated that some people did live in the warehouses, often using businesses as fronts for cheap accommodation, so she didn't want to draw attention to herself. She was grateful that Nicola didn't believe in alarm systems; it would be difficult to prove that someone broke in without actually breaking in. Plus, most alarm systems either keep track of when the alarm is turned on or off, or they offer individual codes per employee. Also, most were silent alarms these days and it would shorten her time allowed inside without getting caught.

She made her way into Nicola's office and slid the chalkboard to the side, revealing Nicola's stalker chart. It had been a few days since she helped with it, but it had already grown immensely. She was impressed. She knew that the stalker hit in random intervals and often left large amounts of time between his 'affection', but when he did he laid it out heavily upon Nicola. Nothing on the chart actually led anywhere. However, there were enough clues to not only potentially indicate that there were in fact two stalkers now, but that Patsy might be one of them. She knew it was only a matter of time before Nicola would put two and two together, and if she figured it out too soon she wouldn't be open to understanding Patsy's reasoning behind her actions.

Patsy went to the desk and grabbed the post-its and sharpies. She proceeded to make a few changes. Nothing major, just stuff like hair colour or the location of a clue. She even changed a couple of post-its, keeping the major details the same but changing minor information on them. She doubted Nicola would notice it right away, if at all. Satisfied, she slid the chalkboard back to where she found it and had just opened the drawer in the desk when she heard the rattling of the office's front door.

She looked up quickly, the rattling and clinking of keys echoing loudly throughout the office. She wondered if it was Nicola, but realized it shouldn't be as her sisters were both in town visiting her that weekend. It was the wrong day for the cleaning lady, but no one else had keys. Slowly she slid the drawer shut and rushed over to Nicola's open office door. She closed the door most of the way and peered out, trying to see through the darkness to the front door. She heard the sound of the deadbolt unlocking with a loud thud. Patsy looked towards the bathroom. She could reach it in time if she ran. But if it was the cleaning lady, that was the first room she'd go to. However, if it was Nicola, the office was her likely destination. But considering it shouldn't be either of them, she had no idea where they might be going and therefore where she should hide.

The doorknob slowly turned as she agonized over what to do. She scanned the room quickly, looking for anywhere she could possibly hide. The door creaked as it opened and Patsy looked down, suddenly realizing her flashlight was still on. She fumbled trying to turn it off and it fell out of her hands, clanking onto the ground and rolling off into the darkness. She froze and held her breath. There was nothing but complete silence. She clasped her hands over her mouth and tried to slow her breathing, but all she could hear was the thundering of her beating heart. Seconds passed that felt like hours until she finally heard the sound of the deadlock engaging followed by the sound of footsteps.

They were very faint, but she could just make out the sound of someone walking in the direction of Nicola's office. By the time she ascertained what she was hearing, she realized that the mystery person was already past her desk and halfway to Nicola's office. She quickly slipped out of her shoes and scanned the room in a near panic. The only thing she could make out in the dark was the moonlight casting through the window. As quickly as she could, she quietly made her way to the window, shoving her shoes into her purse as she did so.

Without hesitating, she tried to open the window, but it wouldn't budge. The footsteps were practically outside the office now. She looked back at the door and muttered some obscenities under her breath, realizing she had forgotten to close the door to Nicola's office. She glanced back to the window and tried to open it again, begging it to open. She could hear the soft breathing of someone stopped just outside Nicola's office door, mere feet away from her. She tugged once more, straining her back and arm muscles, panic rising in her heart and tears growing at the corners of her eyes—when she suddenly realized the window was locked. She accidentally let out a loud sigh of relief before noticing her error, and quickly bit her lip to hush herself. She hurriedly unlocked the window and peered out.

The ledge was barely six inches wide, but she didn't have much of a choice. She stepped out onto the ledge, crawling to get herself outside and out of view. She saw a drain pipe beside the window and she used it to hold onto as she knelt down and looked back inside the office. She could see the door open and a dark shadow enter the office as she slid the window shut most of the way. She pulled herself towards the drain pipe just as the mysterious shadow came into full view.

The wind was whipping violently at her hair and clothes, slapping at her painfully. In the short time since she had come upstairs it had started raining. Not heavily, but enough to slick the building down, and the wind had picked up since she had crawled out the window just moments ago. She looked to either side and saw the window she just exited on her left, and a few feet past that she saw a balcony. She looked to her right and saw that the ledge just continued on. She cursed under her breath, realizing the error in her haste. Afraid to look back into the window and be discovered, she admitted defeat and continued along the ledge away from the window. She moved slowly and carefully, her stocking feet slipping with each step that she took. She got about ten feet further away when she heard the sound of the window opening.

She forced herself against the wall so quickly that she almost slipped and fell off the building. She willed herself to be one with the wall and risked a peek towards the window.

A pair of arms stuck out of the window, as if they were just feeling the rain. Then elbows rested on the window ledge and she could make out the side profile of a face. She couldn't tell who it was, or whether it was a man or a woman. Patsy could only tell that he or she was not looking at her, or hopefully, for her. She started to shiver as the rain began to fall harder. She closed her eyes and silently begged the intruder to leave. After what seemed like hours, the mysterious person finally left. Patsy counted to a hundred before slowly inching her way back towards the window.

She was halfway there when she heard the distinctive sound of the window shutting, followed by the click of it locking. She stopped briefly, then in a frenzy inched her way towards the window. She stopped just before it, closed her eyes and forced herself to count to a hundred again. She opened her eyes and as she put a hand on the window she heard the slamming of a door. Looking down she saw someone exiting the warehouse. He (or she) was wearing a long, dark trench coat and a strange looking fedora hat. She strained her eyes, trying to make out who it could be. The person stopped at her still-waiting taxi, knocked on the window and leaned into the window to talk to the driver. The intruder handed something over to the driver, probably money, then stepped back as the window closed. The mystery person then opened the passenger door and started to step into the car, then abruptly stopped midway. The stranger turned around, looked up towards Patsy and waved. Surprised, Patsy almost waved back, but watched in shock as the stranger then got into her cab and drove off.

CHAPTER EIGHTEEN

The elevator seemed to crawl as usual. Nicola knew that she should have taken the stairs. Even though they were the only ones who had access to this specific elevator, it always crawled its way down, every bit as slow as the day it was first installed back in the forties. She grabbed the cage door and shook it, the rattle echoing in the old warehouse, willing it to move faster. It came to a stop with a lurch and she threw the gate open. Running quickly into a sprint, she dashed down the street. She had received yet another letter in the mail from her stalker and this one had information pertaining to Karim. She knew she should just call or text Karim, but things had been so strained between them lately that he might just blow her off.

She weaved her way through the warehouses. A tiny part of her was aware of Patsy's attack being somewhere within this vicinity but she didn't care. She had to find Karim. She lowered her head and put all of her energy into sprinting and jumping over the obstacles and hurdles that lay in her path: pallets, bags of fertilizer, knocked down garbage bins. Finally she burst free of the warehouses and popped out into a busy city street. Now, unable to run due to the overcrowded sidewalks, she settled for a power walk, this time dodging oncoming pedestrians, strollers, dogs and the occasional determined city jogger. She pressed on, eager to catch Karim before his brunch was over. She debated on cutting through some of the alleys but remembered that half the time they were either dead ends, blocked by dumpsters misplaced by careless city workers, or home to cardboard houses for the homeless.

Finally she came to the diner, hoping to find him there. It was lunch time and he usually only dined in two or three different places. She looked through the window. As always, it was packed with a lineup almost as large as the space available in the restaurant. She scanned the crowd quickly and saw that he was nowhere to be seen. She poked her head inside to see Herb's smiling face. He noticed the stressed look on her face and quickly came to her side. After a quick conversation she discovered that not only was Karim not there now, but hadn't been in weeks. Herb hadn't seen Karim since the last time she was there with him. And that he had also in fact dropped out of the Sunday morning brunch.

Outside the diner, she clenched her fists at her side and gritted her teeth. A lie. Karim was lying to her. She couldn't believe it. If he wasn't even going to the brunches, then what was he doing on the weekends? And why hadn't he told her about it? How could she find him? Impulsively, she walked in an eastward direction, towards the more artsy part of town. She knew he liked that part of town and spent a lot of time there. The two of them had spent most of their earlier dating days there almost every evening.

Despite her stress she smiled as she walked down the street. She hadn't been in this neighbourhood much since they moved in together and she got her new office on the other side of town. Both work and the condo renovations had kept them so busy they didn't wander far from home, and it quickly became a pattern. It was like walking down memory lane. The 'One Stop Cakery' had expanded to include the store next door and an outdoor terrace that had pink metal garden tables with matching white and pink chairs, and adorned with large pink- and white-striped umbrellas. The smell of freshly roasting coffee beans filled the air as she realized that the new store addition was a coffee shop complete with its own bean roaster.

Next to it was her favourite secondhand shop. Not only was her wardrobe almost completely filled from this store, but the contents of her bachelor pad had been amassed with decorations and antiques she had found there. She paused to look in the window display. From the back of the stop the clerk saw her, recognized her, and waved. Nicola smiled and waved back but continued down the street.

Across the street was a used record shop. Every record known to mankind was either in this shop or would just magically appear days later upon request. It was here that she had first met Karim. She was browsing for records for a client who had wanted to surprise his wife on their fiftieth anniversary with records of the songs they had played at their wedding. Nicola had heard good things about this store, both in quality and variety, and decided to give it a try first. When she had walked into the store, she saw it was filled from floor to ceiling with records, and the crooning of John Lennon filled her ears. List in one hand, chai latte in the other, her jaw dropped slightly in shock and she remembered thinking to herself that she had come to to right place. She had barely stepped into the store when a good looking man her age came up to her. He had shoulder-length jet black hair and piercing blue eyes. He was wearing semi-broken in denim jeans and a shirt partially unbuttoned with an untied tie. He snatched her chai and sniffed it. Satisfied, he handed it back to her.

'No froufrou drinking babes allowed. But this is acceptable', he had said, then he snatched the list from her other hand. He hemmed and hawed as he looked the list over. He started wandering through the store, plucking records from the stacks and making a pile in the centre of the store on a row of records. After about five minutes he had found everything on the list. He put the records next to the till and ushered her over.

'How do you know I didn't want to browse for them myself?' she had asked defiantly.

'Real collectors don't carry a list in their hand, they carry it in their head.'

She laughed at him and shook her head. He bagged the records as she paid for them and put the receipt in her bag. He had given her the bag with a wink and she left the store smiling. Only later when retrieving the receipt did she find the list with his phone number on it.

Nicola smiled, remembering that day fondly. It was almost as if she could hear his voice right now. Then she realized she actually could. She broke out of her day dream and looked around. Coming out of the café was Karim and a woman, who was eating a cupcake, with him taking small nibbles out of it. The woman was young, probably around nineteen-years-old. She was blonde with long big curls that fell past her shoulders. Her skin was clear and she had a big bright smile filled with perfect pearly-white teeth. She was curvy and had an obvious boob job. Most likely a client. Nicola hesitated, not wanting to interfere with his work, especially if he was just trying to sign her.

She bit her lower lip, considering whether or not she should interrupt them accidentally, on purpose, or not at all, when the woman giggled loudly. She had frosting on her lips. Karim leaned in and licked the icing off of her lips. Nicola gasped. She was sure of what she saw. But she knew she shouldn't jump to conclusions. At least not yet. The woman giggled again and Karim put an arm around her waist. The woman leaned in and the two headed away from Nicola. She decided to follow them and see where they would end up.

The couple didn't wander far, only down the block to the nearest taxi stand. There was no line so they popped into a cab and drove off. Nicola dashed forward and jumped into the next cab in line and in a hurried voice said, "Follow that cab," pointing to the one that had just left.

Neither Karim nor Nicola had noticed that across the street, sitting in front of an Italian restaurant was Patsy, watching Karim and taking photos. As Karim got into the cab, Patsy quickly put her camera away and ran over to her scooter, so she didn't see Nicola get into the cab behind him.

Twenty minutes later the cab pulled in front of a locally known love motel that rented by the hour only. Nicola asked the cab driver to wait as she watched Karim and the woman, now all super cuddly, get out of the taxi and go into the motel. After fifteen minutes of waiting the couple hadn't come back out so Nicola asked the driver to take her to her office.

Patsy slid onto the bench seat of the table. It was at the back of a dimly lit, artsy-type café on the other side of town. The walls were adorned with a variety of modern art, all with hefty price tags and poor in taste and style for her. They were garish and overly bold. The café itself, however appeared to be more attractive and friendly despite this. The ceiling was high and filled with wood beams that were decorated with rope lights, candles and small lanterns. The walls free of artwork were a bright, shiny and new-looking maple that almost seemed like syrup was pouring down the walls, and they created a variety of shadows in the dim lighting. Upbeat yet romantic music filled the air, and the overall vibe was quite pleasant. It was a mixture of artsy folk and business folk that appeared to bend the normal rules of social hierarchy and co-exist peacefully amongst each other.

The other huge perk of the café was its amazing selection of baked goods. All items were made in-house in a fire brick oven. Their speciality was custom pizzas. At the counter you could buy pizza dough, either pre-rolled or do-it-yourself. Just past the counter was a buffet table filled with a variety of ingredients. Along with the dough you bought a time slot. Then made your pizza, put it in the tray cart and it would get cooked.

Patsy had just put in a mushroom and pepperoni pizza with extra cheese and sat down with two beers. She looked at her watch. It was quarter past nine. Her pizza should be done by nine-thirty, right when Gregory would arrive. She took a swig of her beer and pulled out her laptop. Already on it were the pictures she had taken earlier that week. She scrolled through them, shaking her head. She opened a blank calendar and started writing down the times and the different women on the calendar, creating a bit of a time flow of Karim's horrendous activity. The more she filled it in, the more she couldn't believe that Nicola hadn't noticed. In the past few months he had taken his mistress to the hotel twice a week and also slept with a minimum of one other woman, most often two separate women on top of that. Nicola had never talked about Karim being an animal in bed or having a voracious sexual appetite. And Nicola was more than happy to dish out intimate details after a glass or two of wine. Patsy was just jotting down the last entry when her order was called. She left her laptop on the table and went to retrieve her pizza.

When she returned, Gregory was sitting at the table, drinking his beer and looking at the pictures. She smiled and set down the pizza. Along with it she had chili flakes and parmesan cheese. She held them up and Gregory nodded. She poured a generous amount of both onto the pizza and slid in next to him, putting a hand on his thigh.

"Disgusting, isn't it," she murmured.

"Yes, it really is. Sorry for the hasty text, I just couldn't wait to see the proof in print. Seeing it with your own eyes is one thing, you can easily convince yourself it hadn't happened," he said.

She shrugged her shoulders then took a slice of pizza and gobbled it down quickly. She blushed as she realized how rude this might be but he was heavily engrossed in the pictures. She grabbed a second slice and nibbled at it.

"You have to wonder how she hasn't noticed already. I mean you figured it out pretty easily didn't you?" she said casually.

"Hmmm. Yeah. There are so many. How does he find the time?"

"Or the excuses to be away so much," she retorted.

He grabbed a slice of pizza and ate it with great thought. "How many of these are just during the day though?"

"Just the casuals. So far, he's only checked in with his mistress once during the day. Mostly they get together Tuesday evenings and Saturday mornings. I'm guessing on Saturday it's when Nicola is out race training," said Patsy.

"She's training still?" he asked.

"Yeah, she's running a marathon later this year. Her first full."

"Oh, right. I had forgotten," mumbled Gregory.

"Have you gotten in touch with her recently?" Patsy asked, eyeing him suspiciously.

"We had coffee the other day. She's getting more and more distraught and is reaching out to me more and more. It might be time to intervene soon," he said hopefully.

Patsy nodded in agreement. He closed the laptop abruptly. Patsy stopped mid-bite and looked up at him. He brushed her face with his fingers.

"You are so adorably cute," he said, causing her to blush madly. He took the pizza out of her hand and she swallowed deeply. He held up her beer and she took it. He grabbed his beer and held it up high.

"To our growing friendship," he said with a wink. They cheered, took a drink and set their bottles down. He leaned over and kissed her hard. He held her face close to his, not letting his lips leave hers. When they finally broke apart it was only for a quick moment, to catch a breath, and he pulled her back in again.

Sarah pounded heavily on the front door. Her hair was dishevelled, her clothes slept-in, and her face void of make up. Despite the late hour that Nicola had texted her, she was still wide awake. She had merely thrown on her shoes and raced out the door, car keys barely hanging from her fingers. The empty highway had made for a quick drive, but still she worried that Nicola had either cried herself to sleep or had done something drastic. Sarah pounded on the door again and violently pushed the doorbell. She was just about to pull out her phone to text Nicola when the door slowly swung open.

Nicola stood in front of her, dressed only in one of Karim's shirts, panties and brightly coloured ankle socks. Her face was a mess of tears and she stared off into the space behind Sarah. Her eyes were glazed and vacant. Sarah rushed through the door, embracing her sister tightly. Nicola let herself be dragged backwards so the door could close behind them.

After Sarah broke off the hug, she took one of Nicola's hands and led her to the living room, making a pit stop in the kitchen to grab a glass of water. In the living room she found what she expected—tissues everywhere and a mostly empty bottle of white wine. She sat Nicola down on the couch and forced her to drink most of the glass of water she had brought over. She left Nicola alone long enough to check the other rooms, determining that Karim wasn't home.

Sarah sat back down beside Nicola and took her hands, asking where Karim was and if he had responded to her messages yet. Slowly, with great effort but an overwhelming lack of care, Nicola proceeded to tell Sarah that she hadn't texted Karim at all and was waiting for him to return. But then he didn't come home. Then she remembered it was his night out with the guys, so she waited more. But he still hadn't come home. So then she called Sarah because she couldn't stop crying. But she was done crying now. She was out of tears.

Sarah looked up at the clock on the wall and discovered it was almost five in the morning. She looked back at Nicola, who had gone from stoney-faced grim, to about to burst out into tears. Sarah pulled her into a tight embrace as Nicola burst into tears again.

The office was unusually quiet. Patsy had the day off since they were up-to-date with their current orders and nothing new had come up in the last few days for them. Technically, Nicola could have taken the day off too, but being at home depressed her. She and Karim hadn't talked in days.

She decided now would be a good time to review her stalker profile board. He'd been unusually quiet the last couple of weeks but she knew a new look might provide a fresher insight. She slid the chalkboard to the left, revealing the partially-filled corkboard behind it. She had nothing new to add to it, but she wanted to review what she already had, maybe refresh old leads.

Nicola looked under the section of clues she had. Nothing much had come up from the voice messages other than that the voice was obviously altered through some filtering device. Without a better quality message or knowledge of the original filtering program, Sarah was unable to deduce much more than that it was either a young female voice or a significantly older male voice. But Sarah had had the crazy idea to start ruling people out, so she, Patsy, Nicola, and Cassandra had provided samples. It was more to help her test out the software than to actually 'prove their innocence' as she had jokingly said.

Nicola had a section called 'fingerprints'. Sarah had come by the office and searched for fingerprints everywhere in the office. Then she had taken Patsy's and Nicola's fingerprints to rule them out. Even with fancy software it would take days to input all of the data and cross-reference it. Almost three months in already, and Sarah's CSI groupie friends had still turned up nothing and were only through ten percent of all of the fingerprints they had collected.

At the very top of the corkboard was a big question mark followed by actual clues pertaining to the stalker's identity. Nicola looked over the list and crossed her arms. Something seemed wrong, the order looked off. So either there were facts missing or things had slightly changed. She had a remarkably good memory, and it was telling her that something was amiss. She looked over the list again and again, and suddenly pointed her finger at it. There. Under 'hair' was written 'brown blonde'. She distinctly remembered writing 'honey blonde'. She erased 'brown' and rewrote 'honey' before she could doubt the change in her mind.

Tapping her fingers on her chin, she wondered what else might have been written down wrong or how she could have made such silly mistakes like that. Or perhaps Patsy had just misheard her when taking notes. Most likely that was it. When they worked on the wall together, Nicola liked to walk around just spouting ideas out; she had probably said 'brown' at one point by mistake.

Nicola started scanning every detail on the board looking for any other discrepancies, when she heard a small click followed by a whoosh of air and then a fairly loud thunk. At least a fairly loud thunk for mail. She turned on her heels quickly to go get the mail when she heard the sound of a metallic object rolling along the floor as she kicked something small by accident. Getting onto her hands and knees, she looked under her desk. Past it and under the filing cabinet she could see a dark shadow. She crawled towards the cabinet and peered under it. Unable to make out what she was seeing, she reached under and grappled around until she could feel it with her fingers. She pulled it out and discovered she was holding a tiny flashlight. She shrugged her shoulders and set it on her desk, disappointed that it wasn't something more exciting. She left it behind to go investigate her 'loud' mail drop.

She found a few newspapers fliers, junk mail and a large brown manila envelope. She picked up the latter and saw it was addressed 'to occupant'. It was relatively hefty in weight and size. She gathered the remaining mail, throwing the majority of it out and placing the rest on Patsy's desk. However, she took the large envelope back to her office. She sat down and opened the envelope carefully, just in case she had to send it back. Although it was addressed 'to occupant', a package this big must be intended for someone who needed it.

She slid the contents of the package onto her desk. Inside, Nicola found three smaller envelopes that were numbered one through three. Curious, she opened the first envelope and inside she found a deck of playing cards. Single words, written with a sharpie, were written on several cards. She sorted through the whole deck, separating the cards with words and without. She then took the pile with words and spread them out in front of her. They were all different numbers, different suits and each with a different word written on them. Slowly she mixed the words around, trying to arrange them in a readable and logical sentence. After a few attempts she put the cards in numerical order. It spelled out 'Don't stop now. You're getting closer. Look outside your door'.

She looked up from her desk and towards the office door, half expecting to see someone out there. But of course, the office was empty, except for her. She slowly got to her feet and walked over to the door. She looked around the office again, but of course she saw nothing. Cautiously, she made her way to the front door, wishing that they had a peephole or even partially frosted glass walls so she could see if anyone was lurking outside. She crouched down to the mailbox slot, and holding herself to the side of it, slowly opened it. When nothing happened, she pulled out her phone and turned on the camera. She aimed the phone at the mail slot and used it to look through it. Satisfied that no one was directly in front of her door, she moved over and looked outside the slot herself. She couldn't make much out, but there appeared to be a brown object just below the mail slot.

She stood up and opened the door. There was indeed a package in front of the door. The mailman must have left it there when he dropped off the mail. She picked up the package and examined the hallway. Nothing and no one. She took the package back inside the office and made sure to carefully lock the office door.

Setting it down on the desk she was unsure if she should open the package first or continue on with the envelopes. She examined the box and aside from her mailing address, it too was addressed 'to occupant'. She looked at her pile of cards and flipped them over. The first seven were blank, but then the last three had writing on them in very tiny letters that read 'Open the package'.

She took out a pen, and using the tip, she sliced open the brown packing tape. The contents of the box were very much like the contents of the envelope, separately wrapped and numbered one through seven. She took the package labeled '1' and opened it. Inside was a baby's bib covered in a reddish-brown stain. She looked it over, puzzled, not sure what it was supposed to mean. So she took the next package and opened it. It contained a jar of dirt that looked relatively fresh. There were no indications or writing anywhere on the jar. She pulled a piece of scrap paper out of her drawer and set it on the desk. She opened the jar and dumped the dirt onto the paper. Nothing inside the dirt.

Nicola stopped and surveyed her desk. It suddenly dawned on her that this package was probably from her stalker. It wasn't his usual MO, but it reeked of him. She stood up and removed all of her own personal items off of the desk and put them into the drawer. She then separated the two packages from each other and arranged them more neatly on her desk. She took the large box and set it on the floor next to her. On the right she placed the envelope on top of its wrapping so the number '1' was visible. She set the jar with the dirt next to it.

She opened the third package to find that it simply contained a note that read 'Go back to number 2'. She looked at the pile of dirt, confused. She looked from the dirt to the note then back to the dirt, then slowly turned her gaze back to the first envelope. Next to the sentence that was made with the specially-labeled playing cards sat the pile of remaining cards. Next to it were the other two envelopes, and one of them was labelled '2'. She took it and opened it. Inside she found a folded up piece of paper. She set the envelope down and unfolded the paper. It was a white piece of paper with a black chalk rubbing on it. She turned it around a couple of times before she realized what it was. It was a tombstone rubbing. One that she had never seen, but knew.

Her hands shaking, she folded the rubbing up and put it back in the envelope. Nicola crossed her hands around her chest and shivered. She knew she should stop. She should call the police. This was obviously from her stalker. She should stop touching it and let them open the rest. She reached into her desk drawer to grab her phone, pulling it out with fumbling hands that caused it to jump out of her hands and drop onto the floor. She cursed under her breath as she picked it up. She started to dial the police when she stopped. No, she thought to herself, they haven't done much to help her. Sure, they might be able to do more with this now. But if she let them take all of this away now she wouldn't know what the rest of the contents were and it would hinder her investigation. She trusted Sarah's CSI groupies more than the actual police. Despite their lack of findings, they actually wanted to help her figure things out.

She put her phone back into the drawer. She would call the police after she had opened everything. Technically, nothing was a threat to her so why would she call them over creepy presents. No longer caring about the numerical order, she opened the third envelope. Inside was a thin baby blanket. Folded inside the baby blanket was a note. It read, 'You know you did it'.

She gasped involuntarily and set the blanket beside the rubbing. She felt she knew where this was going. Nicola knew she should stop before old memories threatened to overtake her, but she couldn't help herself. Besides, she knew how it would look to the police. She reached into the other package, afraid to continue on, but she willed all of her strength together. She knew what the theme was. If she could just push the emotion back long enough so she could open up the rest. Package three was small. It contained a locket with pictures of two children. She gasped softly as her hands continued to shake and tremble violently. This locket was her mother's! No one had seen it for years. Nicola assumed her mother had thrown it away before Cassandra was born. Things suddenly became very, very personal, and very specific. Why was he doing this to her? Why had he suddenly turned mean?

Nicola's heart was racing and pounding loudly. The stalker not only knew her, but he knew her past. He must have known her for a long time. How else could he have known about the locket? She was afraid that the stalker was someone she knew personally. This no longer felt like a stranger. He had always been nice to her, with flowers, candies and love notes. What had changed? Had she done something to upset him?

She opened the fourth package to find an assortment of brand new baby water toys: rubber duckies and toy boats. Tears filled Nicola's eyes. She fought to hold them back, telling herself that there were only three more packages, that she could do this—except her heart ached with a misery that threatened to engulf her whole. The fifth package held a blue onesie. The sixth package was empty except for a note that read 'Like my heart', and the last package contained a tiny bouquet of flowers with a note that read 'To go with number 2…'

She looked up at the tombstone rubbing and then back to the pile of dirt. She held the bouquet up, and then it it slowly dawned on her. If the stalker was there to take a rubbing from the tombstone, then he could have also taken dirt from the grave.

She pushed her chair away from the desk and flung herself out of it. She tripped over the box that she had put there, and fell crashing down to the floor. She heaved, and clasped a hand over her mouth. She got back to her feet and dashed for the bathroom. She barely made it there before she vomited what little breakfast she had eaten that day. Groaning, she collapsed down beside the toilet and finally let the tears fly free.

CHAPTER NINETEEN

Patsy sat in her car outside the hotel she had seen Karim often frequent, the one in which she had rented a room and installed a couple of cameras. She knew she should remove them soon, that she had more than enough proof. But she couldn't help herself, it had become an obsession. She had gotten the cameras from Sarah under the ruse of wanting to install them in their office. Patsy had convinced Sarah not tell Nicola as to not worry her further. After the incident with the mysterious intruder who had taken her cab, she had wanted to determine if the intruder was who she thought it was. Sarah was so excited at this prospect that she had given Patsy enough cameras to set up the entire building, and a quick lesson on how to record, rewrite and access the cameras online. Patsy had set up the ones in the office to simply watch, and linked them to her computer. She had only recently set them up to actually record. The ones in the hotel ran 24/7, and in order to hide them from housekeeping, were quite tiny and therefore only able to broadcast live. In order to record them, she had to be close enough to access them so she could record everything live on her laptop.

So now she sat in her car, in the parking lot on the other side of the hotel where Karim and Miranda had just entered. She sat right outside their room and could see their window, two floors above. Patsy watched on her laptop as they entered the room, and then from her car she saw him close the curtains.

The first time she had watched the footage she had expected them to jump straight to sex and only that, but she had watched in shock as they proceeded to spend the majority of the afternoon cuddling, watching television, and talking. She had always thought that Karim was cheating on Nicola. Not because he was a bad guy—she actually liked him very much—but mainly because his job entailed him spending hours upon hours around several young, attractive women who were constantly throwing themselves at him in attempts to win him over and have him represent them or give them the good gigs. Patsy figured any man would have caved in by now. The pictures she had taken previously showed just that. Him with multiple young things, never any repeats. Even with this Miranda girl. Her earlier recordings had shown their visits to be over relatively quickly.

But it had slowly become a different situation. This was more real, more wrong. Karim was no longer just sleeping with this woman. He was having an actual relationship with her. He was actually cheating on Nicola in all possible aspects. For the first time since Gregory had asked for her help, she felt fully justified. Her heart broke for Nicola, but she finally didn't feel dirty because she was snooping where she wasn't supposed to. Nicola was not only her boss but her friend, and she deserved to know the truth.

Patsy hit 'record' and hoped that her laptop had enough space since she felt this would go on all night long. She was grateful that she wasn't going to be the one to deliver the news, but also curious as to when Gregory would finally reveal the truth. She knew the difficulty involved, but she was also impatient as well.

I stormed into the warehouse kicking everything that crossed my path. A plastic bucket went sailing down the hallway, a bag of old carpet puffed out clouds of dirt and dust, and a stuffed bunny squeaked as I kicked it with full force out of my way. Fumbling with my keys, I dropped them twice as my hands shook with rage. I finally got the door unlocked and stormed inside, slamming the door behind me, making the walls tremble and shake.

I made my way to the kitchen and pulled out a bottle of beer from the fridge. I slammed the bottle down on the counter before pulling out the bottle opener from the drawer. As I opened the beer it exploded, fizzing and foaming out in abundance, spraying everywhere. Screaming, I hurled the bottle across the empty room and it smashed into several pieces, spraying beer all over the wall. Still cursing, I put my hands to my head and knelt down on the floor. I cursed her out loud in every way possible and uttered several threats. Part of me wished she was here so I could take her scrawny neck and throttle it. Teach her a lesson in respect.

The moment passed and I was finally a bit calmer, so I grabbed myself another beer. After opening it more successfully than the last, I took a long drink. I ran a hand through my hair and stared out at the now beer-stained wall, already barely noticeable compared to the other bits of dirt and grime still on it.

I was shocked and appalled. I couldn't believe that she was reacting this way! Her behaviour and sudden desire to take such control was unexpected. She was moving much faster than I had originally anticipated and not at all how I had planned. I knew that I had to do something about it but I wasn't sure what. I couldn't talk to her—that was completely out of the question right now. But I had to send her the right message. I paced about the kitchen until I could hear the sound of broken glass crunching beneath my feet, then I left to wander the living room.

"What can I do? What can I do?" I muttered to myself, over and over again like a broken record. I ran my hands through my hair as I pondered the possibilities. My mind wandered from what I could do to what I wanted to do. How I wanted to hold her in my arms, feel the warmth of her skin next to mine. The taste of her lips on mine. I stopped pacing and stood rocking on my heels as I thought about undressing her, whether or not she would smile for me as I did so.

I shook my head to clear it. I had to stop letting my mind wander like that, else I might get ahead of myself. There was time for all of that later—when I finally revealed myself to her completely. I knew that she suspected the truth. That she was much closer to it than she realized. I wondered if she would actually, truly, be surprised by the truth.

But right now, I had to think. I had to come up with a suitable punishment for her and I had to do it soon.

CHAPTER TWENTY

Nicola was sitting on a park bench in the middle of Triangle Park, a fairly small and obviously triangular-shaped park that was decorated with stone walkways and flower boxes around the edges of it. There were several benches lining the walkway, but ironically very few trees. It resembled more of a glorified parking lot than a tree-filled park. But it was popular, and during the summer several food vendors would make it their home along with other small carnival-type events.

She was sitting alone, staring off into the space around her, unsure of when or how she had gotten there or how long she had been sitting on the bench. The last few days had been rough. The police department's lacklustre interest in her case, despite the new evidence, discouraged her greatly. Despite their own efforts, they had no leads, no potential suspects—nothing. Karim's continued absence made her feel empty. She had chided herself at her lack of courage to finally confront him when he had returned the following day. She let the weeks slip by without saying anything and she could feel him withdrawing from her. She even felt like Patsy felt was growing estranged.

The package she had last received from the stalker tore at her heart in ways she hadn't known possible. She had forgotten so much of that part of her life to the point that she had wondered, from time to time, if the memories were nothing more than a bad dream. That if maybe the nightmares she remembered were nothing more than that—nightmares. She had always tried so hard when growing up, and knew that no matter how she tried, it would be for nothing. She would never be forgiven, never be allowed to forget and she would always be an outsider.

She felt the tears tugging at her heart make their way to her eyes. She was gently wiping her face when a pair of arms suddenly embraced her from the back. She hugged them tightly and fondly as Sarah leaned her head into hers. Sarah kissed her on the cheek then hopped over the park bench and sat down next to her. Nicola looked up at her, a confused smile on her face.

"Sorry I'm late," Sarah said as Nicola looked at her, perplexed.

"I know I'm a terrible sister," Sarah continued, "B-u-u-u-t does this make up for it?" she asked as she produced a box from Nicola's favourite bakery.

Nicola's eyes lit up as she nodded and opened the box to reveal an assortment of chocolate pastries. They both popped a mini donut into their mouths and Nicola closed her eyes, leaning back with a smile.

Sarah coughed in an unsubtle manner and Nicola looked at her again with question. Sarah pouted and mimed drinking while Nicola looked around the bench frantically, wondering what exactly Sarah had expected. She was still trying to figure out why Sarah was here, when she herself didn't even know why she was here. As she looked behind the bench, Sarah coughed again and nudged her foot. Looking down under the bench she saw a paper bag. Opening it, she found iced drinks inside and pulled them out with a dramatic flourish, trying to hide her confusion. She couldn't recall purchasing them, let alone arranging to meet with Sarah. She could taste the delicate aroma of alcohol on her straw as she drank, but not in her drink. She wondered if she had been drinking. She looked at her watch, seeing that it was almost three in the morning.

"We've never really done stuff like this until recently, have we?" asked Sarah, and Nicola slowly nodded her head, agreeing. "When did things change?"

Nicola looked at her sister briefly, then back at the sky.

"When you guys both moved out of the house," she said softly. She pulled her knees up to her chest and shivered.

Sarah turned herself to face Nicola, who was still staring into the sky. "Why did things have to be like that when we were growing up?" she asked Nicola.

Nicola swallowed loudly, a faint shimmer growing in her eyes.

"I don't know," she replied.

Sarah put her hand on Nicola's shoulder, and she trembled at her touch.

"Nic—" Sarah started but Nicola cut her off mid-sentence.

"It was what it was. But that's over. The future is what we want to make of it."

Sarah leaned to the side, trying to look into Nicola's eyes, but she was avoiding Sarah's avid gaze.

What little Sarah could see frightened her. Pain and fear was quite obviously written all over Nicola's face. She took her hand from Nicola's shoulder and turned away from her. The two sat in silence for several minutes. Nicola turned her back away from Sarah, then leaned against Sarah and pulled her knees to her chest so both girls were leaning against each other. Sarah sighed softly.

"You never did say why you wanted to meet up," Nicola said absently, part of her hoping Sarah had messaged her first and not the other way around.

Sarah laughed. "You messaged me first silly. It was well past midnight... again. I know better than to disturb your beauty sleep."

Sarah looked down at her phone and the documents on it. She sighed heavily and shut her phone.

Nicola looked at the watch on her wrist again.

"Oops. Must be texting in my sleep again," she said, laughing nervously.

"Nic, are you okay? I mean, other than the obvious?" Sarah asked quietly.

Nicola turned to face Sarah and saw the concern written into her wrinkled brow. She playfully swatted her sister on the shoulder and then grabbed her, pulling her into a giant hug.

"Yeah, of course I am," she said, laughing as she tried to tackle Sarah down to the ground.

Patsy was sitting at her desk surfing the internet. Nothing interesting in the land of Facebook or the world wide web. She pondered about updating her relationship status to say 'in a complicated relationship', but knew that would provoke too many questions that she didn't want to answer, and Nicola would be likely to notice. Of all the technological things Nicola could have actually known about on her own, which were very few, Facebook was one of them. Nicola had started a Facebook page even before she started her business, and used Facebook to promote her business when she first started.

Patsy browsed the local sites for random and unusual items, unable to resist working during her lunch break. Nothing extraordinary or special, like usual. She and Nicola found most of their more rare items while browsing garage sales and going-out-of-business sales. She usually only found things online when she was looking for something specific. She sighed with boredom. It had been days since she had heard from Gregory. She wanted to see him again, but over the past few weeks their outings had been scattered and few.

Her phone chirped and she heard a knock on the office door simultaneously. She ignored her phone to answer the door. Opening it, she discovered a large bouquet of flowers in front of her. They moved to the left and she saw the pale, pimply face of a teenaged boy.

"For Nicola?" she asked as the messenger boy shook his head.

"Nope. For a Miss Patsy Klein."

A small smile curled up around her lips. She held her hands out and he put the flowers in them.

"Just sign here," he said, producing a slip of paper.

She signed it and he left, closing the door behind him. She walked over to her desk and her phone chirped again. She sat down, the flowers on her lap, and picked up her phone from beside the laptop. There were two new messages from a blocked number. The first one read

'Congratulations on a job well done'. The second read 'Thinking of you'. She held the phone to her chest and smiled. She wasn't sure if he had actually noticed or not, and now she knew.

Nicola cautiously poked her head out of her office and looked at Patsy, who was sporting the biggest, silliest grin on her face.

"Can I presume from your face that the knock was good news?" Nicola asked hesitantly.

Patsy immediately flushed, turning bright red all the way down to her roots. Nicola laughed and ventured over to her desk. She noticed the flowers and leaned over to inhale their sweet fragrance.

"Soooo?" Nicola coyly asked, sitting on the edge of the desk. "Are these from your beau?"

Patsy nodded, sneaking one last quick glance at her cell phone before putting it away in the top drawer of her desk. Nicola fingered the flowers lightly.

"He must really like you, not that I blame him," she said softly.

Patsy looked up and asked her why.

"These," Nicola said, carefully caressing the beautiful purple petals, "Are, if I'm not mistaken, saffron crocuses."

Patsy looked at her and shrugged her shoulders.

"This, my darling Patsy—" Nicola started but paused long enough to pick up the bouquet, hem and haw while moving it from hand to hand then finally setting it back down. "Probably cost almost as much as a teenaged boy's first beater car."

Patsy's eyes grew wide and her mouth formed a giant 'O'. "Are you serious?" she asked.

Nicola nodded. "Ask your Google," she said chuckling. "But believe me, I'm jealous."

Patsy, her face expressing clear disbelief, whipped out her phone and after a few seconds she put it away, shock and awe written on her face. She leaned back in her chair and slumped down in it. Nicola laughed at her, and Patsy sat up abruptly.

"How on earth did you know?" Patsy asked incredulously.

"I saw a picture of these flowers years ago when I was a small child. I fell in love with them and when prom came around I asked my date if he could find them. His mother happened to be a florist. Right after I made the request he started acting odd. Then a couple of days before prom he asked me if I knew anything about them. I admitted I did not, only that they were beautiful. He finally confessed that he had asked his mother about them and she told him how much one would cost. And while he could afford it, it would mean no limo and no tux for him. So I happily settled for a custom dyed purple orchid instead," Nicola answered smugly.

Patsy smiled, curling her legs up onto her chair and snuggling into her knees. She looked over at Nicola. "Is everything okay?" she asked.

Nicola nodded. She told Patsy how she had been trying to Skype Cassandra the last few days but she had always had 'company' so it wasn't possible. Nicola complained that her stalker was giving her more attention than Karim, and how she was feeling lonely because she hadn't been able to see either of her sisters in days.

"I'm free tonight, if you want," Patsy offered.

"Aww, thanks. But I'm going to try and Skype Cassandra again. 'Company' is supposed to be leaving sometime today," Nicola said.

"Oh. Okay," Patsy answered softly. "How's the investigation going? We haven't done anything with it in forever," she said quickly, sitting upright in her chair.

"Hmm, not much to do. Sarah's CSI groupies are investigating all of the clues I have but haven't turned up anything solid and there isn't much to add to the chart."

Patsy slumped back into her chair. "Oh, okay."

"Do you think I should invite Cassandra over this weekend? Just her, no kids? So we can catch up? We don't have any big orders, do we?" Nicola asked.

"Just a delivery on Saturday," Patsy answered.

"If Cassandra is free, would you be able to do the delivery?" Nicola asked, pulling her cell phone out and shooting off a text off to Cassandra.

"Yeah, sure. Not like I have any plans," Patsy answered. "You certainly don't seem to want to hang out with me anymore, apparently," she muttered under her breath.

Nicola looked up from her phone. "Sorry, what was that? I didn't hear you."

Patsy plastered a huge smile on her face. "Sure. No problem."

Nicola's cell chirped. She looked at her message and stood up from the desk.

"That's great. Cassandra says the weekend is a go. Thanks, Patsy," she said, smiling, before walking back into her office.

Patsy gave an annoyed looked to Nicola's back before sticking her tongue out at her. She looked back at her flowers and smiled.

"At least someone still wants me," she said.

Nicola and Karim were sitting at the kitchen island. As usual, they were eating Chinese take out, but the air was thick with tension. Nicola sat uncomfortably upright, sneaking peeks at Karim, trying to read him. He was glued to his phone, adamantly avoiding conversation. When he came home with the dinner, he had dumped the bag down and proclaimed 'work' as he surfed his phone. She had unpacked the bag, separating the containers in silence.

"Karim?" she asked softly.

"Hmm? Can it wait? I'm in the middle of a something," he muttered.

She sighed. It was their first meal together in weeks, and yet she felt all alone as usual. She shoved her chopsticks into the rice and began playing. She stabbed them in as one, then slowly pulled them apart. She repeated this over and over again. Hopeful, she looked up at Karim, expecting a scolding of some kind, but received nothing. He'd either not noticed or was actually ignoring her.

The doorbell rang, breaking the awkward silence. Nicola smiled and hopped to her feet. She wasn't expecting anyone, but judging by Karim's lack of reaction, neither was he. She walked to the door as it rang a second time. She opened the door and smiled a greeting. On the other side of the door was a large bouquet of flowers. A tiny male head poked out to one side of the bouquet. She giggled as she realized the man was practically fully engulfed by the bouquet.

"Nicola VanBurgen?" he asked. She answered 'yes' as he handed the flowers to her, tipped his hat, and left.

Nicola walked back to the island and set the flowers down next to her food. She went over to the cupboard and began opening doors, looking for a vase. Karim finally came to life and set his phone down.

"You ordered flowers?" he asked.

She shook her head 'no' as she moved the flowers to the counter and opened another cupboard door.

"Can you reach this for me please?" she asked, reaching her arms up towards the top shelf.

Slowly, Karim came over to the cupboard and grabbed the vase that her outstretched fingers were barely touching. He handed it down to her and she yanked it out of his hands. She danced her way over to the sink, filled the vase full of water and set it to the side. She grabbed a pair of scissors and went back to her bouquet. She brought it to the sink and began to take it apart and reassemble it into the vase. The whole time Karim was intently watching her.

"Who's it from?" he asked, leering over her shoulder.

Nicola pushed him away before examining the flowers for a card, but unable to find one, she shrugged her shoulders and pushed him away as he hovered over her trying to comb through the flowers. She swatted his hand away.

"Don't break them. There's no card." She smiled as she arranged the flowers.

"The delivery man didn't say anything?" he asked, agitation rising in his voice.

"No, does it matter? Maybe I have a secret admirer," she said with a smirk.

"Maybe it's from your stalker," he said facetiously.

She stopped her arranging and looked at him with wonder. "Do you really think so?" she said softly, her hands starting to tremble.

He muttered a curse under his breath and grabbed her hands, pulling her in close. "I was being a jerk. Sorry."

Nicola closed her eyes and sighed softly.

"Whoever gave them to you was obviously grateful for something. The delivery boy probably lost the card. You must have made a client very happy," he said, the words rushing out of his mouth.

Nicola broke away from his embrace and put the flower that had been in her hand, now crushed, into the sink. She grabbed a new one and put it in the vase.

"It looks beautiful, doesn't it?" she asked.

Karim put a hand around her waist. "Yeah, babe, it does."

◇◇◇

"About time you answered girlie girl. You've missed our last two Skype dates," Nicola said, her voice full of mocking disapproval.

Cassandra made a face, apologizing profoundly. She plead the fifth since she figured they didn't need to Skype this week with her coming over in a couple of days. Nicola batted her eyelashes and made a mock pouting face.

"Being cute won't help you," Cassandra said and Nicola sighed loudly.

"It's okay. Things have been hectic enough around here to keep me distracted," Nicola said with a weak smile.

She knew that Cassandra was unaware of the how serious and uncertain things were getting with Karim. She also knew that Sarah hated being the only one who knew something; she had a hard time keeping secrets.

"Ha! You think you're busy now? Just you wait, soon you will realize what hectic really means," Cassandra said.

"Yeah," Nicola said absently.

"Hey. What's up? What's wrong? You don't seem your usual annoyingly perky self."

"Nothing, everything, I don't know anymore," Nicola said throwing her hands up in the air with frustration before letting them fall heavily into her lap.

"Is it the baby thing? Don't get discouraged, it'll happen at the right time and when you least expect it."

Nicola let out a loud breath of air, her bangs fluffing upwards as she put her chin into her hands. "It's not."

"What do you mean? You've changed your mind?" Cassandra asked.

"No. It's just that I don't think Karim is really into it anymore, and not just because of the stalker."

"So you guys aren't trying anymore?" Cassandra asked.

"Apparently I've been driving Karim nuts with it," Nicola said.

"I hate to say it, but I kind of agree with him. You've become as obsessed with having a baby as you were when you first declared you were never going to have a baby."

"Really?" Nicola asked, a bit surprised.

"Nic, I hate to ask this, but Sarah and I have been talking. We're worried about you." Cassandra said.

"About what?" Nicola asked, her hands slowly curling into fists.

"We're worried about your reason for wanting a baby..." Cassandra said, letting the last word hang, not wanting to continue.

Nicola abruptly sat up, her back rigid and goosebumps appearing on her arms. Her voice grew prickly. "What do you mean, my 'reason'?"

"Nic, don't get mad at me, we're just concerned. We want to make sure you're doing this for the right reasons," Cassandra said.

"Why exactly do you think I want to have baby?" Nicola spoke each word slowly and carefully, reining in her anger.

"For the same reason you never wanted kids... because of—" she started but Nicola cut her off.

"Don't even go there. How dare you bring that up again."

"Nic. C'mon. You know we wouldn't bring it up under normal circumstances. It's ju—"

Nicola cut her off again. "Just what?!? I suddenly wanted to become a mother? I wanted what most women in their lives want?" she shrieked as she slammed her fists onto the coffee table.

Cassandra grew silent. Nicola then jammed her fists in between her thighs and glared at her sister. Cassandra took a deep breath and let it out slowly.

"We're just worried about you. You're behaving exactly the same as you did before. We just thought that maybe it was bothering you again. That maybe mother was getting to you again. I'm sorry."

"Maybe you should mind your own business. Both of you," Nicola said softly.

"You know we love you. No matter what happened."

"I know," Nicola said sharply as tears were filling her eyes. "I have to go now. Talk to you later."

"Nicola, no, please wait—" Cassandra started but Nicola ended the call mid-sentence. She flipped her iPad screen down, put her head in her hands and cried. She'd never be able to forget. No one would let her forget.

CHAPTER TWENTY ONE

I was nine years old when my whole life as I knew it came crashing down upon me. I hadn't realized then the significance of the events about to happen to me. Or the damage it would do to everyone. Or just how much more fragile we all would become.

We lived on a farm. We raised chickens. A lot of chickens. It was the best time of my life. The day before my eighth birthday my parents pulled me out of school, put me in a bathing suit and placed me deep into the barn. It smelled sweet and the sawdust-like fibres beneath my feet tickled when I walked on them. The entire floor was covered in soft, yellow, fluffy and scratchy sawdust in large clumps and pieces. There were three rows that ran as far down as the eye could see. The rows were created by a long, continuous strip of plywood that ran the entire length of the barn. The far right and left rows were separated into over a dozen sections each, by shorter pieces of plywood that sat beneath a barn-long water and food trough for the chickens. Inside each section, my uncles were placing cardboard boxes. The centre row stood empty except for us.

My father picked me up and tossed me onto his shoulders. He walked me down to the end of the row, explaining to me the significance of the job he was about to bestow upon me.

"I have an important job for you. It's something only a big kid can do. I know you're smart and that we can trust you. So, do you think you're ready to help us out?"

I nodded.

My father tilted his head towards me. "Was that a yes?" he chuckled.

"Yes!" I shouted happily, eager to please my father and even happier to be in my bathing suit in a very warm barn in the middle of the cold September outside.

We got to the end of the row and the first small section. He dropped me inside the section next to the box. I put my head on the box and listened quietly. Small, tiny peeps could be hear from within. My dad laughed softly. He pulled me back and took the lid off the box. Inside it was full of baby chicks. Cute, adorable, yellow, baby chicks. I gasped and squealed. The chicks fluttered about at the sound of my voice. I reached inside the box and picked one up. I rubbed its softness against my cheek and giggled.

My dad took my hand and looked at me very seriously. I gulped and put the chick back in the box.

"Now, there are a lot of chicks here in the barn. Even more than you can count."

"More than a hundred?"

He chuckled, "Yes, a lot more."

"Wow! A million?"

"No, not quite that many. Only about ten thousand."

My eyes felt like there were ready to jump out of my head. I wasn't sure if ten thousand was more or less than a million. Only that it was a big number.

"What I need you to do is to take each chick out of the box and count it. When you get to a hundred I want you to draw a line on the wood. Do you understand?"

I took the box of crayons out of his hands and nodded 'yes'. "Can I name them?"

He smiled at me fondly. "As long as it doesn't slow you down from counting, yes of course."

I sat down and started counting. My father reached down to stop me. "There is one other thing honey."

I looked up him with question.

"Remember how I said I know that you're all grown up?"

I nodded.

"You saw the truck outside, right? That's the truck that the chicks rode in to get here. However, they are babies and babies aren't always very strong. So some of them might not have made it."

I tried to understand what he was telling me. "They're sleeping? Like my cousin?"

He drew in a breath sharply and stood upright. He was surprised at my recollection of my cousin, whom I'd never met, and who had passed away at birth when I was five. When I think about it, I can recall several moments like this where my maturity and acceptance of the world as it was, shocked my father immensely.

"Yes, like David. Sleeping. If you find any that are sleeping, just leave them in the box and don't count them."

"Ok, daddy." I sat down and started counting aloud. "One – Charlie, two – Fred, three – Henry."

My dad laughed, "Darling, you know that the chicks are gi—"

I cut him off—"There aren't enough girl names for all of them. I don't want them to have to share."

My uncles overheard this and the whole barn filled with adult laughter. My father patted me on the head and went to the other end of the barn to help bring in more chicks. I continued my counting and naming of the chicks.

The whole day passed away like a dream. I was in my own little heaven surrounded by yellow, fluffy, cotton balls of love. I completed an entire row by myself. To reward myself I burrowed myself into the sawdust and beneath the chicks. They crawled over my legs, my stomach, my arms and face. I giggled and kissed each and every one I could reach. My father laughed and plucked me out of the remaining section and twirled me into the air.

"Now go get dressed and find your mother. Tell her we're about to come in for dinner."

I stuck my lower lip out and tried to whimper. My father put his hands on his hips and stared me down. I took my stance and stared back, intent on winning this battle. Money exchanged hands behind my father, distracting me from my focus. I could hear the seconds tick on my father's watch. The men behind him chuckled. I bit my lip and tried to keep on task. Then I blinked. They roared with laughter as my father swatted my bottom and I ran down the aisle and towards my clothes. As I threw on my shirt and jumper quickly, I slipped on my shoes and darted out of the barn, my jacket dangling from my hands.

The sun beat down on me brightly through the cloudless autumn sky. Brilliant reds and pinks filled the sky as the sun was setting for the day. I ran the long way, past the other barn and through the cow field. The ground was dimpled with divots caused by the cows feeding and stomping when we forced them inside at night. I skipped over the divots and cartwheeled through the larger clumps of grass. I stopped once to grab Betsy's teats and squirt milk into my mouth. She mooed in protest and shot me an annoyed look, having already been milked twice that day. I petted her on the side of her head and kissed her cheek and ran off towards the house.

"Mommmm!" I hollered from the mud room. I kicked off my shoes and hung my jacket on a free coat hook. I expected to smell the start of dinner but there was nothing. I closed the outside door and went through to the kitchen. There were fresh carrots cut up on the cutting board, an empty bloody plate next to it, and Chico, our dog, *was licking his lips. A lone pot sat on the stove, smoke starting to rise from it. I pulled the step-stool up to the stove and looked inside it. It was empty and burnt. I took it off the burner and turned the gas off. "Mom?" I asked out loud, unsure of what was happening.*

A crash followed by a sudden cry from the living room broke me out of my uncertainty. I ran to the living room and found one of my sisters smashing my toy cars onto the dining table and into mother's vases. She drove another car across the table and took out a second vase, sending it flying off the table. She clapped her hands in glee. I rushed over and took her off the table and spanked her on her bottom.

"Bad girl. We don't play on the table."

She looked at me with shock as her lower lip trembled briefly before she broke out loudly into tears. As I walked over to put her in the play area, I realized her pants were sopping wet. She was five-years-old and potty trained. I looked at her clothes and saw that she was wearing overalls with clasps which I knew she couldn't undo herself.

"Why didn't you ask mommy to help you? Why did you pee your pants? I thought you were a big girl."

She looked up at me with large, sad eyes. "Mommy gone." And she started crying again.

I sighed. Mother must be outside somewhere. I took her upstairs to her room and undressed her. We walked together to the bathroom and I turned on the shower.

She looked at me with surprise. "I'm a big girl?"

"Yes, today, you can be a big girl. Be quick. I have to help mommy make dinner. Daddy is almost done in the barn." I gently pushed her into the shower and handed her the soap. "I'll be right back. I'm going to pick out clean clothes for you, ok?" She nodded and began to sing as she cleaned himself.

I went back to her room and put the dirty clothes into the hamper. I pulled fresh clothes out and set them onto her bed. I grabbed a towel from the back of the door and went back to the bathroom.

"All done?" I asked and she grinned as she shot the soap at me. I batted it back at her and turned off the shower. Holding out the towel she jumped into my arms, sending the two of us crashing to the ground. She giggled and ran off, naked, towards her room. I chased her down and tackled her onto the bed, wrapping her like a sausage in the towel. I rubbed her hard and rolled her around the bed until I felt she was dry. Her laughter echoed through the halls. I barely noticed how empty the house seemed.

"Okay, you can get dressed by yourself, okay? I need to find mommy and start dinner."

I leaned over the bed and looked out the front window. You could see both barns and the entire front yard from this room. They both stood quite empty, even the well was unoccupied. Maybe, she was in the back yard tending to the animals? It was a bit early still, but perhaps she was putting the cows inside?

I crossed to my parents room to take a look at the back yard. Their door stood wide open and I walked back to the bay window that overlooked the backyard and the animals. The cows were still grazing and mother was nowhere in sight.

"Where are you?" I muttered to myself as I turned to leave the room when I saw her, lying down on the bed sleeping. "Mother?" I asked out loud but got no response. I called out to her again before hopping onto the bed and shaking her shoulder. "Mother, wake up. Time to make dinner," I said in a sing-song voice as I shook her harder and harder, not realizing that I was starting to scream.

My sister called out to me from her room, asking if mommy was okay.

"Stay in your room!" I screamed at her. I looked around the bed, taking everything in, trying hard to process what was going on. On

the nightstand was a bottle of pills lying on its side. Empty. A half-full glass of water stood next to it. Mother sleeping. Mother cold. So very, very cold. Mother. Not. Sleeping.

I ran out of my parents' room and into my sister's room. I grabbed my sister, still half naked, and took her in my arms. She looked at me with confusion and fear at the near hysteria in my eyes. I ran down the stairs, dragging her along with me, afraid to leave her upstairs alone. I ran out the front door, not even stopping to grab shoes, and clutching my sister tightly in my arms. I ran towards the barn screaming. My father and the truck driver stood outside the barn, the transport truck's engine revving, drowning out my screams, but still I kept at it. My sister suddenly started bawling and wet her pants, the pee trickling down the front of my clothes, but I paid it no attention. All of my effort was on getting to father and not dropping her. The driver of the truck shook my fathers hand and went to hop into his truck when he suddenly stopped and stared out at me. He must have said something to my father as he suddenly dropped whatever was in his hands and they both ran for me.

My father reached me first as I collapsed to my knees. Clutching my sister tight to my chest, I struggled to catch my breath amidst my tears.

"Dear god child, what is wrong?" he asked

I opened my mouth to try and talk but nothing came out.

My father took me by the shoulders and gave me a shake. "Child, what is the matter?"

I put my hands over my sister's ears. "Mother," I whispered, "Is sleeping."

My father looked at me quizzically. Then I saw the fog abruptly clear behind his eyes as the realization of my statement hit him. He took off towards the house like his pants were on fire. My uncles came out of the barn just in time to see him run off. They both broke *out in a run after him. I could hear him hollering out to them to call an ambulance as he ran inside the house.*

I sat on the ground, rocking my sobbing sister in my arms, crying along with her.

Nicola was lying on her back, unsure if she was on her bed or the floor. It was too difficult to tell. A cool breeze swept through the room and she wondered if she had left a window open. Her head hurt but her body felt light. Her head felt as thick as syrup and pounded as she struggled to remember what had happened. She remembered it was Tuesday, so Karim was out with the boys. She remembered Skyping Cassandra. But her mind was a blank after that. She couldn't even remember when she had left the living room or what time it was. She heard a noise coming from behind her followed by silence.

A slow trickling of warm liquid flowed softly over her skin, down her face and onto her neck. She reached up and gingerly touched the top of her head, wincing at the pain it evoked. She could feel a sticky substance on her fingertips. Opening her eyes slowly, she panicked as she realized she couldn't see. She blinked several times only to feel the rustling of her eyelashes against fabric. A wave of nausea rolled through her and she tried to turn onto her side, but found herself unable to move.

Cruel laughter filled the room as a hand clamped firmly down onto her wrist. She cried out as fiery pain exploded up her arm. A taunting voice asked her if it hurt and laughed at her as she begged to be let go. Instead he squeezed her wrist more, laughing harder as she winced in pain, tears pouring out of her eyes. He let go of her wrist and slowly traced his finger around her face, his breath hot and humid against her cheek. She fought to remain still as his sour and pungent breath invaded her nostrils, causing her to flinch. He slid his fingers down her cheek, her throat and then under the top of her blouse. She could feel his pulse quickening and his breath started to grow more rapid as he licked her lips through the fabric, and roughly cupped her breast in his hand. She tried not to squirm but found it impossible to not be repulsed by his touch as he softly kissed her lips.

"I can play nice, if you really want me to. But I'd rather not," he said, panting heavily between his words.

She heard the chink of a blade popping and involuntarily gasped, and he burst into a fit of hysterical giggles. Suddenly, he was everywhere. All she could hear was his laughter. In her head, beside her, above her, behind her. Then just as quickly, everything grew still. The wind died and the breeze was gone. His voice was gone and the air was empty with silence. She could only hear the pounding of her own heart and her raspy breath as she gulped air with every other swallow. She forced herself to slowly count to ten, and with each number her breath grew calmer and her heart more still. Once she hit ten she strained herself to hear where he had gone. But nothing. Slowly she reached her hands to the blindfold on her face.

Then suddenly he was on top of her. Her hips cried out in pain as he landed forcefully on her and thrust his knife against her chin, pushing her head upwards with the hand that held the knife while the other ripped her blouse open. He slid the cold steel down her throat and over her bosom.

"Such a waste" he murmured as his slid the knife into the top layer of her skin. She screamed and jerked underneath him. He put his hand over her mouth.

"Shhhhh. It's only going to get worse," he said.

He slid his body down over her legs, the tip of the blade carving a path down her stomach, stopping just above her navel. She whimpered and begged him again, her tears saturating the blindfold. But he ignored her pleas and grabbed at her pants, gently tugging at them, then quickly ripped them off with his knife. She felt her pants fall to her sides and slide out from beneath her as he lowered his knife hand back onto her navel, and thrust his face into her groin. He murmured with delight and began to lick her panties.

She couldn't hold back anymore; she cried, she screamed, she squirmed and tried to kick him off, desperately trying to free herself from his grasp. He giggled like a schoolgirl, happy at her pathetic attempts to stop him. He ripped her panties off like they were paper and quickly thrust his hard self into her. She screamed at the sudden intrusion and pain. Harder and harder he shoved himself into her, laughing as she cried in pain and misery beneath him. He pawed at her body as he came closer and closer to his climax, the knife nicking her constantly with each passing thrust. Suddenly he clamped one hand onto her throat and the other over her mouth and nose. Panicking, she began to squirm and writhe about. He moaned with delight at her 'participation' and pounded into her even harder. He released his hands and she hungrily gulped in the air with deep gasping breaths. Again, he covered her face and she immediately began to panic and thrash about once more against her will. Tears streamed down her face, and with disgust she realized that he was forcing her body to enjoy this. She tried to fight against her body, to hold it still and not participate. But he kept repeating the strangulation and gasping for air again and again until her body involuntarily was about to climax. He moaned loudly as he orgasmed and laughed as her body followed suit.

As she reached the highest point of her climax, he pushed a damp cloth onto her mouth and whispered, "Nighty-night princess."

Then everything was dark.

CHAPTER TWENTY TWO

The fluorescent lights flickered and shook as the subway ran along the tracks nearby. A cool breeze flitted through the hallway, and the curtains separating the beds swayed to and fro. The room was filled with voices calling out to each other, barking orders, and people crying. The clank of wheels rolling along the floor and the metallic clatter of equipment-filled carts rushed along with them. A periodic beeping of equipment roamed through the air. A young woman screeched through the halls with a distraught and wailing child in her arms.

Nicola, in a flimsy hospital gown, lay on her back with her legs in stirrups. Her face was covered with fresh bruising, spattered with cakes of dried blood on her forehead, and drenched with dried tears. A young female doctor was at her feet, talking her through her the procedure and attempting to keep Nicola calm. Nicola tried to focus on the noise around her to keep herself out of the horror of her situation. She had never felt so alone and violated in her life. The doctor made the occasional grunting noise as she continued her procedure and talked to Nicola. Nicola numbly mumbled the odd 'yes' and 'uh huh', pretending to listen to the doctor while her mind was a million miles away.

Karim's angry voice suddenly filled the hallway. She could hear him arguing with the police officer that had brought her here. She managed a small half smile. Her saviour, her prince. Their voices suddenly grew quieter and she could no longer hear them anymore. She reached a hand out towards the curtain.

"Karim—" she mumbled. But the doctor was too absorbed in the procedure to notice her. As the doctor was finishing up, Nicola could hear the sound of feet approaching and then stopping just outside the curtain.

A female voice, a different officer than earlier, cleared her throat outside the curtain. The doctor looked up from her tray.

"Yes?" she asked briskly as she finished the exam and helped Nicola lower her legs out of the stirrups.

"It's Officer O'Hara, Doctor. I have Ms. VanBurgen's boyfriend, Karim, here. May we come in to see Ms. VanBurgen?" she asked.

The doctor slid the curtain open slightly and ushered the officer in. She was younger than Nicola, barely out of the academy by the looks of it, and her features were soft and caring. She wore latex gloves, had a camera strung around her neck, and a small briefcase in her hands.

"Hello Ms. VanBurgen, my name is Officer O'Hara. I'm with the crime department of sexual offences and I'm here to take pictures of your injuries sustained and collect any other evidence from you, if that's all right."

Nicola pulled herself to a sitting position and nodded slowly. Karim lingered behind at the curtain, avoiding her gaze.

"Can I see Karim?" she asked timidly, mentally urging him to look up at her from where he stood in the corner, but his gaze was turned downwards.

"As soon as I'm finished we can, but we can't risk him contaminating any evidence. I've allowed him in just to see that you are okay, but he needs to remain outside until we are finished. Do you understand?"

Nicola nodded absently.

"I'm right here, babe," he said meekly before exiting the curtained room.

Tears sprung from her eyes as she saw his feet just past the curtain. She wanted him to hold her so badly, to tell her that she would be okay.

The officer stepped closer and carefully looked Nicola over. She instructed her to hold her arms out in front of her and Nicola complied as the officer took pictures. The she turned her arms over and the officer took more pictures. She took pictures of Nicola's face, head and legs. She also took several close-ups of her head injury and of the wound inflicted on her navel. After setting the camera down, she pulled the briefcase out from behind her and placed it on the table that flipped down from the hospital bed. She opened it up to reveal several vials, swabs, jars, baggies and a large assortment of other small tools and instruments. Nicola tried to laugh inside weakly as she thought of how excited Sarah would be if she could see this real forensic kit.

The officer told her that she was going to take some samples from her scalp, fingernails and skin, in order to not only help decipher the weapon used on her, but for any trace evidence that the assailant might have left behind. She stood quite close to Nicola and started to carefully comb through her hair. She filled a few vials with blood, dander and other items she found. She scraped her fingernails and swabbed a piece of tissue along Nicola's mouth, explaining that while the other officers not only smelled chloroform on her and found the rag used, they wanted to match the two as absolute proof. She took another thorough look over Nicola's body. She plucked a couple of stray hairs and closed her vial bag. The officer gathered her things, thanked Nicola and left the curtained room.

Nicola stared at the curtain blankly and realized that she was all alone. The doctor had left at some point and she couldn't hear Karim's voice, nor see his shoes beneath the curtain. She started to cry softly at first, and then her tears fell rapidly down her face. The curtain suddenly flew open and Karim burst in. He rushed to her, pulled her into a tight embrace and she burst into loud, raucous sobs. She could finally let out the fear and loneliness she had been holding in all night. She sobbed and sobbed as he kept soothing her, stroking her hair and talking to her softly. Finally her tears subsided and she let herself be calmed down as she felt the steady rhythm of his heart. It was then that she noticed that they were no longer alone. The two officers that had shown up at her house were now standing behind Karim. She broke away from Karim slightly, and noticing, he too turned to face the officers.

"Ms. VanBurgen, I'm sorry, but there are a few more things we need to clarify before you leave," one of the officers said, pausing briefly as she looked between Nicola and Karim.

Nicola noticed the pause, and looking up at Karim she saw that he looked grim. She suddenly felt confused and unsure.

"You said that you were home alone when the perpetrator broke into your home, is that correct?" asked the officer, and Nicola slowly nodded her head. She had already answered this question and many others before they had even let her see the doctor.

"While it's still too early to make solid conclusions, there appears to be no evidence of forced entry anywhere in the house, and there were no opened or unlocked windows. Along with the fact that your condo is four stories above ground," he said.

"We often leave the windows unlocked," Karim retorted impatiently.

"I understand. We did check all of the windows, but they were all locked. Are you sure you locked the front door when you entered?" the officer asked.

"The door closes and locks automatically. I purposely installed a lock like that since we're both a little forgetful. You need a second key, which only I have a copy of, to unlock it from the inside. I've already told you this," Nicola said.

The officers whispered something between themselves. "All right, we understand. Is it possible then that you left the door ajar? Or that you let someone in that evening prior to your attack?"

Nicola shook her head. "The door swings shut on its own. I was alone the entire evening."

The officers jotted down more notes and whispered amongst each other again. "Do you recall if the rapist wore a condom?" he asked.

"I don't know… Maybe? I wasn't exactly paying attention. Why?" Nicola asked.

"Well ma'am, the doctor wasn't able to find any traces of semen from you and the officers weren't able to find any used condoms in your home."

"What are you suggesting?" Nicola asked, her voice growing shrill and her body trembling.

She couldn't understand why Karim wasn't jumping into their conversation anymore and why he wasn't defending her. She had the suspicious feeling that things were looking grim for her and she couldn't understand why or how things were suddenly moving in this direction.

"What about my bruises? My cuts?" she asked defensively.

"The doctor says that the evidence she has gathered is inconclusive, and until all of the tests have been run, the evidence neither agrees nor disagrees with your statement," the officer said.

"So what are you trying to say exactly? Do you think I made this up? Are you that desperate that you can't even wait for the evidence to process before you try pinning it on me?" she said, her voice steadily rising up to a near shriek.

"Karim?" she said, and he looked at her uncomfortably.

"I don't know, Nicola. I really don't know. Something seems wrong about this," he said meekly.

"What's wrong is that my boyfriend should be defending me! My boyfriend should be pissed off that someone broke into our home and raped his girlfriend!" she hissed at him.

She turned back to the officers. "And you two should be doing a better job finding some evidence that will lead you to my rapist! If either of you had half a brain you'd know that I've been stalked for months now and maybe perhaps my stalker did this! Do your damn job!!!" she spat at them as she pushed herself out of Karim's now weak embrace and off of the hospital bed.

She stormed off towards the receptionist counter. "I want my clothes!" she yelled out loud and to no one in particular.

The officers looked at each other, in the direction that Nicola had stormed off, and then back to Karim.

"We're not saying this didn't happen, but that there is a lack of evidence supporting her claims. It is obvious she is under a lot of stress from this stalker. Without any conclusive evidence, it is hard to say what really happened to your girlfriend. We will continue our investigation and let you know what we find," one of the officers said.

"She's right," Karim said, and the officers looked up at him, surprised. "It's assholes like you and me that jump to conclusions without processing all of the information at hand. We are the reason so many women who get raped never say anything about it. And can you blame them? We jump to blame the victim and not the jerk that violated them. I'm ashamed to have let you sway my opinion like that," he said, and he left the two officers behind in the room, embarrassed and surprised at his sudden outburst.

◇◇◇

She sat on the edge of the chair, elbows on the island, sipping her coffee and nibbling on toast. Karim sat across from her, drinking his coffee. Neither spoke to each other yet neither had their phones out. She was glaring at him, attempting to stab daggers into him with her eyes, and he occasionally looked over at her, watching as she quickly looked away and then resumed staring into his coffee. They hadn't spoken to each other in almost a week. She had been sleeping on the couch since they returned from the hotel a couple of days ago and the tension was so thick it could be cut with a knife.

He took a sip of coffee and gently set his mug down. "This is ridiculous," he said.

"The only thing that is ridiculous is that my boyfriend thinks I faked my rape attack for attention," Nicola said.

"I never said that," he said softly.

"No, but you certainly let the police say that. Mere hours after being raped, you let them assault me to my face," she retorted.

He sat there quietly, letting her vent.

"You let them humiliate me. Cops like them are the reason so many women who get raped never report it," she spat out angrily.

He sighed. He knew that she was right. He had failed his duty as a loyal boyfriend. He should have stood by her. But he was tired. Tired of the arguing. Tired of always feeling like he was wrong and that he was the bad guy.

"I'm going to the doctor's today," he said, trying to change the topic.

Nicola looked up at him. "Awww, are you sick? Poor little baby," she said mockingly.

"I'm going to the fertility specialist," he said defiantly.

Nicola slammed her coffee on the island counter so abruptly that it sloshed over the top and spilled onto the counter. "What? Really? Why?" she asked suspiciously.

"I know I said we should wait until things calm down. But who knows when they actually will. You've been through so much lately, maybe a step towards good news will make things better." He took her hands in his. "We'll make it through this together, okay?"

She fidgeted in her seat, her eyes fluttering everywhere except on him. She tried to gently pull away from his hands, but he kept his grip tight. He pulled her hands toward his, lowered his head onto her hands and kissed them. She looked away uncomfortably. He took one of his hands and placed it under her chin. He pulled her towards him, forcing her to look into his eyes.

"I'm sorry, Nicola," he said and she squirmed uncomfortably in her chair. She knew that this was what she wanted from him, but for reasons unbeknownst to her, she wasn't ready to hear them. Not now.

"I'm very sorry I wasn't there for you when I should have been."

She squirmed a bit more but he maintained his grip on her face, so she reluctantly stopped fidgeting.

"Apology accepted," she mumbled and he let her chin go, kissing her on the forehead.

"I'm going to see the doctor at lunch time. I'll message you later today to check up on you, okay?"

She nodded and mumbled a vague reply about going to work and checking in on Patsy, to make sure she was holding down the fort. He stood up from his seat and nodded in agreement as he slung his bag over his left shoulder. He squeezed her hand one more time before grabbing his keys, and walked over to the front door.

"Love you, honey," he said over his shoulder as the door closed behind him.

She murmured a goodbye but felt remarkably empty. Despite his entire speech, she felt like his adoration was more of a 'goodbye' than a 'see you later'.

Nicola sat at her desk and stared at the enormous pile of paperwork. Despite Patsy's great efforts this past week, the number of new clients that suddenly appeared out of the woodwork had overwhelmed her a bit. At least Patsy had kept the orders on time and convinced most of the new clients to accept a one-time short delay with a minimal explanation. The relationship that Nicola created with her ongoing clients was usually a very close and personal one—a relationship that allowed the simple explanation of 'personal trauma' from Patsy that left them wanting to know more, but respectfully not asking while offering their condolences.

Patsy also seemed less on edge than she had been a few days ago when she had come by the hotel to visit her. Nicola felt that Patsy also agreed with the police officers and that the rape was faked, although she had no idea why. It had created an awkward tension that had never existed before between the two women. Nicola felt that the only people who truly supported her from the get-go were Sarah and Cassandra.

When she had come into the office that morning Patsy was already there. They had exchanged brief hellos before Patsy dove back into her computer work. The only consolation that Nicola felt was that Patsy at least looked relieved to see Nicola come in. Only a few minutes after she had entered her office, Patsy knocked timidly on her door. She held a large stack of paperwork in one hand and a lukewarm chai in the other.

"May I come in?" she asked softly.

"Of course," Nicola said.

Patsy set the paperwork on the desk and the chai beside it.

"I'm going out to do the deliveries for today. After tomorrow we should be caught up on all of our regulars. We will still need more time to catch up with our newer clients. I've not been able to find everything. I tried to sort the pile out as best I could. The top is mostly new scribbled post-its on the paperwork from new clients and other notes I haven't been able to get to," she said quickly.

"Thank you Patsy for doing so much. It's good to know I can count on you."

Patsy looked down at her feet awkwardly, then smiled briefly and left. Nicola looked at her and shook her head.

It saddened her to know that her trusted friend and colleague didn't even believe her. She hoped that Patsy could work past this and the two of them could resolve their differences over this matter quickly. She almost called Patsy back into the office just to tell her that the police found evidence that supported her rape accusation. They had found a window that was tampered with after all, and the doctor corroborated that with the rape kit. Although there were no traces of semen, the doctor had been able to prove that Nicola had had rough, non-consensual intercourse. Since Karim had immediately voiced that he had not had sex with Nicola in the past week, that along with the human hair traces they had found supported Nicola's original statement. Karim had already apologized left, right and centre for days now. Everyday he had brought home flowers and practically begged for forgiveness. Even the police officers, when delivering the news, offered meek apologies for the way they treated her in the hospital. She had stood her ground and urged them to take all rape accusations more seriously in the future as not all victims were as strong and stubborn as she was. And that their behaviour could cause a victim to crumble and let a rapist go free.

However, she had decided that her first day back in the office was not the time to inform Patsy of that now, so she decided to dive into the paperwork. A few pages in, she realized that Patsy had done a better job than she had initially expected. She knew how much Patsy hated doing paperwork—about as much as Nicola hated her computer at first. But Nicola had insisted that they first create actual hard copies before inputing anything officially into the computer. It was one of the few ongoing battles they had about work. Nicola had still not warmed up to trusting computers entirely just yet.

The first folder was all new clients so she decided to put that off until later, wanting to catch up on the bills as she knew most were due the past week. She found the folder marked 'bills' and slowly started making her way through it. The day crawled by but she finally made her way through the majority of the paperwork. Bills got paid and confirmed, she updated her ongoing clients' folders and added more contacts to their database. Now it was time to tackle the new clients. She looked at her clock and saw that it was after six in the evening. She should stop for the day, but she felt like she was on a roll and she knew that Karim would be home late that night, as usual.

She had just flipped open the folder when her iPad chirped, indicating a new email. She flipped the cover up and the two lines read an unknown email address and *'Karim's test results'*. She studied the email address again, positive it was neither his work nor professional address. Curious, she unlocked her iPad, went to her mail folder and opened the new email. Other than the subject line all it contained were two attachments. She clicked on the first one and a medical document popped up. It was many pages long, but thankfully the sender had highlighted the appropriate parts. It took a few minutes before she realized that these medical papers were from a few years ago, before she and Karim had even met and started dating. She had to Google a few of the words, but finally she understood that it was results from a fertility test. From what the doctor wrote, Karim had had an infection in his late teens 'down there' and they had done several tests to help understand the infection. One of the tests was a fertility test and the result was that he was infertile.

Nicola stared at the screen numbly, her hands covering her mouth. He had already known that he was infertile. It wasn't that he didn't want to have kids, he never could. Maybe he did want to have kids but pretended he didn't because he was ashamed? But why hadn't he told her? Why had he kept this a secret for so long, and why not tell her the truth after she had decided she wanted to try and have kids?

She closed the file and went to shut off her iPad when she remembered that there was another attachment. She cautiously clicked it open to reveal a single page document. It was the same form she saw the doctor fill out for her when she went to the fertility clinic. It had today's date and Karim's name on it. Other than that it only had a few notes. No indication that he was there for a fertility test or anything else other than a brief chat. He didn't even do a check-up with the doctor. Simply written on the bottom was *'Met with Nicola's partner. Seems supportive and eager'*.

She stared at her iPad in disbelief. Even with the facts in front of her she couldn't believe her eyes. All this time he had been hiding the truth from her, he had been lying to her. Tears welled up in her eyes and she wiped them away, refusing to give in. She balled her fists and trembled. Her phone beeped and she whipped it out, half expecting another email even though it wasn't her iPad that chirped. She looked at the screen and saw a text from a blocked number. She opened the message and read *'Wonder what else he has lied about…'*.

CHAPTER TWENTY THREE

Almost three weeks had passed since the rape, and everything was finally beginning to resemble a more quiet, peaceful and drama-free time. Things with Patsy had literally cleared up overnight, and things with Karim, despite his lack of admitting the truth to her yet, were rolling along relatively well. They still seldom saw one another, but when they did he was more attentive than usual and her feelings of him leaving had evaporated.

Patsy and Nicola walked out of the café together. It was one of those rare mornings where the two had crossed paths en route in the morning. Nicola snatched the paper bag out of Patsy's hand and dangled it above her head. She waved it back and forth, singing and mocking Patsy's short stature.

"Never gonna get it," Nicola sang as she did a little twirl and danced away. Patsy dashed after her and kicked her in the rear with her very pointed high heels. Nicola stopped abruptly and Patsy walked right into her. She lowered the bag and Patsy yanked it out of her hand.

"I'm never buying you breakfast again," Patsy retorted as she bit into the pastry meant for Nicola.

"Hey!" Nicola shouted and yanked the danish out of her mouth. "That's mine."

She examined it quickly before taking a bite herself as Patsy stuck her tongue out at her and dashed off ahead. Nicola ran after her, but even in heels, Patsy could easily outrun her.

Patsy slowed down when they entered the warehouse district and leaned against a building, huffing and puffing as she tried to catch her breath.

"Whew," she exclaimed, fanning her face with her hand as she turned around to see Nicola not too far behind her. "I thought you were a runner," she said laughing.

Nicola stopped behind her and pinched her butt.

"I'm not the one out of breath," she laughed as she waltzed by the still gasping-for-air Patsy. "Besides, I already ran ten kilometres this morning," she shouted over her shoulder.

Patsy shot her a dirty look but remained hunched over, trying to catch her breath. When she was finally able to compose herself, she walked quickly, trying to catch up with Nicola.

Nicola was holding the gate open, waiting in the elevator for her. Patsy walked in with a breathless 'thank you'.

"You have no idea how tempted I was to go up and make you wait hours just for it to return," Nicola teased.

Patsy glared at her and rolled her eyes. "I would have called in sick first before waiting for this beastie." Both laughed as the elevator lurched upwards.

Still in high spirits, they got off the lift and let themselves into the office. Nicola opened the door with a grand gesture and curtsied as Patsy tiptoed in like a ballerina. She attempted a pirouette and stopped suddenly. Nicola, still laughing, stepped inside the office.

"That wasn't a very go—" she started but cut herself off abruptly as her chai tea fell out of her hand and fell to the floor. As if in slow motion, the lid popped off as the cup clattered loudly to the ground, tea splashing in all directions. Her arms fell lifelessly to her side as she turned herself in a slow semi-circle, looking the room over, and her purse slid off her shoulder, falling to the floor with a soft thud. Her face fell slack as she mouthed the word 'no' and her eyes grew wide.

Patsy stepped towards the wall and touched one of the articles tacked on it. She started to ask what they were when Nicola suddenly appeared in front of her and slapped her hand off the article.

"Don't touch it!" she shrieked and Patsy stepped away from the wall, mumbling an apology and gingerly clutching the hand Nicola had hit in front of her chest, thoroughly confused. Nicola shook her head.

"Just don't touch it. Don't read it, just go," she stammered, her words coming out in a jumbled rush. Patsy put a hand on Nicola's shoulder but Nicola shrugged her off. "Call the police please. Then just go outside. Wait for them outside."

Patsy looked at her, curious and concerned, but she slowly took her cell phone out of her purse and dialled 9-1-1. She left the office, went downstairs, and left Nicola alone.

Although she knew better than to hope her stalker had finished with her, she hadn't expected this. She stepped up to the article Patsy had been about to read, and careful not to touch it, she looked at the headline. It read '*Baby Drowns in Bathtub Accident*'. Nicola hugged herself tight and shivered. She didn't have to read the article to know what it was about. She had recognized the grainy black-and-white photo of herself when she had first had stepped into the office. Although she had never read any of the articles herself, she had known when she saw the office and the picture of herself, what they had to be about. She was only four when it had happened. Not old enough to read or to even know what a newspaper or reporters were. Not even old enough to know what death was.

She wanted to rip them off the wall. Her terrible ordeal with the police was still fresh in her mind. Even with the more definitive evidence in her rape assault, she knew that they looked at her with anger and disgrace. That somehow they just knew she was guilty and was, somehow, as much the accused as she was the victim. Their continued lack of leads and dead ends brought about doubt, and she could see it every time she had to deal with them.

Even way back then, when the drowning happened, they had stared at her as if she were guilty and thought that she had gotten away with something horrible just because she was a child. She had never talked to Karim or anyone else about it. Not then, now, or even with all that the stalker had suggested with his gifts. She was avoiding calls from her sisters, and Patsy, bless her heart, had known something really bad had happened but was good enough to not ask her anything about it. Patsy was the one thing holding her sanity together. And now Patsy had almost found out her ugly truth. What would she do if Patsy found out what Nicola had done?

She clutched herself tightly again and shuddered. She looked up at the walls. She couldn't believe how many different articles there were. Curious, she looked at another and gasped. The headline read *'Mother's Negligence Kills'*. She shook her head. She couldn't believe what she was reading. She looked at another article that started off with *'A community lies saddened at the death of a baby that could have been prevented if only a mother had paid attention to her children instead of answering the phone'*. Nicola skimmed through the article. The only mention of her was as the other child in the tub left alone with a baby. *'A baby with a baby'*, it read. Another article sympathized with her, arguing that the mother's negligence would leave the child, Nicola, with permanent mental issues due to survivor's guilt.

She continued reading article after article, surprised at what she was reading. All of them had the same underlying tone: the mother was to blame; the mother was negligent; the surviving child was to be sympathized with. Some even suggested that the only reason the police didn't press charges was because the mother was already pregnant with her third child. The last article Nicola read before the police arrived stated that the only reason social services didn't step in and take Nicola away was because her father had stood by her mother and supported her through the entire ordeal. He had also publicly announced that he would take responsibility for his children and prevent further mishaps like this from happening. And to prove his point, the first thing he did was disconnect their telephone.

Nicola recalled growing up with no means of communication to the outside world aside from school and mail. She tried to recall when they had finally gotten a telephone.

Nicola was sitting on the floor of the office when the police finally arrived. Patsy walked them as far as the office door, but remained outside. She could see Nicola sitting there, shell shocked. She turned her back to Nicola, hiding the tiniest of smirks.

Nicola looked up at the police officers and saw it was the same two from when her office was littered with pictures of herself. She looked up at them, her face wracked with misery, and tears hinting at the corners of her eyes. Her lips trembled and her face twitched. The female officer bent down to talk to her as the male officer looked over the articles, switching between taking pictures, writing down notes and cursing under his breath.

"Your colleague tells me that you asked her to leave right after you both walked in and saw the walls filled with these articles. Can you tell me why?" the female officer asked her.

Nicola shook her head and cradled it further into her lap, her knees now pulled up to her chest. "I was afraid," she muttered, slowly rocking back and forth.

"Afraid of what?" the officer asked but Nicola could only mumble as she gestured to the articles on the wall. "Do you know what these are about?" the officer asked gently.

Nicola shook her head no as she whispered 'me'. The officers looked at her quizzically.

"It's me in the pictures," she said more loudly, but still barely audible.

The officer looked up above Nicola. The other officer handed her an article featuring a picture of a young girl and a baby boy. She showed it to Nicola.

"Is this you?" she asked incredulously and Nicola nodded. The two officers looked at each other with concern and then out at Patsy, who still had her back to them, standing in the hall. The female officer leaned in closer and asked in a very quiet voice. "Does your colleague know about this?"

Nicola shook her head as she finally lifted her head out of her lap and answered in a very clear voice. "No one knows. No one."

The male officer slowly walked over to the office door, said a few words to Patsy and then closed the door. He nodded at the female officer.

"How about your family? Your sisters? Your boyfriend?" she asked.

"We moved to another city after it happened. We even changed our last name. But we have never talked about it. Ever. But they found out," Nicola whined.

"Who found out?" the officer asked.

"My sisters. At least, I think they did. I don't know. I don't want to talk about it. Please." Nicola buried her head back into her lap.

The female officer put a hand on her shoulder. "We can talk about it later if you like. But for right now, is there anyone you want us to call?"

Nicola looked up at them, her face wracked with anger, heartbreak and confusion. She shook her head back and forth violently, then put her head back into her lap and cried.

CHAPTER TWENTY FOUR

Nicola opened the door to greet her sisters, only to discover it was just Cassandra. Cassandra held out an armful of baked goods mixed amongst large paper bags loaded full of snacks. They had a momentary awkward juggle as Nicola tried to help lighten her load. They struggled a bit but managed to safely make it to the kitchen island. Nicola started poking though the bags, looking at all of the treats her sister had brought. She had brought her favourite cake, devil's food cake, and liquid chai tea mix, along with a ton of fresh fruit, vegetables, and fish, obviously from the island market they all loved. She smiled as she noticed that the chai mix was the same brand that Patsy bought for her.

Cassandra yanked the cake out of Nicola's hands before she could stick a finger in the icing and promptly put it into the refrigerator.

"Really, still five are we?" Nicola pouted and Cassandra put on the kettle. "Sarah says she'll be by later. She has a few errands to run."

Nicola grabbed two mugs, poured milk into them, put them into the microwave and set it for a minute. Cassandra started emptying the bags out onto the counter. She put the fruit directly into the fridge and the vegetables and fish onto the counter. While Nicola made the chai tea lattes, her sister set the fish to marinate and chopped up the vegetables.

Nicola inhaled the strong aroma of the chai. She loved the island market's chai mix. They made it themselves from scratch and only sold a few hundred a week to maintain freshness. She handed a mug to her sister who sipped at it cautiously.

"I didn't make yours as strong as mine. Promise."

Her sister still sipped carefully. Then, after two sips, she was satisfied and took a bigger drink. Nicola offered to help with dinner, but Cassandra shook her head no at first, then changed her mind and handed her two large purple onions, instructing her to dice them.

They settled into a rhythm of chopping vegetables, and a comfortable silence settled over them. They put the fish into a casserole dish and covered it with the raw vegetables. It sat on one side of the oven while a small tray of finely chopped up potatoes slathered in butter and onions was already cooking on the other side. They sat down at the island with their drinks.

"It's been awhile since we've cooked dinner like this," Cassandra said softly.

Nicola nodded, absorbed in her chai. She knew that Patsy must have talked to her sisters about the office incident. She hadn't told anyone else about it, not even Karim. She had even refused the free counselling the police had offered her. She tried to push it behind her and had told Patsy to forget about it, but two days later her sisters suddenly wanted a weekend together with her. She had tried to refuse, but Cassandra was a force to be reckoned with.

"It's been awhile since I've been free from the kids for this long, but I think I could get used to this," she said with a wink.

Nicola laughed. "In three years they'll be in school and it'll be almost as liberating."

"I was thinking about enrolling them in preschool next year," Cassandra said.

Nicola peeked at her from over her mug.

"We took them to get assessed. Apparently they're in the high percentile of potentially gifted toddlers," Cassandra chuckled. "There's a special school for preschoolers that helps them to develop their potential early. We've been thinking about sending them there."

Nicola looked at her in shock. "Wow, that's amazing. I knew my niece and nephew were little prodigies."

Her sister laughed. "We'll see."

The timer went off and Cassandra opened the oven, pulled out the potatoes, flipped them over, put them back in and reset the timer. She sat down again, reached a hand out to take Nicola's free hand and squeezed it. Nicola looked at her with question, trying to hide the suspicion growing inside her.

"I've been going over and over this in my head, trying to figure out how to say this to you. We both have," Cassandra started.

Nicola gingerly set her mug back down and took a slow deep breath.

"But there is no nice way to say this, and honestly, I wish we had known about it years ago."

Nicola grew tense; she knew what her sister was about to say. She knew it the moment both of them said they wanted to visit her together. She started to shake her head.

"There's nothing to say. Please," Nicola said softly.

"It needs to be said. Do you know how much it hurts to see you in so much pain?" asked Cassandra.

Nicola jumped to her feet and ran off towards the living room. Cassandra caught her hand and stopped her. "Nic, listen to me. We know what happened. It wasn't your fault."

Nicola tried to pull free. "Yes, it was. Mother said so, father said so, everyone said so," she cried. "Besides, shouldn't we wait for Sarah to get here? It's not a proper girls night with her missing."

"Stop trying to change the topic. Besides, you're wrong," Cassandra said sternly.

"You wouldn't know, you weren't even born," Nicola spat at her.

"I know that we had no idea for years why Mother hated you. I know that no one would tell us anything. No one, not even father would say anything to us. No one told us why we didn't have any relatives outside of our immediate family. Now I know that they cut us off after father chose to take her side," Cassandra said.

Nicola stared at Cassandra, her face full of tears, gently trying to tug her hand free. "Please, Cass. Don't," she pleaded.

Cassandra stood her ground. "You need to hear this. It's. Not. Your. Fault," she said emphatically.

"It is. She said so," Nicola wept.

"You were four! How the hell could it be your fault?" Cassandra asked.

"She said I was a big girl," Nicola said, her eyes growing a glazed-over look and her voice going child like.

Cassandra grabbed her by the arms and shook her. Nicola fought against her and tried to pull away but Cassandra wouldn't loosen her grip.

"It was my fault. That's why you had to stay away from me. I was dangerous," she whimpered.

"No. You were just a baby."

Despite her continued fighting, Cassandra easily overpowered Nicola and pulled her into a tight embrace. Nicola felt herself losing her composure and let herself fall into her sister, the two of them collapsing down to their knees. Cassandra stroked her hair, tears falling down both their faces.

"Why did you never tell us, Nic? Why did you let them hurt you like that?"

"My fault, my fault, my fault," Nicola muttered through her tears like a broken record.

Cassandra hugged her tighter, stroked her hair, and in response kept saying, "No it's not, it never was. No it's not, it never was…."

"Bubbles?" Nicola asked eagerly, leaning her naked body over the edge of the bathtub, gazing in with excitement. She loved bath time. Mommy let her play with lots of toys and her baby brother, George.

"Use your words," her mother said.

"May I have bubbles?" Nicola asked again.

"Manners?" her mother said.

"May. I. Have. Bubbles. Please."

Her mother smiled and tousled her hair. "Yes, but only a little. We don't want George to get sick from eating them."

Nicola wrinkled her nose. She couldn't understand why George liked to eat the bubbles. They tasted gross.

Mommy set George's chair into the bath tub, watching the water level slowly rise. She kept dipping her elbow in the water, testing the temperature. Nicola leaned over herself, trying to reach her elbow in. Mommy laughed at her when she couldn't reach, she could barely touch the water with her fingertips and she was leaning over so much her feet were off the floor. Once the chair was half covered with water, Mommy turned off the taps.

"Here," Mother said, grabbing Nicola by the waist and lowering her slightly. "Feel with your hand first."

Nicola obeyed and splashed her hand in the bathtub.

"Now, use your elbow. I'll help you," she said as she lowered Nicola towards the tub so she could put her elbow in.

Once in, Nicola's eyes opened wide. "It's hotter!"

Mommy nodded. "Your elbow is more sensitive, like George's skin."

Nicola nodded her head, not really understanding what Mommy was telling her. She grabbed her rubber duckies and her bath Barbies, and put them into the bathtub before climbing in herself. Mommy left to go get George who was still lying in his playpen.

Nicola began to have a parade with her duckies, with Barbie being the cheerleader up front. After a few minutes mother brought a naked George in and set him in his chair. He flailed his arms up and down, splashing water everywhere. Nicola laughed and splashed him back.

"Gentle splashes," her mother said.

Nicola resorted to using just her fingers to make splashes at George. She played with her duckies, driving them around George, up George, and even gave him one so he could splash it in the tub before trying to eat it.

"Hold your brother," Mother said.

Nicola obediently let go of her duckies and grabbed onto George's torso. She scrunched her eyes closed and tipped her head back as Mommy put one hand on her forehead, and with her other hand dumped a pitcher of bathwater onto Nicola's head, her hand guiding the water away from Nicola's eyes. Once the water had stopped Nicola opened her eyes. George was shrieking hysterically. He loved watching the water splash. Mommy went about washing Nicola's hair while Nicola discovered that if she dipped her one hand in the water with the other still holding George, and then held it over his head and wiggled her fingers, she could splash tiny bits of water over his head. He shrieked and giggled as she did this.

"Head up," Mother said as she rinsed the shampoo out.

George splashed and kicked and shrieked. Nicola laughed and almost got soap in her eye. Mommy kissed her on the forehead.

"Good girl. Now let's wash Georgie's hair."

Nicola held George while Mommy used a washcloth instead of the pitcher to wet his hair. Mommy let her wash his hair, reminding her to be gentle. He got very quiet when she washed his hair, almost as if he wasn't sure if what was happening was good or bad. It made Nicola giggle that he could be so quiet.

Once his hair was done Nicola saw that all of the bubbles were gone. "Bubbles?" she asked.

Mommy shook her head. "Bath time is almost done."

Nicola pouted but lowered her head into the bathtub water and snorted. Bubbles appeared in the water and she raised her head, laughing. George shrieked and almost kicked her in the face. She scooted back away from him, lowered her head and made more bubbles. George shrieked even more and even Mommy laughed.

From afar they could hear the telephone ring. Nicola looked up abruptly. "Daddy?" she asked.

"No sweetie, Daddy's at work. It's probably nobody important."

The telephone continued to ring and ring. Then it finally stopped.

"See," Mother said. "If it was important they wouldn't have hung up."

The telephone started to ring again. This time it rang even longer before the caller finally hung up. After another moment it began to ring again. Mommy looked between the bathtub, where Nicola was just finishing washing herself with the wash cloth, and outside the bathroom door.

"Can you be a big girl and hold George for a few minutes? Mommy has to get the telephone," she asked and Nicola nodded. She grabbed onto George's torso as her Mommy got up and left the bathroom.

George kicked and shrieked a little but quickly petered down. Nicola looked around the tub but all of her toys had floated far away and Mommy had already taken the Barbies out and put them in the basket too high for her to reach when she was holding George. George looked around and started to cry.

"Shhh. Don't cry George," she said as she let go of George with one hand, turned to the side and put her face in the water to make bubbles. George laughed and splashed his hands in the water. She lifted her face out and he stopped splashing, his face beginning to tremble again. She put her face in the water again and made more bubbles. Again he shrieked with excitement, but this time he kicked her in the face. She accidentally let go of him and he slid down his chair and into the water. His face fell under the water and when he breathed out he made bubbles himself. Nicola grabbed him and tried to slide him back up into his chair. When she got his face out of the water he looked shocked but excited. He clapped his hands and she smiled.

"Yay! Georgie made bubbles!" she laughed. "Want to make more?" she asked him.

He splashed the water. She lowered him into the water again and he made more bubbles. She lifted him out and he choked and coughed a little but shrieked and kicked about. Nicola lowered her head into the water and made more bubbles herself. Then she lowered George in again. She kept alternating back and forth between herself and George. But then suddenly George wasn't making bubbles anymore. He had fallen asleep.

"Wake up Georgie," she said, lifting him higher in his seat.

Mommy finally came back into the bathroom.

"Sorry sweetie, I didn't mean to be—" she stopped abruptly as she saw George. She immediately lifted him out of the bathtub.

"George?" she whispered.

"Mommy?" Nicola asked.

Mommy ignored her and ran out of the bathroom screaming George's name. Nicola sat in the bathtub, confused. She didn't want to keep playing anymore because the water was cold and Mommy's screaming was scaring her. She crawled out of the bathtub and walked out of the bathroom.

She went into her bedroom and crawled under the sheets, shivering and hiding from Mommy who was still screaming. She closed her eyes and tried to hide away from the screams. Soon she heard the sound of sirens. They kept getting closer and closer until they were outside her house. Red lights flickered through her bedroom window and she could hear the front door burst open.

Karim sat on the bed next to Nicola. He stroked the hair off of her forehead, her face was dirty with tears and snot. When he had come home, he saw the two of them huddled into a tight embrace, bawling their eyes out like some high school girls who had just lost their first love. When he had tried to figure out what had happened, Cassandra only shook her head at him. After the crying had finally subsided, he helped a sleepy Nicola to her feet. She literally collapsed into his arms and had passed out from exhaustion by the time he had taken her to their room. He kissed her gently on the forehead and went to check on Cassandra.

In the living room he found she had already set up camp on the pull-out couch. Cassandra was already in her pajamas and was brushing her teeth. She disappeared into the kitchen, where he heard her spit and rinse out her mouth. She returned only to ignore him and crawl into her bed. He sat down next to her and tapped her on the shoulder.

"Do you mind letting me in on what the hell just happened?"

Cassandra shook her head. "I'm exhausted. If Nic is up to it maybe we can talk about it in the morning. Goodnight Karim," she blew him a kiss, turned over and closed her eyes.

He shook his head and went back into the bedroom. Nicola was fast asleep. He got undressed, crawled into bed next to her and turned off the light.

Nicola tossed and turned in her sleep. Abruptly, she stopped tossing and her eyes popped open. She caught her breath and slapped her hands over her mouth before she could scream out loud. Still looking up at the ceiling she willed herself to slow her breath down until she could no longer hear the pounding of her heart. She slowly moved her hands down from her mouth. She could hear Karim snoring beside her. Carefully, she slid the sheets off of her body and towards the middle of the bed. She tumbled off the bed and onto the floor. Peeking up she saw that Karim was still sound asleep. Cautiously she stood up and tiptoed towards the open closet. She grabbed her bathrobe and crept into the bathroom. She closed the door adjoining the bedroom and then opened the other door that led into the hallway.

She caught her reflection in the mirror and saw how bad she looked. She turned the water on lightly, and using a washcloth she quickly cleaned her face and then left the bathroom.

In the hallway she looked towards the living room and could hear Cassandra, also fast asleep. Sarah apparently had not made it yet. She made her way down the hallway to their office. She opened the door, let herself in and closed the door with a quiet click.

Turning on only the desk lamp, the room looked eerie. Shadows danced on the walls and mixed with the moonlight. She opened the closet and emptied out the entire contents that covered the floor of the closet. She felt along the edge of the closet floor until she felt a slight difference in the hardwood panels. Then she counted three panels over to the right and pressed down and back on it. She then counted over another five panels, pushed down once, then back one panel and pressed down twice. On the second press the whole floor popped open on a hinge. When she had started her business, one of her first clients was a magician who also happened to be a carpenter in his early career days. After she had found him some very rare doves, he offered her a bonus of installing secret panels in her apartment to hide things from burglars. He happened to incorporate these illusionary panels into his earlier carpentry work, trying to sell them, but they had not taken off quite as well as his magical career had. Not only did she hire him to do most of the renovations with her, but she got him to install four of these panels without telling Karim. There was one in the floor of both of the closets, one behind the bathroom cabinet and one in the hallway behind the bookshelf.

Inside this compartment was an assortment of baby clothes, toys and accessories. Slowly, she pulled out the items one by one and set them around her. Bibs, cloth diapers, a diaper pail, scented baby wipes. An assortment of toys including teething rings, stuffed animals, and other soft plush toys. She hugged the Baby Elmo tightly. Then, without pause, she proceeded to grab its arms and pull. She pulled harder and harder until it finally started to rip apart slowly. She pulled it completely apart into two sections and then proceeded to pull the stuffing out of it. When she finished with it, she grabbed another stuffed animal and tore it apart. Then she got up and went to the desk. She rifled through the desk drawers until she found a pair of scissors. She went back to the pile of baby things and began to cut everything. She cut the remaining parts of Elmo and the other stuffed animals until they were nothing more than a large pile of tiny scraps. She cut the bibs into many pieces, she scratched the plastic toys until they were barely recognizable and punctured holes into the teething rings. She discovered she could rip the cloth diapers after just cutting the top edge and she tore them apart, one by one, growing more and more frenzied with each rip. When she finally finished destroying all that she could she threw the scissors into the compartment, then pushed the large pile of scrap baby stuff into the compartment. She tossed them angrily and shoved them down as hard as she could. When it was all finally in she forced the lid down and closed it.

Satisfied, she took a deep breath. Naively, she had waited for Karim to tell her the result of his visit to the doctors weeks ago. When more than a couple of weeks had passed, she had brought the topic up herself and he had blatantly lied, saying all was good on his end. She had thought of showing him the email and calling him out on it, but for reasons unbeknownst to her she couldn't. She had tried to convince herself it was a lie from her stalker trying to provoke her, and she decided to not care about it. Her face was flushed red, her breathing was erratic, and her hair was a mess, flying everywhere. She drew her fingers through her hair, collecting it briefly and then let it fall back down. She calmly put the contents of the bottom of the closet back in place. She closed the closet door, turned off the desk lamp, went back to the bedroom and crawled back into bed.

Patsy was already seated at the little Italian place in their reserved table at the back. She was doing a final look-over of herself, making sure she looked absolutely perfect. It had been almost a month since she had last seen Gregory. Their get-togethers had become so erratic with no sense of logic or planning. He'd go days without contacting her then text her all day. He kept going through different phone numbers, claiming to keep having issues with his credit and stuck with prepaid options that weren't enough for what he needed—which made contacting him difficult if he didn't reach out first. His email address was the only permanent means of contact that she had. But when he did contact her he was so overwhelmingly attentive that it always made up for the lack of free time that he had. He was always busy with his various charities. He refused to tell her which ones other than that they were cancer-related. He said he was always anonymous when dealing with the charities, and felt embarrassed if anyone found out what he was doing since he didn't do it for credit or gratification. He did this work as a thank you to the doctors who had saved his life. She knew his stories were just that, stories. But she also knew that when he was ready he'd be able to share the truth with her. Share his secret that she already knew. She loved him enough to be patient. She smiled as she recalled that his last text had simply read, 'Can't wait to see you. Usual spot and time'.

She had floated on cloud nine all day at work until she could rush home to get ready. She had originally opted for a dress, but remembered how restricting it could be compared to a skirt and shirt. Instead she chose a flowing knee-length skirt covered with red flowers and a sheer tank top under a button-up cardigan. She took special care with her makeup, less bold and more subdued. She knew he preferred natural, but she was unfortunately not a natural beauty and required a fair amount of work to look 'au natural'. Her hair was in a loose braid and the excess pulled back with a couple of clips.

Patsy had already ordered a bottle of wine and was halfway through her first glass when Gregory arrived. She didn't even have to try, a giant smile came naturally to her lips as soon as she saw him. She knew she was beginning to glow and he hadn't done much more than smile back at her. She waved her hand a little and he sat down beside her. She wiggled over to get closer to him but he put a hand on her knee and stopped her. She looked up at him with startled eyes and hesitated at first, but then slowly slid back to her side of the bench.

"Have you ordered anything else other than the wine?" he asked curtly.

"No-o-o—," she stammered, surprised at his tone of voice.

"Good," he said as he poured himself a glass of wine.

He swallowed the whole glass in one take then poured himself another. She stared at him, her eyes wide with surprise. Suddenly she clenched her hands in her lap and began to twiddle her fingers around each other nervously. Her eyes darted briefly from side to side before settling onto her half-empty wine glass. She opened her mouth to speak, but quickly closed it again.

Gregory stared out into space and seemed to be contemplating something with deep thought. He sat tall, his body rigid and his eyebrows furrowed. Finally, after what seemed like hours but was actually only seconds, he turned and spoke to her.

"You have no idea do you?" he asked.

Slowly she looked up at him and when their eyes met she winced. She could see great anger pouring out of his eyes and straight at her. Despite his calm outer appearance, she could see a faint tremble in his hands. He appeared to be holding great restraint. Afraid to speak, she merely shook her head from side to side and looked down at her lap. He took a sip of wine and set the glass back down onto the table with such force that the wine nearly sloshed out of the glass. Patsy started to slide farther away from him but he reached out with such fierceness and speed that she paused, startled, and he caught her hand. He began to squeeze it, slowly crushing her fingers.

"What have you been doing?" he snarled at her, his voice starting to pitch.

"I— uh— What you've asked me to do?" she whimpered.

He squeezed her hand harder.

"Don't lie to me," he said, still looking straight ahead, an angry snarl on his lips. He picked up his glass with his free hand and took another sip. "What have you been doing to her?"

Patsy whimpered again but he wouldn't release his grip on her hand.

"I wanted to help you—" she started and he slammed her hand down into the table, causing both their glasses to shake and tumble over.

He caught his easily but hers fell over and wine spilled all over her skirt. She went to jump up out of the way of the spilling wine but he grabbed her chin and forced her to look at him.

"I'm talking to you," he growled.

She looked into his eyes and the rage behind them was strong. Her face hurt where he was holding her, but she knew he would only let her go when he was ready.

"I'm sorry?" she said softly.

He pulled her face close to his. "Sorry isn't good enough," he said, spitting in her face with each word, then roughly let her go.

She pulled away from him and looked down at the ground. Her skirt was now ruined but she could barely register enough thought to care about it. Her eyes clouded over.

"I won't do it again," she mumbled, risking a glance up at him. She could see him shaking. She couldn't tell if it was because of how angry he was at her or because he was having trouble holding himself together. This wasn't what she wanted. She wanted to help him. Help him become stronger.

"Why did you do it?" he asked.

"Do what?" she asked meekly, afraid to confess to what he might not already know.

"Don't play dumb with me, Patsy. What did you think it would accomplish? None of what you've done on your own is helping prove Karim's guilt," he said with a sudden calm.

"I wasn't trying to, I don't know— I thought you were trying to push her farther. I thought I was helping. Honest."

"Torturing her doesn't help her," he said, "It only hurts her. I don't want to hurt her," he said more softly.

"But you said—" she started to say but stopped herself quickly, realizing the implications of her own words. She looked at the tenderness in his eyes and felt both a pang of jealousy and relief, as he had neither heard her but was obviously no longer thinking about her. She looked down at her skirt again she mumbled another vague apology.

He looked over at her and snapped his fingers near her face and she jumped, looking up at him quickly.

"Make sure it doesn't happen again." He said as he abruptly got up and left.

Patsy watched as he left, her meekness quickly turning into anger. Slowly she clenched her fists in her lap as her breath slowly hissed through her teeth and she forced herself to slow her breathing. When she finally felt calm enough, she picked up her tipped-over glass and set it upright. She filled it with the remaining wine and took a long sip.

She set the glass down onto the table and said, "You will be mine, Gregory. One way or another, you will be mine."

CHAPTER TWENTY FIVE

Cassandra carefully backed out of her parking spot; the number of hungover or still-drunk students milling on the street was always high at her sister's place, especially after a weekend of binge drinking. Sarah had made it to Nicola's a day late so both sisters decided to stay a couple of extra days. They didn't talk about the past, just merely lazed about and watched movies. It was a long weekend so Cassandra's hubby was home to look after the kids, and neither Nicola nor Sarah had to work on the weekend. Cassandra successfully made it onto the street and a block away without running anyone over before she felt it safe to increase her speed to that of the legal limit. Thankfully for her, Nicola's condo was not only on the outskirts of town but also on the north-eastern side, which was where the highway she wanted to use intersected nearby to get her home easily. She never minded the drive since she could bypass the city core entirely and have a carefree, non-rush-hour-traffic drive there and back almost any time of the day.

Like tonight, she not only easily got onto the highway, but it was relatively empty despite it being the last day of the long weekend. Nothing but truckers and herself.

Thinking she was lucky, she quickly put her car into cruise control and started playing with the radio with the control on her steering wheel. Of course, the first thing that popped on was a children's sing along. She laughed and switched to **BBC**. She didn't care much for music, she just wanted the white noise in the background.

Up ahead she saw several trucks pulling out of the truck stop. She sped up, hoping to pass the truck stop before the long line of trucks could join the highway as it narrowed down to one lane shortly after the truck stop exit. Just as she thought she was in the clear, a truck changed lanes in front of her, forcing her to slow down.

Only she wasn't slowing down. A quick look at the dash board revealed that her car was still in cruise control, hovering just above the speed limit. She pushed hard on the brake. Nothing. She pushed the arrows down to decrease her speed, yet still nothing. She slammed on the brakes with all the strength she could muster, and the car kept hurtling forward, the truck's rear end suddenly looming in front of her. She grabbed the hand brake with both of her hands and yanked it with all of her might, forcing her car into a tail spin. It spun in circles as the brakes squealed, smoke pouring out of them as the wheels burned rubber, trying to stop. She looked up through her windshield in time to see the passenger side of the car slam into the truck in front of her. Instinctively she covered her face as the airbag deployed and the passenger window exploded. Her face struck the airbag with such force that blackness engulfed her immediately.

Nicola rushed through the emergency room doors. She was dressed in fuzzy teddy bear pajama pants, a tank top, a thin dark purple cardigan and tennis shoes. Her hair was still done up neatly and her face, as always, free of makeup. The ER was extraordinarily busy. Several people had gotten hurt in her sister's car accident, along with the usual nightly visitors: the drunk-themselves-to-a-stupor college students, the odd mom with a sick child, and a few regulars who preferred the ER doctors to a regular doctor. The hallway was filled with several people whose injuries ranged from minor lacerations or broken bones to full-on unconscious, heavily bleeding, almost dying or already dead. The ER was a bustle of yelling voices, crying people and the sound of crash carts being wheeled everywhere.

Nicola rushed over to the nurses' reception counter. When she finally saw a potentially free nurse she waved her down.

"My name is Nicola VanBurgen. My sister, Cassandra VanBurgen, was brought in her. She was in the accident on highway eleven," she said, her body shaking and her hands trembling. She hugged herself, trying to shake herself free of the chill inside.

The nurse held up a single finger, indicating that Nicola wait a moment while she checked her computer.

"Can I see your ID please?" the nurse asked.

Nicola looked at her strangely before fumbling through her purse. "I don't understand. Is that a new policy?" she asked as she produced her driver's license.

The nurse took it, looked it over and handed it back to her. "Sorry about that Miss VanBurgen, this was a big accident and we have to make sure you're not press sneaking in. Plus, your sister is in the ICU."

Nicola put a hand to her mouth and drew a breath in sharply.

"No," she said softly under her breath, but the nurse didn't seem to notice her reaction or simply was immune to it.

"Third floor. Be prepared to show your ID again," she said before quickly disappearing.

Nicola numbly walked towards the elevator. ICU. She wondered how bad it meant Cassandra was. She looked at her phone and saw that Karim still hadn't read the message she had sent him. She tried to recall what he did again on Tuesday nights, but she couldn't remember what club or group he was in, so she could only reach him on his cell. The elevators doors were closing before she realized she was already in the elevator. She hit the number three on the panel and shook her head to clear it. Pull yourself together she thought, Cassandra needs you.

The doors opened and she walked out into a more clear, clean and less chaotic hallway. Like the ER, the hallway and floor were the usual hospital white. Only the lighting seemed less harsh and there was no obvious waiting room. She saw two nurses manning the desk as she slowly stepped towards them. She repeated to them what she said in ER and they directed her to sit in a small waiting room that was hidden around the corner.

She sat down in a chair and looked around. She was alone. She wondered if Cassandra was the only one hurt enough to be in the ICU. Or perhaps Nicola was just the first to arrive. She lived close by the hospital they had taken the majority of the car accident victims to. She hadn't waited more than a few minutes when a doctor, half dressed in scrubs, came in looking for her.

"Hello. Are you friend or family of Cassandra VanBurgen?" he asked her.

"I'm her older sister, Nicola VanBurgen. Is she alright?" she asked standing up.

"I only have a minute, we're prepping her for surgery. Have you contacted anyone else in your family? Is she married?" he asked.

Nicola looked at him scared and confused. "Surgery?" she asked.

"Yes. She's suffering from internal damage. Are you the only one here?" he asked her.

"Yes," she said. "But have you not called her husband?" she asked, still confused.

A nurse handed the doctor a chart. He looked at it briefly.

"No, Nicola, she has you listed as her emergency contact. No one else. She's not been at this hospital before so we've no previous records other than what's listed as contacts in the state computer." He handed the chart back to the nurse who disappeared as quickly as she had appeared.

"I should call her husband," Nicola said absently.

"Ma'am, I have to go into surgery now. Call her husband and I'll be out to check in with you later, okay?" he said.

"Is she going to be okay?" Nicola asked.

The doctor looked at her with a stony, unreadable face. "I can't say right now, we've only been able to address her superficial wounds. I'll have a better answer after surgery. Call her husband and wait here."

Nicola nodded as he left. She stood in the hallway, unable to process what little information he had given her. She was Cassandra's emergency contact? Why not her husband? She stood lost in her thoughts until one of the nurses came up to her and tapped her shoulder.

"Do you need to use a phone?" she asked gently.

Nicola shook her head but let herself be guided to a corner of the waiting room where there was a phone sitting on a small table.

"It's a direct line out," she said with a smile and left Nicola alone. Nicola sat down, picked up the phone and stared at it like it was a foreign object. After a moment she dialled her sister's home number from memory.

An hour later Philip rushed through the ICU doors. He saw Nicola with Patsy and Sarah. The three women got up and rushed over to him.

"Where is she? How is she? What happened?" he spewed out in a big jumble.

Nicola and Patsy each took an arm and guided him to the couch in the waiting room. He reluctantly let them sit him down on the couch. Patsy disappeared after muttering something about coffee and a long night.

Nicola took his hand in hers.

"Cassandra was in a car accident. The police aren't sure exactly what happened other than she literally drove straight into the semi truck. I've assured them she had not had anything to drink that night before she left. I only saw the doctor briefly when I first got here and all he said was that she needed surgery."

He stared at her blankly. "Is she going to be alright?"

"I don't know. The doctor didn't say," Nicola said.

Patsy returned with hot drinks and some vending machine pastries. She passed them around and they all sat quietly, absorbing the situation. Every time a door opened they all looked up eagerly.

"What do I do?" he asked absently.

Nicola took his hand again and squeezed it. "We wait. We pray," she said softly.

Nicola's phone chirped and she looked at it, hoping it was Karim. But it was only a notification from Instagram. She ignored it and put her phone back into her pocket, but it continued to chirp again and again and again. She pulled it out again to see more notifications from Instagram. She mumbled an apology to no one in particular and turned her phone to vibrate. Still in her hand it started going off like crazy.

"Christ. Patsy, can you turn the notification thingie off for me?" she asked, reaching her phone out towards Patsy.

Patsy took the phone and held it out towards Nicola asking her to enter her password. After Nicola punched it in Patsy opened Instagram and suddenly got very quiet. One of her hands quickly covered her mouth as she softly whispered, "Oh my god."

Nicola looked over at her and asked her what was wrong, doing her best to whisper. But Patsy suddenly tried to hide her cell phone from her. Nicola tried to take it back but Patsy held it away and tried to protest, telling Nicola that it wasn't the best time and she'd show her later. But Nicola hissed at her under her breath, demanding that Patsy come clean on what she found.

Unable to speak, Patsy just held the phone out towards Nicola. Nicola leaned over Philip, who was sitting between the two, and looked at the picture on the phone. Her eyes grew wide and her jaw dropped.

"Where the hell did you get that?" she asked, her voice a mere whisper.

Patsy looked at her awkwardly. "It's from Instagram. One of your friends posted it. And there are more—" she said, her voice trailing off.

Nicola snatched the phone out of Patsy's hand and started scrolling through the pictures, muttering curses and obscenities under her breath as she did. Sarah leaning over her shoulder gasped at the pictures. Philip took notice and asked what was wrong. Nicola, her face now beet red, handed the over phone to him. He started scrolling through the pictures, their eyes slowly growing wider and wider as they realized who was in the pictures.

"Who posted these?" he asked incredulously. "Who's *I'm a douche 14*?".

Nicola shrugged her shaking shoulders, her hands clenched in fists and her teeth gritted.

"I don't know. But who cares. That asshole's been cheating on me!"

The sound of a door opening made them look up, hoping to see Cassandra's doctor, but instead Karim had finally showed up.

Under normal circumstances Nicola wouldn't have noticed anything amiss, but right now her eyes were wide open. Karim's clothes were too neat and clean to have been worn all day or quickly thrown on if he had been asleep. Plus, they looked like his work clothes, not his normal evening wear which usually consisted of khakis or jeans and a short sleeved shirt of some kind. Also considering that it was almost two in the morning, it seemed the wrong attire to her. He also looked like he had just gotten out of the shower, his hair glistening with water droplets and his skin looking rosy and squeaky clean.

He rushed into the waiting room, looking around frantically before he noticed them. He rushed to her side and hugged her. She responded stiffly at first, with her arms at her side and her body rigid before she finally reached her arms up and attempted a half-hearted hug back. He didn't seem to notice until she abruptly pushed him away.

"Where have you been? I've been trying to reach you all evening." her voice bitter and icy.

"I was with the boys, drinking, like I always do on Tuesday nights," he said, his eyes full of apology.

"Your phone doesn't work in a bar?" she asked accusingly.

"It was loud, babe," he said.

"And you didn't bother to check your phone for messages for over four hours? You're as attached to your bloody phone as much as I'm not!" she said, taking a step towards him, so close that they could almost be ready to kiss. Instead her words were spitting in his face.

Subconsciously, he wiped a hand across his face. "What is this? The Spanish Inquisition? This isn't the time. How's—"

"I know you read my first message," she said, cutting him off abruptly. "Then you started to ignore me."

"I don't know what you're talking about babe," he said.

"Messenger says when someone reads your message. Patsy taught me that last week. You read the first two messages right after I sent them. But when you didn't reply I tried to call you. You ignored my calls. If you read the texts you obviously would have heard the calls that came minutes later."

Her voice was starting to rise and grow more and more shrill by the second. Philip took notice, stood up and slowly began to lumber in her direction.

"Babe, I think we should be focusing on your sister right now," Karim said.

"No. I've already focused on my sister. I know her condition. I've already talked to her doctor twice, hours ago!" she hissed through a clenched jaw.

"Calm down, honey," he said, putting his hands on her shoulders.

She shrugged away from him, her body shaking. "No, I won't calm down. Where were you? Why were you ignoring my calls?" she asked.

Both Sarah and Philip were within hands reach while Patsy maintained her distance behind them, a small smile curling at the edge of her lips.

"I already told you I was at the bar with the guys," he said.

"Are you sure? Maybe you've mistaken the boys for her!" She shoved her phone into his face.

He blinked and gently pushed the phone away from his face to get a better look at the screen. He saw a picture of himself with a brunette in a very compromising embrace.

"Where did you get this?" he asked quietly.

"Oh, there's a lot more of those where this came from. Courtesy of, what's his name?" she turned the phone back to face herself and glanced at the screen, then turned it back to face Karim.

" '*I'm a cheatin' douche 14*'," Nicola said as she swiped to the next picture. Karim with a blonde, then a redhead, then another brunette.

He cleared his voice, trying to maintain his composure.

"I'm a casting director, remember? I work with a lot of women," he said.

"One that makes out with his clients?" she said.

"I've never—" he started but Nicola pushed the phone in his face again showing him a picture of him with a sexy young redhead in full embrace. Patsy stepped forward and stood beside Nicola.

"We've seen enough pictures that say otherwise, Karim," she said. Karim started to protest, but Philip put a hand on his shoulder.

"Maybe you should just go home. We'll be fine here. It's just a matter of waiting now," he said, more of an order than a request.

Karim looked the group over. A reluctant Patsy, a disgruntled Sarah, a pissed off Nicola ready to either burst into tears or punch him, and Philip who was definitely ready to take him in the ring. He squared up his shoulders, spun on his heels and left.

CHAPTER TWENTY SIX

The sun rose silently through the windows of the hallowed halls on the ICU floor. Nicola, Philip, Sarah and Patsy were all lying in a giant heap on the lone couch in the waiting room area. Their last update was several hours ago and Cassandra was still fighting strong. Now they were just waiting to see if she would wake up or slip into a coma. They were still only allowed in to see her for short periods of time until she awoke and was stabilized. The day shift was coming and the changing of the guard was commencing as they slept on.

A nurse came out of the ICU unit, her face a stony wall of unreadable emotion. She handed a chart to the day-duty RN floor nurse, said a few words and pointed to the group asleep on the couch. The new nurse nodded and set the chart on the top of the counter. She turned to her other charts and began the preparations for her day. A sudden shrill beeping filled the air causing the nurses to jump to their feet and run into the ICU unit. An orderly with a crash cart quickly followed.

Patsy, Sarah and Nicola abruptly woke up and jumped to their feet. Patsy bumped into Nicola who fell backwards, bumping into Sarah who then fell onto the couch whilst the two others fell to the floor. Nicola got to her knees, rubbing her derriere while Patsy sat on the floor, still not quite awake. The girls looked at each other with fear, their faces pale and in mid-slumber shock. They clutched each other and looked at the ICU with trembling anxiety. Sarah motioned to wake their still sleeping beauty, but Nicola slowly shook her head side to side and mouthed the words 'Not yet'. The three of them, still clutching each other, got to their feet and quietly walked towards the ICU unit. The shrill beeping continued, faltered, then flatlined. They looked at each other in shock for a moment then burst into a full sprint towards the ICU unit.

They plastered themselves against the window, trying to peer in through the partially opened venetian blinds. The room held four patients. Cassandra was in the middle, near the back, right where all of the doctors and nurses were gathered. They couldn't remember which side she was on in the back so they squinted their eyes and pressed their faces to the glass. One of the nurses noticed them, broke away from the pack, went to the window and closed the venetian blinds. They turned their back to the glass, took each other's hands, squeezed them tightly and slid down the wall.

"Could you see…?"

"No. Could you…?"

"No…"

They all looked towards Philip, still asleep on the couch.

"Should we…?"

"No… we don't know who…"

"But what if it is…?"

"What if it's not?"

They gripped each other's hands tightly and then suddenly realized that the noise from the ICU was gone. No shrill beeping, no flatline, no… anything. They look at each other and simultaneously took a deep breath each. The sound of the door opening made them realize they were still holding their breaths and they exhaled in a loud gush. They looked up at the door hopefully.

The group of nurses and doctors that came out didn't look very happy. They were shaking their heads, their eyes full of loss and sorrow. The day RN nurse noticed them, glanced into the room and then at them. She walked over to them but they were unable to pull themselves to a standing position, so she squatted down in front of them. By now their arms were so intertwined together that they were practically one unit. Their breathing had slowed down so much that they could hear their hearts slow down with each breath that they took. The whole world around them tuned out as the nurse asked them if Cassandra was their sister. Nicola and Sarah slowly nodded their heads 'yes' as tears began to form in Nicola's eyes and a large lump grew in her throat. Nicola tried to ask the nurse if Cassandra was okay but she could only manage a small gurgle.

The nurse put a hand on her shoulder.

"Shhh. It's okay. It wasn't her. She's still okay." Nicola stared at the nurse with disbelief as Sarah yelped, hugging her tightly.

"Nicola, she's okay. She's okay!?!"

Nicola slowly looked over to Patsy and it started to dawn on her what the nurse just said. The nurse smiled, then returned to the nurses' station.

Philip yawned out a growl and sat upright.

"What did I miss?" he asked, still lost in his sleep.

Nicola jumped to her feet, ran over to him and threw herself onto him, hugging him tightly with Sarah quick on her heels behind them.

Patsy joined in the hugging, the three of them squealing, "She's okay, it wasn't her! It wasn't her!" He looked at the three of them as if they were crazy and the nurse shushed them.

After the hugging was done he stood up and asked if there was any new information. The women shook their heads and he sighed, proclaiming that he needed a coffee and asked if they wanted anything. Patsy's stomach growled and she laughed, offering to join him as they went on the hunt for something more nourishing than vending machine food. Nicola wished them luck as she sat back down on the couch. Looking at the clock on the wall she saw that it was already seven in the morning. Karim would be awake and getting ready for work. Part of her wanted to call him, but she knew if she did she'd just cave in. She had to be here for her sister and once things with her were okay, she'd deal with Karim.

She pulled out her phone anyways to see if maybe he had called or texted her. She had turned off her phone after he left the hospital. As she pulled the phone out of her pocket a folded up piece of paper fell to the floor. She leaned over to pick it up. It was folded up to be half the size of her palm, much like a note she would have passed in high school. She noticed her name was scribbled on one side of it. Slowly she unfolded it. Inside was written:

'I know you cannot depend on him, but you can depend on me just like you used to. I can be here for you again if you need me. Just let me know'.

It was signed with a heart and a smiley face. She re-read the note over and over again. She looked up and glanced around the waiting room. Aside from them and the nurses it was empty. She checked her other pocket and found it empty. She lifted her arm and looked her cardigan over. It was brand new. She had bought it earlier with Sarah and Cassandra, their one adventure outside the condo that weekend to a little boutique nearby that Cassandra loved but couldn't really afford. They had all bought matching cardigans of different colours. Even the tag was still attached to the sleeve. She had left the cardigan on the kitchen island counter before she went to bed. There was no way the note could have been put in it before she got to the hospital.

Which meant he had been here sometime in the last few hours. She shivered.

"Are you cold?" Patsy asked from behind her. Nicola pulled her hand into a fist, crushing the note inside it. She put her hands into the pockets of her cardigan and scrunched her body in tight and smiled weakly shaking her head 'no'. Patsy held out a paper cup with steam escaping out of it. Nicola unclenched her hands, letting the paper stay in her pocket and pulled them out to take the tea and smiled a thank you. Patsy sat beside her.

"What are friends for?" she said smiling back.

"This way ma'am," the officer said, indicating that Nicola follow him down the hallway. They turned several corners through a maze of corridors until it opened up into a medium-sized room filled with multiple desks. There was a large buzz about the room as half the desks were occupied and the officers at them were either talking on the phone, typing on their computers or doing paperwork. Other officers were milling about, talking to each other or comparing notes.

They weaved their way through the desks until they reached a room in the far back. It resembled a conference room with a long table surrounded by chairs. The officer pointed to a chair and Nicola sat down. He closed the door behind him, leaving her alone in the room.

She looked around the room nervously. The call to come into the station was unexpected. She hadn't heard anything from them in weeks, and although she had been debating earlier whether or not to tell them about the note she found, she knew that the chances of them having something new to report was unlikely. So being called in for an update was quite a surprise. She absently drummed her fingers on the table as she looked around the room. It was relatively stark. A couple of generic prints in black picture frames adorned the walls. There was a clock on one wall and the third wall was filled with windows covered in partially opened venetian blinds.

The door opened and the two officers from her case entered. They were out of uniform and instead wore slacks and button-up shirts. They sat down across from Nicola. The female officer had a file folder that she set down on the table in front of her. She opened it up and flipped through the pages. The male officer leaned back in his chair, slouching in it. Finally the female officer looked up at Nicola.

"I'm sorry we had to call you in, but we didn't feel this was an appropriate conversation to have over the phone."

Nicola shrugged her shoulders, and the officer continued.

"We still don't have any actual suspects, but we've come across some distressing evidence."

Nicola sat up straighter in her chair, her interest suddenly piqued. The officer took out a piece of paper and slid it in front of Nicola. It was basically two columns, each listing the different actions her stalker had taken. The officer pointed to the first column.

"Basically, everything in this column is 'nice'. Flowers, cards, endearing messages, et cetera. Things that someone who likes you would do. Which is often what most stalkers do."

Nicola nodded in agreement.

"But," the officer said, pointing to the other column, "These are things that someone who hates you would do. Now stalkers usually go one way or the other. They either remain nice and friendly, and for the victim they are just an annoyance. They rarely get worse than that. However, once they do it's usually only for a short period of time before they either do something that reveals themselves and they get caught. Or on the rare occasion, they hurt their victim. But, one thing they almost never do, is reverse gears completely. On top of that we've had a profiler from the FBI look over the case and his results are a bit distressing."

"I don't understand, why was the FBI looking at my case?" Nicola asked.

The female officer's face flushed red and she coughed, trying to clear her throat. Her companion tried to stifle his laughter and suddenly grunted as if he had been kicked roughly in the leg. Nicola observed their interaction with even more confusion.

The female officer, now better composed, put her hands on the table in front of her. "Stalkers seldom go from being nice to you and giving you flowers to suddenly abusing and harassing you aggressively."

Nicola looked at her with a mixed look of clarity and confusion.

The male officer suddenly sat upright, leaned forward onto the table and looked point blank at Nicola. "What my partner here is trying to say, is that we think you have two separate stalkers."

Nicola dropped her hands to her lap and looked down at the table. Her eyes blinked rapidly and darted from side to side before she finally she looked up at the officers.

"How is that possible?" she asked softly.

The officers looked at each other awkwardly.

"To be honest ma'am, this would be the first time we've ever heard of it happening," he said, looking at his partner. She nodded in agreement, took the paper back from Nicola and put it back into her folder.

"We are completely baffled. When we showed your case to our profiler friend he suggested that you had two different stalkers. They suggested that the first one is relatively harmless. Annoying, but harmless. But the second one, she's a real bitch. She's out to get you. The only thing that puzzled the profiler is the rape. Either the first stalker has snapped, but then there should have been more evidence left behind since a rape would have been something he did impulsively, not planned. Also, his lack of aggression since then indicates either incredible restraint or that it wasn't him. Your second stalker, while aggressive, is most likely a female. "

Nicola shuddered and wrapped her arms around her chest.

"What am I supposed to do? Do you have any idea who's doing this to me?" Nicola asked.

"I know we've already asked you if you have any enemies, but can you think again? Have you wronged anyone recently? Does your boyfriend work closely with any women that you know? This could be someone who's jealous of you," the officer asked her.

Nicola shook her head. "I never meet any of his clients, so I can't imagine it being any of them. All of my clients are happy with my business, so no, I can't really think of anyone, sorry," she said.

"Can we get another contact number for your boyfriend Karim other than his cell? We'll need to contact him and we've had problems reaching him. See if he's upset any of his clientele. Perhaps someone is angry at him? He's a casting director right? I'm sure there are women who don't get the roles they think they deserve. Perhaps someone is trying to get even with him by using you?" the female officer suggested.

"I doubt any of them would care about me, he's probably fucking all of them," she said haughtily as she fumbled in her purse for her cell. She pulled it out, scrolled through it and produced both his cell and office number.

The officers took down the numbers and exchanged a curious glance between each other.

"Is there something you'd like to tell us?" the officer asked, and Nicola smiled back at them sweetly.

"Only that my boyfriend is a lying cheating sack of shit?"

The male officer gave a look to his partner and opened his mouth in a retort when his his partner kicked him again in the shins. She stood up and extended a hand to Nicola, shaking her hand.

"Thank you for your time ma'am," she said. "An officer will be by shortly to escort you out."

Nicola looked up them meekly. "What should I do?" she asked.

"Be more aware of your surroundings. Call us right away if you notice anything unusual or strange. No matter how insignificant you think it may be."

Nicola slowly nodded and the officers left. On auto pilot, she pulled out her phone and went to text Karim but stopped halfway before realizing what she was doing. She stopped immediately and angrily put her phone away.

The door opened and the same officer that had led her into the room poked his head in. "Ready?" he asked, a smile on his face.

She nodded a yes, got to her feet and followed him out the door.

Nicola pushed the door open with great effort, its weight and her exhaustion holding it back. She dragged herself in just far enough to clear the door before it slid shut behind her with a loud clack as it locked behind her. She sighed. She was exhausted, both mentally and physically. First the four of them had tried taking turns sleeping while waiting for Cassandra to be out of surgery. She had been in surgery for over six hours before the doctor finally came to see them with more positive news. She was going to be all right. She suffered several internal injuries but the surgery was successful. She was groggy by the time they let them see her, but she was alive. She would heal in time and everything would be okay. When Nicola got to see her, they were only allowed in for a few minutes each and one at a time. Nicola told her that she would move in and look after the kids until she got out of the hospital. Then Sarah would help once she was out. Instead of protesting, Cassandra was well enough to joke about getting a vacation from the family and that she might ask the doctors to extend her visit her. Nicola smiled, knowing that if Cassandra could joke, then she really was okay.

Then, along with the whole Karim incident that had happened in the middle of night, and then the phone call from the police right after Cassandra had gotten out of surgery—all of this had pushed her to complete exhaustion. So, just before she left for the police station, Philip said that Nicola could go home, sleep and come by in the evening. The kids were at his parents', and would be okay there until the evening. She knew she should probably pack first, but she was too tired. She dropped her purse onto the island and stumbled towards the bedroom. Halfway there she walked into a suitcase. It went rolling down the hallway.

"Karim?" she called out, but no one answered.

She went into the bedroom and saw another suitcase on the bed, a smaller one, opened and filled with his clothes and toiletries. A look into the closet revealed that most of his clothes were probably in the suitcase she had just run into. Their bathroom door was ajar and she could hear the faucet running. She slowly slid the door open and Karim was leaning over the sink, examining his freshly shaved face. He looked back at her for a moment then back at the mirror.

"Aren't you even going to ask how my sister is?" she asked.

"Oh, now I'm allowed to care?" he retorted.

She crossed her arms over her chest, then sighed and let her arms drop. She knew she should be angry at him, but she was too exhausted to put up a fight. She went over to him and leaned against his body.

"I don't want to fight. I'm too tired," she said.

"So am I," he said, agreeing with her.

She sighed and hugged him from behind but he gently pulled her arms off of him and went into the bedroom. She was suddenly aware that he had gathered the remaining toiletries and was putting them into the suitcase. She followed him and sat on their bed.

He sighed heavily, then closed the suitcase. They stayed like that, him at his suitcase and her sitting, the silence growing thick and heavy around them.

"You were right," he finally said.

She looked up at him, her eyes full of tears. Slowly she shook her head.

"No. No, I can't be right. Please. No," she said.

He lifted the suitcase onto the floor and extended the handle.

"I'm sorry, Nicola. I never wanted children because I can't have them. I'm sterile. Which I'm guessing you've probably already figured out on your own by now. I never told you because you didn't want kids either. And when you suddenly did, I hoped that it was just a phase," he said as Nicola wrapped her arms around her chest, shaking her head back and forth, tears spilling from her eyes.

"No," she said softly, more to herself than to him.

"But you kept at it. Nagging me day in and day out. You never even asked me if I wanted them, you just assumed I wanted them because you did. I had hoped that when you didn't get pregnant you would stop trying. But then it was doctors and pills and schedules and having sex was no longer about us. It was about 'it'. About the baby. I was tired of having to have sex with you."

He slammed the suitcase out the door so violently that it crashed into the hallway and Nicola jumped. Karim turned around and stormed over to the bed next to Nicola. He leaned over her, placing a hand on either side of her so his face was mere inches from hers. She could feel the anger emanating from him and she shuffled herself backwards, away from him as his voice grew louder and louder as he continued yelling at her.

He followed her until her back was pinned against the headboard, her knees pulled halfway to her chest, his body straddling over hers and his hands on either side of her head.

"This is all your fault! If you just once thought about someone else other than yourself maybe you would have noticed how much agony you were putting me through! Did you not think that I have always wanted to do anything I could to make you happy? Do you not think that if I could have kids I would have changed my mind for you? Do you know how I felt? Like I wasn't even a man. You made me feel worthless!" he yelled, smashing his fist into the headboard close to her head.

Nicola stared at him wide-eyed, holding her breath, afraid to move. He lowered his head so that it almost sat on her chest and knees. Her heart was racing a million miles a minute. Slowly she raised a hand, as if to comfort him, but hesitated just before she touched his head. She held it there, hovering, afraid. Finally he lifted his head and she snapped her hand back to her side but he didn't notice. He crawled off the bed and stood up. He ran a hand through his hair and turned back to look at her.

"We're over," he said

"Karim. Please, no. I don't need a baby. I just—" she started, but he cut her off.

"It's too late for that now. I'm done. I can't do this anymore. You've ruined me," he said, leaving the bedroom.

Nicola sat on the bed in shock. She heard the sound of the suitcases rolling along the floor followed by the sound of the front door closing. She curled herself into a ball, muffling her screams into the bedsheets, and pounded the mattress.

CHAPTER TWENTY SEVEN

Gregory hit 'send' on his phone, impulsively inviting Patsy to his place. It would be the first time he had visitors. Well, technically his second. Although Nicola wasn't really a visitor, it was as much her place as his, as far as he was concerned. He smiled at her, knowing she wouldn't remain unconscious for long, but hoped she wouldn't put up too much of a fight. She belonged with him now and she would come to realize that fact now very quickly.

He looked around his flat, realizing it could use some tidying up. He did suppose that it wasn't extremely flattering, but it was all he could afford at the time. And he was always the minimalist type. He tidied up the kitchen area and poured two glasses of red wine, one full and the other half empty. He prepared a small tray of cheese and grapes. He took both to the living area, where a small couch sat behind a makeshift table, a piece of frosted glass on top of two wooden apple boxes. He had pinched them from a film set during a walk one day. Behind the couch in the far corner was a desk, a chair and his main computers where he did most of his work.

There was a loud rapping on the metal door. He smiled fondly as he walked over to the door, casting a quick glance over his shoulder, making sure that he could neither see nor hear any traces of Nicola before opening the door. A flushed Patsy smiled, holding a small box from her favourite pastry place. He leaned towards her and kissed her cheek, gesturing inwards.

"Welcome to my simple, but humble abode," he said as Patsy, grinning ear-to-ear, stepped inside, looking around the room. He walked her to the couch and took her jacket after she put the box of pastries on the table.

She looked at the wine glasses and pointed to the half empty one.

"Got a head start?" she asked.

He sat down beside her and put a hand on her thigh, squeezing it. "I hope you don't mind," he said.

She shook her head and grabbed the full wine glass and took a generous sip. "I'll just have to catch up."

He smiled, grabbed a piece of cheese and popped it into his mouth. He lightly traced a finger along her thigh and she smiled brightly at him. She finished her glass of wine and as he poured her another glass, he snuck a quick look at his watch. He took a piece of cheese and popped it seductively in her mouth and she giggled. She leaned towards him, licking her lips softly. He slid his arm around her and pulled her closer. But instead of kissing her, he turned her body ever so gently so that she ended up leaning against his chest. He glanced at his watch again, almost time he thought.

"Gregory—" she started but stopped when he suddenly pushed her away from him. She looked at up him as he slid across to the other side of the couch. "What's wrong? Was it something I said?" she asked, but he only shook his head.

- 327 -

Ignoring her he looked at his watch again.

"Why do you keep looking at your damn watch? Are you expecting someone else?!" she asked, becoming agitated.

He chuckled. "No dear, I'm just waiting for the show to start. More wine?"

She nodded her head slowly and he went into the kitchen briefly, returning with another bottle of red wine, already opened, and poured them both another full glass.

"What show?" she asked looking around the room. "I don't see a television anywhere."

He smiled an unearthly wicked smile, his lips curling up to his ears as he pulled out his cell phone.

"You'll see soon enough. Well, to be honest, I'll see," he took another sip of wine as the glass suddenly fell from Patsy's hand and immediately shattered into a million pieces on the concrete floor. Gregory smiled and hit 'send' on his phone.

Karim stared at his phone. He had gotten two texts simultaneously. One from Nicola and one from a blocked number. He ignored the one from Nicola and read the latter. It simply read *'Answer her'*. As he pondered this a moment another text came from the blocked number. *'Tick Tock'*, it read. He opened the message from Nicola. It read *'Answer my call, my life depends on it'*. He almost dropped his phone when it started to ring in his hands. He had an incoming video call from Nicola. He hesitated a moment then hit 'accept'.

His screen filled with the image of Patsy sitting on a small couch and a glass coffee table in front of her. It took him a moment before he realized that she was apparently choking and that he could see her hands clinging to her throat. The image got bigger, zooming in closer to Patsy. The screen flickered as it went from fuzzy to clear. He could see white foam coming out of Patsy's mouth.

What the hell was Nicola thinking, he thought to himself. What were they doing? Was this some lame attempt to get him back? He was about to end the call when a rough male voice filled the phone.

"Not the prettiest way to go, huh?" he asked comically.

Patsy flailed off of the couch and onto the coffee table. She hit it with enough force that it broke easily under her weight and she fell through it to the floor.

Karim gasped, suddenly realizing that this wasn't staged. This was actually real.

"What the hell are you doing to her—"

"Unless you want your girl to end up like this faithless whore, come to this address, alone," Gregory said, interrupting Karim. "Scream for your man, Nicola."

Karim could hear him slapping her and she screamed in response.

Patsy flailed about, her arms bouncing against the apple boxes and her body slowly seeping with blood from the broken glass she was now unwillingly rolling around in.

"If I hear sirens, Nicola dies," he said and ended the call.

Karim stared at his phone in shock. An address popped up in a text from Nicola and he immediately tried to call her back but a computerized voice said that her phone was no longer in service.

He immediately began to punch 9-1-1 into his phone but quickly stopped. He knew he should call the police, but the man said not to. He was obviously Nicola's stalker and he was probably dangerous, but the police had done nothing in over six months. No leads, no real attempt at helping her, and little support as far as he was concerned. Even if he managed to convince them to arrive quietly, it would take too much time to convince them to do so, and the stalker would have realized that he had gone to the police and would probably kill her.

He looked down at the address and realized it was one of the warehouses in the same area that Nicola's office was in. He grabbed his jacket and raced out of his hotel room.

Karim stood outside the door of the warehouse that the address had led him to. He had walked around the whole building, but only one entrance wasn't boarded up. There were no windows at ground level and no other apparent way in. He held up his hand to knock, then hesitated before shaking his head. He put a hand on the door knob and held his ear up close to the door. Hearing nothing, he slowly turned the door knob and it opened easily.

He stepped into a dark hallway, lit solely by a lightbulb hanging from an old cord. He appeared to be in an office hallway. An incomplete ceiling was above his head, wires dangling down and the framing unfinished. Continuing down the hallway, he tried each door he passed. But each was closed and locked tight. The sounds of his footsteps echoed loudly around him. The hallway opened up into what appeared to be a waiting room. It was about ten feet by fifteen feet, had a couch, a table and a desk still remaining in it. To the right and behind the desk he could see one last door. He stopped and cocked his head, listening. The warehouse was eerily silent. No sound of Nicola or the stalker. He walked over to the door, unable to hide the sound of his footsteps, and put his hand on the door knob.

"It's open," a male voice sang from the other side of the door.

Karim opened the door. Inside he could see a couch and in front of it two wooden boxes and Patsy collapsed between them on a bed of glass. He rushed inside a few steps then quickly stopped. To the left of Patsy was a chair and some rope on it and to the right of the couch was someone hiding in the shadows.

Karim turned to face the shadow. "Where is she?" he asked.

"She's hiding, why don't you come and find her," Gregory said in a sing-song voice.

Karim took a step inside and scanned the room. Gregory took a step closer, his face still obscured by the shadows.

"Why don't you show yourself?" Karim said, his voice steady but hesitant.

"All in due time," Gregory said. "What's your hurry?"

Karim took another step towards Patsy, and Gregory took a step away from the couch. Karim slowly made his way towards Patsy while Gregory just stood in the shadows and watched him. Keeping an eye on Gregory, Karim knelt down and felt for a pulse.

"Waste of time. She died shortly after I called you," Gregory said.

"What the hell do you want!?!" Karim shouted. "Where is Nicola!?!"

"I told you, she's hiding. Come and find her," Gregory mocked.

Karim stood up and rushed Gregory. He put a hand to Gregory's throat as he pushed him up hard against the wall and Gregory choked out a laugh.

"Where is she?" Karim demanded.

"Closer than you think. Can't you see her?" Gregory said between gasps.

He looked down at Gregory's face, now splashed with a sliver of light from amongst the shadows. His eyes glittered a bright green as if there were small fragments of metal in his eye colour. Something about the way he smiled, the softness behind his eyes made Karim release his grip slightly. With his free hand he traced his hand along Gregory's lips, past his cheek and to his hair. He ran his fingers through Gregory's hair softly, then gripped it more tightly and started to pull.

"Who are—" he started when suddenly his mouth formed a large 'O'. He stared into Gregory's eyes, now a cold steely green, as Gregory leaned forward, brushed his lips against Karim's cheek and whispered into his ear.

"Found her," he whispered as he pulled away, sliding the knife that was now in Karim's stomach out and back in again and again. Karim stood in shock, then gurgled, blood pouring out of his mouth. He clumsily put his hands to his stomach as Gregory pulled the kitchen knife out for the last time and dropped it on the floor. Blood soaked through Karim's shirt, through his fingers and down his pants. Karim looked down at his stomach and muttered a small groan. He looked up at Gregory inquisitively, confusion in his eyes. He mouthed the word 'why?' as he slowly collapsed to the ground.

"You never deserved her anyway," Gregory said and walked away from the dying Karim. "Now where is my girl?" he called out to Nicola.

CHAPTER TWENTY EIGHT

Nicola opened her eyes again, unsure of how long she had been unconscious this time. The room was still dark. Slowly she raised her pounding head up and looked around the room she was in. She craned her head all the way to the right and swore she could see someone on the floor behind her.

"Hello?" she called out to the shadows, but no one replied.

She pulled at her hands that were tied behind her back. Snug but also strangely loose. She slowly wriggled her hands, and realized they weren't actually tied or roped to the chair. She stretched her legs out, one by one, realizing that they, too, were not tied down. Confused but relieved, she tried to stand up. Her hands got caught on the back of the chair and she fell back down, almost tipping herself and the chair over completely. Once stable, she tried again. This time she slowly spread her legs out to either side of the chair and gradually brought herself upwards, standing while straddling the chair and attempting to keep her body as straight as possible. Her hands finally cleared the back of the chair and she stepped forward past it.

Partially free, she turned herself around in a complete circle scanning for whomever put her there. Satisfied that no one else appeared to be here in the room with her at the moment, she tried to untie her hands that were still behind her back. She struggled and stumbled, falling down to her knees, and moaned as she put her head between her knees. Her head racked in pain and her eyes threatened to be engulfed by the darkness yet again.

"No, Nicola. You can do this. Concentrate," she said, urging herself on.

She lowered herself down to the floor completely and took a deep breath. Sliding her hands downwards towards her butt, she simultaneously pulled her rear upwards while sliding her hands beneath it. She bowed her arms while pulling her hands apart as much as possible as she attempted to slide them down around her butt. Finally her hands popped past her rear end and she was another moment closer to freedom. She paused for a moment, but then quickly resumed moving her hands past her feet, pulling one leg through at a time.

Sitting up, her hands now in front of her she scanned the room once again. Still nothing and no one. She quickly untied her hands, a knot so easy she could have done it herself. As she untied the knot, she looked down at herself and noticed that she was wearing Karim's pants and one of his shirts. Both were soaked in blood. She examined herself quickly but found no wounds of any kind.

Frantic, she quickly stood up and rushed towards where she thought she might have seen a person a moment ago. Fearing what she might see but unable to stop herself, she continued towards the person on the ground, calling out to them. Glass crunched beneath her feet as she got closer to the couch. A person was lying in the pile of glass and in between two wooden boxes.

Putting a hand on their shoulder but not really expecting yet hoping for a reply, she shook them gently and called out to them. When she got silence in return she rolled the body over and shrieked, falling to the ground and landing in glass. Not noticing the pain nor the glass embedded in her skin, she clasped both of her hands to her mouth in shock and pedalled herself away from the body, which she now recognized as Patsy.

Patsy's face was contorted in agony. Dried bits of foam clung to her lips and spattered droplets traced her throat. There were scratches down her throat, like she had been trying to claw it open. Her entire body was covered in cuts and her clothes were torn to shreds. She had apparently rolled around in the glass as she had died.

Nicola stood up, realizing her hands were bloody and full of glass. Carefully she brushed the glass off of her hands and stepped away from Patsy. She looked around the room frantically, searching for a phone or a way out. She wiped her hands absently on her pants and felt a lump in her pocket. She reached inside and found two phones. One was hers, but the other she didn't recognize. Immediately she turned her phone on and dialled 9-1-1.

"Hello 9-1-1, ambulance, police or fire department?" a male voice answered.

"All of them. Help me," Nicola said.

"Ma'am, please try to stay calm. Can you tell me what the problem is?" he asked.

"She's dead. She's dead! And I was tied up. You have to help me," she said in a rush.

"Ma'am, I've got the police and the ambulance on the line, ready to go. Do you know where you are?" he asked.

"I'm in a room. It's dark," she answered, the words spilling out between choked sobs.

"Do you know the address where you are? Is there anyone else there with you?" he asked.

"No. Just Patsy. But she's dead. I'm all alone," she said, now crying.

"Ma'am please remain calm. If you're able, can you get outside? Or find something in the house that tells you where you are. Is there any mail lying around? A flyer perhaps?" he asked.

She looked around the room. She could make out a desk behind the couch and moved towards it. Halfway there she screamed, dropping her phone onto the ground.

"Ma'am. M'am! Are you alright?" he asked.

Nicola fell down to her knees and into the puddle of blood that Karim now lay in. He lay on his side, facing her. She put her hands to his face.

"Karim?" she whispered to him. "Karim? Are you okay?" she asked absently, knowing he wouldn't answer.

She looked from his face and down to his stomach, her hand covering her mouth. She started to push herself away from the horror in front of her, but then she stopped. She could see something in his hand. Her left hand supported her weight as she leaned in over him and plucked it from his hand. Holding it out in front of her she saw it was a blonde wig. She blinked her eyes and suddenly she was standing in her office.

She knew that Patsy had left for the day and thought that Nicola had left an hour before her. But Nicola had hidden in a room the floor below, waiting to hear the elevator leave with Patsy in it. It was

Tuesday so Karim was out with the boys so he wouldn't notice her coming home late. On her desk was a file folder. She opened it up to reveal pictures of herself. She pulled a roll of scotch tape out of her purse and took a picture from the folder. One by one she filled her office with them.

Nicola shook her head and stared at the blond wig in front of her like it would suddenly come to life. She knew this wig. She turned it inside out and read the tag inside. She had bought this wig. For her old school friend Gregory. What was it doing here? Was Gregory here too? She got to her feet, her phone was face up in Karim's blood, the 9-1-1 operator calling out to her. She felt like she was on the verge of remembering something crucial as she stumbled backwards, a sudden breeze blowing through her hair.

The wind and rain blew violently in through her office window. She knew she had closed it before she had left earlier that day. She knew who had opened it. She cocked an ear towards the window. She could hear that someone was slowly scraping against the wall outside. She smiled and walked over silently to the window. Part of her felt like sticking her head out the window and yelling 'boo'. But she knew the results could be hazardous. Instead she simply closed the window and engaged the lock. She smiled again as the rain pelted against the glass.

Lightning suddenly struck past the window and she flinched before she realized she wasn't standing in front of it but lying down on her bed. Her blouse was ripped open and her skirt was hiked up. In her right hand was a kitchen knife and she held it up against her own neck. She took a deep breath and gasped as she sliced herself slightly. Stars danced around her head as she quickly sat up. Her legs still wide open, she pulled an oversized dildo out from between her legs.

She gasped as more stars danced and the lights briefly grew dim, then flickered, and she looked up.

The hallway flickered with the lone light bulb above her head. How had she ended up here? She looked around realizing that she was no longer in the living room area. Behind her she could see an oven and cupboards. In front of her were two more doors. The first one was a sliding door in the wall. She slid it open and looked inside.

She saw that Karim had left a few of his suits behind, older ones she hadn't seen him wear in ages. She stripped completely naked and pulled out a pair of his pants. She grabbed one of her belts hanging in the closet and slid it into the belt loops. She put the pants on and tightened the belt so they wouldn't fall off. She reached inside and grabbed a shirt. She buttoned it up quickly and went to their office closet.

It was a closet built into the wall. Inside were several pants, shirts, t-shirts, ties and other mens' clothing. Clothes for a man smaller than Karim. She fingered the clothes lightly and continued down the hall towards the other door and pushed it open. She took a second glance back over her shoulder. She could see an opened bottle of wine sitting on the counter.

She popped the wine open, one of the few remaining brands that still used cork. She loved the smell of freshly-opened wine. She pulled two glasses out of the cupboard and filled both of them half full. One of the glasses she set close to the sink, the other she set a spoon beside. She reached back into the cupboard and pulled out a ziplock baggie filled with white powder. She took the spoon and scooped a generous spoonful and dumped it into the wine glass. She stirred it until all of the powder had dissolved. Then she topped the glass up generously and smiled.

She stepped through the doorway and into the bathroom.

Kneeling on the floor she threw everything out of the closet between her and the hidden panel. She didn't care about the mess, Karim wouldn't be back to see it anytime soon. She flung the hidden panel open. There, amongst all of the destroyed baby items was a lone box. She pulled it out and set it on her lap. Carefully she opened the lid to reveal a blonde wig. She gingerly took it her hands. Tears were still flowing down as her face twisted with pain and her hands shook. She wiped the tears from her face, grabbed the wig and slowly pulled it down onto her head.

Looking into the bathroom mirror she saw herself wearing the same blonde wig. His wig. Gregory's wig. Her hands trembled in front of her and she looked down to see a blood soaked knife in her hand. The same knife that had killed Karim. She screamed out and the knife clattered in the sink as her face contorted and her knees buckled. She fell to the floor, hitting her head on the sink as she did. Staring up at the ceiling, she watched as the light bulb slowly swayed back and forth. The darkness crept into her head and overtook her. The last thing she heard was the faint shrill of sirens in the distance.

A police officer gently pushed Nicola's head down to ease it under the roof of the car as she got into the back seat of the police car. Her arms were cuffed behind her. She looked back up towards the warehouse, her face streaked with dried blood and tears.

Inside the warehouse, an older detective stepped into the room, carefully surveying the grim scene already being tagged and photographed by his fellow officers. The detective taking pictures noticed him enter and looked up at him.

"Did she say anything useful?" he asked.

The older detective shook his head. "She just kept muttering, 'It was Gregory, it wasn't me, it was Gregory'."

EPILOGUE

Cassandra let herself be guided into common room of the St. Augustine Psychiatric Hospital. She could see Nicola sitting at a table all by herself, staring absently into the open space in front of her. Cassandra's heart broke and her eyes watered at the sight of what remained of her sister. She sat down at the table with Nicola, and the orderly took a few steps back and stood against the wall, his hands held together loosely at his waist.

"Nicola. It's me, Cassandra," she said. Nicola just gazed off into space, staring right through her. Cassandra put a hand on her sister's and gently squeezed it.

"Nicola, honey. Can you hear me?" she pleaded.

Nicola blinked and slowly turned her face towards Cassandra's face. She stared into her eyes, penetrating them with an icy coolness and emptiness. Cassandra held her breath, afraid to move, suddenly realizing that Nicola was gripping her hand back tightly.

"Nicola," she whispered.

"It was George all along. He grew up," Nicola said softly, her eyes full of certain clarity. "George became Gregory."

Then she released her grip on Cassandra's hand, turned her head slightly and her eyes grew vacant again.

Cassandra choked back a sob and got up from the table. Her head hung low as she left the common room. As she stepped back into the hallway a doctor put his hand on her shoulder and asked, "Miss, do you know who George is?"

Cassandra slowly shook her head, trying to hold back the tears. "I always thought he was her imaginary friend," she said softly as she left the hospital.

9 7 8 0 9 9 4 8 6 5 6 0 1